"DEVASTATINGLY POWERFUL . . . RICH AND IMPRESSIVE . . . A REVOLUTIONARY WORK!"

—*Washington Post Book World*

"Suzy Charnas turns her strange story back upon itself—and upon her readers. With wry gallows humor, with sympathy for her alien, born-again monster, Charnas asks who are the predators and who are the prey?"

—*L.A. Times Book Review*

"Clever, chilling . . . a complex and disturbing tale . . . thoroughly believable."

—*School Library Journal*

"A superior, grandly detailed vampire story . . . Charnas uses the inhuman condition to explore the specialness of humankind—and the result is both a gripping psychological portrait and smashingly deft entertainment."

—*Kirkus Reviews*

THE VAMPIRE TAPESTRY

SUZY McKEE CHARNAS

PUBLISHED BY POCKET BOOKS NEW YORK

ALL CHARACTERS IN THIS BOOK ARE FICTITIOUS. ANY RESEMBLANCE TO ACTUAL PERSONS, LIVING, DEAD, OR UNDEAD, IS PURELY COINCIDENTAL—BARRING A BRIEF APPEARANCE BY THE AUTHOR'S MOTHER-IN-LAW, WITH THE GRACIOUS PERMISSION OF THE SAME.

The portion of this book entitled "The Ancient Mind at Work" appeared in *Omni*, February 1979. © 1979 Omni Publications International Ltd.

 POCKET BOOKS, a Simon & Schuster division of
GULF & WESTERN CORPORATION
1230 Avenue of the Americas, New York, N.Y. 10020

Acknowledgments

MY GRATITUDE TO THOSE who read for me while this work was in progress: Stephen (first, last, and always); Marge, Joanna, and Vonda; Janet, Sondra, Michael, Esther, Juliet, Mara, Ned, Maggie, and Jo and her friends of the mini-reading in their mini-dining room at Evergreen; Robin, Patty, Liza, Sally, and associates. Thanks also to some who read parts of this book in the light of particular expertise (errors that survived their attentions are entirely my own responsibility): Marion London and Claudine Wilder, therapists; Jon Charnas for advice on the layouts of apartments in New York, his town; Bruce Stringer, veterinarian; Bill and Kay Weinrod, formerly on the administrative staff of the Santa Fe Opera, and Drew Field, technical director; Eric Rose and Eva Friedlander, anthropologists; Virginia Kidd, agent, whose enthusiasm and eye for detail were so helpful; David Hartwell, an editor who knows when work can be made better and gives fruitful suggestions to that end; and special thanks to Harry Nadler for the use of his Panama hat.

To the memory of Loren Eiseley. We never met, but his writing first opened to me the vast perspectives of geologic time. From those distances eventually emerged the figure of the vampire as envisioned in this book.

Contents

I
The
Ancient Mind
at Work

ON A TUESDAY MORNING Katje discovered that Dr. Weyland was a vampire, like the one in the movie she'd seen last week.

Jackson's friend on the night cleaning crew had left his umbrella hooked over the bike rack outside the lab building. Since Katje liked before starting to work to take a stroll in the dawn quiet, she went over to see if the umbrella was still there. As she started back empty-handed through the heavy mist she heard the door of the lab building boom behind her. She looked back.

A young man had come out and started across the parking lot. Clearly he was hurt or ill, for he slowed, stopped, and sank down on one knee, reaching out a hand to steady himself on the damp and glistening tarmac.

Behind him, someone else emerged from the building and softly shut the heavy door. This man, tall and gray-haired, stood a moment touching to his mouth a white handkerchief folded into a small square. Then he put the handkerchief away and walked out onto the lot. Passing behind the kneeling figure, he turned his head to look—and continued walking without hesitation. He got into his shimmering gray Mercedes and drove off.

Katje started back toward the lot. But the young man pushed himself upright, looked around in a bewildered manner, and making his way unsteadily to his own car also drove away.

So there was the vampire, sated and cruel, and there was his victim, wilted, pale, and confused; although the movie vampire had swirled about in a black cloak, not a raincoat, and had gone after bosomy young females. Walking over the lawn to the Club, Katje smiled at her own fancy.

What she had really seen, she knew, was the eminent anthropologist and star of the Cayslin Center for the Study of Man, Dr. Weyland, leaving the lab with one of his sleep subjects after a debilitating all-night session. Dr. Weyland must have thought the young man was stooping to retrieve dropped car keys.

The Cayslin Club was an old mansion donated years before to the college. It served now as the faculty club. Its grandeur had been severely challenged by the lab building and attendant parking lot constructed on half of the once-spacious lawn, but the Club was still an imposing place within.

Jackson was in the green room plugging leaks; it had begun to rain. The green room was a glassed-in terrace, tile-floored and furnished with chairs of lacy wrought iron.

"Did you find it, Mrs. de Groot?" Jackson said.

"No, I'm sorry." Katje never called him by his name because she didn't know whether he was Jackson Somebody or Somebody Jackson, and she had learned to be careful in everything to do with blacks in this country.

"Thanks for looking, anyway," Jackson said.

In the kitchen she stood by the sinks staring out at the dreary day. She had never grown used to these chill, watery winters, though after so many years she couldn't quite recall the exact quality of the African sunlight in which she had grown up. It was no great wonder that Hendrik had died here. The gray climate had finally quenched even his ardent nature six years ago, and she had shipped him back to his family. Katje had possessed his life; she didn't need his bones and didn't want a grave tying her to this dark country. His career as a lecturer in the sociology of medicine here and at other schools had brought in a good income, but he had funneled all he could of it into the Black Majority Movement back home. So he had left her little, and she had expected that. To the amazement and resentment of certain faculty wives, she had taken this job and stayed on.

Her savings from her salary as housekeeper at the Cayslin Club would eventually finance her return home. She needed enough to buy not a farm, but a house with a garden patch somewhere high and cool—she frowned, trying to picture the ideal site. Nothing clear came into her mind. She had been away a long time.

While she was wiping up the sinks Miss Donelly burst in, shrugging out of her dripping raincoat and muttering, "Of all the highhanded, goddamn— Oh, hello, Mrs. de Groot; sorry for the language. Look, we won't be having the women's faculty lunch here tomorrow after all. Dr. Weyland is giving a special money pitch to a group of fat-cat alumni and he wants a nice, quiet setting—our lunch corner here at the Club, as it turns out. Dean Wacker's already said yes, so that's that."

"Why come over in the rain to tell me that?" Katje said. "You should have phoned."

"I also wanted to check out a couple of the upstairs bedrooms to make sure I reserve a quiet one for a guest lecturer I'm putting up here next month." Miss Donelly hesitated, then added, "You know, Mrs. de Groot, I've been meaning to ask whether you'd be willing to be a guest lecturer yourself in my Literary Environments course—we're reading Isak Dinesen. Would you come talk to my students?"

"Me? About what?"

"Oh, about colonial Africa, what it was like growing up there. These kids' experience is so narrow and protected, I look for every chance to expand their thinking."

Katje wrung out the sink rag. "My grandfather and Uncle Jan whipped the native boys to work like cattle and kicked them hard enough to break bones for not showing respect; otherwise we would have been overrun and driven out. I used to go hunting. I shot rhino, elephant, lion, and leopard, and I was proud of doing it well. Your students don't want to know such things. They have nothing to fear but tax collectors and nothing to do with nature except giving money for whales and seals."

"But that's what I mean," Miss Donelly said. "Different viewpoints."

"There are plenty of books about Africa."

"Try getting these kids to read." Miss Donelly sighed. "Well, I guess I could get the women together over at Corrigan tomorrow instead of here, if I spend an hour on the phone. And we'll miss your cooking, Mrs. de Groot."

"Will Dr. Weyland expect me to cook for his guests?" Katje said, thinking abstractedly of the alumni lunching with the vampire. Would he eat? The one in the movie hadn't eaten.

"Not Weyland," Miss Donelly said dryly. "It's nothing but the best for him, which means the most expensive. They'll probably have a banquet brought in from Borchard's."

She left.

Katje put on coffee and phoned Buildings and Grounds. Yes, Dr. Weyland and six companions were on at the Club for tomorrow; no, Mrs. de Groot wouldn't have to do anything but tidy up afterward; yes, it was short notice, and please write it on the Club calendar; and yes, Jackson had been told to check the eaves over the east bedrooms before he left.

"Wandering raincoat," Miss Donelly said, darting in to snatch it up from the chair where she'd left it. "Just watch out for Weyland, Mrs. de Groot."

"What, a fifty-year-old widow like me? I am not some slinky graduate student trying for an A and the professor also."

"I don't mean romance." Miss Donelly grinned. "Though God knows half the faculty—of both sexes— are in love with the man." Honestly, Katje thought, the things people talked about these days! "To no avail, alas, since he's a real loner. But he will try to get you into his expensive sleep lab and make your dreams part of his world-shaking, history-changing research that he stole off poor old Ivan Milnes."

Milnes, Katje thought when she was alone again; Professor Milnes who had gone away to some sunny place to die of cancer. Then Dr. Weyland had come from a small Southern school and taken over Milnes's dream project, saving it from being junked—or stealing it, in Miss Donelly's version. A person who looked at a thing in too many ways was bound to get confused.

Jackson came in and poured coffee for himself. He leaned back in his chair and flipped the schedules where they hung on the wall by the phone. He was as slender as a Kikuyu youth—she could see his ribs arch under his shirt. He ate a lot of junk food, but he was too nervous to fatten on it. By rights he belonged in a red blanket, skin gleaming with oil, hair plaited. Instead he wore the tan shirt, pants, and zip-up jacket of an "engineer" from Buildings and Grounds, and his hair was a modest Afro, as they called it, around his narrow face.

"Try and don't put nobody in that number-six bedroom till I get to it the end of the week," he said. "The rain drips in behind the casement. I laid out towels to soak up the water. I see you got Weyland in here tomorrow. My buddy Maurice on the cleaning crew says that guy got the best lab in the place."

"What is Dr. Weyland's research?" Katje asked.

" 'Dream mapping,' they call it. Maurice says there's nothing interesting in his lab—just equipment, you know, recording machines and computers and like that. I'd like to see all that hardware sometime. Only you won't catch me laying out my dreams on tape!

"Well, I got to push along. There's some dripping faucets over at Joffey I'm supposed to look at. Hans Brinker, that's me. Thanks for the coffee."

She began pulling out the fridge racks for cleaning, listening to him whistle as he gathered up his tools in the green room.

The people from Borchard's left her very little to do. She was stacking the rinsed dishes in the washer when a man said from the doorway, "I am very obliged to you, Mrs. de Groot."

Dr. Weyland stood poised there, slightly stoop-shouldered, slightly leonine somehow. At least that was the impression Katje got from his alert stance, his still, grave, attentive face from which the wide eyes looked out bright with interest. She was surprised that he knew her name, for he did not frequent the Club.

"There was just a little remaining to do, Dr. Weyland," she said.

"Still, this is your territory," he said, advancing. "I'm sure you were helpful to the Borchard's people. I've never been back here. Are those freezers or refrigerators?"

She showed him around the kitchen and the pantries. He seemed impressed. He handled the accessories to the Cuisinart as if they were artifacts of a civilization he was studying. The thing was a gift to the Club from the Home Ec staff. Many parts were missing already, but Katje didn't mind. She couldn't be bothered, as she told Dr. Weyland, getting the hang of the fancier gadgets.

He nodded thoughtfully. Was he condescending to her, or really in sympathy? "There's no time to master the homely technology of these times, all the machines, what they mean to a modern life . . ."

He was, she realized, unexpectedly personable: lean and grizzled, but with the hint of vulnerability common among rangy men. You couldn't look at him long without imagining the gawky scarecrow he must have been as a boy. His striking features—rugged brow, nose, and jaw—no doubt outsized and homely then, were now united in somber harmony by the long creases of experience on his cheeks and forehead.

"No more scullions cranking the spit," he remarked over the rotisserie. "You come originally from East Africa, Mrs. de Groot? Things must have been very different there."

"Yes. I left a long time ago."

"Surely not so very long," he said, and his eyes flicked over her from head to foot. Why, the man was flirting!

Relaxing in the warmth of his interest, she said, "Are you from elsewhere also?"

He frosted up at once. "Why do you ask?"

"Excuse me, I thought I heard just the trace of an accent."

"My family were Europeans. We spoke German at home. May I sit down?" His big hands, capable and strong-looking, graced the back of a chair. He smiled briefly. "Would you mind sharing your coffee with an institutional fortune hunter? That is my job—persuading rich men and the guardians of foundations to spend a little of their money in support of work that offers no immediate result. I don't enjoy dealing with these shortsighted men."

"Everyone says you do it well." Katje filled a cup for him.

"It takes up my time," he said. "It wearies me." His large and brilliant eyes, in sockets darkened with fatigue, had a withdrawn, pensive aspect. How old was he, Katje wondered.

Suddenly he gazed at her and said, "Didn't I see you over by the labs the other morning? There was mist on my windshield, I couldn't be sure . . ."

She told him about Jackson's friend's umbrella, thinking, Now he'll explain, this is what he came to say. But he added nothing, and she found herself hesitant to ask about the student in the parking lot. "Is there anything else I can do for you, Dr. Weyland?"

"I don't mean to keep you from your work. Would you come over sometime and do a session for me in the sleep lab?"

Just as Miss Donelly had said. Katje shook her head.

"All information goes on tapes under coded I.D. numbers, Mrs. de Groot. Your privacy would be strictly guarded."

His persistence made her uncomfortable. "I'd rather not."

"Excuse me, then. It's been a pleasure talking with you," he said, rising. "If you find a reason to change your mind, my extension is one-sixty-three."

She found herself obscurely relieved at his abrupt departure. She picked up his coffee cup. It was full. She realized that she had not seen him take so much as a sip.

She was close to tears, but Uncle Jan made her strip down the gun again—her first gun, her own gun—and then the lion coughed, and she saw with the wide gaze of fear his golden form crouched, tail lashing, in the thornbrush. She threw up her gun and fired, and the dust boiled up from the thrashings of the wounded cat.

Then Scotty's patient voice said, "Do it again," and she was tearing down the rifle once more by lamplight at the worn wooden table, while her mother sewed with angry stabs of the needle and spoke words Katje didn't bother to listen to. She knew the gist by heart: "If only Jan had children of his own! Sons, to take out hunting with Scotty. Because he has no sons, he takes Katje shooting instead so he can show how tough Boer youngsters are, even the girls. For whites to kill for sport, as Jan and Scotty do, is to go backward into the barbaric past of Africa. Now the farm is producing, there is no need to sell hides to get cash for coffee, salt, and tobacco. And to train a *girl* to go stalking and killing animals like scarcely more than an animal herself!"

"Again," said Scotty, and the lion coughed.

Katje woke. She was sitting in front of the TV, blinking at the sharp, knowing face of the talk-show host. The sound had gone off again, and she had dozed.

She didn't often dream, hardly ever of her African childhood—her mother, Uncle Jan, Scotty the neighboring farmer whom Uncle had begun by calling a damned *rooinek* and ended treating like a brother. Miss Donelly's request for a lecture about Africa must have stirred up that long-ago girlhood spent prowling for game in a landscape of yellow grass.

The slim youngster she had been then, brown-skinned and nearly white-haired from the sun, seemed far distant. A large-framed woman now, Katje worked to avoid growing stout as her mother had. In the gray New England climate her hair had dulled to the color of old brass, paling now toward gray.

Yet she could still catch sight of her child-self in the mirror—the stubborn set of her firm, round jaw and the determined squint of her eyes. She had not, she reflected with satisfaction, allowed the world to change her much.

Miss Donelly came in for some coffee the next afternoon. As Katje brought a tray to her in the long living room, a student rushed past calling, "Is it too late to hand in my paper, Miss Donelly?"

"For God's sake, Mickey!" Miss Donelly burst out. "Where did you get that?"

Across the chest of the girl's T-shirt where her coat gapped open were emblazoned the words SLEEP WITH WEYLAND HE'S A DREAM. She grinned. "Some hustler is selling them right outside the co-op. Better hurry if you want one—Security's already been sent for." She put a sheaf of dogeared pages down on the table beside Miss Donelly's chair, added, "Thanks, Miss Donelly," and clattered away again on her high-heeled clogs.

Miss Donelly laughed and said to Katje, "Well, I never, as my grandma used to say. That man certainly does juice this place up."

"Young people have no respect for anything," Katje grumbled. "What will Dr. Weyland say, seeing his name used like that? He should have her expelled."

"Him? He wouldn't bother. Wacker will throw fits, though. Not that Weyland won't notice—he notices everything—but he doesn't waste his super-valuable time on nonsense." Miss Donelly ran a finger over the blistered paint on the windowsill by her chair. "Pity we can't use some of the loot Weyland brings in to fix up this old place. But I guess we can't complain; without Weyland Cayslin would be just another expensive backwater school for the not-so-bright children of the upper middle class. And it isn't all roses even for him. This T-shirt thing will start a whole new round of backbiting among his colleagues, you watch. This kind of stuff brings out the jungle beast in even the mildest academics."

Katje snorted. She didn't think much of academic infighting.

"I know we must seem pretty tame to you," Miss Donelly said wryly, "but there are some real ambushes and even killings here, in terms of careers. It's not the cushy life it sometimes seems, and not so secure either. Even for you, Mrs. de Groot. There are people who don't like your politics—"

"I never talk politics." That was the first thing

Hendrik had demanded of her here. She had acquiesced like a good wife; not that she was ashamed of her political beliefs. She had loved and married Hendrik not because of but in spite of his radical politics.

"From your silence they assume you're some kind of reactionary racist," Miss Donelly said. "Also because you're a Boer and you don't carry on your husband's crusade. Then there are the ones who're embarrassed to see the wife of a former instructor working at the Club—"

"It's work I can do," Katje said stiffly. "I asked for the job."

Miss Donelly frowned. "Sure—but everybody knows the college should have done better by you, and besides you were supposed to have a staff of people here to help out. And some of the faculty are a little scared of you; they'd rather have a giggly cocktail waitress or a downtrodden mouse of a working student. You need to be aware of these things, Mrs. de Groot.

"And also of the fact that you have plenty of partisans too. Even Wacker knows you give this place tone and dignity, and you lived a real life in the world, whatever your values, which is more than most of our faculty have ever done." Blushing, she lifted her cup and drank.

She was as soft as everyone around here, Katje thought, but she had a good heart.

Many of the staff had already left for vacation during intersession, now that new scheduling had freed everyone from doing mini-courses between semesters. The last cocktail hour at the Club was thinly attended. Katje moved among the drinkers unobtrusively gathering up loaded ashtrays, used glasses, crumpled paper napkins. A few people who had known Hendrik greeted her as she passed.

There were two major topics of conversation: the bio student who had been raped last night leaving the library, and the Weyland T-shirt, or, rather, Weyland himself.

They said he was a disgrace, encouraging commercial exploitation of his name; he was probably getting a cut of the profits. No he wasn't, didn't need to, he had a hefty income, no dependents, and no appetites except for study and work. And driving his beautiful Mercedes-Benz, don't forget that. No doubt that was where he was this evening—not off on a holiday or drinking cheap Club booze, but roaring around the countryside in his beloved car.

Better a ride in the country than burying himself in the library as usual. It was unhealthy for him to push so hard; just look at him, so haggard and preoccupied, so lean and lonely-looking. The man deserved a prize for his solitary-bachelor-hopelessly-hooked-on-the-pursuit-of-knowledge act.

It was no act—what other behavior did people expect of a great scholar? There'd be another fine book out of him someday, a credit to Cayslin. Look at that latest paper of his, "Dreams and Drama: The Mini-Theatre of the Mind." Brilliant!

Brilliant speculation, maybe, like all his work, plus an intriguing historical viewpoint, but where was his hard research? He was no scientist; he was a mountebank running on drive, imagination, a commanding presence, and a lucky success with his first book. Why, even his background was foggy. (But don't ever suggest to Dean Wacker that there was anything odd about Weyland's credentials. Wacker would eat you alive to protect the goose that laid the golden eggs.)

How many students were in the sleep project now? More than were in his classes. They called his course in ethnography "The Ancient Mind at Work." The girls found his formality charming. No, he wasn't formal, he was too stiff-necked and old-fashioned, and he'd never make a first-rate contribution to anthropology. He'd simply appropriated poor Milnes's beautiful adaptation of the Richman-Steinmolle Recording System to the documentation of dreams, adding some fancy terminology about cultural symbols to bring the project into his own field of cultural anthropology. And Weyland thought he knew all about computers too—no wonder he ran his assistants ragged.

Here was Peterson leaving him because of some brouhaha over a computer run. Charming, yes, but Weyland could also be a sarcastic bastard. Sure, he was temperamental—the great are often quarrelsome, nothing new in that. Remember how he treated young Denton over that scratch Denton put on the Mercedes' fender? Gave him a tongue-lashing that could warp steel, and when Denton threw a punch Weyland grabbed him by the shoulder and just about flung him across the street. Denton was bruised for a month, looked as if he'd been on the bottom of a football pile-up. Weyland's a tiger when he's roused up, and he's unbelievably strong for a man his age.

He's a damned bully, and Denton should have gotten a medal for trying to get him off the roads. Have you seen Weyland drive? Roars along just barely in control of that great big machine. . . .

Weyland himself wasn't present. Of course not, Weyland was a supercilious son-of-a-bitch; Weyland was an introverted scholar absorbed in great work; Weyland had a secret sorrow too painful to share; Weyland was a charlatan; Weyland was a genius working himself to death to keep alive the Cayslin Center for the Study of Man.

Dean Wacker brooded by the huge empty fireplace. Several times he said in a carrying voice that he had talked with Weyland and that the students involved in the T-shirt scandal would face disciplinary action.

Miss Donelly came in late with a woman from Economics. They talked heatedly in the window bay, and the other two women in the room drifted over to join them. Katje followed.

". . . from off campus, but that's what they always say," one of them snapped. Miss Donelly caught

Katje's eye, smiled a strained smile, and plunged back
into the discussion. They were talking about the rape.
Katje wasn't interested. A woman who used her sense
and carried herself with self-respect didn't get raped,
but saying so to these intellectual women wasted breath.
They didn't understand real life. Katje went back
toward the kitchen.

Buildings and Grounds had sent Nettie Ledyard over
from the student cafeteria to help out. She was rinsing
glasses and squinting at them through the smoke of her
cigarette. She wore a T-shirt bearing a bulbous fish
shape across the front and the words SAVE OUR WHALES.
These "environmental" messages vexed Katje; only
naïve, citified people could think of wild animals as
pets. The shirt undoubtedly belonged to one of Nettie's
long-haired, bleeding-heart boy friends. Nettie herself
smoked too much to pretend to an environmental
conscience. She was no hypocrite, at least. But she
should come properly dressed to do a job at the Club,
just in case a professor came wandering back here for
more ice or whatever.

"I'll be helping you with the Club inventory during
intersession," Nettie said. "Good thing, too. You'll be
spending a lot of time over here until school starts
again, and the campus is really emptying out. Now
there's this sex maniac cruising the place—though what
I could do but run like hell and scream my head off, I
can't tell you.

"Listen, what's this about Jackson sending you on
errands for him?" she added irritably. She flicked ash
off her bosom, which was pushed high like a shelf by
her too-tight brassiere. "His pal Maurice can pick up
his own umbrella, he's no cripple. Having you wandering around out there alone at some godforsaken
hour—"

"Neither of us knew about the rapist," Katje said,
wiping out the last of the ashtrays.

"Just don't let Jackson take advantage of you, that's
all."

Katje grunted. She had been raised not to let herself be taken advantage of by blacks.

Later, helping to dig out a fur hat from under the coat pile in the foyer, she heard someone saying, ". . . walk off with the credit; cold-bloodedly living off other people's academic substance, so to speak."

Into her mind came the image of Dr. Weyland's tall figure moving without a break in stride past the stricken student.

Jackson came down from the roof with watering eyes. A damp wind was rising.

"That leak is fixed for a while," he said, hunching to blow on his chapped hands. "But the big shots at Buildings and Grounds got to do something better before next winter. The snow will just pile up and soak through again."

Katje polished the silver plate with a gray flannel. "What do you know about vampires?" she said.

"How bad you want to know?"

He had no right to joke with her like that, he whose ancestors had been heathen savages. "What do you know about vampires?" she repeated firmly.

"Not a thing." He grinned. "But you just keep on going to the movies with Nettie and you'll find out all about that kind of crap. She got to have the dumbest taste in movies there ever was."

Katje looked down from the landing at Nettie, who had just let herself into the Club.

Nettie's hair was all in tight little rings like pigs' tails. She called, "Guess what I went and did?"

"Your hair," Katje said. "You got it done curly."

Nettie hung her coat crookedly on the rack and peered into the foyer mirror. "I've been wanting to try a permanent for months, but I couldn't find the spare money. So the other night I went over to the sleep lab." She came upstairs.

"What was it like?" Katje said, looking more closely

at Nettie's face; was she paler than usual? Yes, Katje
thought with sudden apprehension.

"It's nothing much. You just lie down on this couch,
and they plug you into these machines, and you sleep.
They keep waking you up in the middle of your dreams
so you can describe what's going on, and you do some
kind of tests—I don't remember, it's all pretty hazy
afterwards. Next morning there's a sort of debriefing
interview, and you collect your pay and go home.
That's all there is to it."

"How do you feel?"

"Okay. I was pretty dragged out yesterday. Dr.
Weyland gave me a list of stuff I'm supposed to eat to
fix that. He got me the day off, too. Wait a minute, I
need a smoke before we go into the linens."

She lit a cigarette. "Really, there was nothing to it.
I'd go back for another session in a minute if they'd
have me. Good money for no work; not like this." She
blew a stream of smoke contemptuously at the linen-
closet door.

Katje said, "Someone has to do what we do."

"Yeah, but why us?" Nettie lowered her voice. "We
ought to get a couple of professors in there with the
bedding and the inventory lists, and us two go sit in
their big leather chairs and drink coffee like ladies."

Katje had already done that as Hendrik's wife. What
she wanted now was to sit on the *stoep* after a day's
hunting, sipping drinks and trading stories of the kill in
the pungent dusk, away from the smoky, noisy hole of a
kitchen: a life that Hendrik had rebelled against as
parasitical, narrow, and dull. His grandfather, like
Katje's, had trekked right out of the Transvaal when it
became too staid for him and had started over. Katje
thought sometimes that challenging his own people
about the future of the land, the government, and the
natives had been Hendrik's way of striking out afresh.
For herself, she wished only to return to her old
country and its old ways.

Nettie, still hanging back from the linen closet,

ground out her cigarette on the sole of her shoe. "Coming to the meeting Friday?"

Dr. Weyland was giving a lecture that same evening, something about nightmares. Katje had been thinking about attending. Now she must decide. Going to his lecture was not like going to his laboratory; it seemed safe enough. "No union meeting," she said. "I've told you, they're all Reds in those unions. I do all right for myself. I'll be going to Dr. Weyland's open lecture that night."

"Okay, if you think it's fine to make what we make doing this stuff." Nettie shrugged. "Me, I'll skip his lecture and take the bucks for sleeping in his lab. You ought to go over there, you know? There's hardly anything doing during intersession with almost everybody gone—they could take you right away. You get extra pay and time off, and besides Dr. Weyland's kind of cute, in a gloomy way. He leaned over me to plug something into the wall, and I said, 'Go ahead, you can bite my neck any time.' You know, he was sort of hanging over me, and his lab coat was sort of spread, like a cape, all menacing and batlike—except white instead of black, of course—and anyway I couldn't resist a wisecrack."

Katje gave her a startled glance. Nettie, missing it, moved past her into the closet and pulled out the step stool. Katje said cautiously, "What did he say to that?"

"Nothing, but he smiled." Nettie climbed up onto the step stool. "You know how his mouth turns sort of down at the corners? It makes him look grim all the time? Well, real serious anyway. When he smiles you'd be amazed how good he looks; he could really turn a girl on. We'll start up top in this closet, all right? I bet all the guys who work nights at the labs get those kind of jokes all the time. Later he said he was hoping you'd come by."

Taking a deep breath of the sweet, sunshine smell of the clean sheets, Katje said, "He asked you to ask me to go there?"

"He said to remind you."

The first pile of blankets was handed down from the top shelf. Katje said, "He really accepts anyone into this project?"

"Unless you're sick, or if you've got funny metabolism or whatever. They do a blood test on you, like at the doctor's."

That was when Katje noticed the little round Band-Aid on the inside of Nettie's elbow, right over the vein.

Miss Donelly was sharing a jug of cheap wine with three other faculty women in the front lounge. Katje made sure the coffee machine was filled for them and then slipped outside.

She still walked alone on campus when she chose. She wasn't afraid of the rapist, who hadn't been heard of in several days. A pleasurable tension drove her toward the lighted windows of the labs. This was like moving through the sharp air of the bushveldt at dusk. Awareness of danger was part of the pleasure.

The lab blinds, tilted down, let out only threads of light. She could see nothing. She hovered a moment, then turned back, hurrying now. The mood was broken, and she felt silly. Daniel from Security would be furious to find her alone out here, and what could she tell him? That she felt herself to be on the track of something wild and it made her feel young?

Miss Donelly and the others were still talking. Katje was glad to hear their wry voices and gusts of laughter, equally glad not to have to sit with them. She had never been comfortable among Hendrik's highly educated colleagues.

She had more on her mind than school gossip, too, and she needed to think. Her own implusive act excited and astonished her: sallying forth to the lab at dusk at some risk from the rapist (her mind swerved neatly around the other, the imaginary danger), but for what? To sniff the breeze and search the ground for tracks?

The thought of Dr. Weyland haunted her: Dr.

Weyland as the charming, restless visitor prowling the Club kitchen, Dr. Weyland thrusting young Denton aside with contemptuous strength, Dr. Weyland as the heartless predator she had at first thought him that morning in the parking lot of the lab building.

She was walking to the bus stop when Jackson drove up and offered her a lift. She was glad to accept. The lonesomeness of the campus was accentuated by darkness and the empty circles of light around the lampposts.

Jackson pulled aside a jumble of equipment on the front seat—radio parts, speakers and wires—to make room for her. Two books were on the floor by her feet. He said, "The voodoo book is left over from my brother Paul. He went through a thing, you know, trying to trace back our family down in Louisiana. The other one was just laying around, so I brought it along."

The other one was *Dracula*. Katje felt the gummy spot where the price sticker had been peeled off. Jackson must have bought it for her at the discount bookstore downtown. She didn't know how to thank him easily, so she said nothing.

"It's a long walk to the bus stop," Jackson said, scowling as he drove out through the stone gates of the college drive. "They should've fixed it so you could stay on in faculty housing after your husband died."

"Our place was too big for one person," Katje said. Sometimes she missed the house on the east side of campus, but her present lodgings away from school offered more privacy.

He shook his head. "Well, I think it's a shame, you being a foreign visitor and all."

Katje laughed. "After twenty-five years in this country, a visitor?"

He laughed, too. "Yeah. Well, you sure have moved around more than most while you been here: from lady of leisure to, well, maid work." She saw the flash of his grin. "Like my aunt that used to clean for white women up the hill. Don't you mind?"

She minded when she thought working at the Club would never end. Sometimes the Africa that she remembered seemed too vague a place to actually go back to, and the only future she could see was keeling over at the end while vacuuming the Club rugs, like a farmer worn to death at his plow . . .

None of this was Jackson's business. "Did your aunt mind her work?" she snapped.

Jackson pulled up opposite the bus stop. "She said you just do what it comes to you to do and thank God for it."

"I say the same."

He sighed. "You're a lot like her, crazy as that sounds. There's a bunch of questions I want to ask you sometime, about how it was when you lived in Africa; I mean, was it anything like in the movies—you know, *King Solomon's Mines* and like that?"

Katje had never seen that movie, but she knew that nothing on film could be like her Africa. "You should go to Africa and see for yourself," she said.

"I'm working on it. There's your bus coming. Wait a minute, listen—no more walking alone out here after dark, there's not enough people around now. You got to arrange to be picked up. Didn't you hear? That guy jumped another girl last night. She got away, but still. Daniel says he found one of the back doors to the Club unlocked. You be careful, will you? I don't want to have to come busting in there to save you from some de-ranged six-foot pre-med on the rampage, know what I mean?"

"Oh, I take care of myself," Katje said, touched and annoyed and amused all at once by his solicitude.

"Sure. Only I wish you were about fifteen years younger and studying karate, you know?" As Katje got out of the car with the books in her arm he added, "You told me once you did a lot of hunting in Africa when you were a kid; handling guns."

"Yes, a lot."

"Okay. Take this." He pulled metal out of his pocket and put it in her hand. It was a gun. "Just in case. You know how to use it, right?"

She closed her fingers on the compact weight of it. "But where did you get this? Do you have papers for it? The laws here are very strict—"

He yanked the door shut and said through the open window, "You going to holler 'law' at me, you can just give the damn thing back. No? Okay, then, hurry up before you miss your bus."

Dracula was a silly book. She had to force herself to read on in spite of the absurd Van Helsing character with his idiot English—an insult to anyone of Dutch descent. The voodoo book was impenetrable, and she soon gave it up.

The handgun was another matter. She sat at the formica-topped table in her kitchenette and turned the shiny little automatic in the light, thinking, How did Jackson come by such a thing? For that matter, how did he afford his fancy sports car and all that equipment he carried in it from time to time—where did it all come from and where did it go? He was up to something, probably lots of things, what they called "hustling" nowadays. A good thing he had given her the gun. It could only get him into trouble to carry it around with him. She knew how to handle weapons, and surely with a rapist at large the authorities would be understanding about her lack of a license for it.

The gun needed cleaning. She worked on it as best she could without proper tools. It was a cheap .25-caliber gun. Back home your gun was a fine rifle, made to drop a charging rhino in its tracks, not a stubby little nickle-plated toy like this for scaring off muggers and rapists.

Yet she wasn't sorry to have it. Her own hunting gun that she had brought from Africa years ago was in storage with the extra things from the old house on campus. She had missed the presence of that rifle lately. She had missed it because, she realized now with a nervous little jump of the heart, she had become engaged in stalking a dangerous animal. She was stalking Dr. Weyland.

She went to sleep with the gun on the night table next to her bed and woke listening for the roar so she would know in what direction to look tomorrow for the lion's spoor. There was a hot rank odor of African dust in the air and she sat up in bed thinking, He's been here.

It was a dream. But so clear! She went to look out the front window without turning on the light, and it was the ordinary street below that seemed unreal. Her heart drummed in her chest. Not that he would come after her here on Dewer Street, but he had sent Nettie to the Club, and now he had sent this dream into her sleep. Creatures stalking each other over time grew a bond from mind to mind.

But that was in another life. Was she losing her sanity? She read for a little in the Afrikaans Bible she had brought with her from home but so seldom opened in recent years. What gave comfort in the end was to put Jackson's automatic into her purse to carry with her. A gun was supposedly of no use against a vampire —you needed a wooden stake, she remembered reading, or you had to cut off his head to kill him—but the weight of the weapon in her handbag reassured her.

The lecture hall was full in spite of the scarcity of students on campus this time of year. These special talks were open to the town as well.

Dr. Weyland read his lecture in a stiff, abrupt manner. He stood slightly cramped over the lectern, which was low for his height, and rapped out his sentences, rarely raising his glance from his notes. In his tweeds and heavy-rimmed glasses he was the picture of the scholarly recluse drawn out of the study into the limelight. But Katje saw more than that. She saw the fluid power of his arm as he scooped from the air an errant sheet of notes, the almost disdainful ease with which he established his dominion over the audience. His lecture was brief; he fulfilled with unmistakable impatience the duty set every member of the faculty to give one public address per year on an aspect of his work, in this case "The Demonology of Dreams."

At the end came questions from the audience, most of them obviously designed to show the questioner's cleverness rather than to elicit information. The discussions after these lectures were reputed to be the real show. Katje, lulled by the abstract talk, came fully awake when a young woman asked, "Professor, have you considered whether the legends of supernatural creatures such as werewolves, vampires, and dragons might not be distortions out of nightmares at all—that maybe the legends reflect the existence of real, though rare, prodigies of evolution?"

Dr. Weyland hesitated, coughed, sipped water. "The forces of evolution are capable of prodigies, certainly," he said. "You have chosen an excellent word. But we must understand that we are not speaking—in the case of the vampire, for example—of a blood-sipping phantom who cringes from a clove of garlic. Now, how would nature design a vampire?

"The corporeal vampire, if he existed, would be by definition the greatest of all predators, living as he would off the top of the food chain. Man is the most dangerous animal, the devourer or destroyer of all others, and the vampire preys on man. Now, any sensible vampire would choose to avoid the risks of attacking humans by tapping the blood of lower animals, if he could; so we must assume that our vampire cannot. Perhaps animal blood can tide him over a lean patch, as sea water can sustain the castaway for a few miserable days but can't permanently replace fresh water to drink. Humanity would remain the vampire's livestock, albeit fractious and dangerous to deal with, and where they live so must he.

"In the sparsely settled early world he would be

bound to a town or village to assure his food supply. He would learn to live on as little as he could—perhaps a half liter of blood per day—since he could hardly leave a trail of drained corpses and remain unnoticed. Periodically he would withdraw for his own safety and to give the villagers time to recover from his depredations. A sleep several generations long would provide him with an untouched, ignorant population in the same location. He must be able to slow his metabolism, to induce in himself naturally a state of suspended animation. Mobility in time would become his alternative to mobility in space."

Katje listened intently. His daring in speaking this way excited her. She could see he was beginning to enjoy the game, growing more at ease on the podium as he warmed to his subject. He abandoned the lectern, put his hands casually into his pockets, and surveyed his listeners with a lofty glance. It seemed to Katje that he mocked them.

"The vampire's slowed body functions during these long rest periods might help extend his lifetime; so might living for long periods, waking or sleeping, on the edge of starvation. We know that minimal feeding produces striking longevity in some other species. Long life would be a highly desirable alternative to reproduction; flourishing best with the least competition, the great predator would not wish to sire his own rivals. It could not be true that his bite would turn his victims into vampires like himself—"

"Or we'd be up to our necks in fangs," whispered someone in the audience rather loudly.

"Fangs are too noticeable and not efficient for blood-sucking," observed Dr. Weyland. "Large, sharp canine teeth are designed to tear meat. Polish versions of the vampire legend might be closer to the mark: they tell of some sort of puncturing device, perhaps a needle in the tongue like a sting that would secrete an anticlotting substance. That way the vampire could seal his lips around a minimal wound and draw the blood freely, instead of having to rip great, spouting, wasteful holes in his unfortunate prey." Dr. Weyland smiled.

The younger members of the audience produced appropriate retching noises.

Would a vampire sleep in a coffin, someone asked.

"Certainly not," Dr. Weyland retorted. "Would you, given a choice? The corporeal vampire would require physical access to the world, which is something that burial customs are designed to prevent. He might retire to a cave or take his rest in a tree like Merlin, or Ariel in the cloven pine, provided he could find either tree or cave safe from wilderness freaks and developers' bull-dozers. Locating a secure, long-term resting place is one obvious problem for our vampire in modern times."

Urged to name some others, he continued, "Consider: upon each waking he must quickly adapt to his new surroundings, a task which, we may imagine, has grown progressively more difficult with the rapid acceleration of cultural change since the Industrial Revolution. In the last century and a half he has no doubt had to limit his sleeps to shorter and shorter periods for fear of completely losing touch—a deprivation which cannot have improved his temper.

"Since we posit a natural rather than a supernatural being, he grows older, but very slowly. Meanwhile each updating of himself is more challenging and demands more from him—more imagination, more energy, more cunning. While he must adapt sufficiently to disguise his anomalous existence, he must not succumb to current ideologies of Right or Left—that is, to the cant of individual license or the cant of the infallibility of the masses—lest either allegiance interfere with the exercise of his predatory survival skills."

Meaning, Katje thought grimly, he can't afford scruples about drinking our blood. He was pacing the platform now, soundless footfalls and graceful stride proclaiming his true nature. But these people were spellbound, rapt under his rule, enjoying his domina-

tion of them. They saw nothing of his menace, only the
beauty of his quick hawk-glance and his panther-
playfulness.

Emrys Williams raised a giggle by commenting that a
lazy vampire could always take home a pretty young
instructor who would show him any new developments
in interpersonal relations.

Dr. Weyland fixed him with a cold glance. "You are
mixing up dinner with sex," he remarked, "and not, I
gather, for the first time."

They roared. Williams—the "tame Wild Welshman
of the Lit Department" to his less admiring colleagues
—turned a gratified pink.

One of Dr. Weyland's associates in Anthropology
pointed out at boring length that the vampire, born in
an earlier age, would become dangerously conspicuous
for his diminutive height as the human race grew taller.

"Not necessarily," commented Dr. Weyland. "Remember that we speak of a highly specialized physical
form. It may be that during his waking periods his
metabolism is so sensitive that he responds to the
stimuli in the environment by growing in his body as
well as in his mind. Perhaps while awake his entire
being exists at an intense level of inner activity and
change. The stress of these great rushes to catch up all
at once with physical, mental, and cultural evolution
must be enormous. These days he would need his long
sleeps as recovery periods from the strain."

He glanced at the wall clock. "As you can see, by the
exercise of a little imagination and logic we produce a
creature bearing superficial resemblances to the vampire of legend, but at base one quite different from your
standard strolling corpse with an aversion to crosses.
Any questions on our subject—dreams?"

But they weren't willing to drop this flight of fancy. A
young fellow asked how Dr. Weyland accounted for the
superstitions about crosses and garlic and so on.

The professor paused to sip water from the glass at
hand. The audience waited in expectant silence. Katje

had the feeling that they would have waited an hour without protest, he had so charmed them. Finally he said, "Primitive men first encountering the vampire would be unaware that they themselves were products of evolution, let alone that he was. They would make up stories to account for him, and to try to control him. In early times he might himself believe in some of these legends—the silver bullet, the oaken stake. Waking at length in a less credulous age he would abandon these notions, just as everyone else did. He might even develop an interest in his own origins and evolution."

"Wouldn't he be lonely?" sighed a girl standing in the side aisle, her posture eloquent of the desire to comfort that loneliness.

"The young lady will forgive me," Dr. Weyland responded, "if I observe that this is a question born of a sheltered life. Predators in nature do not indulge in the sort of romantic mooning that humans impute to them. Our vampire wouldn't have the time for moodiness. On each waking he has more to learn. Perhaps someday the world will return to a reasonable rate of change, permitting him some leisure in which to feel lonely or whatever suits him."

A nervous girl ventured the opinion that a perpetually self-educating vampire would always have to find himself a place in a center of learning in order to have access to the information he would need.

"Quite right," agreed Dr. Weyland dryly. "Perhaps a university, where strenuous study and other eccentricities of the active intellect would be accepted behavior in a grown man. Even a modest institution such as Cayslin College might serve."

Under the chuckling that followed this came a question too faint for Katje to hear. Dr. Weyland, having bent to listen, straightened up and announced sardonically, "The lady desires me to comment upon the vampire's 'Satanic pride.' Madame, here we enter the area of the literary imagination and its devices where I dare not tread under the eyes of my colleagues from the

English Department. Perhaps they will pardon me if I
merely point out that a tiger who falls asleep in a jungle
and on waking finds a thriving city overgrowing his lair
has no energy to spare for displays of Satanic pride."

Great God, the nerve of him! Katje thought, torn
between outrage and admiration. She wanted him to
look at her, to see knowledge burning in one face at
least, to know that he had not flaunted his reality
tonight only before blind eyes. Surely he sensed her
challenge, surely he would turn—

Williams, intent on having the last word as always,
spoke up once more: "The vampire as time-traveler—
you ought to be writing science fiction, Weyland." This
provoked a growing patter of applause, signal of the
evening's end.

Katje hurried out with the crowd and withdrew to
stand aside under the portico of the Union Building
while her hot heart cooled. Dr. Weyland's car was
across the street, gleaming in the lamplight. To him, she
thought, it was not just a car but his access to physical
mobility and a modern mechanical necessity that he
had mastered. That was how he would think of it, she
was sure. She knew something of his mind now.

With the outwash of departing audience came Miss
Donelly. She asked if Katje needed a lift. Katje explained that a group of women from the staff cafeteria
went bowling together each Friday night and had
promised to swing by and pick her up.

"I'll wait with you just in case," Miss Donelly said.
"You know, Wild Man Williams is a twerp, but he was
right: Weyland's vampire would be a time-traveler. He
could only go forward, of course, never back, and only
by long, unpredictable leaps—this time, say, into our
age of what we like to think of as technological marvels;
maybe next time into an age of interstellar travel. Who
knows, he might get to taste Martian blood, if there are
Martians, and if they have blood.

"Frankly, I wouldn't have thought Weyland could
come up with anything so imaginative extempore like

that—the vampire as a sort of leftover saber-tooth tiger prowling the pavements, a truly endangered species. That's the next term's T-shirt: 'Save the Vampire.' "

There was no point consulting Miss Donelly. She might banter, but she would never believe. It was all a joke to her, a clever mental game invented by Dr. Weyland to amuse his audience. She could not perceive, as Katje could, that he was a monster amusing himself by toying with his prey.

Miss Donelly added ruefully, "You've got to hand it to the man, he's got tremendous stage presence, and he sure knows how to turn on the charm when he feels like it. Nothing too smooth, mind you—just enough unbending, enough slightly caustic graciousness, to set susceptible hearts abeating. You could almost forget what a ruthless, self-centered bastard he can be. Did you notice that most of the comments came from women?

"Is that your lift?"

It was. While the women in the station wagon shuffled themselves around to make room, Katje stood with her hand on the door and watched Dr. Weyland emerge from the building with admiring students at either hand. He loomed above them, his hair silver under the lamplight. For overcivilized people to experience the approach of such a predator as sexually attractive was not strange. She remembered Scotty saying once that the great cats were all beautiful, and maybe beauty helped them to capture their prey.

Dr. Weyland turned his head, and she thought for a moment that he was looking at her as she got into the station wagon.

Fear filled her. What could she do to protect herself from him, how could she alert others to the truth without people thinking she was simply crazy? She couldn't think amid the tired, satisfied ramblings of the bowling friends, and she declined to stay up and socialize with them. They didn't press her.

Sitting alone at home, Katje had a cup of hot milk to

calm herself for sleep. To her perplexity, her mind kept wandering from thoughts of Dr. Weyland to memories of drinking cocoa at night with Hendrik and the African students he used to bring to dinner. They had been native boys to her, dressed up in suits and talking politics like white men, flashing photographs of black kids playing with toy trucks and walkie-talkie sets. Sometimes they had all gone to see documentary films of an Africa full of cities and traffic and black professionals exhorting, explaining, running things, as these students expected to do in their turn when they went home.

She thought about home now. She recalled clearly all those indicators of change in Africa, and she saw suddenly that the old life there had gone. She would return to an Africa largely as foreign to her as America had been at first. Reluctantly she admitted that one of her feelings while listening to Dr. Weyland talk had been an unwilling empathy: if he was a one-way time-traveler, so was she. She saw herself cut off from the old life of raw vigor, the rivers of game, the smoky village air, all viewed from the heights of white privilege. To lose one's world these days one did not have to sleep for half a century; one had only to grow older.

Next morning she found Dr. Weyland leaning, hands in pockets, against one of the columns flanking the entrance to the Club. She stopped some yards from him, her purse hanging heavily on her arm. The hour was early, the campus deserted-looking. Stand still, she thought; show no fear.

He looked at her. "I saw you after the lecture last night and, earlier in the week, outside the lab one evening. You must know better than to wander alone at night; the campus is empty, no one is around—anything might happen. If you are curious, Mrs. de Groot, come do a session for me. All your questions will be answered. Come over tonight. I could stop by here for you in my car on the way back to the lab after dinner.

There's no problem with scheduling, and I would welcome your company. During intersession the lab is empty. I have no volunteers. I sit alone over there these nights hoping some impoverished youngster, unable to afford a trip home at intersession, will be moved by an uncontrollable itch for travel to come to my lab and earn his fare."

She felt fear and excitement knocking sharply in her body. She shook her head, no.

"My work would interest you, I think," he added, watching her. "You are an alert, handsome woman; they waste your qualities here. Couldn't the college find you something better than this job after your husband died? You might consider coming over regularly to help me with some clerical chores until I get a new assistant. I pay well."

Astonished out of her fear at the offer of work in the vampire's lair, she found her voice. "I am a country woman, Dr. Weyland, a daughter of farmers. I have no proper education. We never read books at home, except the Bible. My husband didn't want me to work. I have spent my time in this country learning English and cooking and how to shop for the right things. I have no skills, no knowledge but the little that I remember of the crops, the weather, the customs, the wildlife of another country—and even that is probably out of date. I would be no use in work like yours."

Hunched in his coat with the collar upturned, looking at her slightly askance, his tousled hair gleaming with the damp, he had the aspect of an old hawk, intent but aloof. He broke the pose, yawned behind his large-knuckled hand, and straightened up.

"As you like. Here comes your friend Nellie."

"Nettie," Katje corrected, suddenly outraged: he'd drunk Nettie's blood, the least he could do was to remember her name properly. But he was walking away over the lawn toward the labs.

Nettie came panting up. "Who was that? Did he try to attack you?"

"It was Dr. Weyland," Katje said. She hoped Nettie didn't notice her trembling.

Nettie laughed. "What is this, a secret romance?"

Miss Donelly came into the kitchen toward the end of the luncheon for the departing emeritus. She plumped herself down between Nettie and Katje, who were taking a break and preparing dessert respectively. Katje spooned whipped cream carefully into each glass dish of fruit.

Miss Donelly said, "In case I get too smashed to say this later, thanks. On the budget I gave you, you did just great. The Department will put on something official with Beef Wellington and all the trimmings over at Borchard's. But it was really important for some of us to give Sylvia our own alcoholic farewell feast, which we couldn't have done without your help."

Nettie nodded and stubbed out her cigarette.

"Our pleasure," Katje said, preoccupied. Dr. Weyland had come for her, would come back again; he was hers to deal with, but how? She no longer thought of sharing her fear, not with Nettie with her money worries or with Miss Donelly whose eyes were just now faintly glazed-looking with drink. Weyland the vampire could never be dealt with by a committee.

"The latest word," Miss Donelly added bitterly, "is that the Department plans to fill Sylvia's place with some guy from Oregon; which means the salary goes up half as much again or more inside of six months."

"Them's the breaks," Nettie said, not very pleasantly. She caught Katje's eyes with a look that said, Look who makes all the money and look who does all the complaining.

"Them is," Miss Donelly agreed glumly. "As for me, the word is no tenure, so I'll be moving on in the fall. Me and my big mouth. Wacker nearly fainted at my prescription for stopping the rapes; you entrap the guy, disembowel him, and hang his balls over the front gates. Our good dean doesn't know me well enough to realize that it's all front. On my own I'd be too petrified to try anything but talking the bastard out of it; you know, 'Now you just let me put my dress back on and I'll make us each a cup of coffee, and you tell me all about why you hate women.'" She stood up.

"Did you hear what happened to that girl last night, the latest victim? He cut her throat. Ripped her pants off, but didn't even bother raping her. That's how desperate for sex he is."

Katje said, "Jackson told us about the killing this morning."

"Jackson? Oh, from Buildings and Grounds. Look out, it could even be him. Any of them, damn them," she muttered savagely as she turned away, "living off us, kicking our bodies out of the way when they're through—"

She stumbled out of the kitchen.

Nettie snorted. "She's always been one of those libbers. No wonder Wacker's getting rid of her. Some men act like hogs, but you can't let yourself be turned into a man-hater. A man's the only chance most girls have of getting up in the world, you know?" She pulled on a pair of acid-yellow gloves and headed for the sink. "If I want out of these rubber gloves, I have to marry a guy who can afford to pay a maid."

Katje sat looking at the fruit dishes with their plump cream caps. It was just as the Bible said: she felt it happen—the scales fell from her eyes. She saw clearly and thought, I am a fool.

Bad pay is real, rape is real, killing is real. The real world worries about real dangers, not childish fancies of a night prowler who drinks blood. Dr. Weyland took the trouble to be concerned, to offer extra work, while I was thinking . . . idiot things about him. Where does it come from, this nonsense of mine? My life is dull since Hendrik died; so I make up drama in my head, and that way I get to think about Dr. Weyland, a distinguished and learned gentleman, being interested in me.

She resolved to go to the lab building later and leave

a note for him, an apology for her reluctance, an offer to stop by soon and make an appointment at the sleep lab.

Nettie looked at the clock and said over her shoulder, "Time to take the ladies their dessert."

At last the women had dispersed, leaving the usual fog of smoke behind. Katje and Nettie had finished the cleaning up. Katje said, "I'm going for some air."

Nettie, wreathed by smoke of her own making, drowsed in one of the big living-room chairs. She shook her head. "Not me. I'm pooped." She sat up. "Unless you want me along? It's still light out, so you're safe from the Cayslin Ripper."

"Don't disturb yourself," Katje said.

Away on the far edge of the lawn three students danced under the sailing shape of a Frisbee. Katje looked up at the sun, a silver disk behind a thin place in the clouds; more rain coming, probably. The campus still wore a deserted look. Katje wasn't worried. There was no vampire, and the gun in her purse would suffice for anything else.

The sleep lab was locked. She tucked her note of apology between the lab door and the jamb and left.

As she started back across the lawn someone stepped behind her, and long fingers closed on her arm: it was Dr. Weyland. Firmly and without speaking he bent her course back toward the labs.

"What are you doing?" she said, astonished.

"I almost drove off without seeing you. Come sit in my car, I want to talk to you." She held back, alarmed, and he gave her a sharp shake. "Making a fuss is pointless. No one is here to notice."

There was only his car in the parking lot; even the Frisbee players had gone. Dr. Weyland opened the door of the Mercedes and inserted Katje into the front passenger seat with a deft, powerful thrust of his arm. He got in on the driver's side, snapped down the automatic door locks, and sat back. He looked up at the gray sky, then at his wristwatch.

Katje said, "You wanted to say something to me?"

He didn't answer.

She said, "What are we waiting for?"

"For the day man to leave and lock up the labs. I dislike being interrupted."

This is what it's like, Katje thought, feeling lethargic detachment stealing through her, paralyzing her. No hypnotic power out of a novelist's imagination held her, but the spell cast on the prey of the hunting cat, the shock of being seized in the deadly jaws though not a drop of blood was yet spilled. "Interrupted," she whispered.

"Yes," he said, turning toward her. She saw the naked craving in his gaze. "Interrupted at whatever it pleases me to do with you. You are on my turf now, Mrs. de Groot, where you have persisted in coming time after time. I can't wait any longer for you to make up your mind. You are healthy—I looked up your records—and I am hungry."

The car smelled of cold metal, leather, and tweed. At length a man came out of the lab building and bent to unlock the chain from the only bicycle in the bike rack. By the way Dr. Weyland shifted in his seat Katje knew that this was the departure he had been awaiting.

"Look at that idiot," he muttered. "Is he going to take all night?" Weyland turned restlessly toward the lab windows. That would be the place, Katje thought, after a bloodless blow to stun her—he wouldn't want any mess in his Mercedes.

In her lassitude she was sure that he had attacked that girl, drunk her blood, and then killed her. He was using the rapist's activities as cover. When subjects did not come to him at the sleep lab, hunger drove him out to hunt.

She thought, *But I am myself a hunter!*

Cold anger coursed through her. Her thoughts flew:

she needed time, a moment out of his reach to plan her survival. She had to get out of the car—any subterfuge would do.

She gulped and turned toward him, croaking, "I'm going to be sick."

He swore furiously. The locks clicked; he reached roughly past her and shoved open the door on her side. "Out!"

She stumbled out into the drizzling, chilly air and backed several hasty paces, hugging her purse to her body like a shield, looking quickly around. The man on the bike had gone. The upper story of the Cayslin Club across the lawn showed a light—Nettie would be missing her now. Maybe Jackson would be just arriving to pick them both up there. But no help could come in time.

Dr. Weyland had gotten out of the car. He stood with his arms folded on the roof of the Mercedes, looking across at her with a mixture of annoyance and contempt. "Mrs. de Groot, do you think you can outrun me?"

He started around the front of his car toward her.

Scotty's voice sounded quietly in her ear: "Yours," he said, as the leopard tensed to charge. Weyland too was an animal, not an immortal monster out of legend —just a wild beast, however smart and strong and hungry. He had said so himself.

She jerked out the automatic, readying it to fire as she brought it swiftly up to eye level in both hands, while her mind told her calmly that a head shot would be best but that a hit was surer if she aimed for the torso.

She shot him twice, two slugs in quick succession, one in the chest and one in the abdomen. He did not fall but bent to clutch at his torn body, and he screamed and screamed so that she was too shaken to steady her hands for the head shot afterward. She cried out also, involuntarily: his screams were dreadful. It was long since she had shot anything.

Footsteps rushed behind her, arms flung round her pinning her hands to her sides so that the gun pointed at the ground. Jackson's voice gasped in her ear, "Jesus Christ!"

His car stood slewed where he had braked it, unheard by Katje. Nettie jumped out and rushed toward Katje, crying, "My God, he's shot, she shot him!"

Breaking off his screaming, Weyland tottered away from them around his car and fetched up leaning on the front. His face, a sunken-cheeked, starving mask, gaped at them.

"It's him?" Jackson said incredulously. "*He* tried to rape you?"

Katje said, "No, he's a vampire."

"A vampire!" Jackson exploded. "Have you gone crazy? Jesus!"

Weyland panted, "Stop staring, cattle!"

He wedged himself heavily into the driver's seat of his car. They could see him slumped there, his forehead against the curve of the steering wheel. Blood spotted the hood of the Mercedes where he had leaned.

"Mrs. de Groot, give me the gun," Jackson said.

Katje clenched her fingers around the grip. "No."

She could tell by the way Jackson's arms tightened that he was afraid to let go of her and grab for the gun. A siren sounded. Nettie cried in wild relief, "That's Daniel's car coming!"

Weyland raised his head. His gray face was rigid with determination. He snarled, "The door—one of you shut the door!"

His glaring face commanded them. Nettie darted forward, slammed the door, and recoiled, wiping her hand on her sweater. The engine started. Weyland drove the Mercedes waveringly past them, out of the parking lot toward the gateway road. Rain swept down in heavy gusts. Katje heard the siren again and woke fully to her failure: she had not made a clean kill. The vampire was getting away.

She lunged toward Jackson's car. He held her back,

shouting, "Nothing doing, come on, you done *enough*!"

The Mercedes crawled haltingly down the middle of the road, turned at the stone gates, and was gone.

Jackson said, "*Now* will you give me that gun?"

Katje snapped on the safety and dropped the automatic on the wet paving at their feet.

Nettie was pointing toward the Club. "There's people coming—they must have heard the shooting and called Daniel. Listen, Jackson, we're in trouble. Nobody's going to believe that Dr. Weyland is the rapist—or the other thing either." Her glance flickered nervously at Katje. "Whatever we say, they'll think we're crazy."

"Oh, shit," said Jackson tiredly, letting Katje go at last. He picked up the gun. Katje saw the apprehension in his face as he weighed Nettie's assessment of their situation: a wild story from some cleaning people about the eminent professor.

"We've got to say something," Nettie went on desperately. "All that blood . . ." She fell silent, staring down.

There was no blood. The rain had washed the tarmac clean.

Jackson faced Katje and said urgently, "Listen, Mrs. de Groot, we don't know a thing about any shooting, you hear?" He slipped the gun into an inside pocket of his jacket. "You came over to make an appointment at the sleep lab, only Dr. Weyland wasn't around. You waited for him, and Nettie got worried when you didn't come back, and we drove over here looking for you. We all heard shooting, but nobody saw anything. There was nothing to see. Like now."

Katje was furious with him and with herself. She should have chanced the head shot, she shouldn't have let Jackson hold her back.

She could see Daniel's car now, wheeling into the parking lot.

Jackson said tightly, "I got accepted to computer

school in Rochester for next semester. You can bet they don't do vampires over there, Mrs. de Groot; and they don't do blacks with guns either. Me and Nettie got to live here, we don't get to go away to Africa."

She grew calm; he was right. The connection had been between herself and the vampire all along, and what had happened here was her own affair, nothing to do with these young people.

"All right, Jackson," she said. "There was nothing to see."

"Check," he said. He turned toward Daniel's car.

He would do all right, Katje thought; maybe someday he would come visit her in Africa, in a smart suit and carrying an attaché case, on business. Surely they had computers there now, too.

Daniel stepped out of his car into the rain, one hand on his pistol butt. Katje saw the disappointment sour his florid face as Nettie put a hand on his arm and talked.

Katje picked up her purse from where she had dropped it—how light it felt now, without the gun in it. She fished out her plastic rain hood, though her hair was already wet. Tying the hood on, she thought about her old .350 magazine rifle, her lion gun; about taking it from storage, putting it in working order, tucking it well back into the broom closet at the Club. In case Weyland didn't die, in case he couldn't sleep with two bullets in him and came limping back to hunt on familiar ground—to look for her. He would come next week, when the students returned, or never. She didn't think he would come, but she would be ready just in case.

And then, as she had planned, she would go home to Africa. Her mind flashed: a new life, whatever life she could make for herself there these days. If Weyland could fit himself to new futures, so could she. She was adaptable and determined—like him.

But if he did sleep, and woke again fifty years from now? Each generation must look out for itself. She had done her part, although perhaps not well enough to boast about. Still, what a tale it would make some evening over the smoke of a campfire on the veldt, beginning with the tall form of Dr. Weyland seen striding across the parking lot past the kneeling student in the heavy mist of morning . . .

Katje walked toward Daniel's car to tell the story that Buildings and Grounds would understand.

II
The Land
of
Lost Content

"THESE GUYS FOUND this big old Mercedes-Benz sedan jammed into a clump of bushes in the county park, with the driver collapsed all bloody at the wheel," Wesley said. "They said they'd get the cops or take him to the hospital, but the guy said no. Well, they know Weinberg, and they called him. Figured the Mercedes man had his reasons and Weinberg might be able to make something out of it and tip them for it.

"Weinberg came and got this guy and tucked him up quiet at his U-Store-It near Hartford. He had the car hauled out and cleaned up, and he sold it for a nice price. Whoever this guy is, he took good care of his car."

Wesley paused to unwrap and break in a fresh stick of gum.

"But who is the guy?" he continued. "Nobody knows. I brought down everything they found on him, over in that paper bag. There's no wallet, no I.D., and he wouldn't give any name. Weinberg called this doctor

he knows. The doctor took two slugs out of the
Mercedes man, one here and one here." He touched
his own chest and belly. "And he brought some whole
blood to transfuse so the guy wouldn't drop dead while
Weinberg was still trying to find out who might have a
worthwhile interest in him.

"Now here's the weird part. They hung up the blood
bottle and put the needle in, and the next thing you
know the Mercedes man pulls the needle out again and
busts it off, and he starts sucking the fuckin' tube.
Sucking up the blood, you see what I mean? Drinking
it. That's when Weinberg decided this one was for you,
Roger. He said he didn't know anybody else who'd
know what to do with a goddamn vampire."

Roger laughed delightedly, hugging his knees, and
looked at Mark to see how he was taking all this.

The whole thing sounded to Mark like a loony
hangover from the days when his Uncle Roger had
been, in many of his successive crazes, a good market
for outlandish items from Weinberg's unadvertised
stock. Weinberg the fence was the only crook Mark
knew and his first evidence that there were Jewish
gangsters as well as all the other kinds.

Trust Roger to know people like that. Whenever
things heated up too much between Mark's parents—
this time it was over plans for his summer—he came to
stay with Roger. He reveled in more freedom here than
a fourteen-year-old school kid would be allowed any-
where else.

But what the heck was this? You walk into Roger's
place, unannounced as usual, and everything looks like
always: sliding door open to let in spring air from the
yard, all the living-room plants looking wilted with
neglect, Wesley sprawled on the couch chewing gum,
and Roger perched in the big leather chair bright as a
jungle bird in his scarlet silk shirt and tie-dyed jeans.
Roger owned a string of fashion outlets and liked to
dress off the men's racks.

Then before you even have a chance to put away

your pack and your school briefcase they tell you, straightfaced, that Roger has bought a vampire, and Wesley has just delivered him here, to Roger's garden apartment on the West Side of Manhattan. A vampire.

Mark kept his expression carefully noncommittal.

Roger said to Wesley, "Do you believe the guy really drank blood?"

Wesley shrugged. He was an ex-Marine, working these days as a hospital attendant. In his spare time he did odd jobs for Roger. He said, "I seen guys do real weird things when they're shot."

Roger said, "Did this vampire say anything to them while they kept him at the U-Store-It?"

"Said he couldn't sleep. Who could, with two holes in him and no dope to put him out? Weinberg wanted some for him in case he started yelling, but the doctor said he wouldn't use anything without doing a bunch of tests first because the guy seemed to be built kind of odd, and he didn't know what the drugs would do. Real interested, this doctor was; I bet Weinberg told you that, Roger, to hurry you up—making out like he was worried the doctor would get hold of this vampire first to study him. Uh-huh, thought so. How much did you pay for this character, anyway?"

"Are you still game to help find out if he's worth the money?" Roger countered. Wesley shrugged again. They both got up. "Come on, Mark, you don't want to miss this."

It wasn't a joke. They were serious. All of a sudden the dim hallway to the guest rooms looked scary.

The living room was the center of the apartment. The kitchen and Roger's bedroom and bath were to the right, up front. On the short hallway leading left were closets, a guest bathroom, and two small spare rooms. One of the spare rooms was Mark's when he was staying here. Across the hall from it was a much smaller room, white and bare, with a tiny half-bath adjoining.

Mark opened the door to his own room and glanced in. Bed, dresser, drawing table, bookcase, old map prints hanging on the cool blue walls, window curtains with wild birds on them, Scandinavian striped fur rug on the floor—all reassured him. If use was made of the room in Mark's absence, Roger cleaned up any signs of it afterward. Mark never asked about that. He liked to think of the room as his own.

On the other side of the hallway the wooden door to the smaller bedroom stood open. No wonder the apartment smelled of plaster dust. Wesley had been at work here, installing square pipes flush against the sides of the doorway. Between the pipes hung a tall gate of metal bars. In the back wall there was one barred window glazed with frosted, wire-mesh glass, the kind used to keep out burglars. The bleak little chamber, transformed by the gate into a cage, contained a prisoner.

A man lay on his back on a cot against the wall. He was too tall for the cot; his feet hung over the end, and the blue blanket that covered them came up only to his chest. His face was turned away. He had gray hair. One arm hung down, the hand resting knuckles up on the linoleum.

Mark, inwardly braced to see a dangerous monster, felt relieved and disappointed. But maybe the man's face was awful with fangs and a million wrinkles, like the face on the Dracula book that Mark had browsed through on a Marboro bargain table last week.

Roger, unlocking the gate, must have sensed Mark's reaction. "Doesn't look like much, does he?" he said uneasily. "I wonder if Weinberg's trying to put one over on me."

They went inside and walked over to the cot. The man turned his head. He had a long, lined face with hollow cheeks and sunken eyes that he seemed hardly able to hold open. His mouth looked dark and crusted, and Mark thought, *blood* and felt a twinge of nausea. Then he realized that it must be like when you have a bad fever, and your mouth gets so dry your lips blacken and crack.

Wesley rolled up the sleeve of his blue work shirt. Sitting down carefully at the head end of the cot, he slipped an arm under the man, raising his head and shoulders against his own side. The man's lips curled back in pain, showing plain teeth, no fangs. Wesley said in a soothing, coaxing voice, "Okay now, you want to try a little, ah, drink?"

The man stared at nothing, ignoring the bared arm that Wesley held extended in front of him.

Mark said in a small voice, "Aren't you scared, Wesley?"

"Nope. I got lots of blood. Bled a fuckin' flood when I got hit in Nam, and I'm still here."

"I mean, if he bites you won't you turn into a vampire too?"

Roger said, "Don't be silly, Markie. If that were true, even if there was only one real vampire to start with, pretty soon we'd be all vampires and no people. It can't work like that, it doesn't make any sense. Wesley's safe."

Wesley grunted. "Only no biting on the neck, that's too personal. He can take it from my arm, like at the doctor's."

But the supposed vampire seemed disinclined to take it at all. Roger said furiously, "He's a fake! He must be some pal of Weinberg's who got shot up, so he's looking for a place to hide. I am not running a rest home for incompetent stick-up men or whatever this is—I'd rather sling him out in the street for the cops to find."

The man on the cot made no protest, no plea, but he gathered himself for an effort. His long, thin fingers closed on Wesley's forearm. The sound of his labored breathing filled the little room. He bent his face over the pale inner surface of Wesley's elbow.

Wesley jumped slightly and said, "Son-of-a-bitch!"

Roger stood rapt, lips parted, watching. Wesley sat there holding the man propped against him, watching too, cool again. God, Mark thought, Wesley was something: he never let anything really get to him.

At length the vampire drew back, licked his lips once, and subsided loosely onto the cot with a whispered sigh. Wesley got up, flexing his fingers. "Will you look at that," he said. There was a puncture in the vein in his arm, surrounded by a bruiselike discoloration.

Roger, gaping, said dazedly, "Uh, you want a Band-Aid?"

"No, it's only bleeding a little bit. Damndest thing I ever saw. I better lie down a couple of minutes, though. I feel kind of dopey." Wesley ambled away toward the living room, still looking down at his arm.

They followed him out. "The gate locks automatically when you shut it," Roger said. He looked back at the man on the cot. "Jesus," he breathed, "it's true."

Wesley was lying on the couch. Roger crouched down next to him. "How did it feel?"

"Like giving fuckin' blood, what else?"

"You sure you're okay, Wesley?"

"Sure."

"I want you to get me supplies for him."

Wesley frowned. "I could lose my job, monkeying around with the hospital blood bank."

"I know you'll do what you can, Wesley," Roger said airily; which meant he had something on Wesley and wasn't interested in hearing about his problems. "I can store the stuff in the fridge, right? And if sometimes you can't get blood from the hospital, bring it on the hoof."

"Shit," Wesley said, clenching his fist and crooking his arm up. "I can't do this fountain-of-youth trick too often, you know."

"Then find somebody to fill in for you."

Wesley departed to return the rented van in which he had brought the vampire. Roger hung the key to the barred gate on a nail in a kitchen cabinet. "I'll leave this one here, Mark, but you won't need to use it unless there's an emergency."

Roger, an elfin thirty, had a heart-shaped face, fine-featured and lively. He wore his blue-black hair cut full, and he tossed it off his forehead with a dramatic gesture whenever possible. If angels had dark hair they would look like Roger, Mark thought, though an angel probably wouldn't get himself thrown out of four different schools as Roger had.

Mark knew himself to be plain and gangly and sallow, his appearance not helped at all by owlishly magnifying eyeglasses. He had realized fairly recently that Roger liked to have him around as a foil for Roger's own good looks, but Mark didn't mind much. He knew that he was going to make his own way with his brains. He knew, too, that Roger was a dabbler, never getting the benefit of his own intelligence, too easily bored, too greedy for the taste of the experiences he gobbled up.

Roger left Mark to unpack and in a little while came back down the hall carrying one of the kitchen chairs. This he set down outside the gate, and, sitting astraddle with his arms on the top of the chair back, he faced his new acquisition.

He had a portable tape recorder with him, and he switched it on and began asking questions: What's your name? How did you get to be a vampire? Are you in communication with other vampires? How much blood do you drink at a time? Who shot you?

Every time Mark looked up from arranging his bookshelves, he saw that the vampire was ignoring Roger and following with a sickly gaze what Mark was doing in the bedroom across the hall.

Once Roger had gone off to bed and there would be no interruptions, Mark got the plans for Skytown out of his briefcase and laid them out on the drawing table. This personal project ran currently to forty drawings depicting the systems of his one-man space station. Scientific accuracy was not his main concern, although he kept a tight rein on any impulse to outright fantasy. Mysterious vistas of space and carefully scaled perspectives and details of a space-going home were what fascinated him. Working with his Rapidograph under the fluorescent lamp, he forgot Roger, his parents, and even the vampire.

When he got up to brush his teeth in the bathroom down the hall, he was startled to find the vampire staring at him again. Returning, he shut his door and opened it only when he had turned out his light. Better to leave it open than lie in the dark wondering what was going on out there. Wesley had installed a night light in the cell, enclosed in a little wire cage and connected to a switch in the hallway. The vampire was illuminated, stretched motionless on the cot.

Mark turned on his side and lay listening to the muted sounds of traffic. In his head he tried to picture the details of the energy-gathering vanes of Skytown, sweeping shapes against a background of stars. Maybe there would be a special robot team to tend the vanes; or maybe he would reserve to himself the adventure of working outside in his space suit with stars for company.

Gradually, reluctantly, he became aware of a faint shuffling sound across the hall: movement, effort. Shivering slightly in his underwear, he got up and ghosted barefoot to the doorway.

The vampire stood leaning against the wall, facing in the direction of the little bathroom that adjoined his cell.

Mark sneezed.

The vampire looked at him.

Mark whispered, "I'll go get Roger."

But he didn't. Something in the vampire's posture, a faint shrinking in the already cramped shoulders, made it clear that he sensed what Mark knew—that Roger would make a humiliating joke out of this: a vampire who had to go to the bathroom just like everybody else and couldn't manage it on his own, poor thing. In acute discomfort Mark remembered how that last summer at camp had been. For no reason he'd found himself wetting the bed every night. Every morning he'd had to go rinse out his sheets and hang them outside to dry behind the cabin where everybody could see them. Very funny, ha ha.

He crossed the hallway and whispered through the bars, "I'll help, but if you try anything I'll yell my head off and Roger will come and—and beat you up. He keeps a hunk of lead pipe by his bed for burglars."

He padded toward the kitchen, already regretting the impulse. Cautiously he groped in the dark for the key. Not to wake Roger, not to invite Roger's mean side to come out, was important. He really hated Roger's mean side.

He unlocked the gate and entered the cell warily. He didn't want the vampire to get the idea that he could obtain favors just by looking weak and pathetic. He said, "Roger'd kill me if he knew I came in here. He'd send me home. What do I get for taking that chance?"

The vampire peered at him. Then came his rasping whisper, "You may, if you wish, put yourself on the level of attendant in a public lavatory. I was carrying change in my pockets."

The change would now be in the paper bag that Weinberg had given Wesley. That would do, though the vampire had tried to make it seem grungy to take payment. The main thing was not to let anybody reach you.

Mark moved nearer. The vampire draped a sinewy arm over his shoulders, and for a moment Mark thought in terror that he was being attacked. Then he realized that the man was so weak that he had to lean almost all of his weight on his helper. Maybe walking even these few steps would make him keel over. Maybe he'd die. It would have been better to have wakened Roger. Then if anything went wrong it wouldn't be Mark's fault.

"All right," gasped the vampire, transferring his grip to the corner of the sink.

Mark backed out of the tiny bathroom and stood against the wall. He heard the watery noises, the faint groan of relief, the fumbling for the flush handle. He thought, This is crazy: he pees like me or Roger, but he drinks people's blood.

Helping him back to his cot, Mark noticed that the vampire needed a bath and a change from his stained white shirt and rumpled pants. They had taken away his belt and his shoes.

"Wait," the vampire breathed.

Mark backed toward the gate. "Why?"

"Stay and talk. I must not sleep. If I do, I could easily drop into the sleep of years that takes me from one era to another. Then my life would sink to so low an ebb that my body would be unable to heal itself. I would die. Your Uncle Roger would be annoyed. So talk to me. Tell me things."

God, this was weird. "What things?"

"What do you do all day?"

"I'm in school, ninth grade."

A small silence, and then the vampire murmured, "That seems appropriate. I too am something of a student. Tell me about school."

Mark sat down on the floor across the room from the cot and talked about school. After a while he got a blanket from his closet and folded it under himself, and he brought a glass of water from the kitchen to moisten his throat.

The vampire lay still and listened. If Mark let a little time go by in silence, the vampire said, "Talk to me."

When Mark got back from school the next day Wesley was there. "Your dad called, said he'd like to hear from you."

"Oh, yeah, thanks, Wesley." Both Mark's parents accepted Roger's apartment as Mark's neutral refuge from their endless hassling. Nevertheless they tried to keep tabs on him by phone.

"Okay," Wesley continued, "our friend is bathed and shaved, got clean pajamas on and fresh bandages. He's all set for a couple of days, except for the feeding. Now, you have to go inside his room for that. Even if you shove a glass of blood across the floor at him, he can't lean down and pick it up. He can sit up on his own, though—enough, anyhow, so you won't have to touch him. Carry the glass in and hand it to him, but keep clear of him."

Mark looked into the icebox for something to eat. There were plastic pouches of blood heaped up on the top shelf in back. He blinked fast and looked away. He said, "I thought you weren't scared of him."

"I wasn't scared to give him some of my blood yesterday, but he's healing awful fast. He's scary, all right. He's in a lot better shape than he should be, an old guy with two fuckin' bullet holes in him. Be careful." Wesley, washing his hands at the kitchen sink, laughed suddenly and turned off the water. "Look at me, washing up like after handling a patient at the hospital! I guess I'm just a natural for nursemaiding Roger's vampire, right? Roger sure thinks so."

He shook his head and tucked away the dish towel on which he had dried his hands. "Myself, I liked it better when I was just fixing this place up for Roger." With Wesley's help and at great expense, Roger had reconverted the entire ground floor of the brownstone from two tiny apartments to one comfortable one.

Shutting the icebox door on the sight of the blood, Mark said, "You give it to him cold, right out of the fridge? Isn't that sort of a shock?"

"Well, it's probably not a bad idea to heat the stuff up a little first—but not too hot."

"I know how. I used to heat up the bottle for Aunt Pat's baby that time I stayed with her." At the sink counter Mark spread peanut butter on a slice of bologna.

Wesley unwrapped fresh gum. "You'd make a good hospital attendant, thinking of a thing like that. If you could keep your distance, that is."

Mark felt ashamed that Wesley thought he wasn't cool enough. He considered telling Wesley about helping the vampire at night, how he kept his distance then all right, but decided not to say anything. Wesley might tell Roger.

He politely asked Wesley what was owing for the fresh blood supply, and Wesley went into the living room to wait while Mark got the money box out of the oven. Roger kept it there on the theory that no burglar would look inside a kitchen fixture. He avoided banks because they made reports of interest income for taxes, and he said he preferred to forgo the interest and the taxes both. The money was safe: the apartment was fortified New York City style with barred windows, grilles on the back doors, even strands of wire strung along the top of the wooden fence that enclosed the sour scrap of yard. It was like something out of a prison-camp story. Stalag Manhattan.

With only one prisoner.

As Wesley counted his bills in the hallway by the front door Mark said, "You know, I almost wish Mr. Weinberg's friend the doctor had taken this vampire away for the scientists to study. It feels funny, having somebody locked up here like this."

Wesley, chewing, looked at him. "You figure even a guy who drinks blood has a right not to be grabbed and shut up in Roger's apartment like he was a stray dog, is that it? That's Roger's lookout. You're a minor, you got no say, so don't go feeling all responsible. Stay laid back, all right? Right."

When Mark had the apartment to himself he got the paper bag and spread the vampire's belongings on the coffee table in the golden light of afternoon: a ballpoint pen, blue; a felt-tipped pen, red; two pencils with broken points; four small index cards covered with unreadable handwriting; a rubber band, three paper clips, a horn-handled pocketknife; two keys; one case containing a pair of glasses with dark, heavy rims, the left lens cracked; and two quarters.

Mark passed up the knife after a moment's hesitation and pocketed one of the quarters as payment for last night's favor.

Then his mother phoned. She promised she wouldn't bring up the touchy subject of plans for his summer vacation, and he relaxed a bit. She sounded tired and anxious. How was he, she wanted to know, how was Roger? Did Mark need anything from home? Had his father called? Did Mark have enough pocket money? He was not to become any kind of a drain on Roger. How was school? Was he seeing that nice Maddox boy he'd brought home last week? Was he eating right? When was he planning to come home?

Never, he thought. He said, "I don't know, Mom. I just need to be able to settle down without a bunch of fighting going on all the time. I've got a lot of school work to do before the term ends."

"I wish your father wouldn't phone me when he knows you're probably home. He only does it to—"

"I have to go, Mom. I've got some things to do for Roger."

"Just remember, when your father calls you, you remind him that this little interlude that his foul temper provoked isn't coming off my time with you. When you leave Roger's you come back here to finish our six months together, darling. I love you, Markie."

Love you too, Mom; but you could never say that kind of thing out loud to either of them, because they'd put an edge on it and turn it around and cut you with it. She'd say later, He loves me, not you, he said so; and if Dad believed that even a little he'd think you were on her side. Then he'd take it out on you somehow, and you'd spend your time crying like Mom; crying and complaining.

He said, "Bye, Mom," and hung up. Then he sat there chewing his nails and wondering when he'd get used to his parents hating each other. Other kids got used to it with their folks. Maybe being an only child made it worse. On the other hand, Dad and Roger didn't seem to derive any special benefits from being brothers.

One time, one time only, he'd gone weeping to his

father, begging him to patch it up, put the family back the way it was supposed to be. His father had said, "Is that what you do when you can't get what you want, cry like a girl? Who taught you that, your mother?"

The worst of it was that Mark had spoken as much out of feeling for his father as out of his own misery, knowing that his dad was wretched, too.

Thinking about them didn't help. He got up energetically and went into his room, where he pulled out the drawings for the botanical gardens of Skytown. He was working on plants picked up from different planets, right now one adapted from a book called *A Voyage To Arcturus* which was mostly boring but had this terrific tree that grabbed up small mammals in its branches and ate them. But what kind of an animal would it eat? A rat? A weasel? Weasels were vicious, you wouldn't mind if it ate a weasel. Inside the cage of branches he drew a weasel, working from the picture in his encyclopedia.

At last, reluctantly, he put the Skytown plans aside; there was work more pressing. He had to do a paper for Carol Kelly for her English class on a poem by A. E. Housman. If he didn't get to it soon, there wouldn't be enough time to work on it. Completing the job was important. Carol Kelly was getting awfully chummy lately. There was nothing like a cash transaction to push a relationship back into shape.

He settled down to the poem, trying to make sense of it.

The evening after that, instead of packaged blood Wesley brought Bobbie, one of Roger's former girl friends. Going down the hall between Wesley and Roger, she kept laughing and saying, "It's just one of your theater friends fooling around, right, Roger? Come on, I know you—it's a joke, right?"

Then she was sitting there on the cot in the little white room and not laughing at all. She looked down with wide eyes at the vampire's head bent over her arm.

Mark could only bear to watch out of the corner of his eye.

"Oh," she said softly. And then, still staring, "Oh, wow. Oh, Wesley, he's drinking my blood."

Wesley said, "I told you. No joke."

"Don't worry, Bobbie," Roger said, patting her shoulder. "You won't grow fangs afterward—Wesley hasn't, anyway."

She put out her hand as if to push the vampire's head away, but instead she began to stroke his hair. She murmured, "I read my tarot this morning and I could see there would be fantastic new things, and I should get right behind them and be real positive, you know? But I never thought—oh, this is so far out, this is a real supernova, you know?" Until he finished she sat enthralled, whispering, "Oh, wow," at dreamy intervals.

When the vampire lifted his drowned, peaceful face, she said earnestly to him, "I'm a Scorpio; what's your sign?"

Roger came home, having at last fired a store manager he disliked. He took Mark out for Chinese dinner and talked angrily about the mess the manager was leaving behind—unrecorded orders, evidence of pilfering and jacking around with receipts . . .

Mark handed him a note from school. "They want a signature on this." Roger was good at signing his brother's name.

"Sent home early for sleeping in class? What gives?"

Mark braced himself and explained.

Roger looked at him in openmouthed astonishment and the beginnings of outrage. "You mean you've been having midnight chats with our friend for the three nights he's been with us? What's he told you?"

"Nothing. He just listens. Last night I told him *Childhood's End, The Mysterious Island*, and some Ray Bradbury stories."

"And he doesn't say anything?"

"Nothing much."

Roger's mouth got thin and pressed together. "Tonight you take the tape recorder in with you, and you ask some questions and get some answers before you tell him a goddamn limerick."

Roger had been trying his questions on the vampire for shorter and shorter periods, perhaps because his efforts were always failures. Mark did no better. When he asked his memorized questions that night, they were ignored.

The vampire merely remarked, "Scheherezade has joined the Inquisition, I see. Fortunately, I can manage now without these diversions."

Roger was going away for the weekend, leaving Mark to look after the vampire. You had to keep Roger from taking advantage. He did it without thinking, really, he just sort of forgot about your interests in the pursuit of his own.

"Look, Roger," Mark said, "I'll take care of the place for you—water the plants and do some cleaning up and all that, like before, to pay you back for letting me stay here. But you're away a lot partying or checking out the shops, and that means I'm stuck with . . . him, in there. That's a big responsibility."

Roger was packing a rainbow sweater in nubbleknit acrylic he had borrowed from the uptown store for the weekend. "You can always go home," he said. Mark waited. Roger sighed. "Okay, okay. Five dollars a week."

"Ten."

"Bloodsucker!" Roger said. "All right, ten." So simple, no tearing your guts up over everything like at home. "Listen, there's a special reason why I'm going up to Boston. I want to consult with a few friends about this vampire. There must be ways to get incredibly rich on this thing."

With Roger gone, Mark settled down to the paper for Carol Kelly. Looking for a book of poetry criticism in the living room, he was distracted by a remnant from Roger's fling with super-exotica, *The Two-Duck Pleasure Book: Balkan Folk Wisdom,* by R. Unpronounceable. Beguiled into browsing for enlightening dirty bits (". . . method of contraception is for the woman to get up after intercourse, squat on the floor, and inserting her index finger . . ." Yuucchh), he spent a fascinating half hour.

Then he pulled out a book on Lapland and found the vampire's face looking at him from the back cover of the volume next to it.

No mistake; it was the same man, only in a three-piece suit with a beat-up raincoat slung around his shoulders. He was looking straight into the camera with an assertive stare, as if daring the photographer to soften his imperious features. Mark studied the strong planes of forehead and cheek, the jutting nose, the long, shapely mouth with lips muscular-looking as if slightly compressed on some inner tension. He could look at the photo as long and hard as he liked, while looking at the living man for any length of time made Mark nervous.

The book was called *Notes on a Vanished People*, the diaries of some hitherto unknown German traveler in South America. The translator and editor pictured on the book jacket was Dr. Edward Lewis Weyland, Ph.D., professor of anthropology and director of the Cayslin Center for the Study of Man at Cayslin College upstate. "New light on Pre-Columbian history," proclaimed the blurbs. "A stupendous find for anthropology, with erudite, provocative commentary by Dr. Weyland."

Mark recalled now having seen that forbidding face somewhere else recently—in the news, it had to be. He dug through the piled-up papers and magazines on the end tables until he found what he was looking for in a copy of *Time*. Then slowly, thoughtfully, heart pounding, he went down the hall, the book in his hand.

The vampire dozed, lying on his side with his knees sticking forward off the cot. Wearing pajamas and showing bandages at the opening of the collar, he looked a lot less impressive than in the photograph.

Mark said, "Dr. Weyland?"

The vampire opened his eyes. Mark let him see that he was holding *Notes on a Vanished People*. There was no observable reaction.

"I just thought you might be hungry," Mark said lamely.

"I am."

Mark had bought a stoneware mug so that he wouldn't have to see the blood being drained out of the glass. He stood carefully out of reach while Dr. Weyland drank.

"How'd you get shot?" he asked.

"You know my name. Do a minimum of research: look in the newspapers."

"I did. All anybody says is that you disappeared." Mark added aggressively, "I bet you did something dumb and somebody guessed about you and tried to kill you."

The vampire studied him a moment. "You would win your bet," he said, and he set the mug on the floor and lay back down.

Mark browsed through *Notes on a Vanished People* over a TV dinner that night. A lot of the book was boring, but there were some intriguing sections in the long introduction. Here Dr. Weyland described his suspicions that the German's notebooks existed, the search for them, and the struggle—against doubters whom Dr. Weyland demolished with a keen wit—to establish the authenticity of the documents once they were found. There were also some chilly passages about missionaries of the traveler's day and modern anthropologists. Pretty interesting background reading if you might be the first person to contact the inhabitants of the distant planets on scouting expeditions from Skytown . . .

*

Late on Sunday a stranger came to the door. "Bobbie tells me there's a vampire here," he said. "Show him to me." He stood not exactly with his foot in the door, but turned so that his thick shoulder seemed about to snap the chain.

"I'm sorry," Mark said quickly, "but my uncle isn't back yet from Boston, and I'm not allowed to let in anybody I don't know."

"My name is Alan Reese. Roger knows me. I'm sure he must have mentioned me to you."

"I have to keep the house rules," Mark said, putting a whine into his tone. He was thinking back to when Roger had been into sorcery. This must be the Reese he'd gotten mixed up with about that. Reese looked ready to bulldoze the door down, and capable of it, too, with a powerful torso and a wrestler's neck as broad as the head it supported.

But he only smiled, shrugged, and retired to sit on the steps into the areaway, reading a paperback book from his pocket. Plainly, he was going to wait for Roger.

Mark did the dishes and watched him from the window over the sink. Reese wore whipcord pants and an embroidered Mexican shirt, and he had brought a large black briefcase. His face was puffy and pale, the skin freckled and smooth like a boy's. There was more to be read in his thick hands than in his face. He tore out the pages of the book as he finished them, and before flipping them into the garbage can by the steps he absently crumpled them in his fist.

Leaving him unwatched didn't seem safe somehow. Mark stayed by the sink and sharpened the knives. Then he rearranged all the silver in the drawer.

Finally Roger came, arguing briefly with the cabby over the tip. Mark saw him turn to face Alan Reese with surprise. One of those big paws fell heavily on Roger's shoulder. The two men stood talking. Roger nodded a lot, hesitantly at first, then with vigor.

When he came in, Reese entered behind him, smiling.

"Mark, I want you to meet Alan Reese, an occultist I've known for a long time," Roger said. "He has some suggestions for managing our guest."

"I am, strictly speaking, a Satanist," Alan Reese introduced himself in a measured, theatrical voice. A light of triumph sparkled in his blue eyes, as if Mark had held a castle against him which he had blown down with a breath. "Does that make you nervous, Mark? It shouldn't. Having a vampire in an unprotected house with you is what should make you nervous. I'm going to help you keep control of him, using my knowledge of his Master."

Oh boy, Mark thought. He got the key from the cupboard door and went into the hall ahead of them to unlock the gate, determined to stick close. He wanted to see the man who had written the introduction to *Notes on a Vanished People* take this guy Reese apart with a sharp remark.

Dr. Weyland turned his head to watch them come in.

Ignoring him, Reese slipped on a black gown over his street clothes and took some objects from his briefcase. He murmured over them, kissed them, held them up to the four directions. One, a metal charm on a chain, he put around Roger's neck, its twin around Mark's. The rest—a knife, a ring, a silver bowl, a withered brown thing that Mark couldn't identify—he placed carefully in the corners of the stark white cell.

Then he brought out a nest of trays and lit incense in them, and these Roger set down where Reese directed. Reese talked or chanted the whole time, projecting so that he seemed to fill the room. From a little pouch hung round his neck on a thong he rubbed something onto the window frame, the door frame, the drains of the bathroom appliances, and even the electric outlets. He made markings on the floor with a lump of red chalk.

Mark was given a censer and a candle to hold. He felt

a fool and wished now he'd let them do all this weird stuff without him.

To his surprise and disappointment, Dr. Weyland made no comment. Mark had his first chance to observe the vampire without those chilly eyes staring back at him, and he felt an unpleasant shock. He thought he saw fear.

"All right, he's well bound. That's a start," Reese said finally, standing in the middle of the little room with his feet braced apart as if against a typhoon. He looked about him with a pleased expression.

"The funny thing is," Roger said, "he doesn't seem to have fangs, but he does—well, bite."

"So Bobbie said." Reese pulled back the sleeves of his gown from muscular forearms. "Hold him quiet— he can't hurt you, don't worry—and let me see."

Roger made a nervous grab for the vampire's wrists. Dr. Weyland did not resist, not even when Reese hooked him under the armpits and dragged at him so that his head hung off the end of the cot. There was nothing silly in the scene anymore. Dr. Weyland's fear touched Mark like a cold breath.

Reese bent and clamped the vampire's head hard against his thick thigh with one arm. Seizing him by the jaw, he wrenched his mouth open.

A sound of protest escaped Mark.

Reese looked up. "This being is inhabited by a devil's strength. He only pretends weakness and pain to fool us. I may seem rough with him, but I know what I'm doing. I put all the force I have into encounters like this because that's the only way to keep control. He's all right; it would take a tank to hurt one of these."

Roger said, "You've come across vampires before?"

"I come across all kinds of abstruse things," Reese replied. "It's true there are no fangs, but here—see that? A sort of sting on the underside of the tongue. It probably erects itself at the prospect of dinner, makes the puncture through which he sucks blood, and then folds back out of sight again."

"Sexy," Roger said with new interest. "Maybe that's why he doesn't talk?"

"It shouldn't interfere," Reese said. "Let's have a look at his eyes." He shut the mouth and moved his hand to thumb back one of the vampire's eyelids.

Mark told himself they weren't really hurting Dr. Weyland. They were like zoologists or veterinarians immobilizing a dangerous animal so they could examine it. But Reese gripped and twisted the passive body of the vampire brutally, like a guy wrestling an alligator in a movie about the Everglades. Mark tried not to breathe the sharp odor from the censer and waited miserably for the examination to be over.

At last they finished, leaving the disheveled vampire —who had still spoken no word—stretched out on the cot, one arm over his eyes. Roger looked high, as if exhilarated by the defeat of someone who had scared him. Reese, smiling, packed up his gear and shed his gown. He came and sat in the verdant living room like any casual guest.

"Have you any plans for him?" he asked intently.

Roger scowled. "He's not very cooperative. I've been trying to get him to tell me things. Can you imagine what a best-seller it would be, a real vampire's story from his own lips? But he won't answer questions."

Reese stood up. "I was thinking of something more ambitious—some effort to cut through appearances to his essential self, the black and powerful heart of an existence beyond the laws of the life we know. Some way of taking over and harnessing this arcane and formidable nature to our own uses."

The atmosphere of the room seemed changed— darkened. Reese's bombast should have reduced him to an absurdity, but it didn't. He came across as not silly but scary. His melodramatic style was backed up by his beefy, aggressive muscularity and by the watchful stare of his small, cold eyes as he stood over the two of them.

"You have a marvelous find here," Reese said, "rich in possibilities. My High Priestess is skilled in hypnotism. With that and whatever rites and pressures seem appropriate, we'll have this creature begging to give up his secrets. Believe me, Roger, we'll wring him like a wet rag, he'll be our bridge to realms you can't even guess at yet. On May Eve, the night of April thirtieth, I and my group customarily hold a Great Sabbat, as you may remember. I want to hold it here and include your guest in the proceedings. Good, that's settled, then.

"Meanwhile, try to emphasize fresh supplies, like Bobbie. I know some who'll volunteer for the experience, if I give the word. I agree there's no danger of the occasional donor becoming a vampire, especially now that I've mobilized my protective forces. Some trustworthy students of my arts would even pay to watch a vampire feed. The proceeds . . ."

The whole thing was building a crazy momentum. When Reese paused for breath, Mark cleared his throat and said, "I found out something about him today. His name is Edward Lewis Weyland and he's a famous anthropologist." Well, he certainly had their attention. He explained about the vampire's identity. "It's a kind of kidnapping already, don't you see? We could all get into a lot of trouble. He's not just some crazy tramp, he's an important professor."

Roger began to say something resentful, but Reese cut him off. "Be patient, Roger. Mark's young, he needs careful instruction." Reese's moon face looked placid, but he cracked the knuckles of his hands with muffled crunching noise. "He thinks what we have here is merely an ordinary man, albeit one of prominence, with a freakish taste for human blood—but basically a human being like ourselves to whom the laws of human societies apply.

"However; I am here to tell both of you—and qualified to tell both of you—that what you have behind bars in there is not simply a perverted human being. I felt the aura around it, and I arced my spells to subdue its real, its supernatural nature and render it docile."

"He didn't fight you because he's hurt," Mark blurted.

"Oh, I don't deny that the vampire has a fleshly carapace and that that shell has been damaged. But if you could see beyond the disguise, Mark, as I can, you'd know right away that this isn't a person at all. It's a bloodsucking devil, and it's subject to no laws but those of the Great One whose rites I study."

Argument was hopeless. Mark retreated to his own room, busying himself at his desk until the two men, still talking, left. Then he stepped into the hall, intending to go fix himself some dinner. He hadn't meant to look across into the cell, but he couldn't help himself.

The vampire sat elbows on knees, hands clasped at his mouth as if he'd been gnawing at his knuckles. His wide gaze seemed to leap to meet Mark.

In a low, tense voice Dr. Weyland said, "Let me out."

Face doggedly turned away, Mark shook his head, no.

"Why not?"

"Look," Mark said, "you don't understand. I'm just a kind of a guest here. Roger never messes around with my stuff and I don't mess around with his."

"Alan Reese will kill me."

"Roger wouldn't let anyone get hurt!" Mark was shocked. Did Dr. Weyland really misunderstand Roger so badly?

"Reese will bring a dozen or so of his followers here on May Eve. I think Roger, facing them, will be something less than brave."

"But this is his home. He wouldn't let them."

"He'll have no choice. Don't you recognize the kind of man Reese is?"

"He's just a weird friend of Roger's," Mark said uncomfortably. "Nothing terrible will happen."

"Nothing terrible?" Dr. Weyland seemed to look into space and to speak more to himself than to Mark. "I felt his hands on me, I saw his eyes. He's not the first man to lust after powers he imagines me to have."

Mark's scalp prickled. He said rapidly, "Look, you're forgetting—this is all Roger's idea, he's running things. He's taken care of you so far, hasn't he? I mean, Roger can be sort of inconsiderate and wild and Reese is definitely creepy, but they're not—they're not in a class with the person who shot you, for instance."

Dr. Weyland frowned. "Of course not. That was a matter of poor judgment on my part and self-defense on hers—an incident of the hunt, no more."

"It was a woman?" Mark was fascinated despite himself.

"Yes, a woman of more discernment and competence than I had thought. She acted as any intelligent prey acts. She wanted to escape me, and she succeeded.

"But this man Reese wants . . . to use me, to tear out my life and devour it, as men once ate the hearts of slain enemies in order to acquire their strength and skill in battle."

Overriding the vampire's final words, Mark said loudly, "That doesn't make sense. I'm not going to stand here and listen to a lot of crap that doesn't make sense." His face felt hot. He hurried up the hall to the kitchen.

His appetite was gone. He took off Reese's amulet and threw it into the garbage.

Later when he looked for *Notes on a Vanished People*, which he had used to prove Dr. Weyland's identity, he couldn't find it. Reese must have taken the book.

All the next morning Mark dreaded a resumption of that upsetting conversation with Dr. Weyland. He came home by a roundabout route from school and watched TV a while in the living room, but he couldn't put off the vampire's feeding indefinitely.

He delivered the mugful of blood with a tool that Wesley had contrived for the purpose the last time he was here by twisting a coat hanger around the end of a detachable mop handle. Reaching between the bars with this, Mark carefully pushed the mug across the floor toward the cot.

"Lunch," he announced in a tone he hoped would discourage conversation.

Moving very slowly, Dr. Weyland leaned down and took up the mug, emptied it, and carefully set it down on the floor again. He said, "Might you bring me something to read?"

Caught off balance, Mark blinked foolishly at him. "To read?"

"Yes. To read. Books, magazines, newspapers. Printed matter. Though of course I can't pay you for the service, since you've already 'earned' everything that I owned."

Those three nights of storytelling had transferred the second quarter and the pocketknife into Mark's possession. How else could he have made it unmistakably clear to Dr. Weyland that he operated on a strictly business basis?

"Now Roger pays me to look after you," he mumbled. He went to the living room and collected whatever was on the coffee table. The horn-rimmed glasses he placed on top of the pile before pushing it all into the cell.

Dr. Weyland picked up the glasses and put them on.

God, Mark thought suddenly, he's just an old guy with glasses, like Mr. Merman at school. "The lens was cracked when they came," he said.

He watched while the vampire, sitting with the blue blanket pulled around his shoulders, sorted through the untidy heap. *Harper's. The Village Voice. Women's Wear Daily. The New Yorker. Prevention.* Does your uncle subscribe to everything published, regardless of the contents?"

"He doesn't have time to read most of it anyway," Mark said. "I have to do some homework now." It was long past time to do it, in fact.

He couldn't find his dictionary. Hesitantly he called, "How do you spell 'kinesthetic'?"

"Look it up," replied the vampire.

"Can't find my dictionary."

Dr. Weyland spelled out the word. Then he said, " 'Kinesthetic'? What are you writing?"

"An assigned paper on some mushy poem," Mark said.

"May I see?" Dr. Weyland put aside the magazines.

With the mop handle Mark pushed in the book of poems. Dr. Weyland opened to the place marked with the flattened drinking straw. " 'The Land of Lost Content,' " he murmured. " 'Into my heart an air that kills from yon far country blows . . .' " Mark's outline for the paper was tucked inside the front cover. Dr. Weyland read this swiftly and looked up with a keen glance that made Mark uncomfortable.

"Interesting," the vampire said. "The second paragraph, under the heading 'Kinesthetic Sense,' where you note, 'Poet writes about highways he went on, remembers moving muscles while going on highways . . .' That must be in response to a question from the teacher?"

"Yes, about what senses the poet uses in the poem."

"But when Housman writes of 'an air that kills,' I doubt he means he's smelling the air," Dr. Weyland said. "The deadly breeze seems to me to blow directly into Housman's heart, bypassing his senses altogether."

Mark fidgeted unhappily at the bars. He should have known better; there was nothing worse for school work than a grown-up helping you with it. He said, "Well, without smell there's just sight and the kinesthetic sense. That's only two senses. I need more than that.

The teacher wants at least two whole pages, double-spaced.''

"I see," said Dr. Weyland dryly. "Nevertheless, while the point about muscular memory does have some minor value, you would do better without a paragraph on the senses altogether. Then the outline would flow much more easily from the first paragraph about the fairy-tale atmosphere of the poem, through the second on its childlike simplicity, to your conclusion concerning its meaning."

Mark remained mutinously silent.

Dr. Weyland flicked the edge of the page with his forefinger. "I see that you mean to conclude, 'I like the poem a lot.' But you called it a 'mushy poem' when you first mentioned it to me."

"I hate this assignment!" Mark burst out. "The poem doesn't even make sense. What's 'an air that kills,' anyway, poison gas? It's just dumb, a lot of babyish moaning around for no reason."

"Good, you do realize that you've avoided the main question," said Dr. Weyland; "what, precisely, 'an air that kills' might be and what it destroys in the poet. As for 'moaning around,' have you never had to leave behind an existence that suited you better than the one you moved on to?"

For no reason Mark felt a pressure of tears in his eyes. He turned away, angry and embarrassed.

"I have," Dr. Weyland added meditatively. "Often."

"That doesn't mean a person should go around whining all the time," Mark muttered. "Can I have that stuff back now? I have to go and type the paper up."

"You're not ready to," Dr. Weyland said. "Not until you at least consider the central question."

"I'm only in the ninth grade, you know. I'm not supposed to know everything."

"What is the air that kills?" asked Dr. Weyland inexorably. "Why does he let it into his heart?"

"I guess it's memory," Mark said sullenly, "and he

lets it into his heart because he's a jerk. He's doing it to himself—making himself miserable by thinking about his happy childhood. Only a stupid jerk walks around thinking about his childhood. Most people's childhoods are actually pretty lousy anyhow."

"It isn't necessarily childhood that he means," Dr. Weyland said, "although you make a good case for that in your outline. I think the reference is more general—to the perils of looking backward on other times and the seductiveness of memory. Well." He fell for moment into an abstracted silence. Then he added briskly, "I think, by the way, that if you really dislike the poem you should say so—and why—in your paper."

"I can't," Mark said. "This is for Carol Kelly, and she likes the crummy poem. She would."

"Who is Carol Kelly?"

Suddenly recalling that Dr. Weyland was a teacher himself, Mark tried to brazen it out. "This is her assignment. I'm doing it for her."

"How kind of you," murmured Dr. Weyland, returning the book.

"She's paying me ten dollars. It's a business."

"My God," Dr. Weyland said, "a thesis mill! How old are you—fifteen?"

"Fifteen in June."

"Fifteen and rich, no doubt. Certainly enterprising."

"I'm not greedy," Mark said stoutly. "It's important to have an income of your own, that's all. Then you don't have to depend on other people. You should know—I bet you're rich yourself, I bet you've salted away all kinds of treasure from other times."

"Unfortunately, great wealth, like renown or exalted rank, attracts too much attention, most of it hostile," Dr. Weyland said. "I learned a long time ago to travel unencumbered and to depend on my wits. Now I'm not so sure. What a pity I have no diamonds about me, no purses of pirate gold. If I had, you and I could make a transaction of the kind you like, all business: my freedom for your enrichment."

"Money wouldn't change anything," Mark said. "I told you, I can't let you go."

Dr. Weyland drew back. He said harshly, "Of course. It was a mistake to ask you for help in the first place. I won't ask again."

For some time Mark sat at his drawing table, biting his pencil and working over the paper again and again. He couldn't read the poem now without thinking wretchedly of his parents.

God, Dr. Weyland would drive you crazy if you had him for a class. He was one of those never-satisfied types who beat out your brains under the mistaken impression that they're teaching you to think.

A kid from math class wanted to go to a movie after school. Mark begged off, saying he had chores to do. Actually, Wesley was coming today and would handle the feeding of Dr. Weyland. Mark used the time to go to a film and lecture about coyotes at the Museum of Natural History. He preferred seeing animals stuffed in the museum exhibits or on film to seeing them in a zoo. The zoo depressed him horribly.

The documentary film drove him out before the program was over. It first lovingly detailed the cleverness of the coyote, his beauty and his place as part of nature, and then settled into a barrage of hideous images: poisoned coyotes, trapped coyotes, burned coyotes, and coyotes mangled by ranchers' dogs. Mark didn't think he would ever be cool enough to stand that kind of stuff.

Wesley was still at Roger's when Mark got in. "I cleaned up our friend special for tonight," he said. "Roger called and said don't feed him. There's company coming."

Ugh, maybe that meant Alan Reese. Walking Wesley out, Mark told him about Reese's visit.

Wesley kicked at the base of the brownstone steps. "Shit," he said. "I thought Bobbie had quit running around with all those devil nuts. Didn't Roger and her do a trip with them once before?"

"He's getting into it again," Mark said.

Wesley shook his head. "Tell you one thing: Alan Reese is weird. He likes stagey stuff with all kinds of blood and crazy stunts. Him and his friends did something one time that left a whole apartment in Queens splashed with rooster blood. The chick who played altar for him and his friends that night said if he ever talked to her again she'd sue."

"Wesley, I'm sort of worried."

"Yeah, well, it'll be okay. Roger won't go as far as Reese will want to. It'll be okay." Wesley stuck a wad of gum under the curve of the stoop and went away whistling.

Dr. Weyland sat reading, dressed in dark trousers, socks and slippers. The cuffs of his white shirt were folded back the way Mark did his own cuffs when his arms got too long for the sleeves.

"Roger said not to give you anything to eat."

"Temporarily, I trust," Dr. Weyland said. "I need food badly when I'm healing. My hunger hurts."

Mark met his stare for as long as he could. "I can bring some water," he said. "But Roger said no food."

Just as he was about to settle into his work, Bobbie turned up at the front door with a short, stocky woman in a caftan who carried an embroidered knapsack by one broad strap. Bobbie smiled.

"Hi, Mark. This is my friend Julie. We called Roger and he said we could come see the vampire."

Mark hesitated. Julie had dark, haughty eyebrows and a determined-looking mouth. Bobbie wouldn't dare bring someone over without really getting Roger's permission, and anyway Roger was due back early. Mark let them in but asked them to wait to go back and see the vampire until Roger came.

Julie sat down in the big armchair by the avocado plant and surveyed the living room. "Roger must have good vibrations to be able to keep so many growing beings happy in his home."

Bobbie, curled on a hassock, smiled at Mark. "Mark takes care of it, mostly. When he's not around, it all goes to hell."

Turning to Mark, Julie said, "You wouldn't happen to have anything of the vampire's handy for me to look at while we're waiting—a hairbrush, used clothing? I can tell a lot about a person from those kind of things."

Another nut. Mark went to the cell. "Could you pass me your hairbrush, please?"

Dr. Weyland put down his book and brought the hairbrush from the tiny bathroom. The bare cell seemed more cramped than ever when his tall, stoop-shouldered form moved about in it.

Julie took the brush and drew a gray hair from among the bristles. "A man," she said firmly, "not a demon." She held the brush against her chest. "Tell me about the man, Bobbie."

Mark watered plants, listening as they talked. When he could no longer stand Bobbie's shapeless torrent of "wows" and "terrifics" and other general terms of awe that kept her from ever concluding a thought or a sentence, he relented and took them both down the hall for a quick glimpse of Dr. Weyland. The vampire looked up briefly from his reading but said nothing. The two women exchanged what Mark supposed was a significant glance and returned without comment to the living room. There they sat silent for so long that Mark got bored and went to his own room.

He was winding up a math assignment when he surfaced to an awareness of music—no, chanting. And a funny smell—

At the gate Dr. Weyland said wearily, "You might go and make certain they aren't burning the building down."

The living-room rugs were rolled up and the furniture had been moved back against the walls. Gray smoke curled from incense sticks thrust into the soft earth of the plant pots. All of the taller plants had been grouped in the center of the floor. The two women were prancing, stark naked, in a circle around this huddle of vegetation.

Under the plants lay a little heap of objects. Julie put down a peacock feather and took up a knife. Bearing it aloft in both hands she marched, with Bobbie behind her, first toward one corner of the room, then another.

Mark stood staring at their bodies. Bobbie was slim and tan all over, and Julie was white and chunky. She jiggled. He felt his face get all hot, and he was torn between intense embarrassment and panic. If Roger saw this . . .

"Casting out!" Julie cried. "Banishing the evil, blood-eating spirit by the power of Her dark phase." She held the stubby knife, a sort of mustard spreader with the handle wrapped in black electrician's tape, with the haft pointed at each corner of the room in succession. "By Her life-making loins." She dug a fistful of earth from under the avocado tree and sprinkled it on the floor. "By the power of Her shining face." A white ribbon fluttered through the smoky air.

Bobbie put down the platter she was holding and, hurrying over, whispered to Mark, "We'll be done pretty soon. I mean, I realize this is an imposition sort of, but I felt so bad about telling Alan about—him. Alan might not do anything, but you never can tell once he gets really involved and starts hearing spirits telling him to do things and all that. Alan is very powerful under certain planetary configurations.

"Julie has this different approach, you know, a warmer sort of attitude and these really glowing, positive vibrations."

Julie swayed alone in the middle of the room with her eyes shut, stroking the leaves of the plants.

"Make her stop," Mark pleaded, "and let's start cleaning up before Roger—"

Roger walked in.

Julie raised her arms. "By the power of my aiding

spirits, I declare the caged man free, I cast the curse from him, I drive forth—"

"Jee-sus!" Roger burst into the living room, kicking at the magical objects and slapping down the incense sticks. .

Julie spun around once in the middle of the floor. "So close our songs to the Mother!"

"Get your goddamn clothes on," Roger commanded, redder from his exertions than she was from hers. "There's a kid here, you slut!"

"We are skyclad," Julie retorted fiercely. She pulled on her caftan and started for the door, gathering her belongings and stuffing them into her knapsack. Bobbie, dressed and carrying her sandals, came after.

"Wait a minute," Roger said, grabbing at Bobbie's arm. "Damn it, Bobbie, what about all this mess you two have made here? I've got people coming over in a little while, serious Satanists."

Julie stood in the hallway holding her knapsack in both arms and glaring at him. "I'm sorry," she said icily, "but we're lousy at mundane tasks when our rites have been interrupted. All I can say is, if our work didn't help that poor man, it's your fault. Any fool but Alan could see in a minute that that person isn't a devil, not with a face like that, such a stern, beautiful mouth, so much gravity and wisdom in the eyes—and if it's Alan's friends you're expecting, they're just a bunch of—"

"Stuff it." Roger yanked open the front door and shoved her outside.

Bobbie gave a weak version of her sunny grin, murmured, "Sorry, Roger," and followed.

Roger slammed the door and. snapped the locks. "Come on," he said angrily to Mark, "help me straighten up in here. I'm trying to work this into a real experience for Alan's people, and those two come and turn everything into a cheap, goofy side show! I thought Bobbie was bringing over some kind of exotic medium who'd give us some class, and this is what I get."

The visitors, a chic and chatty group, came soon afterward. To Mark's relief, Alan Reese was not among them. Roger, his good humor regained, told with relish the tale of how the vampire had been found and brought here. When he had them all fidgeting with anticipation, he led them down the hall to the cell.

Mark went, too. His mouth was dry. He didn't like the atmosphere these people brought with them. Roger didn't even seem to know them, he thought; they were like strangers you happen to be standing on line with for a movie.

A plump, nervous-looking woman went into the cell with Roger. When Dr. Weyland looked at her, she began to hang back.

"Come on, Anne," said the people at the gate. "You said you would." "You told Alan you'd do it."

She smiled a scared smile and let Roger position her by the cot. He pressed her shoulder. She perched stiffly beside Dr. Weyland. Roger said softly to him, "Drink, vampire. The people are waiting to see you."

Dr. Weyland's glance moved from face to face. He looked very white. Sweat gleamed on his forehead. Mark felt sick, but he couldn't turn away.

"Come on inside where you can see," Roger told the spectators.

One of the women said, "It's good from here; we don't want to be piled up in each other's way. God, what a tiny room." She lit a cigarette.

"Start drinking," Roger said. "This is all you're going to get."

Dr. Weyland sat very still, looking at the floor now. Mark thought, Don't do it, don't do it in front of them.

"His hair's gray," a man said. "I thought they lived forever and never got old."

The man next to him answered, "Maybe when he drinks he gets younger right in front of us, like in the vampire movies."

"Or maybe something else happens to him that they're not allowed to show you in the movies." They all snickered.

Dr. Weyland reached over and took hold of Anne's arm.

"Ugh," she gasped as he began. "Jesus!" She sat straining as far from him on the cot as she could get, her face twisted with loathing and fright. The spectators pressed closer to the bars and whispered excitedly.

Mark couldn't see past them anymore. He was glad.

Afterward Anne came out crying and was led into the guest bathroom. The others crowded down the hall to the living room, talking and exclaiming. Passing the bathroom, one woman tipped her head in the direction of the sobbing sounds from inside. "If she'd just relaxed and rolled with it, I bet she could have gotten off on that."

The one with the cigarette glanced back at Mark and shushed her, and they giggled together.

Dr. Weyland sat quietly on the cot, his big hands loose and heavy-looking in his lap, his craggy face still. His glance touched Mark remotely like the stare of a resting cat that watches any movement, out of habit: without intention, without desire, without recognition.

Mark went into his bedroom and closed the door.

A letter came for Mark in Roger's mail. It was from Mark's father, and there was money in it. He put the money into a drawer until he could take it down to the bank and add it to the savings account he kept especially for parental bribes. He had vowed never to make a withdrawal from that account. Someday he was going to give the money back to them and let them figure out what to do with it.

He went back to the cell.

"I got your glasses fixed," he said. This had been his own idea; he knew how a bad lens could give you headaches.

Dr. Weyland came to the gate. "That was very fast. I can't repay your expense."

"I told you, Roger's taking care of stuff like that." In fact, Roger would die before he would spend money on something like fixing the vampire's glasses. Mark had paid out of his own earnings. Later he would figure out how to get the money back from Roger. The amount was small. The glasses had turned out to be not prescription but simple magnifiers, the kind you could buy through a catalog to make reading easier on your eyes.

Mark settled down at his drawing table.

Dr. Weyland, still at the gate, said, "What is it that you do at that table for so many hours at a time?"

After that hatchet job on the paper for Carol Kelly, Mark was wary. But by the same token he knew he would get a straightforward response from Dr. Weyland. Nervously he handed over a Skytown drawing. Dr. Weyland spread the paper flat against the wall with a delicate touch of his long, clean hands. Now that he was stronger, he kept himself immaculate. Mark was uncomfortably aware of his own bitten nails and perpetually grubby knuckles.

" 'Gravity plates,' " read Dr. Weyland. "Is this part of a space ship?"

"Space station, with two auxiliary vehicles and a squad of maintenance robots. It's set up for a single human operator."

"And this is a design for the library—how pleasantly old-fashioned, considering that so much information is already kept on microfilm and in computer memories rather than in print."

"Well, a library would be a kind of extra," Mark said.

"But well worth having," replied the vampire. "Electronic storage and retrieval systems are efficient, but efficiency is only one value among many. Books make fine tools and good friends—informative, discreet, controllable. Are there more of these plans?"

He looked at the Skytown drawings for a long time, and in the end he handed them back saying, with no trace of condescension, "I can see that your best thinking has gone into these. They're well worked out and handsomely drawn. You have a gift for visualization and an admirably steady hand."

Mark blushed with pleasure. Suddenly it was worth it to have endured the Great Housman Paper Massacre.

"This has been a much-needed relief from my current reading," Dr. Weyland added, indicating a stack of Roger's new books on the floor by the gate. They were all about magic and witchcraft and worshiping the Devil. On the top volume of this batch was stamped the word KABALLAH in gold. Dr. Weyland nudged the pile disdainfully with the toe of his slipper, exposing a book called *The Grimoire of Gudrun* and another, *Athames and Athanors*. The gaudy colors of the jackets made the white-walled cell seem bleaker than ever.

Mark said, "What's a 'grimoire'?"

Dr. Weyland corrected his pronunciation. "A grimoire is a witch's personal book of spells and procedures. 'Athame' or 'althame' is supposed to be the ancient name for the short-bladed, black-handled ceremonial knife a witch uses in her rituals, according to these texts. However, I seem to recall that this word was actually invented by an imaginative writer rather late in the nineteenth century."

"And 'athanor'?"

"I hope you've found your dictionary, because for the moment the meaning escapes me. At any rate, I'm done with these—I've read as much as I can bear to, and I can't quite bring myself to descend to the level of Gudrun's recipe book. You understand, I am obliged to you for providing these, but frankly they're scarcely readable—self-importantly conspirational, mind-numbing in their repetitions, abominably inaccurate, and foully edited."

"Roger mostly skims what he reads."

"Wise of him," Dr. Weyland said. "With books

like these the choice is clearly sink or skim."

Mark clutched at his stomach and moaned appreciatively. He lifted the books out between the bars. "It's all made up, then? Magic and devils and all that stuff?"

"Primarily. I do think that there are gifted individuals who can accomplish supernormal feats, usually on an erratic and unpredictable basis and therefore to no great effect on the world at large."

"Can you? I mean, can you work magic?"

"I can behave in ways which while natural in me would be highly unnatural in you," said Dr. Weyland. "But magic—no."

Mark said impulsively, "You're very old, aren't you?"

"Yes."

Dr. Weyland would be all right, Mark decided, now that he had his strength back. Even up against Alan Reese.

That night when Dr. Weyland reached for the young man Reese had sent, Roger commanded, "Not the arm. The neck. The people paid to see the real thing. Go for the neck."

For a moment the vampire looked out at them with an unfathomable gaze. Then he took the young man by the shoulders and leaned in and up under his jawline. The watchers gasped. The victim caught ineffectually at Dr. Weyland's wrists and whimpered.

Mark looked away. At the end the people applauded, and he hated them. They gathered in the living room and chattered: the vampire really was an attractive brute, even handsome in a harsh and distant way—that cold reserve, that eagle-stare. Didn't you get shivers watching him press against a person the way he did and suck on their neck like that? That was worth the money. Was it like sex for the vampire? Shh, where is Mark? Washing dishes, he can't hear us over the running water.

Somebody remembered reading that vampire bats sometimes drink so greedily from their prey that they get too heavy to fly and have to walk home. Ho, ha, that was a good one—waddling home at night along the roadside, burping all the way.

Mark finished up in the kitchen and went to bed. He put his pillow over his head to muffle the sound of their laughter.

May Eve was a week and a half away.

Dad called the next day. "Did you get what I sent you?" He often spoke as though he thought the phone line was tapped.

"Yes, Dad. It's in the bank."

"Mark, I've told you a hundred times, when I give you money it's for you to use. I could keep it in the bank myself. Look, I know your mother's given you some spiel about saving up in case I stop sending child support, but that's crap. You know you can depend on me."

"I know, Dad. When are we going to have dinner together?"

His father began to talk about a medical convention he was attending this week. Eminent heart surgeons one, two, and three; Dad was dropping names like crazy again. Mark held the phone between his cheek and shoulder, saying "Uh-huh" in the pauses. He was sitting on the sofa with his toes tucked cozily between the cushions, working on the game-room section of the Skytown plans.

Hearing his father's voice was nice, a reminder that the whole world didn't revolve around the cell down the hall. Maybe if Dad stayed on the phone long enough the time would go by, and then Mark would feed the vampire, and Roger would call too late to announce a live feeding. Then there would be a quiet evening, no sightseers leering into Dr. Weyland's cell.

". . . basketball game on Wednesday, all right? It means I'll have to pass up going to a talk on blah blah blah . . . Dr. Candleman, the transplant man . . . blah . . . We can have a bite first at that place right in the Garden, the steak house. You liked that last time."

While they made arrangements Mark thought about what Dad would say if he remarked suddenly, "Hey, guess what, Dad; we've got this wounded vampire living here. Roger brings home victims so the vampire can drink their blood, and he charges admission for people to watch." A new spectator sport, hot dog. Dad would say a long silence, and then he'd say, Go see Dr. Stimme, I knew it was a mistake for you to stop talking to him, but your mother never liked him because he was too impartial.

Dad said, "How's Roger?"

"He's okay. Busy."

"Mark, don't let so much time go by again without a phone call, okay?"

Mark said goodbye and hung up. Then he put the Skytown plans aside and wandered down the hallway in his stocking feet to Dr. Weyland.

"Are you hungry?" he said.

"Shouldn't you wait with my food until you hear from Uncle Roger?"

Mark lingered. "I'm sorry," he said finally. "About Roger bringing people here."

Dr. Weyland regarded him, chin on hand. "As a performance, it has its unpleasant side; they stand at the gate staring like lions observing their appointed Christian. But fresh nourishment is welcome, and eating in public is common enough."

Mark should have been relieved to see him in this calm mood instead of panicky and full of wild or bitter talk. Yet he found himself resenting the detached tone. Nobody could be that cool about those degrading exhibitions.

"It isn't just eating to the ones who come here. They make it dirty."

"That, as people say nowadays, is their problem."

"I saw you the first time," Mark accused. "You didn't want to. You knew it was rotten—those people staring . . ."

"Have you ever seen a mob at work?" asked Dr.

Weyland. "You would be amazed to learn how many bits of a living body can be detached with the help of a knife, or even teeth and nails, so that people can carry away souvenirs of a memorable event. In these close quarters, five or six people comprise a mob, and I . . . was and remain outside the boundaries of morality. At first I was afraid of what they might do, seeing me at my food. But having you here helps. There are things they would like to do and see in addition to the central attraction, but they refrain from suggesting the worst of them before a child."

The vampire's thoughtful, heavy-lidded gaze at that moment made him seem impossibly ancient.

"At least," he added pensively, "we seem to be past the danger that Roger might simply turn me over to the Central Park Zoo."

"Would that be so bad?" Mark asked cautiously. "If there were somebody—maybe a scientist from the museum—instead of, well, Roger. And Alan Reese."

After a moment Dr. Weyland said softly, "Being forced to grow from a child's faith to an adult's realism so quickly must be painful for you. I appreciate your having given some thought to an alternative to May Eve. However, I must assure you that scientists would be no improvement, though they would be more systematic at first then Reese, who is steered by his lust for power. Men of science would soon learn the easy answers—that my name comes from a tombstone in a New England churchyard, the original bearer having died aged seven; that the accomplishments of my career under that name can be sorted into those I achieved and those I fabricated in spite of the very great obstacles placed in my path by computerized record-keeping systems; also perhaps that I have in the past killed for food or to keep my nature secret, since those are recurrent necessities of my existence. All very thrilling, no doubt—unprecedented, marvelous, the makings of the best-seller Roger would like to write.

"But the inner secret, the secret of staying alive long

after such curious men are dead dust, I can yield in only one way because I don't know that secret myself. Eventually they would lose patience and cut me apart to see whether they might find the answer in my body—in the brain, the heart, the gut, the bones. Science would be as cruel as the mob. The only kindness is freedom."

"Okay, no scientists," Mark said fiercely. "Forget I said anything. Just leave me alone. You said you wouldn't ask me for help again!"

"I ask," said Dr. Weyland in that same low voice, "because I am desperate."

Mark's heart stamped in his ribs. He looked at his watch. "It's four o'clock, time for your meal."

He was at the refrigerator when the phone rang. It was Roger: "Don't feed him."

Alan Reese came that night. He arrived late, when Roger's preliminary remarks "for our newcomers" were over and everyone had moved into the hallway outside Dr. Weyland's cell. Mark was watching uneasily from his doorway. He tried to shrink back out of sight so that Reese wouldn't notice him.

He hated, really hated, that round, self-satisfied face, those quick, calculating, greedy blue eyes. Without his briefcase of magical paraphernalia and dressed in a windbreaker, the man didn't look dangerous. The crowd parted deferentially to let him through to the front, and then people pressed closer behind him in anticipation of something special now that he had come. Roger, unlocking the gate, broke off in the midst of a comment that Mark couldn't hear.

Reese took command without raising his voice. He said in a stern, level tone, "Those of you who see in this cell only a freak do not belong here. You are all confronting a lesson in the depths that lie behind the surface of every 'reality' of your daily lives. Think about this: you look into this room and you see a creature of human appearance. He looks back—and sees you with the immense contempt and cruel appetite of an immortal who feeds his endless life on your tiny lives.

"Fortunately, there are those of us who are experienced and strong enough to render him tractable . . ."

Mark slipped out. He walked up and down Broadway, guilty at having abandoned the vampire to whatever games Reese had in mind for tonight, furious that Dr. Weyland had saddled him somehow with a feeling of responsibility. Wesley said the vampire was Roger's project, and he was right. Roger was responsible.

Anyway, Dr. Weyland wasn't even human, really, so how could he be sure what people were like, what they would or would not do to him?

When Mark returned a few people were hanging around outside talking, doubtless waiting for Reese, who was in the living room with Roger: ". . . from the Coast, influential contacts in the occult world. The arrangements for filming the special Sabbat on May Eve . . ."

Ducking down the hall and into his own bedroom, Mark listened for Reese's departure. When at last the front door shut and the locks turned, he let out a breath he seemed to have been holding for hours.

Roger looked in. "Hey, where'd you go? You should have stayed. Alan put on a great show. He's pretty pushy, likes to take over, but he does have this fantastic sense of drama. He's been building up the vampire, whetting people's appetites for the main event."

"I think Reese is a power freak," Mark mumbled. He sat on his bed hugging his knees, not meeting Roger's eyes. "He's like kids who like to cut up live little animals, you know? Only he calls it a 'rite.' He could do whatever he wanted and nobody could stop him. His hands could rip you up alive while he was explaining to you in all kinds of big words how your ghost needs its freedom so he's really doing you a favor."

"You read too much crappy fiction," Roger said

sharply. "Nothing bad happened to the vampire tonight while you were gone; nothing awful is going to happen, either."

Across the hallway, Dr. Weyland avoided Mark's gaze. The vampire seemed indifferent, remote, but there were stains of fatigue under his eyes, and his shoulders were slumped as if after great tension.

"I think he's scared," Mark said.

"Nobody's scared but you," snapped Roger. "Everybody else knows—even the vampire himself, you can bet on it—everybody else knows it's all just great theater we're doing here, that's all." His voice softened. "Come on Markie, relax. Good night, now."

Mark lay huddled under his blankets thinking about Dr. Weyland. He knew how it felt to pretend composure and confidence in a situation where you were at the mercy of other people. It felt horrible.

Roger brought home a ponytailed young man in ragged cut-offs and a Pakistani cotton shirt. Mark was in bed when they appeared in his doorway. Roger, behind the blond stranger, flicked on the light.

The blond started to turn to Roger, saying, "The kid keeps your stash for you?"

Roger grabbed him around the neck. The blond looked surprised and reached up, but then his eyes rolled back and he collapsed. Roger caught him and reeled against the doorjamb, swearing breathlessly. "Shit, ow, come on, Mark, give me a hand!"

Dazed and squinting, Mark got out of bed and went to help lower the unconscious stranger to the floor. Roger, squatting, began rolling up one sleeve of the Pakistani shirt.

"What did you do? What's the matter with him?" Mark said.

"I knocked him out a little, that's all. He's dinner for our guest. No audience tonight. This is a sort of a present." Roger lowered his voice. "Alan says no more feeding until May Eve."

"But, Roger, that's a week away!"

"Animals can live a month on just water. All you have to do is make sure he has plenty of water to drink. It's no big deal, you know, just a sort of fasting, purifying for the ceremony. Shit." Roger gave up and ripped the cotton to expose the blond's slack arm up to the shoulder. He began dragging him across the hallway, calling, "Feeding time! Come and get him before he gets cold."

He tucked the blond's flopping arm between the bars. Dr. Weyland got up and came over to the gate. He took hold of the bars with both hands and lowered himself over the offering. After a moment, Roger reached between the bars and pushed at the vampire's head so that the light fell on his lips, sealed to the tan skin of the stranger's inner elbow.

Mark whispered, "Don't, Roger."

"Why not? I can't see well enough. When you put on a show you never get a good look at it yourself, and tonight's—" Roger stopped short of saying "the last time." He laughed a little, shivering. "I'm almost tempted to give him a drink myself, it looks so— God, look at that. His eyes are open."

There was a pale glimmer under Dr. Weyland's lowered lids.

The blond man gave a sudden start and a breathy moan, and a sort of shudder ran along his limbs.

"Christ, he's waking up!" said Roger frantically, and he pressed beside the man's windpipe with his fingertips. The blond subsided once more into gape-mouthed slackness, his long hair spread like a halo around his head on the floor.

"What did you do to him?" Mark croaked.

"If you press right there, you can cut off the blood supply to the brain and put a person out. There's another place in the armpit. It's for handling drowning people so they don't drag you down with them; I learned it that summer in lifesaving class. They don't teach it anymore. It's too dangerous—you could turn a guy into a vegetable if you kept up the pressure too long." Roger tugged at the vampire's hair. "Greedy tonight, isn't he. Come on, that's enough—leave the kid some roses in his cheeks."

While Roger was out depositing the young man in the park, Mark heard gagging sounds from the vampire's cell. Dr. Weyland was in his bathroom being sick. Mark stood at the gate, scared to go in. Suppose it was a trick?

"What is it?" he called. "What's the matter?"

Dr. Weyland panted, "Something in the blood . . . bad blood . . ."

When Roger came back Mark hurried to tell him. Dr. Weyland was still in the bathroom. They could hear his hard, strained breathing.

"That guy must have been a pill-popper or something," Roger muttered. "He told me he was just looking for some good grass. Maybe he was really sick."

"What about Dr. Weyland?" Mark said. "That's all he's had to eat today, and he's throwing everything up."

"There's nothing I can do about it—I took the last package of blood from the fridge with me and dumped it; it was spoiled anyway. Listen, it won't kill him to start fasting a day early."

Next afternoon Roger called from one of the shops. "Mark? Listen. Alan just called. There's an item in the paper about a college student found dead this morning in Riverside Park—guess who. That greedy monster you're so worried about took too much. You might give that some thought. Alan wants me to come over—more complicated arrangements for May Eve. I'll see you later."

Mark took his work and a camp chair out into the yard. He couldn't concentrate. Inevitably, he went down the hall.

The vampire sat on the cot with his back against the wall, doing nothing.

"That guy died," Mark said.

He got no reply. Dr. Weyland's shirt looked rumpled. It was buttoned wrong so that the collar stuck up on one side. His gaze was flat and unfocused. A vein stood in his temple like a smear of ink.

"You're like a wild animal," Mark continued. "You hear like a fox, don't you—everything we say around here. You heard Roger say Alan doesn't want him to bring any more people for you, so you tanked up while you had the chance."

"Yes," Dr. Weyland said, "against hunger. I drank what I could while I could, even though I tasted some impurity. I had to eat, I had to try. I protect myself as best I can, as might also be said of you."

His sudden glance seemed to pierce right through Mark. "But I had no profit of it, and I am hungry now; truly hungry, bitterly hungry, with a hunger you know nothing about and never can. Reese, who has his own appetite, guesses. He means to use my hunger to break me to my role in his performance.

"Your uncle was right, you should have stayed the other night to see Reese display the antagonist he means to subdue. In reality I can give Reese nothing—but he can take from me. He 'builds me up,' as Roger put it, in order to stand higher himself when he has cast me down. He presents me as some mystical and powerful being which he alone, the leader, the master, can conquer and destroy." His knuckles whitened where he gripped the side of the cot. "Do you hear, do you understand? Let me out or Reese and his people will kill me."

"Stop saying that! Roger—"

"Stop dodging, face the truth! Roger can't help now even if he wants to. He consoles himself for his loss of control with thoughts of how rich he'll become from Reese's enterprise. Against that the slaughter of a mere animal, an investment made on a whim, weighs very little. Have you noticed, Roger never refers to or addresses me by name? He is preparing himself to be indifferent to my death."

Mark struck the bars with his fist. "Shut up, Roger's not a coward, he'd never let anybody get killed! You're the killer, and you're a dirty liar, you'd say anything to turn me against Roger so I'd let you go! You'd do anything, you freak, you murderer!"

"And you," replied the vampire with weary bitterness, "are clearly Roger's kin. He makes his preparations and you make yours. At the level of name-calling there's nothing to be said or done. Go tend to your school work." He closed his eyes.

Mark turned away. "Old liar," he whispered furiously to himself. "Murdering old lying freak!"

The weather turned warmer. Mark spent as much time away from Roger's as he could, sitting through foolish movies, wandering blankly down quiet museum halls. Neither his school assignments nor Skytown could hold his attention even when he took all his papers to the library and tried to work there. Once he fell asleep on the carpeting in the muted glow of the gem exhibit at the museum. A noisy class of children came in and woke him. He left and found himself walking uptown toward his mother's: running away.

He could no longer remember the college student's face. The young man's death seemed to him now like . . . like a kid getting his arm pulled off by a bear at the zoo, except of course he hadn't stuck his own arm through the bars to the bear. Roger had done that for the man, literally. Alan Reese had sort of done it, too, through Roger. Sometimes Mark scarcely believed it had really happened. He hadn't seen the student die; maybe it was a mistake, maybe the newspapers had gotten the facts wrong or exaggerated for some reason, or maybe Reese had lied to Roger.

All that was taking Mark's mind off what mattered

now: the possibilities of Reese's Great Sabbat on May
Eve.

His thoughts veered away in a panic. What was he
supposed to do, go to the police station and bring the
cops back to Roger's? That might stop Reese, but it
would get Roger into a lot of trouble, and Dr. Weyland
too once people knew what he was. Or should he stay
around in case Dr. Weyland was right about a kid's
presence being a restraint? Suppose being there didn't
help, how was Mark supposed to stand it, watching
Reese do . . . whatever he was going to do? Or should
he let the vampire loose on the city to save him from
Alan Reese?

Mark was only a kid, how could he take it on himself
to do those things? He told himself that none of this
craziness was his own fault. Remember what the school
psychologist had said about the divorce: Not everything
is about you, grown-up people are responsible for their
own lives. And Dr. Stimme had said, You are not in
charge of things that you have no power to change.
Though sometimes you can be a good influence . . .

Mark turned and trudged back toward Roger's.

Roger was away all day and for several evenings,
saying that he had to consult with some people about
maybe opening a new store on the East Side, or
complaining that with May Eve coming up he had to be
at Reese's beck and call all the time over the details.
Mark thought Roger was just not comfortable around
the apartment these days.

So it was Mark, not Roger, who watched the vampire
starve. Dr. Weyland spent his days huddled over,
hugging his hunger, each breath a shaking, exhausted
hiss of pain. It was Mark, not Roger, who came home
Tuesday to find the water pitcher knocked over. He
couldn't tell whether Dr. Weyland had drunk first and
dropped the pitcher afterward, or dropped it first and
had to lap up the spilled water like a dog. After
Tuesday, Mark laid out a row of filled plastic cups each

morning so that the weakened vampire wouldn't have to lift and pour from the heavy pitcher.

It's an act, he told himself. He fakes being so hungry just to get to me.

But he didn't believe it. The vampire seemed curled around his suffering, holding it private to himself—as private as anything could be, when anyone might come and look through the bars into his tiny cell.

On Wednesday evening Mark went to the ball game with his father. He longed for a shared pleasure that would bring him close enough to his dad to—maybe— share the nightmare that waited back at Roger's.

The sharing didn't happen. He wasn't allowed to like the game itself for the speed and grace of the players, the wonderful way they leaped up with everything they had. What his father savored was the violence.

He shouted and sweated, and he pounded Mark's shoulder to drive home to him every ecstatic moment of impact. Mark felt those heavy hands trying to pummel him into some kind of fellowship of force. It was Dad's idea of closeness to a teenage son.

Dad couldn't help it; he had hitter's hands, hands like Alan Reese's.

On the way back to Roger's his father said, "Is there anything you need, Mark? Anything I can do for you? Just say the word."

Sure. "Everything's cool, Dad."

Roger was out, as usual now. When Mark let himself in, he found that the vampire had worked free one of the legs of the cot. The length of pale wood lay by the gate, battered and splintered from his efforts to beat open the gate lock with it.

Dr. Weyland himself sat cramped against the wall, gasping. One of his slippers had been kicked off across the room.

Mark said, "Drink some water, maybe you'll feel better." He got no response.

An hour later Dr. Weyland had not moved, and Roger was still not back.

Mark dialed Wesley's number. Since the blood deliveries had ended, Wesley hadn't come around.

"Wesley, please come over. You've got to help." To his horror he heard a catch in his voice and stopped to gulp down a big breath and steady himself. "It's hurting him really badly, Wesley. Please bring some blood. I'll pay for it myself. Roger won't ever know."

There was a pause. Then Wesley said, "He'd find out. And I don't want to get mixed up with Alan Reese. The vampire's just putting you on, anyhow, trying to soften you up so you'll spring him. You watch out for him."

"I think he's dying, Wesley."

"Look, he's Roger's baby, I told you. Go home, walk out of it. Don't let this thing get to you, Markie. Go on back to your mother's."

"Can you give me Bobbie's phone number?" Carol Kelly had paid for the Housman paper. Mark thought maybe he could bribe Bobbie to help.

Bobbie was home. In a sleepy voice she said Alan Reese was mad about her getting Julie into the vampire deal. He'd put a heavy curse on her so that she was sick. Julie? Julie was smart, she'd taken off for California, out of range of Alan's bad magic. It was too bad about the vampire—if she wasn't so sick, Bobbie said kindly, she would come over and let him do it, you know; you could really groove on that, it was like some dreamy kind of kiss . . . . Had Mark tried talking to Wesley?

He sat by the phone and gnawed at his nails. Tomorrow night was May Eve. He mixed a batch of sweet lemonade and put it in the cups for the vampire. It was all he could think of to do.

On the morning of the last day Mark was too nervous to eat his cereal. He stared at Roger across the kitchen table, hoping he would see some kind of good sign in

Roger's face, some promise that tonight things would go all right. Maybe Dr. Weyland was wrong about Roger.

"You'll be late for school," Roger said, poking at the runny yellow of his breakfast egg with his fork.

"I don't want to go today."

Roger smiled brilliantly. "Big night tonight, right? Okay, don't worry, I'll see that you're all squared away with the school for today."

"I think he's dying, Roger," Mark said. "I'm scared he'll die if we don't feed him something."

"What, feed him and ruin all his conditioning?" Roger got up, dabbing at his chin with his napkin. "Forget it, Markie. Reese said absolutely do not feed the animal, and we're going along with his arrangements. He has the whole thing under control. The man may be an egomaniac, but he does see that things get done right, and this is a show that has to be done right.

"Did I tell you? Alan's invited some hotshots from out of town for tonight. He's so pleased with himself over it that he's picking them up himself at the airport. Then he wants to make the preparations with everybody at his place. I'll be coming back ahead of the others to set up some things he hasn't even told me yet. The performance isn't really due to begin here before nine o'clock. So find yourself something to keep you busy till after dinner, and leave the vampire show to Reese."

Roger himself spent the morning padding about the apartment in his bathrobe neatening up, in a state of jittery cheerfulness that Mark couldn't bear. Near noon there were phone calls from two of the shops and Roger had to go out.

The apartment was no more tolerable with Roger gone than it had been before. It seemed to be empty of all but Dr. Weyland's merciless appetite and the almost palpable agony of Dr. Weyland's fear. Overhearing the breakfast conversation as he overheard everything, Dr. Weyland would know the schedule now, which must make the waiting more terrible, the hunger more keen.

Mark couldn't go down the hall. He felt like an intruder in the apartment. He walked slowly to the public library and sat staring into space a long time, a book uselessly open on the table in front of him. He wandered in the park. Around midafternoon he returned to Roger's.

Dr. Weyland did not seem to have moved at all since morning. He lay silent as death on the collapsed cot, his long body bent in sharp angles like a snapped stick, knees and forehead pressed to the wall.

Mark sat down wearily in his own bedroom, trying not to think ahead to the night.

A sound woke him in his chair, a horn blaring outside. Even without looking at his watch he could tell that hours had passed. The light had changed, dusk was coming on.

Dr. Weyland had moved at last. He sat huddled in a corner of his room, knees raised, head down and buried in his folded arms. Mark could see a tremor in his shoulders and in the taut line of his neck. His left sleeve was torn, pulled back to hang from the thin bicep, above the crook of the elbow where he had his face pressed, where his mouth was tight against the tender inside of the arm with the raised blue veins—from which he was sucking—drinking—

"Don't, don't do that!" the boy shrilled. Into his mind flashed the image of a trapped coyote in the museum film, chewing off its own foot to escape the steel jaws and death by thirst. He saw the mangled limb, clotted blood and bone—

He flew down the hallway for the key, rushed back, fumbled it into the lock with sweaty, shaking fingers. He lunged at Weyland, weeping, and with frantic strength beat his arms down.

There was a dew of blood on Weyland's lips, a red smear on one seamed cheek. His eyes were blank slits in dark sockets. Mark swallowed nausea and, kneeling, pressed his own arm against the bloody mouth. Warm breath flared onto his shrinking skin.

All in one motion, like being hurled down by an ocean tide, he was seized and pinned breathless to the floor. There came a faint sting and a surging sensation in his arm, and then a growing lightness in all his limbs.

Eyes tight shut, he cried, "Don't kill me, please don't kill me, oh please don't, please!" He was borne under, his head full of the wet sound of the vampire swallowing. On a rush of terror he screamed, "Oh, Mom, help!" and beat wildly at Weyland with his free hand. Dark spots spattered his vision.

Silence. With great effort he opened his eyes. He lay alone on the floor of the cell. The gate was open.

After a long, blank time he noticed sounds of locks clicking. Roger called him. He could find no strength to answer. Roger started down the hall, still calling. Then his voice ceased uncertainly, his footsteps paused, retreated, returned more softly. Turning his head, Mark could see Roger hovering outside the gate, carrying the length of lead pipe in his hand.

"Look out," Mark said. Only no sound came out of him.

"Mark?" Roger whispered. "Oh, my God—"

A shadow glided from the doorway of Mark's bedroom and a hand reached out and closed on Roger's throat. The lead pipe thumped to the floor. As Roger folded the vampire caught him, swayed, slid down against the wall, holding him.

Mark struggled to sit up.

In the hallway Weyland sat crosslegged. He had pulled Roger's upper body into his lap and wrapped his lean arms around Roger so that Roger's arms were caught to his sides. The striped blue shirt that Roger wore was torn open down the front. Roger's head hung back nearly to the floor.

Weyland leaned deeply over him, chest to chest, mouth pressed up under Roger's jaw, lips fastened to

Roger's throat. He was drinking not in some blissful dream but fiercely, ravenously, breathing in long, grateful gasps between swallows.

Roger's eyelids fluttered. Roger emitted one faint cry and turned his head painfully, flinching from the vampire's grip. The heels of Roger's shoes scratched feebly at the floor.

Weyland pressed closer, working his jaw to shift and improve his hold, and he drank and drank. Now Roger's legs sagged limp as ropes. Paralyzed with weakness and horror, Mark kept thinking, This is Roger this is happening to, my Uncle Roger, this is Roger.

At last the vampire raised his head and met Mark's gaze. In Weyland's haggard face the eyes glittered keen as stars. He got up abruptly, dumping Roger out of his lap like a brightly wrapped parcel from which the gift has been removed.

"You killed him," Mark moaned.

"Not yet." Weyland had the lead pipe in his hands. As Mark lurched to all fours, trying to rise, he saw Weyland cock the pipe like a golfer prepared to swing.

"No!" he cried.

"Why not?" The vampire paused, looking at Mark.

Seconds seemed to spin out endlessly. Weyland had not moved. Now he straightened and said, "Very well. You've bought the right. It was as good as paying money." He put aside the pipe and stepped over Roger and into the tiny room. His long hands descended and gripped Mark's shoulders. Mark tried to twist free, panic rising. He had no strength, and the vampire was astonishingly, appallingly strong.

"Please," Mark wailed.

"Get up." The lean fingers dragged him to his feet. "Where does that bedding go? The cot? Put the pillows and the blanket away." Mark moved sluggishly to obey, feeling dazed and drowned. Weyland set about gathering up the cot and brought it out to be stowed at the back of the hall closet. "Broom and dustpan," he said. "Shopping bag. Paper towels."

They cleaned up. In the cramped bathroom every surface was wiped down. Toilet articles, used paper towels and Weyland's dirty laundry went into the shopping bag. Weyland swept. He carried out the dustpan, stepping over Roger's inert form as if over a log of wood.

Stumbling in his wake, Mark stopped there, staring at Roger, who lay sprawled face down on the floor.

Weyland said, "No need to worry about your excitable uncle. He'll live." He pulled the gate shut behind him, and the lock clicked on the empty room.

Mark trailed after Weyland up the hall and through the dark living room. In the brightness of Roger's bedroom, the vampire flung open the wall-length closets. Mark sat slumped on the bed while Weyland chose a short-sleeved shirt of cream white polyester. The rest were clearly impossible: Roger's clothes were sized to a smaller frame.

Weyland glanced at the bedside clock and said, "Wait."

Blearily Mark saw that the hands showed eight o'clock. Weyland had time to freshen up.

After a while he emerged from the bathroom looking very much the man of his book-jacket photograph. Shaven, washed, brushed, the rumpled slacks neatened by one of Roger's belts, he was imposing enough so that the bedroom slippers on his feet were scarcely noticeable.

"My things," he said. "Fetch them."

Mark got the paper bag and gave back the knife. Cards, pencils, even paper clips, Dr. Weyland slipped it all into his trouser pockets. "That seems to be everything I came with, minus a few coins." Then he said, "Roger keeps money in the house."

Mark was only distantly sorry for Roger now. He was absorbed in getting his exhausted body to move. He went into the kitchen, opened the oven door, and pulled out the money box.

Dr. Weyland took all the bills and change without counting. "Put the box back. If there's anything that you want from your room, go and get it."

Mark thought of the plans for Skytown, the shelves of books, the comfortable messiness, all empty of comfort now. He thought of Roger lying in the hall, and he had an impulse to go and help, to do something —but what he could do for Roger was already done. Anything more would be up to somebody else.

He shook his head.

"Come, then. Quickly."

It was cool outside. Dr. Weyland was slightly unsteady in mounting the steps of the areaway. On the sidewalk he stopped. "God damn it. My eyeglasses."

Mark sat on the steps with the shopping bag and waited for him. Trying to run away would be stupid: he could barely walk.

The long shadow fell across him. "Ah," Dr. Weyland breathed, head up, tasting the breeze from the west. "The river."

They walked toward Riverside Drive. Dr. Weyland's hand rested firmly on Mark's shoulder.

"You were only pretending," Mark said.

"Not at all," snapped Dr. Weyland. "I pretended nothing: no stoicism, no defiance, nothing." Broodingly he added, "I left the truth of my condition open to you, in hopes of saving my life—but I was sure I had lost, because of that one who died. I was sure. You would budge only so far, and I needed to push you so much further."

They started over the damp grass toward the promenade beside the water. River-smell enveloped them.

"I thought you were dying," Mark whispered.

"I was," came the low reply.

"That was real, when you drank—your own—" Mark shuddered.

"Oh yes, that was real. The great temptation has always been just that. It tasted good; you can't know how good it was." The hand on Mark's shoulder tightened for an instant. "If you hadn't stopped me . . . I was so hungry . . ."

They crossed the pavement and stopped at the rail. There was a rustle of rats on the wet rocks below. Dr. Weyland turned to watch a trio of evening joggers patter past.

He said, "Your young blood restored me. Even so, I could only manage Roger because of his excellent lesson in producing unconsciousness with the pressure of a finger. There's always something new to learn. Needless to say, I never studied lifesaving."

Mark looked across at Jersey, spangles of light above the black, oily water. Tears welled in his eyes, and his breath broke into sobs.

"Stop snuffling," Dr. Weyland said irritably. "You'll attract attention. There's nothing the matter with you. As Roger correctly deduced, I am not contagious. I did you no serious damage and Roger will recover, thanks to you. You saved his life even before you spoke up for him, just by dulling the edge of my need."

All Mark's control was gone. His whole body shook with the force of his crying.

The vampire added sharply, "I told you to stop that. You have work to do. You must use your fertile imagination to design a story for your mother, something to explain your sudden return from Roger's and whatever else may come out of all this. You did Skytown; you can do this."

"You're lying," Mark blubbered. "You're just going to throw me in the river anyway, so I can't tell."

There was a brief, considering pause. "No," said Dr. Weyland at last. "Corpses lead to questions. Besides, killing you would make no difference. Many people know about me now, although without my physical presence the authorities are unlikely to believe any gossip they may hear.

"You must simply go back to your parents, play the innocent, let them think Roger tried to turn you on or whatever other fiction will serve. You live in a culture that treats childhood as a disadvantage; make a strength of that weakness. Sulk, whine, run away a few times if they press you. You won't be so foolish as to speak of me at all, unless you wish to spend the remainder of your adolescence in analysis."

Two women came by, walking their dogs. One of the women gave Dr. Weyland a tiny smile in passing. Mark looked up at him, saw the predatory profile in the lamplight, the intent eyes thoughtfully following the women. He felt tired, chilly, abandoned. Furtively, he wiped his nose on the front of his shirt.

His arm ached faintly where the vampire had drunk. To have someone spring on you like a tiger and suck your blood with savage and single-minded intensity—how could anybody imagine that was sexy? He would never forget that moment's blinding fear. If sex was like that, they could keep it.

The two of them were alone for the moment. Dr. Weyland turned and slung the shopping bag into the river. It bobbed, swirled round slowly twice, and sank.

Mark said, "Are you going to go after Alan Reese?"

"No. When he is dead, I will still be alive. That suffices."

"What are you going to do?"

"Begin again," Dr. Weyland said grimly. "Unless I can invent some tale to keep my present identity alive and useful. I have my own imagining to do, and then work, a great deal of work. How do you get back to your mother's from here?"

There came no inner recoil. The terrors of home were gone, burned away by the touch of something ancient and wild beyond the concerns of this city. "I take the subway," Mark said.

"Have you money?"

He felt in his jeans pocket. He had Carol Kelly's payment. "Yes."

"Of course—the school scribe has his earnings, and a good thing; I need all that I have. My God, even this rank, filthy river smells wonderful after that foul cupboard of a room!"

He was looking past Mark up the river, turning to sweep his gaze along the bridge to the north and down the lamplit mouths of the streets along the Drive. There was an eagerness to the lift of his head that made Mark think he might simply stride off without another word, so clear was Dr. Weyland's impatience to be away, once more free and secret among men.

Mark shivered, flooded with relief and desolation.

Dr. Weyland looked down at him, frowning slightly as if his thoughts had already left Mark behind. "Come on," he said.

They started back across the narrow park.

"Where are we going?"

"I am walking you to the subway," the vampire said.

III

Unicorn
Tapestry

"HOLD ON," Floria said. "I know what you're going to say: I agreed not to take any new clients for a while. But wait till I tell you—you're not going to believe this—first phone call, setting up an initial appointment, he comes out with what his problem is: 'I seem to have fallen victim to a delusion of being a vampire.'"

"Christ H. God!" cried Lucille delightedly. "Just like that, over the telephone?"

"When I recovered my aplomb, so to speak, I told him that I prefer to wait with the details until our first meeting, which is tomorrow."

They were sitting on the tiny terrace outside the staff room of the clinic, a converted town house on the upper West Side. Floria spent three days a week here and the remaining two in her office on Central Park South where she saw private clients like this new one. Lucille, always gratifyingly responsive, was Floria's most valued professional friend. Clearly enchanted with Floria's news, she sat eagerly forward in her chair, eyes wide behind Coke-bottle lenses.

She said, "Do you suppose he thinks he's a revivified corpse?"

Below, down at the end of the street, Floria could see two kids skidding their skateboards near a man who wore a woolen cap and a heavy coat despite the May warmth. He was leaning against a wall. He had been there when Floria had arrived at the clinic this morning. If corpses walked, some, not nearly revivified enough, stood in plain view in New York.

"I'll have to think of a delicate way to ask," she said.

"How did he come to you, this 'vampire'?"

"He was working in an upstate college, teaching and doing research, and all of a sudden he just disappeared —vanished, literally, without a trace. A month later he turned up here in the city. The faculty dean at the school knows me and sent him to see me."

Lucille gave her a sly look. "So you thought, ahah, do a little favor for a friend, this looks classic and easy to transfer if need be: repressed intellectual blows stack and runs off with spacey chick, something like that."

"You know me too well," Floria said with a rueful smile.

"Huh," grunted Lucille. She sipped ginger ale from a chipped white mug. "I don't take panicky middle-aged men anymore, they're too depressing. And you shouldn't be taking this one, intriguing as he sounds."

Here comes the lecture, Floria told herself.

Lucille got up. She was short, heavy, prone to wearing loose garments that swung about her like ceremonial robes. As she paced, her hem brushed at the flowers starting up in the planting boxes that rimmed the little terrace. "You know damn well this is just more overwork you're loading on. Don't take this guy; refer him."

Floria sighed. "I know, I know. I promised everybody I'd slow down. But you said it yourself just a minute ago—it looked like a simple favor. So what do I get? Count Dracula, for God's sake! Would you give that up?"

Fishing around in one capacious pocket, Lucille brought out a dented package of cigarettes and lit up, scowling. "You know, when you give me advice I try to take it seriously. Joking aside, Floria, what am I supposed to say? I've listened to you moaning for months now, and I thought we'd figured out that what you need is to shed some pressure, to start saying no—and here you are insisting on a new case. You know what I think: you're hiding in other people's problems from a lot of your own stuff that you should be working on.

"Okay, okay, don't glare at me. Be pigheaded. Have you gotten rid of Chubs, at least?" This was Floria's code name for a troublesome client named Kenny whom she'd been trying to unload for some time.

Floria shook her head.

"What gives with you? It's weeks since you swore you'd dump him! Trying to do everything for everybody is wearing you out. I bet you're still dropping weight. Judging by the very unbecoming circles under your eyes, sleeping isn't going too well, either. Still no dreams you can remember?"

"Lucille, don't nag. I don't want to talk about my health."

"Well, what about his health—Dracula's? Did you suggest that he have a physical before seeing you? There might be something physiological—"

"You're not going to be able to whisk him off to an M.D. and out of my hands," Floria said wryly. "He told me on the phone that he wouldn't consider either medication or hospitalization."

Involuntarily she glanced down at the end of the street. The woolen-capped man had curled up on the sidewalk at the foot of the building, sleeping or passed out or dead. The city was tottering with sickness. Compared with that wreck down there and others like him, how sick could this "vampire" be, with his cultured baritone voice, his self-possessed approach?

"And you won't consider handing him off to somebody else," Lucille said.

"Well, not until I know a little more. Come on, Luce—wouldn't you want at least to know what he looks like?"

Lucille stubbed out her cigarette against the low parapet. Down below a policeman strolled along the street ticketing the parked cars. He didn't even look at the man lying at the corner of the building. They watched his progress without comment. Finally Lucille said, "Well, if you won't drop Dracula, keep me posted on him, will you?"

He entered the office on the dot of the hour, a gaunt but graceful figure. He was impressive. Wiry gray hair, worn short, emphasized the massiveness of his face with its long jaw, high cheekbones, and granite cheeks grooved as if by winters of hard weather. His name, typed in caps on the initial information sheet that Floria proceeded to fill out with him, was Edward Lewis Weyland.

Crisply he told her about the background of the vampire incident, describing in caustic terms his life at Cayslin College: the pressures of collegial competition, interdepartmental squabbles, student indifference, administrative bungling. History has limited use, she knew, since memory distorts; still, if he felt most comfortable establishing the setting for his illness, that was as good a way to start off as any.

At length his energy faltered. His angular body sank into a slump, his voice became flat and tired as he haltingly worked up to the crucial event: night work at the sleep lab, fantasies of blood-drinking as he watched the youthful subjects of his dream research slumbering, finally an attempt to act out the fantasy with a staff member at the college. He had been repulsed; then panic had assailed him. Word would get out, he'd be fired, blacklisted forever. He'd bolted. A nightmare period had followed—he offered no details. When he had come to his senses he'd seen that just what he feared, the ruin of his career, would come from his running away. So he'd phoned the dean, and now here he was.

Throughout this recital she watched him diminish from the dignified academic who had entered her office to a shamed and frightened man hunched in his chair, his hands pulling fitfully at each other.

"What are your hands doing?" she said gently. He looked blank. She repeated the question.

He looked down at his hands. "Struggling," he said.

"With what?"

"The worst," he muttered. "I haven't told you the worst." She had never grown hardened to this sort of transformation. His long fingers busied themselves fiddling with a button on his jacket while he explained painfully that the object of his "attack" at Cayslin had been a woman. Not young but handsome and vital, she had first caught his attention earlier in the year during an honorary seminar for a retiring professor.

A picture emerged of an awkward Weyland, lifelong bachelor, seeking this woman's warmth and suffering her refusal. Floria knew she should bring him out of his past and into his here-and-now, but he was doing so beautifully on his own that she was loath to interrupt.

"Did I tell you there was a rapist active on the campus at this time?" he said bitterly. "I borrowed a leaf from his book: I tried to take from this woman, since she wouldn't give. I tried to take some of her blood." He stared at the floor. "What does that mean—to take someone's blood?"

"What do you think it means?"

The button, pulled and twisted by his fretful fingers, came off. He put it into his pocket, the impulse, she guessed, of a fastidious nature. "Her energy," he murmured, "stolen to warm the aging scholar, the walking corpse, the vampire—myself."

His silence, his downcast eyes, his bent shoulders, all signaled a man brought to bay by a life crisis. Perhaps

he was going to be the kind of client therapists dream of
and she needed so badly these days: a client intelligent
and sensitive enough, given the companionship of a
professional listener, to swiftly unravel his own mental
tangles. Exhilarated by his promising start, Floria
restrained herself from trying to build on it too soon.
She made herself tolerate the silence, which lasted until
he said suddenly, "I notice that you make no notes as
we speak. Do you record these sessions on tape?"

A hint of paranoia, she thought; not unusual. "Not
without your knowledge and consent, just as I won't
send for your personnel file from Cayslin without your
knowledge and consent. I do, however, write notes
after each session as a guide to myself and in order to
have a record in case of any confusion about anything
we do or say here. I can promise you that I won't show
my notes or speak of you by name to anyone—except
Dean Sharpe at Cayslin, of course, and even then only
as much as is strictly necessary—without your written
permission. Does that satisfy you?"

"I apologize for my question," he said. "The . . .
incident has left me . . . very nervous; a condition that
I hope to get over with your help."

The time was up. When he had gone, she stepped
outside to check with Hilda, the receptionist she shared
with four other therapists here at the Central Park
South office. Hilda always sized up new clients in the
waiting room.

Of this one she said, "Are you sure there's anything
wrong with that guy? I think I'm in love."

Waiting at the office for a group of clients to assemble
Wednesday evening, Floria dashed off some notes on
the "vampire."

Client described incident, background. No history of mental illness, no previous experience of
therapy. Personal history so ordinary you almost
don't notice how bare it is: only child of German

immigrants, schooling normal, field work in anthropology, academic posts leading to Cayslin
College professorship. Health good, finances ade-
quate, occupation satisfactory, housing pleasant
(though presently installed in a N.Y. hotel);
never married, no kids, no family, no religion,
social life strictly job-related; leisure—says he
likes to drive. Reaction to question about drinking, but no signs of alcohol problems. Physically
very smooth-moving for his age (over fifty) and
height; catlike, alert. Some apparent stiffness in
the midsection—slight protective stoop—tighten-
ing up of middle age? Paranoic defensiveness?
Voice pleasant, faint accent (German-speaking
childhood at home). Entering therapy condition
of consideration for return to job.

What a relief: his situation looked workable with a
minimum of strain on herself. Now she could defend to
Lucille her decision to do therapy with the "vampire."

After all, Lucille was right. Floria did have problems
of her own that needed attention, primarily her anxiety
and exhaustion since her mother's death more than a
year before. The breakup of Floria's marriage had
caused misery, but not this sort of endless depression.
Intellectually the problem was clear: with both her
parents dead she was left exposed. No one stood any
longer between herself and the inevitability of her own
death. Knowing the source of her feelings didn't help:
she couldn't seem to mobilize the nerve to work on
them.

The Wednesday group went badly again. Lisa lived
once more her experiences in the European death
camps and everyone cried. Floria wanted to stop Lisa,
turn her, extinguish the droning horror of her voice in
illumination and release, but she couldn't see how to do
it. She found nothing in herself to offer except some
clever ploy out of the professional bag of tricks—dance
your anger, have a dialog with yourself of those days—

useful techniques when they flowed organically as part
of a living process in which the therapist participated.
But thinking out responses that should have been
intuitive wouldn't work. The group and its collective
pain paralyzed her. She was a dancer without a choreographer, knowing all the moves but unable to match
them to the music these people made.

Rather than act with mechanical clumsiness she held
back, did nothing, and suffered guilt. Oh God, the
smart, experienced people in the group must know how
useless she was here.

Going home on the bus she thought about calling up
one of the therapists who shared the downtown office.
He had expressed an interest in doing co-therapy with
her under student observation. The Wednesday group
might respond well to that. Suggest it to them next
time? Having a partner might take pressure off Floria
and revitalize the group, and if she felt she must
withdraw he would be available to take over. Of course
he might take over anyway and walk off with some of
her clients.

Oh boy, terrific, who's paranoid now? Wonderful
way to think about a good colleague. God, she hadn't
even known she was considering chucking the group.

Had the new client, running from his "vampirism,"
exposed her own impulse to retreat? This wouldn't be
the first time that Floria had obtained help from a client
while attempting to give help. Her old supervisor,
Rigby, said that such mutual aid was the only true
therapy—the rest was fraud. What a perfectionist, old
Rigby, and what a bunch of young idealists he'd turned
out, all eager to save the world.

Eager, but not necessarily able. Jane Fennerman had
once lived in the world, and Floria had been incompetent to save her. Jane, an absent member of tonight's
group, was back in the safety of a locked ward, hazily
gliding on whatever tranquilizers they used there.

Why still mull over Jane? she asked herself severely,
bracing against the bus's lurching halt. Any client was

entitled to drop out of therapy and commit herself. Nor was this the first time that sort of thing had happened in the course of Floria's career. Only this time she couldn't seem to shake free of the resulting depression and guilt.

But how could she have helped Jane more? How could you offer reassurance that life was not as dreadful as Jane felt it to be, that her fears were insubstantial, that each day was not a pit of pain and danger?

She was taking time during a client's canceled hour to work on notes for the new book. The writing, an analysis of the vicissitudes of salaried versus private practice, balked her at every turn. She longed for an interruption to distract her circling mind.

Hilda put through a call from Cayslin College. It was Doug Sharpe, who had sent Dr. Weyland to her.

"Now that he's in your capable hands, I can tell people plainly that he's on what we call 'compassionate leave' and make them swallow it." Doug's voice seemed thinned by the long-distance connection. "Can you give me a preliminary opinion?"

"I need time to get a feel for the situation."

He said, "Try not to take too long. At the moment I'm holding off pressure to appoint someone in his place. His enemies up here—and a sharp-tongued bastard like him acquires plenty of those—are trying to get a search committee authorized to find someone else for the directorship of the Cayslin Center for the Study of Man."

"Of People," she corrected automatically, as she always did. "What do you mean, 'bastard'? I thought you liked him, Doug. 'Do you want me to have to throw a smart, courtly, old-school gent to Finney or MaGill?' Those were your very words." Finney was a Freudian with a mouth like a pursed-up little asshole and a mind to match, and MaGill was a primal yowler in a padded gym of an office.

She heard Doug tapping at his teeth with a pen or

pencil. "Well," he said, "I have a lot of respect for him, and sometimes I could cheer him for mowing down some pompous moron up here. I can't deny, though, that he's earned a reputation for being an accomplished son-of-a-bitch and tough to work with. Too damn cold and self-sufficient, you know?"

"Mmm," she said. "I haven't seen that yet."

He said, "You will. How about yourself? How's the rest of your life?"

"Well, offhand, what would you say if I told you I was thinking of going back to art school?"

"What would I say? I'd say bullshit, that's what I'd say. You've had fifteen years of doing something you're good at, and now you want to throw all that out and start over in an area you haven't touched since Studio 101 in college? If God had meant you to be a painter, She'd have sent you to art school in the first place."

"I did think about art school at the time."

"The point is that you're good at what you do. I've been at the receiving end of your work and I know what I'm talking about. By the way, did you see that piece in the paper about Annie Barnes, from the group I was in? That's an important appointment. I always knew she'd wind up in Washington. What I'm trying to make clear to you is that your 'graduates' do too well for you to be talking about quitting. What's Morton say about that idea, by the way?"

Mort, a pathologist, was Floria's lover. She hadn't discussed this with him, and she told Doug so.

"You're not on the outs with Morton, are you?"

"Come on, Douglas, cut it out. There's nothing wrong with my sex life, believe me. It's everyplace else that's giving me trouble."

"Just sticking my nose into your business," he replied. "What are friends for?"

They turned to lighter matters, but when she hung up Floria felt glum. If her friends were moved to this sort of probing and kindly advice-giving, she must be inviting help more openly and more urgently than she'd realized.

The work on the book went no better. It was as if, afraid to expose her thoughts, she must disarm criticism by meeting all possible objections beforehand. The book was well and truly stalled—like everything else. She sat sweating over it, wondering what the devil was wrong with her that she was writing mush. She had two good books to her name already. What was this bottleneck with the third?

"But what do you think?" Kenny insisted anxiously. "Does it sound like my kind of job?"

"How do you feel about it?"

"I'm all confused, I told you."

"Try speaking for me. Give me the advice I would give you."

He glowered. "That's a real cop-out, you know? One part of me talks like you, and then I have a dialog with myself like a TV show about a split personality. It's all me that way; you just sit there while I do all the work. I want something from *you.*"

She looked for the twentieth time at the clock on the file cabinet. This time it freed her. "Kenny, the hour's over."

Kenny heaved his plump, sulky body up out of his chair. "You don't care. Oh, you pretend to, but you don't really—"

"Next time, Kenny."

He stumped out of the office. She imagined him towing in his wake the raft of decisions he was trying to inveigle her into making for him. Sighing, she went to the window and looked out over the park, filling her eyes and her mind with the full, fresh green of late spring. She felt dismal. In two years of treatment the situation with Kenny had remained a stalemate. He wouldn't go to someone else who might be able to help him, and she couldn't bring herself to kick him out, though she knew she must eventually. His puny tyranny couldn't conceal how soft and vulnerable he was . . .

Dr. Weyland had the next appointment. Floria found herself pleased to see him. She could hardly have asked for a greater contrast to Kenny: tall, lean, that august head that made her want to draw him, good clothes, nice big hands—altogether, a distinguished-looking man. Though he was informally dressed in slacks, light jacket, and tieless shirt, the impression he conveyed was one of impeccable leisure and reserve. He took not the padded chair preferred by most clients but the wooden one with the cane seat.

"Good afternoon, Dr. Landauer," he said gravely. "May I ask your judgment of my case?"

"I don't regard myself as a judge," she said. She decided to try to shift their discussion onto a first-name basis if possible. Calling this old-fashioned man by his first name so soon might seem artificial, but how could they get familiar enough to do therapy while addressing each other as "Dr. Landauer" and "Dr. Weyland" like two characters out of a vaudeville sketch?

"This is what I think, Edward," she continued. "We need to find out about this vampire incident—how it tied into your feelings about yourself, good and bad, at the time; what it did for you that led you to try to 'be' a vampire even though that was bound to complicate your life terrifically. The more we know, the closer we can come to figuring out how to insure that this vampire construct won't be necessary to you again."

"Does this mean that you accept me formally as a client?" he said.

Comes right out and says what's on his mind, she noted; no problem there. "Yes."

"Good. I too have a treatment goal in mind. I will need at some point a testimonial from you that my mental health is sound enough for me to resume work at Cayslin."

Floria shook her head. "I can't guarantee that. I can commit myself to work toward it, of course, since your improved mental health is the aim of what we do here together."

"I suppose that answers the purpose for the time being," he said. "We can discuss it again later on. Frankly, I find myself eager to continue our work today. I've been feeling very much better since I spoke with you, and I thought last night about what I might tell you today."

She had the distinct feeling of being steered by him; how important was it to him, she wondered, to feel in control? She said, "Edward, my own feeling is that we started out with a good deal of very useful verbal work, and that now is a time to try something a little different."

He said nothing. He watched her. When she asked whether he remembered his dreams he shook his head, no.

She said, "I'd like you to try to do a dream for me now, a waking dream. Can you close your eyes and daydream, and tell me about it?"

He closed his eyes. Strangely, he now struck her as less vulnerable rather than more, as if strengthened by increased vigilance.

"How do you feel now?" she said.

"Uneasy." His eyelids fluttered. "I dislike closing my eyes. What I don't see can hurt me."

"Who wants to hurt you?"

"A vampire's enemies, of course—mobs of screaming peasants with torches."

Translating into what, she wondered—young Ph.D.s pouring out of the graduate schools panting for the jobs of older men like Weyland? "Peasants, these days?"

"Whatever their daily work, there is still a majority of the stupid, the violent, and the credulous, putting their featherbrained faith in astrology, in this cult or that, in various branches of psychology."

His sneer at her was unmistakable. Considering her refusal to let him fill the hour his own way, this desire to take a swipe at her was healthy. But it required immediate and straightforward handling.

"Edward, open your eyes and tell me what you see."

He obeyed. "I see a woman in her early forties," he said, "clever-looking face, dark hair showing gray; flesh too thin for her bones, indicating either vanity or illness; wearing slacks and a rather creased batik blouse —describable, I think, by the term 'peasant style'— with a food stain on the left side."

Damn! Don't blush. "Does anything besides my blouse suggest a peasant to you?"

"Nothing concrete, but with regard to me, my vampire self, a peasant with a torch is what you could easily become."

"I hear you saying that my task is to help you get rid of your delusion, though this process may be painful and frightening for you."

Something flashed in his expression—surprise, perhaps alarm, something she wanted to get in touch with before it could sink away out of reach again. Quickly she said, "How do you experience your face at this moment?"

He frowned. "As being on the front of my head. Why?"

With a rush of anger at herself she saw that she had chosen the wrong technique for reaching that hidden feeling: she had provoked hostility instead. She said, "Your face looked to me just now like a mask for concealing what you feel rather than an instrument of expression."

He moved restlessly in the chair, his whole physical attitude tense and guarded. "I don't know what you mean."

"Will you let me touch you?" she said, rising.

His hands tightened on the arms of his chair, which protested in a sharp creak. He snapped, "I thought this was a talking cure."

Strong resistance to body work—ease up. "If you won't let me massage some of the tension out of your facial muscles, will you try to do it yourself?"

"I don't enjoy being made ridiculous," he said, standing and heading for the door, which clapped smartly to behind him.

She sagged back in her seat; she had mishandled him. Clearly her initial estimation of this as a relatively easy job had been wrong and had led her to move far too quickly with him. Certainly it was much too early to try body work. She should have developed a firmer level of trust first by letting him do more of what he did so easily and so well—talk.

The door opened. Weyland came back in and shut it quietly. He did not sit again but paced about the room, coming to rest at the window.

"Please excuse my rather childish behavior just now," he said. "Playing these games of yours brought it on."

"It's frustrating, playing games that are unfamiliar and that you can't control," she said. As he made no reply, she went on in a conciliatory tone, "I'm not trying to belittle you, Edward. I just need to get us off whatever track you were taking us down so briskly. My feeling is that you're trying hard to regain your old stability.

"But that's the goal, not the starting point. The only way to reach your goal is through the process, and you don't drive the therapy process like a train. You can only help the process happen, as though you were helping a tree grow."

"These games are part of the process?"

"Yes."

"And neither you nor I control the games?"

"That's right."

He considered. "Suppose I agree to try this process of yours; what would you want of me?"

Observing him carefully, she no longer saw the anxious scholar bravely struggling back from madness. Here was a different sort of man—armored, calculating. She didn't know just what the change signaled, but she felt her own excitement stirring, and that meant she was on the track of—something.

"I have a hunch," she said slowly, "that this vampirism extends further back into your past than you've told me and possibly right up into the present as well. I think it's still with you. My style of therapy stresses dealing with the now at least as much as the then; if the vampirism is part of the present, dealing with it on that basis is crucial."

Silence.

"Can you talk about being a vampire: being one now?"

"You won't like knowing," he said.

"Edward, try."

He said, "I hunt."

"Where? How? What sort of—of victims?"

He folded his arms and leaned his back against the window frame. "Very well, since you insist. There are a number of possibilities here in the city in summer. Those too poor to own air-conditioners sleep out on rooftops and fire escapes. But often, I've found, their blood is sour with drugs or liquor. The same is true of prostitutes. Bars are full of accessible people but also full of smoke and noise, and there too the blood is fouled. I must choose my hunting grounds carefully. Often I go to openings of galleries or evening museum shows or department stores on their late nights—places where women may be approached."

And take pleasure in it, she thought, if they're out hunting also—for acceptable male companionship. Yet he said he's never married. Explore where this is going. "Only women?"

He gave her a sardonic glance, as if she were a slightly brighter student than he had at first assumed.

"Hunting women is liable to be time-consuming and expensive. The best hunting is in the part of Central Park they call the Ramble, where homosexual men seek encounters with others of their kind. I walk there too at night."

Floria caught a faint sound of conversation and laughter from the waiting room; her next client had probably arrived, she realized, looking reluctantly at the clock. "I'm sorry, Edward, but our time seems to be—"

"Only a moment more," he said coldly. "You asked; permit me to finish my answer. In the Ramble I find someone who doesn't reek of alcohol or drugs, who seems healthy, and who is not insistent on 'hooking up' right there among the bushes. I invite such a man to my hotel. He judges me safe, at least: older, weaker than he is, unlikely to turn out to be a dangerous maniac. So he comes to my room. I feed on his blood.

"Now, I think, our time is up."

He walked out.

She sat torn between rejoicing at his admission of the delusion's persistence and dismay that his condition was so much worse than she had first thought. Her hope of having an easy time with him vanished. His initial presentation had been just that—a performance, an act. Forced to abandon it, he had dumped on her this lump of material, too much—and too strange—to take in all at once.

Her next client liked the padded chair, not the wooden one that Weyland had sat in during the first part of the hour. Floria started to move the wooden one back. The armrests came away in her hands.

She remembered him starting up in protest against her proposal of touching him. The grip of his fingers had fractured the joints, and the shafts now lay in splinters on the floor.

Floria wandered into Lucille's room at the clinic after the staff meeting. Lucille was lying on the couch with a wet cloth over her eyes.

"I thought you looked green around the gills today," Floria said. "What's wrong?"

"Big bash last night," said Lucille in sepulchral tones. "I think I feel about the way you do after a session with Chubs. You haven't gotten rid of him yet, have you?"

"No. I had him lined up to see Marty instead of me last week, but damned if he didn't show up at my door at his usual time. It's a lost cause. What I wanted to talk to you about was Dracula."

"What about him?"

"He's smarter, tougher, and sicker than I thought, and maybe I'm even less competent than I thought, too. He's already walked out on me once—I almost lost him. I never took a course in treating monsters."

Lucille groaned. "Some days they're all monsters." This from Lucille, who worked longer hours than anyone else at the clinic, to the despair of her husband. She lifted the cloth, refolded it, and placed it carefully across her forehead. "And if I had ten dollars for every client who's walked out on me . . . Tell you what: I'll trade you Madame X for him, how's that? Remember Madame X, with the jangling bracelets and the para- keet eye makeup and the phobia about dogs? Now she's phobic about things dropping on her out of the sky. Just wait—it'll turn out that one day when she was three a dog trotted by and pissed on her leg just as an over- passing pigeon shat on her head. What are we doing in this business?"

"God knows." Floria laughed. "But am I in this business these days—I mean, in the sense of practicing my so-called skills? Blocked with my group work, beating my brains out on a book that won't go, and doing something—I'm not sure it's therapy—with a vampire . . . You know, once I had this sort of natural choreographer inside myself that hardly let me put a foot wrong and always knew how to correct a mistake if I did. Now that's gone. I feel as if I'm just going through a lot of mechanical motions. Whatever I had once that made me useful as a therapist, I've lost it."

Ugh, she thought, hearing the descent of her voice into a tone of gloomy self-pity.

"Well, don't complain about Dracula," Lucille said.

"You were the one who insisted on taking him on. At least he's got you concentrating on his problem instead of just wringing your hands. As long as you've started, stay with it—illumination may come. And now I'd better change the ribbon in my typewriter and get back to reviewing Silverman's latest best-seller on self-shrinking while I'm feeling mean enough to do it justice." She got up gingerly. "Stick around in case I faint and fall into the wastebasket."

"Luce, this case is what I'd like to try to write about."

"Dracula?" Lucille pawed through a desk drawer full of paper clips, pens, rubber bands and old lipsticks.

"Dracula. A monograph . . ."

"Oh, I know that game: you scribble down everything you can and then read what you wrote to find out what's going on with the client, and with luck you end up publishing. Great! But if you are going to publish, don't piddle this away on a dinky paper. Do a book. Here's your subject, instead of those depressing statistics you've been killing yourself over. This one is really exciting—a case study to put on the shelf next to Freud's own wolf-man, have you thought of that?"

Floria liked it. "What a book that could be—fame if not fortune. Notoriety, most likely. How in the world could I convince our colleagues that it's legit? There's a lot of vampire stuff around right now—plays on Broadway and TV, books all over the place, movies. They'll say I'm just trying to ride the coattails of a fad."

"No, no, what you do is show how this guy's delusion is related to the fad. Fascinating." Lucille, having found a ribbon, prodded doubtfully at the exposed innards of her typewriter.

"Suppose I fictionalize it," Floria said, "under a pseudonym. Why not ride the popular wave and be free in what I can say?"

"Listen, you've never written a word of fiction in your life, have you?" Lucille fixed her with a bloodshot gaze. "There's no evidence that you could turn out a best-selling novel. On the other hand, by this time you have a trained memory for accurately reporting therapeutic transactions. That's a strength you'd be foolish to waste. A solid professional book would be terrific— and a feather in the cap of every woman in the field. Just make sure you get good legal advice on disguising your Dracula's identity well enough to avoid libel."

The cane-seated chair wasn't worth repairing, so she got its twin out of the bedroom to put in the office in its place. Puzzling: by his history Weyland was fifty-two, and by his appearance no muscle man. She should have asked Doug—but how, exactly? "By the way, Doug, was Weyland ever a circus strong man or a blacksmith? Does he secretly pump iron?" Ask the client himself— but not yet.

She invited some of the younger staff from the clinic over for a small party with a few of her outside friends. It was a good evening; they were not a heavy-drinking crowd, which meant the conversation stayed intelligent. The guests drifted about the long living room or stood in twos and threes at the windows looking down on West End Avenue as they talked.

Mort came, warming the room. Fresh from a session with some amateur chamber-music friends, he still glowed with the pleasure of making his cello sing. His own voice was unexpectedly light for so large a man. Sometimes Floria thought that the deep throb of the cello was his true voice.

He stood beside her talking with some others. There was no need to lean against his comfortable bulk or to have him put his arm around her waist. Their intimacy was long-standing, an effortless pleasure in each other that required neither demonstration nor concealment.

He was easily diverted from music to his next favorite topic, the strengths and skills of athletes.

"Here's a question for a paper I'm thinking of writing," Floria said. "Could a tall, lean man be exceptionally strong?"

Mort rambled on in his thoughtful way. His answer seemed to be no.

"But what about chimpanzees?" put in a young clinician. "I went with a guy once who was an animal handler for TV, and he said a three-month-old chimp could demolish a strong man."

"It's all physical conditioning," somebody else said. "Modern people are soft."

Mort nodded. "Human beings in general are weakly made compared to other animals. It's a question of muscle insertions—the angles of how the muscles are attached to the bones. Some angles give better leverage than others. That's how a leopard can bring down a much bigger animal than itself. It has a muscular structure that gives it tremendous strength for its streamlined build."

Floria said, "If a man were built with muscle insertions like a leopard's, he'd look pretty odd, wouldn't he?"

"Not to an untrained eye," Mort said, sounding bemused by an inner vision. "And my God, what an athlete he'd make—can you imagine a guy in the decathlon who's as strong as a leopard?"

When everyone else had gone Mort stayed, as he often did. Jokes about insertions, muscular and otherwise, soon led to sounds more expressive and more animal, but afterward Floria didn't feel like resting snuggled together with Mort and talking. When her body stopped racing, her mind turned to her new client. She didn't want to discuss him with Mort, so she ushered Mort out as gently as she could and sat down by herself at the kitchen table with a glass of orange juice.

How to approach the reintegration of Weyland the eminent, gray-haired academic with the rebellious vampire-self that had smashed his life out of shape?

She thought of the broken chair, of Weyland's big hands crushing the wood. Old wood and dried-out glue, of course, or he never could have done that. He was a man, after all, not a leopard.

The day before the third session Weyland phoned and left a message with Hilda: he would not be coming to the office tomorrow for his appointment, but if Dr. Landauer were agreeable she would find him at their usual hour at the Central Park Zoo.

Am I going to let him move me around from here to there? she thought. I shouldn't—but why fight it? Give him some leeway, see what opens up in a different setting. Besides, it was a beautiful day, probably the last of the sweet May weather before the summer stickiness descended. She gladly cut Kenny short so that she would have time to walk over to the zoo.

There was a fair crowd there for a weekday. Well-groomed young matrons pushed clean, floppy babies in strollers. Weyland she spotted at once.

He was leaning against the railing that enclosed the seals' shelter and their murky green pool. His jacket, slung over his shoulder, draped elegantly down his long back. Floria thought him rather dashing and faintly foreign-looking. Women who passed him, she noticed, tended to glance back.

He looked at everyone. She had the impression that he knew quite well that she was walking up behind him.

"Outdoors makes a nice change from the office, Edward," she said, coming to the rail beside him. "But there must be more to this than a longing for fresh air." A fat seal lay in sculptural grace on the concrete, eyes blissfully shut, fur drying in the sun to a translucent water-color umber.

Weyland straightened from the rail. They walked. He did not look at the animals; his eyes moved continually over the crowd. He said, "Someone has been watching for me at your office building."

"Who?"

"There are several possibilities. Pah, what a stench—though humans caged in similar circumstances smell as bad.'' He sidestepped a couple of shrieking children who were fighting over a balloon and headed out of the zoo under the musical clock.

They walked the uphill path northward through the park. By extending her own stride a little Floria found that she could comfortably keep pace with him.

"Is it peasants with torches?" she said. "Following you?"

He said, "What a childish idea."

All right, try another tack, then: "You were telling me last time about hunting in the Ramble. Can we return to that?"

"If you wish." He sounded bored—a defense? Surely —she was certain this must be the right reading—surely his problem was a transmutation into "vampire" fantasy of an unacceptable aspect of himself. For men of his generation the confrontation with homosexual drives could be devastating.

"When you pick up someone in the Ramble, is it a paid encounter?"

"Usually."

"How do you feel about having to pay?" She expected resentment.

He gave a faint shrug. "Why not? Others work to earn their bread. I work, too, very hard, in fact. Why shouldn't I use my earnings to pay for my sustenance?"

Why did he never play the expected card? Baffled, she paused to drink from a fountain. They walked on.

"Once you've got your quarry, how do you . . ." She fumbled for a word.

"Attack?" he supplied, unperturbed. "There's a place on the neck, here, where pressure can interrupt the blood flow to the brain and cause unconsciousness. Getting close enough to apply that pressure isn't difficult."

"You do this before or after any sexual activity?"

"Before, if possible," he said aridly, "and instead of." He turned aside to stalk up a slope to a granite outcrop that overlooked the path they had been follow-

ing. There he settled on his haunches, looking back the
way they had come. Floria, glad she'd worn slacks
today, sat down near him.

He didn't seem devastated—anything but. Press him,
don't let him get by on cool. "Do you often prey on
men in preference to women?"

"Certainly. I take what is easiest. Men have always
been more accessible because women have been walled
away like prizes or so physically impoverished by
repeated childbearing as to be unhealthy prey for me.
All this has begun to change recently, but gay men are
still the simplest quarry." While she was recovering
from her surprise at his unforeseen and weirdly skewed
awareness of female history, he added suavely, "How
carefully you control your expression, Dr. Landauer—
no trace of disapproval."

She did disapprove, she realized. She would prefer
him not to be committed sexually to men. Oh, hell.

He went on, "Yet no doubt you see me as one who
victimizes the already victimized. This is the world's
way. A wolf brings down the stragglers at the edges of
the herd. Gay men are denied the full protection of the
human herd and are at the same time emboldened to
make themselves known and available.

"On the other hand, unlike the wolf I can feed
without killing, and these particular victims pose no
threat to me that would cause me to kill. Outcasts
themselves, even if they comprehend my true purpose
among them they cannot effectively accuse me."

God, how neatly, completely, and ruthlessly he
distanced the homosexual community from himself!
"And how do you feel, Edward, about their purposes—
their sexual expectations of you?"

"The same way I feel about the sexual expectations
of women whom I choose to pursue: they don't interest
me. Besides, once my hunger is active, sexual arousal is
impossible. My physical unresponsiveness seems to
surprise no one. Apparently impotence is expected in a
gray-haired man, which suits my intention."

Some kids carrying radios swung past below, trailing a jumble of amplified thump, wail, and jabber. Floria gazed after them unseeingly, thinking, astonished again, that she had never heard a man speak of his own impotence with such cool indifference. She had induced him to talk about his problem all right. He was speaking as freely as he had in the first session, only this time it was no act. He was drowning her in more than she had ever expected or for that matter wanted to know about vampirism. What the hell: she was listening, she thought she understood—what was it all good for? Time for some cold reality, she thought; see how far he can carry all this incredible detail. Give the whole structure a shove.

She said, "You realize, I'm sure, that people of either sex who make themselves so easily available are also liable to be carriers of disease. When was your last medical checkup?"

"My dear Dr. Landauer, my first medical checkup will be my last. Fortunately, I have no great need of one. Most serious illnesses—hepatitis, for example—reveal themselves to me by a quality in the odor of the victim's skin. Warned, I abstain. When I do fall ill, as occasionally happens, I withdraw to some place where I can heal undisturbed. A doctor's attentions would be more dangerous to me than any disease."

Eyes on the path below, he continued calmly, "You can see by looking at me that there are no obvious clues to my unique nature. But believe me, an examination of any depth by even a half-sleeping medical practitioner would reveal some alarming deviations from the norm. I take pains to stay healthy, and I seem to be gifted with an exceptionally hardy constitution."

Fantasies of being unique and physically superior; take him to the other pole. "I'd like you to try something now. Will you put yourself into the mind of a man you contact in the Ramble and describe your encounter with him from his point of view?"

He turned toward her and for some moments regard-

ed her without expression. Then he resumed his surveillance of the path. "I will not. Though I do have
enough empathy with my quarry to enable me to hunt
efficiently, I must draw the line at erasing the necessary
distance that keeps prey and predator distinct.

"And now I think our ways part for today." He stood
up, descended the hillside, and walked beneath some
low-canopied trees, his tall back stooped, toward the
Seventy-second Street entrance of the park.

Floria arose more slowly, aware suddenly of her
shallow breathing and the sweat on her face. Back to
reality or what remained of it. She looked at her watch.
She was late for her next client.

Floria couldn't sleep that night. Barefoot in her bathrobe she paced the living room by lamplight. They had
sat together on that hill as isolated as in her office—
more so, because there was no Hilda and no phone. He
was, she knew, very strong, and he had sat close
enough to her to reach out for that paralyzing touch to
the neck—

Just suppose for a minute that Weyland had been
brazenly telling the truth all along, counting on her to
treat it as a delusion because on the face of it the truth
was inconceivable.

Jesus, she thought, if I'm thinking that way about
him, this therapy is more out of control than I thought.
What kind of therapist becomes an accomplice to the
client's fantasy? A crazy therapist, that's what kind.

Frustrated and confused by the turmoil in her mind,
she wandered into the workroom. By morning the floor
was covered with sheets of newsprint, each broadly
marked by her felt-tipped pen. Floria sat in the midst of
them, gritty-eyed and hungry.

She often approached problems this way, harking
back to art training: turn off the thinking, put hand to
paper and see what the deeper, less verbally sophisticated parts of the mind have to offer. Now that her

dreams had deserted her, this was her only access to those levels.

The newsprint sheets were covered with rough representations of Weyland's face and form. Across several of them were scrawled words: "*Dear Doug, your vampire is fine, it's your ex-therapist who's off the rails. Warning: Therapy can be dangerous to your health. Especially if you are the therapist. Beautiful vampire, awaken to me. Am I really ready to take on a legendary monster? Give up—refer this one out. Do your job— work is a good doctor.*"

That last one sounded pretty good, except that doing her job was precisely what she was feeling so shaky about these days.

Here was another message: "*How come this attraction to someone so scary?*" Oh ho, she thought, is that a real feeling or an aimless reaction out of the body's early-morning hormone peak? You don't want to confuse honest libido with mere biological clockwork.

Deborah called. Babies cried in the background over the Scotch Symphony. Nick, Deb's husband, was a musicologist with fervent opinions on music and nothing else.

"We'll be in town a little later in the summer," Deborah said, "just for a few days at the end of July. Nicky has this seminar-convention thing. Of course, it won't be easy with the babies . . . I wondered if you might sort of coordinate your vacation so you could spend a little time with them?"

Baby-sit, that meant. Damn. Cute as they were and all that, damn! Floria gritted her teeth. Visits from Deb were difficult. Floria had been so proud of her bright, hard-driving daughter, and then suddenly Deborah had dropped her studies and rushed to embrace all the dangers that Floria had warned her against: a romantic, too-young marriage, instant breeding, no preparation for self-support, the works. Well, to each her own, but it was so wearing to have Deb around playing the emptyheaded hausfrau.

"Let me think, Deb. I'd love to see all of you, but I've been considering spending a couple of weeks in Maine with your Aunt Nonnie." God knows I need a real vacation, she thought, though the peace and quiet up there is hard for a city kid like me to take for long. Still, Nonnie, Floria's younger sister, was good company. "Maybe you could bring the kids up there for a couple of days. There's room in that great barn of a place, and of course Nonnie'd be happy to have you."

"Oh, no, Mom, it's so dead up there, it drives Nick crazy—don't tell Nonnie I said that. Maybe Nonnie could come down to the city instead. You could cancel a date or two and we could all go to Coney Island together, things like that."

Kid things, which would drive Nonnie crazy and Floria too before long. "I doubt she could manage," Floria said, "but I'll ask. Look, hon, if I do go up there, you and Nick and the kids could stay here at the apartment and save some money."

"We have to be at the hotel for the seminar," Deb said shortly. No doubt she was feeling just as impatient as Floria was by now. "And the kids haven't seen you for a long time—it would be really nice if you could stay in the city just for a few days."

"We'll try to work something out." Always working something out. Concord never comes naturally—first we have to butt heads and get pissed off. Each time you call I hope it'll be different, Floria thought.

Somebody shrieked for "oly," jelly that would be, in the background—Floria felt a sudden rush of warmth for them, her grandkids for God's sake. Having been a young mother herself, she was still young enough to really enjoy them (and to fight with Deb about how to bring them up).

Deb was starting an awkward goodbye. Floria replied, put the phone down, and sat with her head back against the flowered kitchen wallpaper, thinking, Why do I feel so rotten now? Deb and I aren't close, no comfort, seldom friends, though we were once. Have I said everything wrong, made her think I don't want to see her and don't care about her family? What does she want from me that I can't seem to give her? Approval? Maybe she thinks I still hold her marriage against her. Well, I do, sort of. What right have I to be critical, me with my divorce? What terrible things would she say to me, would I say to her, that we take such care not to say anything important at all?

"I think today we might go into sex," she said.

Weyland responded dryly, "Might we indeed. Does it titillate you to wring confessions of solitary vice from men of mature years?"

Oh no you don't, she thought. You can't sidestep so easily. "Under what circumstances do you find yourself sexually aroused?"

"Most usually upon waking from sleep," he said indifferently.

"What do you do about it?"

"The same as others do. I am not a cripple, I have hands."

"Do you have fantasies at these times?"

"No. Women, and men for that matter, appeal to me very little, either in fantasy or reality."

"Ah—what about female vampires?" she said, trying not to sound arch.

"I know of none."

Of course: the neatest out in the book. "They're not needed for reproduction, I suppose, because people who die of vampire bites becomes vampires themselves."

He said testily, "Nonsense. I am not a communicable disease."

So he had left an enormous hole in his construct. She headed straight for it: "Then how does your kind reproduce?"

"I have no kind, so far as I am aware," he said, "and I do not reproduce. Why should I, when I may live for centuries still, perhaps indefinitely? My sexual equipment is clearly only detailed biological mimicry, a form of protective coloration." How beautiful, how simple a solution, she thought, full of admiration in spite of herself. "Do I occasionally detect a note of prurient interest in your questions, Dr. Landauer? Something akin to stopping at the cage to watch the tigers mate at the zoo?"

"Probably," she said, feeling her face heat. He had a great backhand return shot there. "How do you feel about that?"

He shrugged.

"To return to the point," she said. "Do I hear you saying that you have no urge whatever to engage in sexual intercourse with anyone?"

"Would you mate with your livestock?"

His matter-of-fact arrogance took her breath away. She said weakly, "Men have reportedly done so."

"Driven men. I am not driven in that way. My sex urge is of low frequency and is easily dealt with unaided—although I occasionally engage in copulation out of the necessity to keep up appearances. I am capable, but not—like humans—obsessed."

Was he sinking into lunacy before her eyes? "I think I hear you saying," she said, striving to keep her voice neutral, "that you're not just a man with a unique way of life. I think I hear you saying that you're not human at all."

"I thought that this was already clear."

"And that there are no others like you."

"None that I know of."

"Then—you see yourself as what? Some sort of mutation?"

"Perhaps. Or perhaps your kind are the mutation."

She saw disdain in the curl of his lip. "How does your mouth feel now?"

"The corners are drawn down. The feeling is contempt."

"Can you let the contempt speak?"

He got up and went to stand at the window, positioning himself slightly to one side as if to stay hidden from the street below.

"Edward," she said.

He looked back at her. "Humans are my food. I draw the life out of their veins. Sometimes I kill them. I am greater than they are. Yet I must spend my time thinking about their habits and their drives, scheming to avoid the dangers they pose—I hate them."

She felt the hatred like a dry heat radiating from him. God, he really lived all this! She had tapped into a furnace of feeling. And now? The sensation of triumph wavered, and she grabbed at a next move: hit him with reality now, while he's burning.

"What about blood banks?" she said. "Your food is commercially available, so why all the complication and danger of the hunt?"

"You mean I might turn my efforts to piling up a fortune and buying blood by the case? That would certainly make for an easier, less risky life in the short run. I could fit quite comfortably into modern society if I became just another consumer.

"However, I prefer to keep the mechanics of my survival firmly in my own hands. After all, I can't afford to lose my hunting skills. In two hundred years there may be no blood banks, but I will still need my food."

Jesus, you set him a hurdle and he just flies over it. Are there no weaknesses in all this, has he no blind spots? Look at his tension—go back to that. Floria said, "What do you feel now in your body?"

"Tightness." He pressed his spread fingers to his abdomen.

"What are you doing with your hands?"

"I put my hands to my stomach."

"Can you speak for your stomach?"

" 'Feed me or die,' " he snarled.

Elated again, she closed in: "And for yourself, in answer?"

" 'Will you never be satisfied?' " He glared at her. "You shouldn't seduce me into quarreling with the terms of my own existence!"

"Your stomach is your existence," she paraphrased.

"The gut determines," he said harshly. "That first, everything else after."

"Say, 'I resent . . .' "

He held to a tense silence.

" 'I resent the power of my gut over my life,' " she said for him.

He stood with an abrupt motion and glanced at his watch, an elegant flash of slim silver on his wrist. "Enough," he said.

That night at home she began a set of notes that would never enter his file at the office, notes toward the proposed book.

> Couldn't do it, couldn't get properly into the sex thing with him. Everything shoots off in all directions. His vampire concept so thoroughly worked out, find myself half believing sometimes—my own childish fantasy-response to his powerful death-avoidance, contact-avoidance fantasy. Lose professional distance every time—is that what scares me about him? Don't really want to shatter his delusion (my life a mess, what right to tear down others' patterns?)—so see it as real? Wonder how much of "vampirism" he acts out, how far, how often. Something attractive in his purely selfish, predatory stance—the lure of the great outlaw.

> Told me today quite coolly about a man he killed recently—inadvertently—by drinking too much from him. *Is* it fantasy? Of course—the victim, he thinks, was college student. Breathes there a professor who hasn't dreamed of murdering some representative youth, retaliation for years of

classroom frustration? Speaks of teaching with
acerbic humor—amuses him to work at cultivating the minds of those he regards strictly as
bodies, containers of his sustenance. He shows
the alienness of full-blown psychopathology, poor
bastard, plus clean-cut logic. Suggested he find
another job (assuming his delusion at least in part
related to pressures at Cayslin); his fantasy-
persona, the vampire, more realistic than I about
job-switching:

"For a man of my apparent age it's not so easy
to make such a change in these tight times. I
might have to take a position lower on the ladder
of 'success' as you people assess it." Status is
important to him? "Certainly. An eccentric professor is one thing; an eccentric pipe-fitter, another. And I like good cars, which are expensive to
own and run." Then, thoughtful addition, "Although there are advantages to a simpler, less
visible life." He refuses to discuss other "jobs"
from former "lives." We are deep into the
fantasy—where the hell going? Damn right I
don't control the "games"—preplanned therapeutic strategies get whirled away as soon as we
begin. Nerve-wracking.

Tried again to have him take the part of his
enemy-victim, peasant with torch. Asked if he felt
himself rejecting that point of view? Frosty reply:
"Naturally. The peasant's point of view is in no
way my own. I've been reading in your field, Dr.
Landauer. You work from the Gestalt orientation
—" Originally yes, I corrected; eclectic now. "But
you do proceed from the theory that I am projecting some aspect of my own feelings outward onto
others, whom I then treat as my victims. Your
purpose then must be to maneuver me into accepting as my own the projected 'victim' aspect of
myself. This integration is supposed to effect the

freeing of energy previously locked into maintaining the projection. All this is an interesting insight into the nature of ordinary human confusion, but I am not an ordinary human, and I am not confused. I cannot afford confusion.'' Felt sympathy for him—telling me he's afraid of having own internal confusions exposed in therapy, too threatening. Keep chipping away at delusion, though with what prospect? It's so complex, deepseated.

Returned to his phrase "my apparent age." He asserts he has lived many human lifetimes, all details forgotten, however, during periods of suspended animation between lives. Perhaps sensing my skepticism at such handy amnesia, grew cool and distant, claimed to know little about the hibernation process itself: "The essence of this state is that I sleep through it—hardly an ideal condition for making scientific observations."

Edward thinks his body synthesizes vitamins, minerals (as all our bodies synthesize vitamin D), even proteins. Describes unique design he deduces in himself: special intestinal microfauna plus superefficient body chemistry extracts enough energy to live on from blood. Damn good mileage per calorie, too. (Recall observable tension, first interview, at question about drinking—my note on possible alcohol problem!)

Speak for blood: " 'Lacking me, you have no life. I flow to the heart's soft drumbeat through lightless prisons of flesh. I am rich, I am nourishing, I am difficult to attain.' " Stunned to find him positively lyrical on subject of his "food." Drew attention to whispering voice of blood. " 'Yes. I am secret, hidden beneath the surface, patient, silent, steady. I work unnoticed, an unseen thread of vitality running from age to age—beautiful, efficient, self-renewing, self-cleansing, warm, filling—' " Could *see* him getting worked up. Finally he stood: "My appetite is pressing. I must leave you." And he did.

Sat and trembled for five minutes after.

New development (or new perception?): he sometimes comes across very unsophisticated about own feelings—lets me pursue subjects of extreme intensity and delicacy to him.

Asked him to daydream—a hunt. (Hands—mine —shaking now as I write. God. What a session.) He told of picking up a woman at poetry reading, 92nd Street Y—has N.Y.C. all worked out, circulates to avoid too much notice any one spot. Spoke easily, eyes shut without observable strain: chooses from audience a redhead in glasses, dress with drooping neckline (ease of access), no perfume (strong smells bother him). Approaches during intermission, encouraged to see her fanning away smoke of others' cigarettes—meaning she doesn't smoke, health sign. Agreed in not enjoying the reading, they adjourn together to coffee shop.

"She asks whether I'm a teacher," he says, eyes shut, mouth amused. "My clothes, glasses, manner all suggest this, and I emphasize the impression—it reassures. She's a copy editor for a publishing house. We talk about books. The waiter brings her a gummy-looking pastry. As a non-eater, I pay little attention to the quality of restaurants, so I must apologize to her. She waves this away—is engrossed, or pretending to be engrossed, in talk." A longish dialog between interested woman and Edward doing shy-lonesome-scholar act—dead wife, competitive young colleagues who don't understand him, quarrels in professional journals with big shots in his field—a version of what he first told me. She's attracted (of course—lanky, rough-cut ele-

gance plus hints of vulnerability all very allur-
ing, as intended). He offers to take her home.

Tension in his body at this point in narrative—
spine clear of chair back, hands braced on thighs.
"She settles beside me in the back of the cab,
talking about problems of her own career—
illegible manuscripts of Biblical length, mulish
editors, suicidal authors—and I make comforting
comments, I lean nearer and put my arm along
the back of the seat, behind her shoulders. Traffic
is heavy, we move slowly. There is time to make
my meal here in the taxi and avoid a tedious
extension of the situation into her apartment—if I
move soon."

How do you feel?

"Eager," he says, voice husky. "My hunger is
so roused I can scarcely restrain myself. A powerful hunger, not like yours—mine compels. I embrace her shoulders lightly, make kindly-uncle
remarks, treading that fine line between the game
of seduction she perceives and the game of friendly interest I pretend to affect. My real purpose
underlies all: what I say, how I look, every
gesture is part of the stalk. There is an added
excitement, and fear, because I'm doing my hunting in the presence of a third person—behind the
cabbie's head."

Could scarcely breathe. Studied him—intent
face, masklike with closed eyes, nostrils slightly
flared; legs tensed, hands clenched on knees.
Whispering: "I press the place on her neck. She
starts, sighs faintly, silently drops against me. In
the stale stench of the cab's interior, with the
ticking of the meter in my ears and the mutter of
the radio—I take hold here, at the tenderest part
of her throat. Sound subsides into the background
—I feel the sweet blood beating under her skin,
I taste salt at the moment before I—strike.
My saliva thins her blood so that it flows out, I

draw the blood into my mouth swiftly, swiftly, before she can wake, before we can arrive . . ."

Trailed off, sat back loosely in chair—saw him swallow. "Ah. I feed." Heard him sigh. Managed to ask about physical sensation. His low murmur, "Warm. Heavy, here—" touches his belly—"in a pleasant way. The good taste of blood, tart and rich, in my mouth . . ."

And then? A flicker of movement beneath his closed eyelids: "In time I am aware that the cabbie has glanced back once and has taken our—embrace for just that. I can feel the cab slowing, hear him move to turn off the meter. I withdraw, I quickly wipe my mouth on my hand-kerchief. I take her by the shoulders and shake her gently; does she often have these attacks, I inquire, the soul of concern. She comes around, bewildered, weak, thinks she has fainted. I give the driver extra money and ask him to wait. He looks intrigued—'What was that all about,' I can see the question in his face—but as a true New Yorker he won't expose his own ignorance by asking.

"I escort the woman to her front door, support-ing her as she staggers. Any suspicion of me that she may entertain, however formless and hazy, is allayed by my stern charging of the doorman to see that she reaches her apartment safely. She grows embarrassed, thinks perhaps that if not put off by her 'illness' I would spend the night with her, which moves her to press upon me, unasked, her telephone number. I bid her a solicitous good night and take the cab back to my hotel, where I sleep."

No sex? No sex.

How did he feel about the victim as a person? "She was food."

This was his "hunting" of last night, he admits afterward, not a made-up dream. No boasting in it, just telling. Telling me! Think: I can go talk to Lucille, Mort, Doug, others about most of what matters to me. Edward has only me to talk to and that for a fee—what isolation! No wonder the stone, monumental face—only those long, strong lips (his point of contact, verbal and physical-in-fantasy, with world and with "food") are truly expressive. An exciting narration; uncomfortable to find I felt not only empathy but enjoyment. Suppose he picked up and victimized—even in fantasy—Deb or Hilda, how would I feel then?

Later: truth—I also found this recital sexually stirring. Keep visualizing how he looked finishing this "dream"—he sat very still, head up, look of thoughtful pleasure on his face. Like handsome intellectual listening to music.

Kenny showed up unexpectedly at Floria's office on Monday, bursting with malevolent energy. She happened to be free, so she took him—something was definitely up. He sat on the edge of his chair.

"I know why you're trying to unload me," he accused. "It's that new one, the tall guy with the snooty look—what is he, an old actor or something? Anybody could see he's got you itching for him."

"Kenny, when was it that I first spoke to you about terminating our work together?" she said patiently.

"Don't change the subject. Let me tell you, in case you don't know it: that guy isn't really interested, Doctor, because he's a fruit. A faggot. You want to know how I know?"

Oh Lord, she thought wearily, he's regressed to age ten. She could see that she was going to hear the rest whether she wanted to or not. What in God's name was the world like for Kenny, if he clung so fanatically to her despite her failure to help him?

"Listen, I knew right away there was something flaky about him, so I followed him from here to that hotel where he lives. I followed him the other afternoon too.

He walked around like he does a lot, and then he went into one of those ritzy movie houses on Third that open early and show risqué foreign movies—you know, Japs cutting each other's things off and glop like that. This one was French, though.

"Well, there was a guy came in, a Madison Avenue type carrying his attaché case, taking a work break or something. Your man moved over and sat down behind him and reached out and sort of stroked the guy's neck, and the guy leaned back, and your man leaned forward and started nuzzling at him, you know—kissing him.

"I saw it. They had their heads together and they stayed like that a while. It was disgusting: complete strangers, without even 'hello.' The Madison Avenue guy just sat there with his head back looking zonked, you know, just swept away, and what he was doing with his hands under his raincoat in his lap I couldn't see, but I bet you can guess.

"And then your fruity friend got up and walked out. I did, too, and I hung around a little outside. After a while the Madison Avenue guy came out looking all sleepy and loose, like after you-know-what, and he wandered off on his own someplace.

"What do you think now?" he ended, on a high, triumphant note.

Her impulse was to slap his face the way she would have slapped Deb-as-a-child for tattling. But this was a client, not a kid. God give me strength, she thought.

"Kenny, you're fired."

"You can't!" he squealed. "You can't! What will I—who can I—"

She stood up, feeling weak but hardening her voice. "I'm sorry. I absolutely cannot have a client who makes it his business to spy on other clients. You already have a list of replacement therapists from me."

He gaped at her in slack-jawed dismay, his eyes swimmy with tears.

"I'm sorry, Kenny. Call this a dose of reality therapy and try to learn from it. There are some things you simply will not be allowed to do." She felt better: it was done at last.

"I hate you!" He surged out of his chair, knocking it back against the wall. Threateningly he glared at the fish tank, but, contenting himself with a couple of kicks at the nearest table leg, he stamped out.

Floria buzzed Hilda: "No more appointments for Kenny, Hilda. You can close his file."

"Whoopee," Hilda said.

Poor, horrid Kenny. Impossible to tell what would happen to him, better not to speculate or she might relent, call him back. She had encouraged him, really, by listening instead of shutting him up and throwing him out before any damage was done.

Was it damaging, to know the truth? In her mind's eye she saw a cream-faced young man out of a Black Thumb Vodka ad wander from a movie theater into daylight, yawning and rubbing absently at an irritation on his neck . . .

She didn't even look at the telephone on the table or think about whom to call, now that she believed. No; she was going to keep quiet about Dr. Edward Lewis Weyland, her vampire.

Hardly alive at staff meeting, clinic, yesterday—people asking what's the matter, fobbed them off. Settled down today. Had to, to face him.

Asked him what he felt were his strengths. He said speed, cunning, ruthlessness. Animal strengths, I said. What about imagination, or is that strictly human? He defended at once: not human only. Lion, waiting at water hole where no zebra yet drinks, thinks "Zebra—eat," therefore performs feat of imagining event yet-to-come. Self experienced as animal? Yes—reminded me that humans are also animals. Pushed for his early memories; he objected: "Gestalt is here-and-now, not history-taking." I insist, citing anomalous nature of his situation, my own refusal to be bound by any one theoretical framework. He defends tensely: "Suppose I became lost there in memory, distracted from dangers of the present, left unguarded from those dangers."

Speak for memory. He resists, but at length attempts it: " 'I am heavy with the multitudes of the past.' " Fingertips to forehead, propping up all that weight of lives. " 'So heavy, filling worlds of time laid down eon by eon, I accumulate, I persist, I demand recognition. I am as real as the life around you—more real, weightier, richer.' " His voice sinking, shoulders bowed, head in hands—I begin to feel pressure at the back of my own skull. " 'Let me in.' " Only a rough whisper now. " 'I offer beauty as well as terror. Let me in.' " Whispering also, I suggest he reply to his memory.

"Memory, you want to crush me," he groans. "You would overwhelm me with the cries of animals, the odor and jostle of bodies, old betrayals, dead joys, filth and anger from other times—I must concentrate on the danger now. Let me be." All I can take of this crazy conflict, I gabble us off onto something else. He looks up—relief?—follows my lead—where? Rest of session a blank.

No wonder sometimes no empathy at all—a species boundary! He has to be utterly self-centered just to keep balance—self-centeredness of an animal. Thought just now of our beginning, me trying to push him to produce material, trying to control him, manipulate—no way, no way; so here we are, someplace else—I feel dazed, in shock, but stick with it—it's real.

Therapy with a dinosaur, a Martian.

"You call me 'Weyland' now, not 'Edward.' " I said first name couldn't mean much to one with no memory of being called by that name as a child, silly to pretend it signifies intimacy where it

can't. I think he knows now that I believe him.
Without prompting, told me truth of disappearance from Cayslin. No romance; he tried to drink
from a woman who worked there, she shot him,
stomach and chest. Luckily for him, small-caliber
pistol, and he was wearing a lined coat over
three-piece suit. Even so, badly hurt. (Midsection
stiffness I noted when he first came—he was still
in some pain at that time.) He didn't "vanish"—
fled, hid, was found by questionable types who
caught on to what he was, sold him "like a
chattel" to someone here in the city. He was
imprisoned, fed, put on exhibition—very
privately—for gain. Got away. "Do you believe
any of this?" Never asked anything like that
before, seems of concern to him now. I said my
belief or lack of same was immaterial; remarked
on hearing a lot of bitterness.

He steepled his fingers, looked brooding at me
over tips: "I nearly died there. No doubt my
purchaser and his diabolist friend still search for
me. Mind you, I had some reason at first to be
glad of the attentions of the people who kept me
prisoner. I was in no condition to fend for myself.
They brought me food and kept me hidden and
sheltered, whatever their motives. There are always advantages . . ."

Silence today started a short session. Hunting
poor last night, Weyland still hungry. Much restless movement, watching goldfish darting in tank,
scanning bookshelves. Asked him to be books.
" 'I am old and full of knowledge, well made to
last long. You see only the title, the substance is
hidden. I am a book that stays closed.' " Mali-
cious twist of the mouth, not quite a smile: "This
is a good game." Is he feeling threatened, too—
already "opened" too much to me? Too strung
out with him to dig when he's skimming surfaces

that should be probed. Don't know how to *do* therapy with Weyland—just have to let things happen, hope it's good. But what's "good"? Aristotle? Rousseau? Ask Weyland what's good, he'll say "Blood."

Everything in a spin—these notes too confused, too fragmentary—worthless for a book, just a mess, like me, my life. Tried to call Deb last night, cancel visit. Nobody home, thank God. Can't tell her to stay away—but damn it—do not need complications now!

Floria went down to Broadway with Lucille to get more juice, cheese and crackers for the clinic fridge. This week it was their turn to do the provisions, a chore that rotated among the staff. Their talk about grant proposals for the support of the clinic trailed off.

"Let's sit a minute," Floria said. They crossed to a traffic island in the middle of the avenue. It was a sunny afternoon, close enough to lunchtime so that the brigade of old people who normally occupied the benches had thinned out. Floria sat down and kicked a crumpled beer can and some greasy fast-food wrappings back under the bench.

"You look like hell but wide awake at least," Lucille commented.

"Things are still rough," Floria said. "I keep hoping to get my life under control so I'll have some energy left for Deb and Nick and the kids when they arrive, but I can't seem to do it. Group was awful last night—a member accused me afterward of having abandoned them all. I think I have, too. The professional messes and the personal are all related somehow, they run into each other. I should be keeping them apart so I can deal with them separately, but I can't. I can't concentrate, my mind is all over the place. Except with Dracula, who keeps me riveted with astonishment when he's in the office and bemused the rest of the time."

A bus roared by, shaking the pavement and the benches. Lucille waited until the noise faded. "Relax about the group. The others would have defended you if you'd been attacked during the session. They all understand, even if you don't seem to: it's the summer doldrums, people don't want to work, they expect you to do it all for them. But don't push so hard. You're not a shaman who can magic your clients back into health."

Floria tore two cans of juice out of a six-pack and handed one to her. On a street corner opposite, a violent argument broke out in typewriter-fast Spanish between two women. Floria sipped tinny juice and watched. She'd seen a guy last winter straddle another on that same corner and try to smash his brains out on the icy sidewalk. The old question again: What's crazy, what's health?

"It's a good thing you dumped Chubs, anyhow," Lucille said. "I don't know what finally brought that on, but it's definitely a move in the right direction. What about Count Dracula? You don't talk about him much anymore. I thought I diagnosed a yen for his venerable body."

Floria shifted uncomfortably on the bench and didn't answer. If only she could deflect Lucille's sharp-eyed curiosity.

"Oh," Lucille said. "I see. You really are hot—or at least warm. Has he noticed?"

"I don't think so. He's not on the lookout for that kind of response from me. He says sex with other people doesn't interest him, and I think he's telling the truth."

"Weird," Lucille said. "What about *Vampire on My Couch*? Shaping up all right?"

"It's shaky, like everything else. I'm worried that I don't know how things are going to come out. I mean, Freud's wolf-man case was a success, as therapy goes. Will my vampire case turn out successfully?"

She glanced at Lucille's puzzled face, made up her mind, and plunged ahead. "Luce, think of it this way:

suppose, just suppose, that my Dracula is for real, an honest-to-God vampire—"

"Oh *shit!*" Lucille erupted in anguished exasperation. "Damn it, Floria, enough is enough—will you stop futzing around and get some help? Coming to pieces yourself and trying to treat this poor nut with a vampire fixation—how can you do him any good? No wonder you're worried about his therapy!"

"Please, just listen, help me think this out. My purpose can't be to cure him of what he is. Suppose vampirism isn't a defense he has to learn to drop? Suppose it's the core of his identity? Then what do I do?"

Lucille rose abruptly and marched away from her through a gap between the rolling waves of cabs and trucks. Floria caught up with her on the next block.

"Listen, will you? Luce, you see the problem? I don't need to help him see who and what he is, he knows that perfectly well, and he's not crazy, far from it—"

"Maybe not," Lucille said grimly, "but you are. Don't dump this junk on me outside of office hours, Floria. I don't spend my time listening to nut-talk unless I'm getting paid."

"Just tell me if this makes psychological sense to you: he's healthier than most of us because he's always true to his identity, even when he's engaged in deceiving others. A fairly narrow, rigorous set of requirements necessary to his survival—that *is* his identity, and it commands him completely. Anything extraneous could destroy him. To go on living, he has to act solely out of his own undistorted necessity, and if that isn't authenticity, what is? So he's healthy, isn't he?" She paused, feeling a sudden lightness in herself. "And that's the best sense I've been able to make of this whole business so far."

They were in the middle of the block. Lucille, who could not on her short legs outwalk Floria, turned on her suddenly. "What the hell do you think you're doing, calling yourself a therapist? For God's sake,

Floria, don't try to rope me into this kind of professional irresponsibility. You're just dipping into your client's
fantasies instead of helping him to handle them. That's
not therapy, it's collusion. Have some sense! Admit
you're over your head in troubles of your own, retreat
to firmer ground—go get treatment for yourself!"

Floria angrily shook her head. When Lucille turned
away and hurried on up the block toward the clinic,
Floria let her go without trying to detain her.

Thought about Lucille's advice. After my divorce
going back into therapy for a while did help, but
now? Retreat again to being a client, like old days
in training—so young, inadequate, defenseless
then. Awful prospect. And I'd have to hand over
W. to somebody else—who? I'm not up to handling him, can't cope, too anxious, yet with all
that we do good therapy together somehow. I
can't control, can only offer; he's free to take,
refuse, use as suits, as far as he's willing to go. I
serve as resource while he does own therapy—
isn't that therapeutic ideal, free of "shoulds,"
"shouldn'ts"?

Saw ballet with Mort, lovely evening—time out
from W.—talking, singing, pirouetting all the way
home, feeling safe as anything in the shadow of
Mort-mountain; rolled later with that humming
(off-key), sun-warm body. Today W. says he saw
me at Lincoln Center last night, avoided me
because of Mort. W. is ballet fan! Started attending to pick up victims, now also because dance
puzzles and pleases.

"When a group dances well, the meaning is
easy—the dancers make a visual complement to
the music, all their moves necessary, coherent,
flowing. When a gifted soloist performs, the
pleasure of making the moves is echoed in my
own body. The soloist's absorption is total, much
like my own in the actions of the hunt. But when a

man and a woman dance together, something else happens. Sometimes one is hunter, one is prey, or they shift these roles between them. Yet some other level of significance exists—I suppose to do with sex—and I feel it—a tugging sensation, here—" touched his solar plexus—"but I do not understand it."

Worked with his reactions to ballet. The response he feels to pas de deux is a kind of pull, "like hunger but not hunger." Of course he's baffled—Balanchine writes that the pas de deux is always a love story between man and woman. W. isn't man, isn't woman, yet the drama connects. His hands hovering as he spoke, fingers spread toward each other. Pointed this out. Body work comes easier to him now: joined his hands, interlaced fingers, spoke for hands without prompting: " 'We are similar, we want the comfort of like closing to like.' " How would that be for him, to find—likeness, another of his kind? "Female?" Starts impatiently explaining how unlikely this is— No, forget sex and pas de deux for now; just to find your like, another vampire.

He springs up, agitated now. There are none, he insists; adds at once, "But what would it be like? What would happen? I fear it!" Sits again, hands clenched. "I long for it."

Silence. He watches goldfish, I watch him. I withhold fatuous attempt to pin down this insight, if that's what it is—what can I know about his insight? Suddenly he turns, studies me intently till I lose my nerve, react, cravenly suggest that if I make him uncomfortable he might wish to switch to another therapist—

"Certainly not." More follows, all gold: "There is value to me in what we do here, Dr. Landauer, much against my earlier expectations. Although people talk appreciatively of honest speech they generally avoid it, and I myself have found scarcely any use for it at all. Your straightforwardness with me—and the straightforwardness you require in return—this is healthy in a life so dependent on deception as mine."

Sat there, wordless, much moved, thinking of what I don't show him—my upset life, seat-of-pants course with him and attendant strain, attraction to him—I'm holding out on him while he appreciates my honesty.

Hesitation, then lower-voiced, "Also, there are limits on my methods of self-discovery, short of turning myself over to a laboratory for vivisection. I have no others like myself to look at and learn from. Any tools that may help are worth much to me, and these games of yours are—potent." Other stuff besides, not important. Important: he moves me and he draws me and he keeps on coming back. Hang in if he does.

Bad night—Kenny's aunt called: no bill from me this month, so if he's not seeing me who's keeping an eye on him, where's he hanging out? Much implied blame for what *might* happen. Absurd, but shook me up: I did fail Kenny. Called off group this week also; too much.

No, it was a *good* night—first dream in months I can recall, contact again with own depths—but disturbing. Dreamed myself in cab with W. in place of the woman from the Y. He put his hand not on my neck but breast—I felt intense sensual response in the dream, also anger and fear so strong they woke me.

Thinking about this: anyone leans toward him sexually, to him a sign his hunting technique has maneuvered prospective victim into range, maybe arouses his appetite for blood. *I don't want that.* "She was food." I am not food, I am a person. No thrill at languishing away in his arms in a taxi while he drinks my blood—that's disfigured sex, masochism. My sex response in dream signaled to me I would be his victim—I rejected that, woke up.

Mention of *Dracula* (novel). W. dislikes: meandering, inaccurate, those absurd fangs. Says he himself has a sort of needle under his tongue, used to pierce skin. No offer to demonstrate, and no request from me. I brightly brought up historical Vlad Dracul—celebrated instance of Turkish envoys who, upon refusing to uncover to Vlad to show respect, were killed by spiking their hats to their skulls. "Nonsense," snorts W. "A clever ruler would use very small thumbtacks and dismiss the envoys to moan about the streets of Varna holding their tacked heads." First spontaneous play he's shown—took head in hands and uttered plaintive groans, "Ow, oh, ooh." I cracked up. W. reverted at once to usual dignified manner: "You can see that this would serve the ruler much more effectively as an object lesson against rash pride."

Later, same light vein: "I know why I'm a vampire; why are you a therapist?" Off balance as usual, said things about helping, mental health, etc. He shook his head: "And people think of a vampire as arrogant! You want to perform cures in a world which exhibits very little health of any kind—and it's the same arrogance with all of you. This one wants to be President or Class Monitor or Department Chairman or Union Boss, another must be first to fly to the stars or to transplant the human brain, and on and on. As for me, I wish only to satisfy my appetite in peace."

And those of us whose appetite is for competence, for effectiveness? Thought of Green, treated eight years ago, went on to be indicted for running a hellish "home" for aged. I had helped him stay functional so he could destroy the helpless for profit.

W. not my first predator, only most honest and direct. Scared; not of attack by W., but of process we're going through. I'm beginning to be up to it (?), but still—utterly unpredictable, impossible to handle or manage. Occasional stirrings of inward choreographer that used to shape my work so surely. Have I been afraid of that, holding it down in myself, choosing mechanical manipulation instead? Not a choice with W.—thinking no good, strategy no good, nothing left but instinct, clear and uncluttered responses if I can find them. Have to be my own authority with him, as he is always his own authority with a world in which he's unique. So work with W. not just exhausting —exhilarating too, along with strain, fear.

Am I growing braver? Not much choice.

Park again today (air-conditioning out at office). Avoiding Lucille's phone calls from clinic (very reassuring that she calls despite quarrel, but don't want to take all this up with her again). Also meeting W. in open feels saner somehow—wild creatures belong outdoors? Sailboat pond N. of 72nd, lots of kids, garbage, one beautiful tall boat drifting. We walked.

W. maintains he remembers no childhood, no parents. I told him my astonishment, confronted by someone who never had a life of the previous generation (even adopted parent) shielding him from death—how naked we stand when the last shield falls. Got caught in remembering a death dream of mine, dream it now and then—couldn't concentrate, got scared, spoke of it—a dog tumbled under a passing truck, ejected to side of the road where it lay unable to move except to lift head and shriek; couldn't help. Shaking nearly to tears—remembered Mother got into dream somehow—had blocked that at first. Didn't say it now. Tried to rescue situation, show W. how to work with a dream (sitting in vine arbor near band shell, some privacy).

He focused on my obvious shakiness: "The air vibrates constantly with the death cries of countless animals large and small. What is the death of one dog?" Leaned close, speaking quietly, instructing. "Many creatures are dying in ways too dreadful to imagine. I am part of the world; I listen to the pain. You people claim to be above all that. You deafen yourselves with your own noise and pretend there's nothing else to hear. Then these screams enter your dreams, and you have to seek therapy because you have lost the nerve to listen."

Remembered myself, said, Be a dying animal. He refused: "You are the one who dreams this." I had a horrible flash, felt I was the dog—helpless, doomed, hurting—burst into tears. The great therapist, bringing her own hangups into session with client! Enraged with self, which did not help stop bawling.

W. disconcerted, I think; didn't speak. People walked past, glanced over, ignored us. W. said finally, "What is this?" Nothing, just the fear of death. "Oh, the fear of death. That's with me all the time. One must simply get used to it." Tears into laughter. Goddamn wisdom of the ages. He got up to go, paused: "And tell that stupid little man who used to precede me at your office to stop following me around. He puts himself in danger that way."

Kenny, damn it! Aunt doesn't know where he is, no answer on his phone. Idiot!

Sketching all night—useless. W. beautiful beyond the scope of line—the beauty of singularity, cohesion, rooted in absolute devotion to demands of his specialized body. In feeding (woman in taxi), utter absorption one wants from a man in sex—no score-keeping, no fantasies, just hot urgency of appetite, of senses, the moment by itself.

His sleeves worn rolled back today to the elbows—strong, sculptural forearms, the long bones curved in slightly, suggest torque, leverage. How old?

Endurance: huge, rich cloak of time flows back from his shoulders like wings of a dark angel. All springs from, elaborates, the single, stark, primary condition: he is a predator who subsists on human blood. Harmony, strength, clarity, magnificence—all from that basic animal integrity. Of course I long for all that, here in the higgledy-piggledy hodgepodge of my life! Of course he draws me!

Wore no perfume today, deference to his keen, easily insulted sense of smell. He noticed at once, said curt thanks. Saw something bothering him, opened my mouth seeking desperately for right thing to say—up rose my inward choreographer, wide awake, and spoke plain from my heart: thinking on my floundering in some of our sessions—I am aware that you see this confusion of mine. I know you see by your occasional impatient look, sudden disengagement—yet you continue to reveal yourself to me (even shift our course yourself if it needs shifting and I don't do it). I think I know why. Because there's no place for you in world as you truly are. Because beneath your various façades your true self suffers; like all true selves, it wants, needs to be honored as real and valuable through acceptance by another. I try to be that other, but often you are beyond me.

He rose, paced to window, looked back, burning at me. "If I seem sometimes restless or impatient, Dr. Landauer, it's not because of any professional shortcomings of yours. On the contrary—you are all too effective. The seductiveness, the distraction of our—human contact worries me. I fear for the ruthlessness that keeps me alive."

Speak for ruthlessness. He shook his head. Saw tightness in shoulders, feet braced hard against floor. Felt reflected tension in my own muscles.

Prompted him: " 'I resent . . .' "

"I resent your pretension to teach me about myself! What will this work that you do here make of me? A predator paralyzed by an unwanted empathy with his prey? A creature fit only for a cage and keeper?" He was breathing hard, jaw set. I saw suddenly the truth of his fear: his integrity is not human, but my work is specifically human, designed to make humans more human— what if it does that to him? Should have seen it before, should have seen it. No place left to go: had to ask him, in small voice, Speak for my pretension.

"No!" Eyes shut, head turned away.

Had to do it: Speak for me.

W. whispered, "As to the unicorn, out of your own legends—'Unicorn, come lay your head in my lap while the hunters close in. You are a wonder, and for love of wonder I will tame you. You are pursued, but forget your pursuers, rest under my hand till they come and destroy you.' " Looked at me like steel: "Do you see? The more you involve yourself in what I am, the more you become the peasant with the torch!"

Two days later Doug came into town and had lunch with Floria.

He was a man of no outstanding beauty who was nevertheless attractive: he didn't have much chin and his

ears were too big, but you didn't notice because of his air
of confidence. His stability had been earned the hard
way—as a gay man facing the straight world. Some of his
strength had been attained with effort and pain in a
group that Floria had run years earlier. A lasting affec-
tion had grown between herself and Doug. She was intensely glad to see him.

They ate near the clinic. "You look a little frayed
around the edges," Doug said. "I heard about Jane
Fennerman's relapse—too bad."

"I've only been able to bring myself to visit her once
since."

"Feeling guilty?"

She hesitated, gnawing on a stale breadstick. The
truth was, she hadn't thought of Jane Fennerman in
weeks. Finally she said, "I guess I must be."

Sitting back with his hands in his pockets, Doug
chided her gently. "It's got to be Jane's fourth or fifth
time into the nuthatch, and the others happened when
she was in the care of other therapists. Who are you to
imagine—to demand—that her cure lay in your hands?
God may be a woman, Floria, but She is not you. I
thought the whole point was some recognition of
individual responsibility—you for yourself, the client
for himself or herself."

"That's what we're always saying," Floria agreed.
She felt curiously divorced from this conversation. It
had an old-fashioned flavor: Before Weyland. She
smiled a little.

The waiter ambled over. She ordered bluefish. The
serving would be too big for her depressed appetite,
but Doug wouldn't be satisfied with his customary
order of salad (he never was) and could be persuaded
to help out.

He worked his way around to Topic A. "When I
called to set up this lunch, Hilda told me she's got a
crush on Weyland. How are you and he getting along?"

"My God, Doug, now you're going to tell me this
whole thing was to fix me up with an eligible suitor!"

She winced at her own rather strained laughter. "How soon are you planning to ask Weyland to work at Cayslin again?"

"I don't know, but probably sooner than I thought a couple of months ago. We hear that he's been exploring an attachment to an anthropology department at a Western school, some niche where I guess he feels he can have less responsibility, less visibility, and a chance to collect himself. Naturally, this news is making people at Cayslin suddenly eager to nail him down for us. Have you a recommendation?"

"Yes," she said. "Wait."

He gave her an inquiring look. "What for?"

"Until he works more fully through certain stresses in the situation at Cayslin. Then I'll be ready to commit myself about him." The bluefish came. She pretended distraction: "Good God, that's too much fish for me. Doug, come on and help me out here."

Hilda was crouched over Floria's file drawer. She straightened up, looking grim. "Somebody's been in the office!"

What was this, had someone attacked her? The world took on a cockeyed, dangerous tilt. "Are you okay?"

"Yes, sure, I mean there are records that have been gone through. I can tell. I've started checking and so far it looks as if none of the files themselves are missing. But if any papers were taken out of them, that would be pretty hard to spot without reading through every folder in the place. Your files, Floria. I don't think anybody else's were touched."

Mere burglary; weak with relief, Floria sat down on one of the waiting-room chairs. But only her files? "Just my stuff, you're sure?"

Hilda nodded. "The clinic got hit, too. I called. They see some new-looking scratches on the lock of your file drawer over there. Listen, you want me to call the cops?"

"First check as much as you can, see if anything obvious is missing."

There was no sign of upset in her office. She found a phone message on her table: Weyland had canceled his next appointment. She knew who had broken into her files.

She buzzed Hilda's desk. "Hilda, let's leave the police out of it for the moment. Keep checking." She stood in the middle of the office, looking at the chair replacing the one he had broken, looking at the window where he had so often watched.

Relax, she told herself. There was nothing for him to find here or at the clinic.

She signaled that she was ready for the first client of the afternoon.

That evening she came back to the office after having dinner with friends. She was supposed to be helping set up a workshop for next month, and she'd been putting off even thinking about it, let alone doing any real work. She set herself to compiling a suggested bibliography for her section.

The phone light blinked.

It was Kenny, sounding muffled and teary. "I'm sorry," he moaned. "The medicine just started to wear off. I've been trying to call you everyplace. God, I'm so scared—he was waiting in the alley."

"Who was?" she said, dry-mouthed. She knew.

"Him. The tall one, the faggot—only he goes with women too, I've seen him. He grabbed me. He hurt me. I was lying there a long time. I couldn't do anything. I felt so funny—like floating away. Some kids found me. Their mother called the cops. I was so cold, so scared—"

"Kenny, where are you?"

He told her which hospital. "Listen, I think he's really crazy, you know? And I'm scared he might . . . you live alone . . . I don't know—I didn't mean to make trouble for you. I'm so scared."

God damn you, you meant exactly to make trouble for me, and now you've bloody well made it. She got him to ring for a nurse. By calling Kenny her patient and using "Dr." in front of her own name without qualifying the title she got some information: two broken ribs, multiple contusions, a badly wrenched shoulder, and a deep cut on the scalp which Dr. Wells thought accounted for the blood loss the patient had sustained. Picked up early today, the patient wouldn't say who had attacked him. You can check with Dr. Wells tomorrow, Dr.—?

Can Weyland think I've somehow sicked Kenny on him? No, he surely knows me better than that. Kenny must have brought this on himself.

She tried Weyland's number and then the desk at his hotel. He had closed his account and gone, providing no forwarding information other than the address of a university in New Mexico.

Then she remembered: this was the night Deb and Nick and the kids were arriving. Oh, God. Next phone call. The Americana was the hotel Deb had mentioned. Yes, Mr. and Mrs. Nicholas Redpath were registered in room whatnot. Ring, please.

Deb's voice came shakily on the line. "I've been trying to call you." Like Kenny.

"You sound upset," Floria said, steadying herself for whatever calamity had descended: illness, accident, assault in the streets of the dark, degenerate city.

Silence, then a raggedy sob. "Nick's not here. I didn't phone you earlier because I thought he still might come, but I don't think he's coming, Mom." Bitter weeping.

"Oh, Debbie. Debbie, listen, you just sit tight, I'll be right down there."

The cab ride took only a few minutes. Debbie was still crying when Floria stepped into the room.

"I don't know, I don't know," Deb wailed, shaking her head. "What did I do wrong? He went away a week ago, to do some research, he said, and I didn't hear from him, and half the bank money is gone—just half, he left me half. I kept hoping . . . they say most runaways come back in a few days or call up, they get lonely . . . I haven't told anybody—I thought since we were supposed to be here at this convention thing together, I'd better come, maybe he'd show up. But nobody's seen him, and there are no messages, not a word, nothing."

"All right, all right, poor Deb," Floria said, hugging her.

"Oh God, I'm going to wake the kids with all this howling." Deb pulled away, making a frantic gesture toward the door of the adjoining room. "It was so hard to get them to sleep—they were expecting Daddy to be here, I kept telling them he'd be here." She rushed out into the hotel hallway. Floria followed, propping the door open with one of her shoes since she didn't know whether Deb had a key with her or not. They stood out there together, ignoring passersby, huddling over Deb's weeping.

"What's been going on between you and Nick?" Floria said. "Have you two been sleeping together lately?"

Deb let out a squawk of agonized embarrassment, "Mo-*ther!*" and pulled away from her. Oh, hell, wrong approach.

"Come on, I'll help you pack. We'll leave word you're at my place. Let Nick come looking for you." Floria firmly squashed down the miserable inner cry, How am I going to stand this?

"Oh, no, I can't move till morning now that I've got the kids settled down. Besides, there's one night's deposit on the rooms. Oh, Mom, what did I do?"

"You didn't do anything, hon," Floria said, patting her shoulder and thinking in some part of her mind, Oh boy, that's great, is that the best you can come up with in a crisis with all your training and experience? Your touted professional skills are not so hot lately, but this bad? Another part answered, Shut up, stupid, only an idiot does therapy on her own family. Deb's come to her mother, not to a shrink, so go ahead and be Mommy. If only Mommy had less pressure on her right now—but that was always the way: everything at once or nothing at all.

"Look, Deb, suppose I stay the night here with you."

Deb shook the pale, damp-streaked hair out of her eyes with a determined, grown-up gesture. "No, thanks, Mom. I'm so tired I'm just going to fall out now. You'll be getting a bellyful of all this when we move in on you tomorrow anyway. I can manage tonight, and besides—"

And besides, just in case Nick showed up, Deb didn't want Floria around complicating things; of course. Or in case the tooth fairy dropped by.

Floria restrained an impulse to insist on staying; an impulse, she recognized, that came from her own need not to be alone tonight. That was not something to load on Deb's already burdened shoulders.

"Okay," Floria said. "But look, Deb, I'll expect you to call me up first thing in the morning, whatever happens." And if I'm still alive, I'll answer the phone.

All the way home in the cab she knew with growing certainty that Weyland would be waiting for her there. He can't just walk away, she thought; he has to finish things with me. So let's get it over.

In the tiled hallway she hesitated, keys in hand. What about calling the cops to go inside with her? Absurd. You don't set the cops on a unicorn.

She unlocked and opened the door to the apartment and called inside, "Weyland! Where are you?"

Nothing. Of course not—the door was still open, and he would want to be sure she was by herself. She stepped inside, shut the door, and snapped on a lamp as she walked into the living room.

He was sitting quietly on a radiator cover by the

street window, his hands on his thighs. His appearance here in a new setting, her setting, this faintly lit room in her home place, was startlingly intimate. She was sharply aware of the whisper of movement—his clothing, his shoe soles against the carpet underfoot—as he shifted his posture.

"What would you have done if I'd brought somebody with me?" she said unsteadily. "Changed yourself into a bat and flown away?"

"Two things I must have from you," he said. "One is the bill of health that we spoke of when we began, though not, after all, for Cayslin College. I've made other plans. The story of my disappearance has of course filtered out along the academic grapevine so that even two thousand miles from here people will want evidence of my mental soundness. Your evidence. I would type it myself and forge your signature, but I want your authentic tone and language. Please prepare a letter to the desired effect, addressed to these people."

He drew something white from an inside pocket and held it out. She advanced and took the envelope from his extended hand. It was from the Western anthropology department that Doug had mentioned at lunch.

"Why not Cayslin?" she said. "They want you there."

"Have you forgotten your own suggestion that I find another job? That was a good idea after all. Your reference will serve me best out there—with a copy for my personnel file at Cayslin, naturally."

She put her purse down on the seat of a chair and crossed her arms. She felt reckless—the effect of stress and weariness, she thought, but it was an exciting feeling.

"The receptionist at the office does this sort of thing for me," she said.

He pointed. "I've been in your study. You have a typewriter there, you have stationery with your letterhead, you have carbon paper."

"What was the second thing you wanted?"

"Your notes on my case."

"Also at the—"

"You know that I've already searched both your work places, and the very circumspect jottings in your file on me are not what I mean. Others must exist: more detailed."

"What makes you think that?"

"How could you resist?" He mocked her. "You have encountered nothing like me in your entire professional life, and never shall again. Perhaps you hope to produce an article someday, even a book—a memoir of something impossible that happened to you one summer. You're an ambitious woman, Dr. Landauer."

Floria squeezed her crossed arms tighter against herself to quell her shivering. "This is all just supposition," she said.

He took folded papers from his pocket: some of her thrown-aside notes on him, salvaged from the wastebasket. "I found these. I think there must be more. Whatever there is, give it to me, please."

"And if I refuse, what will you do? Beat me up the way you beat up Kenny?"

Weyland said calmly, "I told you he should stop following me. This is serious now. There are pursuers who intend me ill—my former captors, of whom I told you. Whom do you think I keep watch for? No records concerning me must fall into their hands. Don't bother protesting to me your devotion to confidentiality. There is a man named Alan Reese who would take what he wants and be damned to your professional ethics. So I must destroy all evidence you have about me before I leave the city."

Floria turned away and sat down by the coffee table, trying to think beyond her fear. She breathed deeply against the fright trembling in her chest.

"I see," he said dryly, "that you won't give me the notes; you don't trust me to take them and go. You see some danger."

"All right, a bargain," she said. "I'll give you whatever I have on your case if in return you promise to go straight out to your new job and keep away from Kenny and my offices and anybody connected with me—"

He was smiling slightly as he rose from the seat and stepped soft-footed toward her over the rug. "Bargains, promises, negotiations—all foolish, Dr. Landauer. I want what I came for."

She looked up at him. "But then how can I trust you at all? As soon as I give you what you want—"

"What is it that makes you afraid—that you can't render me harmless to you? What a curious concern you show suddenly for your own life and the lives of those around you! You are the one who led me to take chances in our work together—to explore the frightful risks of self-revelation. Didn't you see in the air between us the brilliant shimmer of those hazards? I thought your business was not smoothing the world over but adventuring into it, discovering its true nature, and closing valiantly with everything jagged, cruel, and deadly."

In the midst of her terror the inner choreographer awoke and stretched. Floria rose to face the vampire.

"All right, Weyland, no bargains. I'll give you freely what you want." Of course she couldn't make herself safe from him—or make Kenny or Lucille or Deb or Doug safe—any more than she could protect Jane Fennerman from the common dangers of life. Like Weyland, some dangers were too strong to bind or banish. "My notes are in the workroom—come on, I'll show you. As for the letter you need, I'll type it right now and you can take it away with you."

She sat at the typewriter arranging paper, carbon sheets, and white-out, and feeling the force of his presence. Only a few feet away, just at the margin of the light from the gooseneck lamp by which she worked, he leaned against the edge of the long table that was twin to the table in her office. Open in his large hands was the notebook she had given him from the table drawer. When he moved his head over the notebook's pages, his glasses glinted.

She typed the heading and the date. How surprising, she thought, to find that she had regained her nerve here, and now. When you dance as the inner choreographer directs, you act without thinking, not in command of events but in harmony with them. You yield control, accepting the chance that a mistake might be part of the design. The inner choreographer is always right but often dangerous: giving up control means accepting the possibility of death. What I feared I have pursued right here to this moment in this room.

A sheet of paper fell out of the notebook. Weyland stooped and caught it up, glanced at it. "You had training in art?" Must be a sketch.

"I thought once I might be an artist," she said.

"What you chose to do instead is better," he said. "This making of pictures, plays, all art, is pathetic. The world teems with creation, most of it unnoticed by your kind just as most of the deaths are unnoticed. What can be the point of adding yet another tiny gesture? Even you, these notes—for what, a moment's celebrity?"

"You tried it yourself," Floria said. "The book you edited, *Notes on a Vanished People*." She typed: ". . . temporary dislocation resulting from a severe personal shock . . ."

"That was professional necessity, not creation," he said in the tone of a lecturer irritated by a question from the audience. With disdain he tossed the drawing on the table. "Remember, I don't share your impulse toward artistic gesture—your absurd frills—"

She looked up sharply. "The ballet, Weyland. Don't lie." She typed: ". . . exhibits a powerful drive toward inner balance and wholeness in a difficult life situation. The steadying influence of an extraordinary basic integrity . . ."

He set the notebook aside. "My feeling for ballet is

clearly some sort of aberration. Do you sigh to hear a cow calling in a pasture?"

"There are those who have wept to hear whales singing in the ocean."

He was silent, his eyes averted.

"This is finished," she said. "Do you want to read it?"

He took the letter. "Good," he said at length. "Sign it, please. And type an envelope for it." He stood closer, but out of arm's reach, while she complied. "You seem less frightened."

"I'm terrified but not paralyzed," she said and laughed, but the laugh came out a gasp.

"Fear is useful. It has kept you at your best throughout our association. Have you a stamp?"

Then there was nothing to do but take a deep breath, turn off the gooseneck lamp, and follow him back into the living room. "What now, Weyland?" she said softly. "A carefully arranged suicide so that I have no chance to retract what's in that letter or to reconstruct my notes?"

At the window again, always on watch at the window, he said, "Your doorman was sleeping in the lobby. He didn't see me enter the building. Once inside, I used the stairs, of course. The suicide rate among therapists is notoriously high. I looked it up."

"You have everything all planned?"

The window was open. He reached out and touched the metal grille that guarded it. One end of the grille swung creaking outward into the night air, like a gate opening. She visualized him sitting there waiting for her to come home, his powerful fingers patiently working the bolts at that side of the grille loose from the brick-and-mortar window frame. The hair lifted on the back of her neck.

He turned toward her again. She could see the end of the letter she had given him sticking palely out of his jacket pocket.

"Floria," he said meditatively. "An unusual name—is it after the heroine of Sardou's *Tosca*? At the end, doesn't she throw herself to her death from a high castle wall? People are careless about the names they give their children. I will not drink from you—I hunted today, and I fed. Still, to leave you living . . . is too dangerous."

A fire engine tore past below, siren screaming. When it had gone Floria said, "Listen, Weyland, you said it yourself: I can't make myself safe from you—I'm not strong enough to shove you out the window instead of being shoved out myself. Must you make yourself safe from me? Let me say this to you, without promises, demands, or pleadings: I will not go back on what I wrote in that letter. I will not try to recreate my notes. I mean it. Be content with that."

"You tempt me to it," he murmured after a moment, "to go from here with you still alive behind me for the remainder of your little life—to leave woven into Dr. Landauer's quick mind those threads of my own life that I pulled for her . . . I want to be able sometimes to think of you thinking of me. But the risk is very great."

"Sometimes it's right to let the dangers live, to give them their place," she urged. "Didn't you tell me yourself a little while ago how risk makes us more heroic?"

He looked amused. "Are you instructing me in the virtues of danger? You are brave enough to know something, perhaps, about that, but I have studied danger all my life."

"A long, long life with more to come," she said, desperate to make him understand and believe her. "Not mine to jeopardize. There's no torch-brandishing peasant here; we left that behind long ago. Remember when you spoke for me? You said, 'For love of wonder.' That was true."

He leaned to turn off the lamp near the window. She

thought that he had made up his mind, and that when
he straightened it would be to spring.

But instead of terror locking her limbs, from the
inward choreographer came a rush of warmth and
energy into her muscles and an impulse to turn toward
him. Out of a harmony of desires she said swiftly,
"Weyland, come to bed with me."

She saw his shoulders stiffen against the dim square
of the window, his head lift in scorn. "You know I can't
be bribed that way," he said contemptuously. "What
are you up to? Are you one of those who come into
heat at the sight of an upraised fist?"

"My life hasn't twisted me that badly, thank God,"
she retorted. "And if you've known all along how
scared I've been, you must have sensed my attraction to
you too, so you know it goes back to—very early in our
work. But we're not at work now, and I've given up
being 'up to' anything. My feeling is real—not a bribe,
or a ploy, or a kink. No 'love me now, kill me later,'
nothing like that. Understand me, Weyland: if death is
your answer, then let's get right to it—come ahead and
try."

Her mouth was dry as paper. He said nothing and
made no move; she pressed on. "But if you can let me
go, if we can simply part company here, then this is
how I would like to mark the ending of our time
together. This is the completion I want. Surely you feel
something, too—curiosity at least?"

"Granted, your emphasis on the expressiveness of
the body has instructed me," he admitted, and then he
added lightly, "Isn't it extremely unprofessional to
proposition a client?"

"Extremely, and I never do; but this, now, feels
right. For you to indulge in courtship that doesn't end
in a meal would be unprofessional, too, but how would
it feel to indulge anyway—this once? Since we started,
you've pushed me light-years beyond my profession.
Now I want to travel all the way with you, Weyland.
Let's be unprofessional together."

She turned and went into the bedroom, leaving the lights off. There was a reflected light, cool and diffuse, from the glowing night air of the great city. She sat down on the bed and kicked off her shoes. When she looked up, he was in the doorway.

Hesitantly, he halted a few feet from her in the dimness, then came and sat beside her. He would have lain down in his clothes, but she said quietly, "You can undress. The front door's locked and there isn't anyone here but us. You won't have to leap up and flee for your life."

He stood again and began to take off his clothes, which he draped neatly over a chair. He said, "Suppose I am fertile with you; could you conceive?"

By her own choice any such possibility had been closed off after Deb. She said, "No," and that seemed to satisfy him.

She tossed her own clothes onto the dresser.

He sat down next to her again, his body silvery in the reflected light and smooth, lean as a whippet and as roped with muscle. His cool thigh pressed against her own fuller, warmer one as he leaned across her and carefully deposited his glasses on the bedtable. Then he turned toward her, and she could just make out two puckerings of tissue on his skin: bullet scars, she thought, shivering.

He said, "But why do I wish to do this?"

"Do you?" She had to hold herself back from touching him.

"Yes." He stared at her. "How did you grow so real? The more I spoke to you of myself, the more real you became."

"No more speaking, Weyland," she said gently. "This is body work."

He lay back on the bed.

She wasn't afraid to take the lead. At the very least she could do for him as well as he did for himself, and at the most, much better. Her own skin was darker than his, a shadowy contrast where she browsed over his body with her hands. Along the contours of his ribs she felt knotted places, hollows—old healings, the tracks of time. The tension of his muscles under her touch and the sharp sound of his breathing stirred her. She lived the fantasy of sex with an utter stranger; there was no one in the world so much a stranger as he. Yet there was no one who knew him as well as she did, either. If he was unique, so was she, and so was their confluence here.

The vividness of the moment inflamed her. His body responded. His penis stirred, warmed, and thickened in her hand. He turned on his hip so that they lay facing each other, he on his right side, she on her left. When she moved to kiss him he swiftly averted his face: of course—to him, the mouth was for feeding. She touched her fingers to his lips, signifying her comprehension.

He offered no caresses but closed his arms around her, his hands cradling the back of her head and neck. His shadowed face, deep-hollowed under brow and cheekbone, was very close to hers. From between the parted lips that she must not kiss his quick breath came, roughened by groans of pleasure. At length he pressed his head against hers, inhaling deeply; taking her scent, she thought, from her hair and skin.

He entered her, hesitant at first, probing slowly and tentatively. She found this searching motion intensely sensuous, and clinging to him all along his sinewy length she rocked with him through two long, swelling waves of sweetness. Still half submerged, she felt him strain tight against her, she heard him gasp through his clenched teeth.

Panting, they subsided and lay loosely interlocked. His head was tilted back; his eyes were closed. She had no desire to stroke him or to speak with him, only to rest spent against his body and absorb the sounds of his breathing, her breathing.

He did not lie long to hold or be held. Without a word he disengaged his body from hers and got up. He

moved quietly about the bedroom, gathering his clothing, his shoes, the drawings, the notes from the workroom. He dressed without lights. She listened in silence
from the center of a deep repose.

There was no leavetaking. His tall figure passed
and repassed the dark rectangle of the doorway, and
then he was gone. The latch on the front door clicked
shut.

Floria thought of getting up to secure the deadbolt.
Instead she turned on her stomach and slept.

She woke as she remembered coming out of sleep as a
youngster—peppy and clearheaded.

"Hilda, let's give the police a call about that break-
in. If anything ever does come of it, I want to be on
record as having reported it. You can tell them we don't
have any idea who did it or why. And please make a
photocopy of this letter carbon to send to Doug Sharpe
up at Cayslin. Then you can put the carbon into
Weyland's file and close it."

Hilda sighed. "Well, he was too old anyway."

He wasn't, my dear, but never mind.

In her office Floria picked up the morning's mail
from her table. Her glance strayed to the window
where Weyland had so often stood. God, she was going
to miss him; and God, how good it was to be restored to
plain working days.

Only not yet. Don't let the phone ring, don't let the
world push in here now. She needed to sit alone for a
little and let her mind sort through the images left
from . . . from the pas de deux with Weyland. It's the
notorious morning after, old dear, she told herself; just
where have I been dancing, anyway?

In a clearing in the enchanted forest with the unicorn, of course, but not the way the old legends have it.
According to them, hunters set a virgin to attract the
unicorn by her chastity so they can catch and kill him.
My unicorn was the chaste one, come to think of it, and
this lady meant no treachery. No, Weyland and I met

hidden from the hunt, to celebrate a private mystery of our own. . . .

Your mind grappled with my mind, my dark leg over your silver one, unlike closing with unlike across whatever likeness may be found: your memory pressing on my thoughts, my words drawing out your words in which you may recognize your life, my smooth palm gliding down your smooth flank . . .

Why, this will make me cry, she thought, blinking. And for what? Does an afternoon with the unicorn have any meaning for the ordinary days that come later? What has this passage with Weyland left me? Have I anything in my hands now besides the morning's mail?

What I have in my hands is my own strength, because I had to reach deep to find the strength to match him.

She put down the letters, noticing how on the backs of her hands the veins stood, blue shadows, under the thin skin. How can these hands be strong? Time was beginning to wear them thin and bring up the fragile inner structure in clear relief. That was the meaning of the last parent's death: that the child's remaining time has a limit of its own.

But not for Weyland. No graveyards of family dead lay behind him, no obvious and implacable ending of his own span threatened him. Time has to be different for a creature of an enchanted forest, as morality has to be different. He was a predator and a killer formed for a life of centuries, not decades; of secret singularity, not the busy hum of the herd. Yet his strength, suited to that nonhuman life, had revived her own strength. Her hands were slim, no longer youthful, but she saw now that they were strong enough.

For what? She flexed her fingers, watching the tendons slide under the skin. Strong hands don't have to clutch. They can simply open and let go.

She dialed Lucille's extension at the clinic.

"Luce? Sorry to have missed your calls lately. Listen,

I want to start making arrangements to transfer my practice for a while. You were right, I do need a break, just as all my friends have been telling me. Will you pass the word for me to the staff over there today? Good, thanks. Also, there's the workshop coming up next month. . . : Yes. Are you kidding? They'd love to have you in my place. You're not the only one who's noticed that I've been falling apart, you know. It's awfully soon—can you manage, do you think? Luce, you are a brick and a lifesaver and all that stuff that means I'm very, very grateful."

Not so terrible, she thought, but only a start. Everything else remained to be dealt with. The glow of euphoria couldn't carry her for long. Already, looking down, she noticed jelly on her blouse, just like old times, and she didn't even remember having breakfast. If you want to keep the strength you've found in all this, you're going to have to get plenty of practice being strong. Try a tough one now.

She phoned Deb. "Of course you slept late, so what? I did, too, so I'm glad you didn't call and wake me up. Whenever you're ready—if you need help moving uptown from the hotel, I can cancel here and come down. . . . Well, call if you change your mind. I've left a house key for you with my doorman.

"And listen, hon, I've been thinking—how about all of us going up together to Nonnie's over the weekend? Then when you feel like it maybe you'd like to talk about what you'll do next. Yes, I've already started setting up some free time for myself. Think about it, love. Talk to you later."

Kenny's turn. "Kenny, I'll come by during visiting hours this afternoon."

"Are you okay?" he squeaked.

"I'm okay. But I'm not your mommy, Ken, and I'm not going to start trying to hold the big bad world off you again. I'll expect you to be ready to settle down seriously and choose a new therapist for yourself.

We're going to get that done today once and for all. Have you got that?"

After a short silence he answered in a desolate voice, "All right."

"Kenny, nobody grown up has a mommy around to take care of things for them and keep them safe—not even me. You just have to be tough enough and brave enough yourself. See you this afternoon."

How about Jane Fennerman? No, leave it for now, we are not Wonder Woman, we can't handle that stress today as well.

Too restless to settle down to paperwork before the day's round of appointments began, she got up and fed the goldfish, then drifted to the window and looked out over the city. Same jammed-up traffic down there, same dusty summer park stretching away uptown—yet not the same city, because Weyland no longer hunted there. Nothing like him moved now in those deep, grumbling streets. She would never come upon anyone there as alien as he—and just as well. Let last night stand as the end, unique and inimitable, of their affair. She was glutted with strangeness and looked forward frankly to sharing again in Mort's ordinary human appetite.

And Weyland—how would he do in that new and distant hunting ground he had found for himself? Her own balance had been changed. Suppose his once perfect, solitary equilibrium had been altered too? Perhaps he had spoiled it by involving himself too intimately with another being—herself. And then he had left her alive—a terrible risk. Was this a sign of his corruption at her hands?

"Oh, no," she whispered fiercely, focusing her vision on her reflection in the smudged window glass. Oh, no, I am not the temptress. I am not the deadly female out of legends whose touch defiles the hitherto unblemished being, her victim. If Weyland found some human likeness in himself, that had to be in him to begin with. Who said he was defiled anyway? Newly discovered capacities can be either strengths or weaknesses, depending on how you use them.

Very pretty and reassuring, she thought grimly; but it's pure cant. Am I going to retreat now into mechanical analysis to make myself feel better?

She heaved open the window and admitted the sticky summer breath of the city into the office. There's your enchanted forest, my dear, all nitty-gritty and not one flake of fairy dust. You've survived here, which means you can see straight when you have to. Well, you have to now.

Has he been damaged? No telling yet, and you can't stop living while you wait for the answers to come in. I don't know all that was done between us, but I do know who did it: I did it, and he did it, and neither of us withdrew until it was done. We were joined in a rich complicity—he in the wakening of some flicker of humanity in himself, I in keeping and, yes, enjoying the secret of his implacable blood hunger. What that complicity means for each of us can only be discovered by getting on with living and watching for clues from moment to moment. His business is to continue from here, and mine is to do the same, without guilt and without resentment. Doug was right: the aim is individual responsibility. From that effort, not even the lady and the unicorn are exempt.

Shaken by a fresh upwelling of tears, she thought bitterly, Moving on is easy enough for Weyland; he's used to it, he's had more practice. What about me? Yes, be selfish, woman—if you haven't learned that, you've learned damn little.

The Japanese say that in middle age you should leave the claims of family, friends, and work, and go ponder the meaning of the universe while you still have the chance. Maybe I'll try just existing for a while, and letting grow in its own time my understanding of a universe that includes Weyland—and myself—among its possibilities.

Is that looking out for myself? Or am I simply no

longer fit for living with family, friends, and work?
Have *I* been damaged by *him*—by my marvelous,
murderous monster?

Damn, she thought, I wish he were here, I wish we
could talk about it. The light on her phone caught her
eye; it was blinking the quick flashes that meant Hilda
was signaling the imminent arrival of—not Weyland—
the day's first client.

We're each on our own now, she thought, shutting
the window and turning on the air-conditioner.

But think of me sometimes, Weyland, thinking of
you.

IV

A Musical
Interlude

IN A CARREL of the university library tower a student slept. Over him stood Dr. Weyland, respected new member of the faculty, pressed by hunger to feed.

The air was warm despite the laboring of the cooling system. Quiet reigned; summer courses brought few students into the stacks. On his preliminary tour of this tower level, silent in crepe-soled shoes, Weyland had noted the presence of only two: this sleeping youth and a young woman sitting on the floor reading in the geology section.

In nervous haste Weyland moved: he rendered the sleeper unconscious by briefly pressing shut an artery to the brain. Then, delicately tipping the lolling head to fully expose the throat, he leaned close and drank without a sound. When he was done, he patted his lips with his handkerchief and left as silently as he had come.

The youth whose blood he had drunk breathed a gusty, complaining sigh across the page on which his pale cheek rested. He dreamed of being unprepared for a history exam.

In the men's room on the ground floor Weyland washed the scent of his victim from his hands. Damp-palmed, he smoothed back his vigorous iron-gray hair, which in this climate tended to stick up in wiry tufts. He frowned at his reflection, at the tension lines around his mouth and eyes.

In his second week in New Mexico, he was still feeling upset from his recent experiences in the East. Yet now he must behave with calm and self-confidence. He could not afford mistakes. No odd rumors or needless animosity must attach themselves to him here. All modern cities seemed so large to him that he had miscalculated about this one: Albuquerque was smaller than he had expected. He missed the anonymity of New York. No wonder he couldn't shake this nervousness. Walking back through the somnolent afternoon for a nap in his temporary quarters, the home of an assistant professor, would relax him. Then he could sleep, as his digestion obliged him to, on the meal he had just taken in the library.

As part of the department head's efforts to settle him comfortably in his new surroundings, social arrange-ments had been made in advance for him. Tonight he was to attend the opera in Santa Fe with some friends of the department head's wife, people who ran an art gallery here in Albuquerque. Weyland hoped the eve-ning would contribute to his image as an austere but approachable scholar. The strain of sociability would be supportable, given the all-important nap.

He walked out into the brilliant summer sunlight.

The tourists ambled through the opera house. From the ridge on which the building lay they could look south toward Santa Fe, east and west toward moun-tains. Even on hot days breezes cooled the opera hill. The deep, concrete-enclosed spaces of the house were wells of shadow. The house manager, who was guiding the tour, led the visitors through the wings and down an open stair. They emerged onto a sunny concrete deck that backed the entire building—stage area in the middle and flanking work areas—in a north–south sweep.

Raising his voice above hammering sounds and a whine of power tools, the guide said, "Most of the technical work gets done here on the deck level." He pointed out the paint and electrical shops and, just behind and below the stage, the big scenery lift between the two open staircases.

The group drifted onto the shaded southern end of the deck, which became a roofed veranda adjoining the wig and costume shop. They stood like passengers at the rail of a cruise ship, looking westward. Someone asked about the chain-link fence that ran behind the opera house near the base of the hill.

The house manager said, "The fence marks off the property of the opera itself from the land that the founder, John Crosby, had the foresight to buy as a buffer against growth from Santa Fe. Nobody will ever be able to build close enough to give us problems with noise or light, or wreck our acoustical backdrop—that hillside facing us across the arroyo at the bottom of our hill."

The tourists chatted, lingering on the shady veranda; even with a breeze, it was hot out on the exposed deck. Cameras clicked.

Looking down, a man in a safari suit asked disapprovingly, "What's all that trash down there?"

The others moved to look. On the deck they stood perhaps thirty feet above a paved road that ran below the back of the opera house along the west face of the hill. Beneath them the road gave access to a doorway and a garage entry, on either side of which huge piles of lumber and canvas were heaped high against the stucco wall.

"That's discarded sets," the guide said. "We have only so much storage space. Old productions get dumped there until we either cannibalize them for new sets or haul them away."

A woman, looking back the way they had come, said, "This building is really a fantastic labyrinth. How does everyone keep track of where they're supposed to be and what they should be doing during a performance?"

The guide said, "By the music. You remember the stage manager's console in the right wings, with the phones and the mike and the TV monitors? The whole show is run from right there by the numbers in a marked copy of the score. Our stage manager, Renée Spiegel, watches the conductor's beat on the monitor, and according to that she gives everybody their cues. So the music structures everything that happens.

"Now, when we want to shut out the view of the mountains, for an indoor scene, say, we use movable back walls . . ."

"Dr. Weyland? I'm Jean Gray, from the Walking River Gallery. Albert McGrath, my partner, had to go to Santa Fe earlier today, so we'll meet him at the opera. You just sit back and enjoy the scenery while I drive us up there."

He folded his height into the front passenger seat without speaking or offering his hand. What's this, Jean wondered, doesn't the great man believe in hobnobbing with the common folk? Her friend the department head's wife had impressed upon her in no uncertain terms that this was indeed a great man. He fitted the part: a dark, well-tailored jacket and fawn slacks, gray hair, strong face—large, intense eyes brooding down a majestic prow of a nose, a morose set to the mouth and the long, stubborn jaw.

They also said he'd been ill back East; give a guy a break. Jean nosed the car out past striped sawhorses and piled rubble, exclaiming cheerfully, "Look at this mess!"

In precise and bitter tones Dr. Weyland replied, "Better to look at it than to listen to it being made. All afternoon I had to endure the bone-shattering thunder of heavy machinery." He added in grudging apology, "Excuse me. I customarily sleep after eating. Today a nap was impossible. I am not entirely myself."

"Would you like a Rolaid? I have some in my purse."

"No, thank you." He turned and put his coat on the back seat.

"I hope you have a scarf or sweater as well as your raincoat. Santa Fe's only sixty miles north of Albuquerque, but it's two thousand feet higher. The opera is open-air, so because of the lighting nothing starts till after sunset, about nine o'clock. Performances run late, and the nights can get chilly."

"I'll manage."

"I keep a blanket in the trunk just in case. At least the sky's nice and clear; we're not likely to be rained out. It's a good night for *Tosca.* You know that marvelous aria in the third act where Cavaradossi sings about how the stars shone above the cottage where he and Tosca used to meet—"

"The opera tonight is *Tosca?*"

"That's right. Do you know it well?"

After a moment he said distantly, "I knew someone in the East who was named after Floria Tosca, the heroine of the story. But I've never seen this opera."

After last night's performance of *Gonzago,* a dissonant modern opera on a bloody Renaissance theme, the *Tosca* lighting sequence had to be set up for tonight. Having worked backward through Acts Three and Two, the crew broke for dinner, then began to complete the reversed sequence so that when they finished at eight o'clock the lights and the stage would be set for the start of Act One.

Everyone was pleased to abandon the dreadful *Gonzago,* this season's expression of the Santa Fe Opera's commitment to modern works, in favor of a dependable old warhorse like Puccini's *Tosca.* Headsets at the stage manager's console, in the lighting booth, in the patch room and at the other stations around the house, hummed with brisk instructions, numbers, comments.

Renée Spiegel, the stage manager, pored over her carefully marked score. She hoped people hadn't forgotten too many cues since *Tosca* last week, what with doing three other operas since. She hoped everything would run nice and tight tonight, orderly and by the numbers.

Jeremy Tremain gargled, spat, and stared in the mirror at the inside of his throat. It looked a healthy pink.

Nevertheless he sat down discontentedly to his ritual pre-performance bowl of chicken broth. Tonight he was to sing Angelotti, a part which ended in the first act. By the opera's end the audience would remember the character, but who would recall having heard Tremain sing? He preferred a house that did calls after each act; you could do your part, take your bows, and go home.

The part he coveted was that of the baritone villain, Scarpia. Tremain was beginning to be bored with the roles open to him as a young bass—ponderous priests and monarchs and the fathers of tenor heroes. He had recently acquired a new singing teacher who he hoped could help him enlarge the top of his range, transforming him into a bass baritone capable of parts like Scarpia. He was sure he possessed the dark, libidinous depths the role demanded.

He got up and went in his bathrobe to the mirror again, turning for a three-quarter view. You wanted a blocky look for Scarpia. If only he had more jaw.

Weyland stared balefully out the car window. His library meal weighed in his midsection like wet sand. Being deprived of rest after eating upset his system. Now in addition he'd been cooped up for an hour in this flashy new car with an abominably timid driver. At least she had stopped trying to make conversation.

They overtook the cattle truck behind which they

had been dawdling, then settled back to the same maddeningly slow pace.

He said irritably, "Why do you slow down again?"

"The police watch this road on Friday nights."

He could hardly demand to take over the driving; he must be patient, he must be courteous. He thought longingly of the swift gray Mercedes he had cherished in the East.

They took a stop-light-ridden bypass around Santa Fe itself and continued north. At length Jean Gray pointed out the opera house, tantalizingly visible beyond a crawling line of cars that snaked ahead of them past miles of construction barriers.

"Isn't there another road to the opera?" Weyland said.

"Just this one; and somehow during opera season it does tend to get torn up." She chattered on about how Santa Feans had a standing joke that their streets were regularly destroyed in summer solely to annoy the tourists.

Weyland stopped listening.

In the parking lot young people in jeans and windbreakers waved their flashlights, shouting, "This way, please," to incoming drivers. People had formed a line at the standing-room window. The ushers stood, arms full of thick program books, talking in the sunken patio beyond the ticket gate.

Tremain checked in with the stage manager, who told him that the costume shop had finished mending the shirt for the dummy of Angelotti used in Act Three. That meant that tonight Tremain wouldn't have to strip after his part was over in Act One, give up his costume to the dummy, and then change back again for curtain calls. He took this for a good sign and cheerfully went down to the musicians' area to pick up his mail.

Members of the orchestra lounged down here, talking, playing cards in the practice rooms, getting their instruments from the cage in back and tuning up. Tremain flirted with one of the cellists, teasing her into coming to the party after the show tonight.

In the narrow conductor's office off the musicians' area, Rolf Anders paced. He wished now for just one more run-through with the backstage chorus in Act Two. The assistant conductor, working from a TV monitor, had to keep his backstage players and singers a fraction ahead of Anders and a fraction sharp for their music to sound right out front.

Anders looked forward to shedding his nervousness in the heat of performance. Some people said that every opera conductor should do *Tosca* each season to discharge his aggressions.

Three ticket-takers stationed themselves beside the slotted stub boxes, and the long iron gate swung wide. The people who had pooled on the steps and round the box office began to stream down into the sunken patio in front of the opera house. First comers sat down on the raised central fountain or the low walls containing foundation plantings of white petunias. From these vantage points they observed the clear but fading light flooding the sky, or watched and discussed the passing pageant.

Here an opera cape from another era, the crushed black velvet setting off an elegant neck; there blue jeans and a down-filled vest. Here a suit of Victorian cut complete with waistcoat, flowered buttonhole and watch chain, the wearer sporting between slim, ringed fingers an even slimmer cane; there a rugby shirt. Here a sport jacket in big orange-and-green checks over green slacks—and there, unbelievably, its double just passing in the opposite direction on a larger man who clearly shopped at the same men's store. Everywhere was the gleam of heavy silver, the sky hardness of turquoise, sparkle of diamond, shimmer of plaited iridescent feathers, glitter of baroquely twisted gold.

A church group of white-haired women, come for the

evening in a chartered bus, stood goggling, a bouquet of pastel polyester flowers.

The house manager, in sober evening dress, moved nimbly through the crowd, sizing up the house, keeping track of mood and movement and the good manners of his ushers.

Jean, standing on her toes, spotted McGrath—stumpy, freckled, thinning on top—at the fountain. He had with him young Elmo Archuleta, a painter he was wooing for the gallery.

"That's Albert McGrath; would you mind going over and introducing yourself?" she said to Dr. Weyland. "I have to make a dash for the ladies' room." Jean and McGrath were at odds over her plans to leave the gallery and return to the East. These days she spent as little time as she could around McGrath.

Dr. Weyland grunted disagreeably, tucked his raincoat over his arm, and went to join them.

God save us, thought Jean, from the grouchy great.

"Pleased to meet you, Professor," McGrath said. So this was the hotshot anthropologist the university people were crowing about; handsome, in a sour, arrogant way, and he still had his hair. Some guys got all the luck.

McGrath introduced Elmo, who was scarred with acne and very shy. He explained that Elmo was a hot young local artist. Jean was undoubtedly trying to steer the kid away from the gallery, to retaliate for McGrath's refusal to let her walk out on their partnership. McGrath let slip no chance to praise Elmo, whose work he really liked. He flourished his enthusiasm.

The professor looked with undisguised boredom at Elmo, who was visibly shrinking into himself.

"Nice ride up?" McGrath said.

"An exceedingly slow ride."

Here comes Jean, thank God, McGrath thought. "Hiya, Jean-girl!" She was little and always fighting her

weight, trying at thirty-two to keep looking like a kid.
And sharp—you'd never guess how sharp from her
round, candid face and breathless manner. Smart and
devious, that was Easterners for you.

The professor said, "I think the altitude has affected
me. I'd like to go in and sit down. No, please, all of you
stay and enjoy the parade here. I'll see you later inside.
May I have my ticket stub, please?"

He left them.

Jean smiled at Elmo. "Hi, Elmo. Is this your first
time at the opera?"

"Sure is," McGrath answered. "I got him a seat
down front at the last minute. And speaking of last-
minute luck, I've wangled an invitation to a party
afterward. Lots of important people will be there." He
paused. She was going to let him down, he could see it
coming.

"Oh, I wish I'd known earlier," she said. "I have to
be back in Albuquerque early tomorrow morning to
meet some clients at the gallery."

McGrath smiled past Jean at a couple he knew from
someplace. "I'll take Elmo and the professor with me,
then. He doesn't seem exactly friendly, this Weyland.
Anything wrong?"

"He barely said a word on the way up. All I know is
what I hear: this is a high-powered academic with a
good book behind him; bachelor, tough in class—a
workaholic, recently recovered from some kind of
breakdown."

McGrath shook his head. "I don't know why they
hire these high-strung, snotty Easterners when there's
plenty of good local men looking for jobs." Giving Jean
no time to respond, he walked away to talk to the
couple he knew from someplace.

Jean said, "Is McGrath treating you okay, Elmo?"

"He's like all gallery people. They treat you nice
until you sign up with them, and then they bring out the
whip." Elmo flushed and looked down at his shiny boot

toes; he liked Jean. "I didn't mean you. Are you still trying to get clear of McGrath?"

She sighed. "He won't let me out of the contract. He keeps saying New Mexico needs me. That's what happens when you're dumb enough to make yourself indispensable."

"How come you don't like it out here anymore?"

"I'm not as adaptable as I thought I was," she said ruefully. "The transplant just isn't working."

Elmo studied her brown hair, its soft, dull sheen. She was ten years his senior, which somehow made it easy for him to like her. He hoped she wouldn't go back East. That felt like a bad wish toward her, so he said impulsively, "Why don't you just up and go? You got enough money to fly back to New York."

She shook her head. "I need to go home with at least as much as I brought out here. You can't live in New York on the stub of a plane ticket."

Weyland took his seat. The theater was quiet, the stage set—there was no curtain—was softly illuminated. The house doors had just been opened, and most of the people were still out on the patio.

He definitely did not feel right. The tedious trip had put an edge on his fatigue. And they always wanted to talk; all the way up he had felt the pressure of Jean Gray's desire for conversation distracting him from the restful sweep of the land and sky.

Now, here, the fashionable crowd had reminded him uncomfortably of something—Alan Reese's followers, the spectators at the cell door . . . All left behind now. He thrust away the thought and leaned back to look a long time through the open roof at the deepening evening. If he could only walk out now into the dark, quiet hills, his keen night vision would aid him to find a hollow where he could lie down and settle his system with a nap—though at best sleep was difficult for him. By nature perpetually on the alert, he was roused by the least disturbance. Still, he could try—he wondered whether anyone would notice if he rose and slipped away.

Too late: another blink of the house lights, and the crowd came drifting down among the stepped rows of seats. Jean Gray sat down next to him, McGrath next to her.

She said to Weyland, "Well, what do you think? It's not a great big opera house like the Met in New York, but it has charm."

He knew he should respond, should make some effort to ingratiate himself. But he could bring himself to offer only a curt syllable of assent, followed by sullen silence.

With Anders standing ready beside her, Renée Spiegel said into the console mike, "Places, everyone, please."

The backstage speakers echoed, "Places, everyone, please."

She signaled the final blinking warnings of the house lights and then dispatched Anders to the podium. His image walked onto her TV monitor screen.

There was no foot-shuffling applause from the musicians when Anders entered the pit; he had lost his temper with them too often during rehearsals. The audience applauded him. He bowed. He turned and opened his score.

Spiegel, watching him on the monitor, called the lighting booth: "Warning, Light Cue One . . ."

Anders breathed deeply and gave the down beat.

"Cue One—"

Out crashed the first of the chords announcing the power of the dreaded Minister of Police, Baron Scarpia.

"Go!" Spiegel said.

The lights came up on an interior portion of the Church of Sant' Andrea della Valle in Rome, the year 1800. Scarpia's chords were transformed into the staggering music of flight. Tremain, as the escaped political prisoner Angelotti, rushed onstage into the church to hide.

In the lighting booth between the two sections of the balcony seating, a technician hit the switch that started the tape player. A cannon shot boomed from the house speakers. The technician grinned to herself, remembering the time her partner, stepping inside to relay a cue invisible from within the booth, had put a foot among the wires and yanked them out. The cannon shots of Act One had been drums that night.

Things could go wrong, things did go wrong, but it was never what you expected.

Floria Tosca on this stage bore no resemblance to the thin, dark woman named Floria whom Weyland had known in New York. This singer probably wasn't even a brunette—her eyes looked blue to him. His uneasy curiosity allayed, Weyland watched inattentively. He was turning over and over in his mind the layout of the university buildings, reviewing the hunting methods he could employ there until less risky opportunities to secure his prey developed.

Something onstage caught his attention. Scarpia was addressing Tosca for the first time, offering her on his own fingertips holy water from the stoup. He lifted his hand slightly as she withdrew hers, so that their contact was prolonged. After a startled glance of distaste at him, Tosca plunged again into jealous anxiety over her lover Cavaradossi's unexpected absence from the church. Scarpia moved downstage behind her, step for step, singing a polite inquiry into the cause of her distress. His tone was caressingly sensual and insinuating over a lively pealing of bells and courtly flourishes in the strings.

Intrigued by Scarpia's calculated maneuvering, Weyland lost interest when Tosca flew into a tantrum. He went back to pondering his new hunting ground.

*

The Te Deum, the great close of the first act, began. What a spectacle it was, Jean thought admiringly. The small stage seemed enlarged by the pageant in white, black, and scarlet entering at a grave, swaying pace behind Scarpia's back.

Scarpia mused on his own plans, oblivious to all else. He had deduced that Tosca's lover Cavaradossi was aiding the fugitive Angelotti out of sympathy with the latter's support of Bonaparte. Now Scarpia hoped that Tosca would go to Cavaradossi, and Scarpia's men would follow her without her knowledge and take the quarry.

The Police Minister's soliloquy, the lighter bells sounding the theme of his first suave approaches to Tosca, the great B-flat bell tolling, the organ, the choral voices, the measured booming of the cannon, all combined to thrilling effect; and the rich public virtue of the religious procession was set off against Scarpia's private villainy. As his sinuous melody wove around the solid structure of the celebrants' Te Deum, the long crescendo built.

Scarpia's voice seemed to ring effortlessly over the music, first an iron determination to recapture Angelotti; then a glowing outpouring of lust, luxuriant, powerful with assurance that soon Tosca would lie in his own arms—"*Illanguidir*," the voice glided down then surged upward with erotic strength on the final syllable; "*—d'amor . . .*"

Waking abruptly to his surroundings, he joined the chorus in full voice, and suddenly the morality of the State, as conveyed by the liturgy, and the personal evil of Scarpia were also united: one the underside of the other, both together the essence of official hypocrisy.

Scarpia knelt. Three times brass and drums shouted the savage ascent of whole tones declaring his implacable ferocity, the lights vanished, the first of the three acts was over.

Jean sat back, sighing deeply. Around her people

began to clap, standing, shouting, or turning to talk excitedly to one another.

Applauding, she turned also, but Dr. Weyland had gone.

Weyland walked in the parking lot. People moved among the cars under pools of light from the tall lampposts, talking and laughing, singing snatches of melody. They took from their cars scarves, gloves, blankets, hats. The breeze had an edge now.

Facing the wind, Weyland opened his jacket, unknotted his tie, and undid the top button of his shirt. He felt unpleasantly warm, almost feverish, and very tired. Even if he were to plead illness and retire to the back seat of the car, he knew he was too restless now to sleep.

He turned uneasily back toward the patio, a concourse of loud, volatile humanity. Crowds of people, their feelings and bodies in turbulent motion, always seemed threatening to him—unpredictable, irrational, as easily swept to savagery as to tears. And the music had been powerful; even he had felt his hackles stir.

Why? Art should not matter. Yet he responded—first to the ballet, back in New York, and now to this. He was disturbed by a sense of something new in himself, as if recent events had exposed an unexpected weakness.

Best to arrange the possibility of an unobtrusive exit during the next act, in case he should find himself too uncomfortable to sit it out.

In the musicians' area people drifted and talked. Tremain, done performing for the evening but still in costume, stood reading over the shoulder of a flutist who was absorbed in a battered paperback titled *The Revenge of the Androids*.

The conductor sat in his room massaging the back of his neck, trying to regain his calm without going flat. Now that everyone was warmed up, the evening was taking shape as one of those rare occasions when the opera's life, which is larger than life, fills the house, electrifying audience and performers alike and including them all in one magnificent experience. He felt the temptation to give in before the excitement and rush the tempi, which would only throw everyone off and spoil the performance.

Relax. Relax. Anders took deep breaths and yawned at last.

People congregated around the Opera Guild booth, where posters, T-shirts, and other souvenirs were being sold.

"I know Scarpia's an awful monster," said a woman in a tailored wool suit, "but he has such wonderful music, so mean and gorgeous, it makes the old heart go pitapat. I'm always a little bit ashamed of loving Puccini's operas—there's that current of cruelty—but the melodies are so sensuous and so lyrical, your better judgment just melts away."

The younger woman to whom she spoke smiled vaguely at her.

"The second act is a real grabber," continued the wool-suited woman. "First Scarpia tells how he likes caveman tactics better than courting with flowers and music. Then he has the poor tenor, Cavaradossi I mean, tortured until Tosca gives in and tells where Angelotti's hiding, and they haul Cavaradossi off to prison. And *then* Scarpia says if she wants to save Cavaradossi from execution for treason, she has to come to bed with him. He has this absolutely palpitating, ecstatic music—"

The young man who was her escort drawled, "Rutting music."

The young woman smiled vaguely. High again, thought the wool-suited woman disgustedly; where does she think she is, some damn rock concert?

"Come on," the wool-suited woman said. "We have to buy a T-shirt for Brother. A friend of mine is selling for the Guild tonight: her—that little lady with the short white hair and bright eyes. See the magenta sari she's wearing? She got that in India; she's been to China too; a great traveler. Hi, Juliet, let me introduce my sister . . ."

Jean took her intermission coffee black, which was bad-tasting but not fattening. "What a show we're getting tonight—a perfect introduction to opera for you, Elmo."

"I didn't like it," Elmo said unhappily. "I mean, it was like watching an animal in church pretending to be a man."

"You know," Jean said, "I read somewhere that Puccini had a strong primitive streak. He loved hunting, shooting birds and such. Maybe it wouldn't be too far off to see his Scarpia as a sort of throwback to a more bestial, elemental type." Elmo looked lost. Jean shifted gears: "You know the costume Tosca wore, the plumed hat, the dress with rustling skirts, the long cane? It's traditional; the first singer to play the role wore a similar outfit at the opening in Rome, in 1900."

Unexpectedly Dr. Weyland spoke close beside her: "Sarah Bernhardt wore the same in Sardou's play *La Tosca* more than ten years earlier. She carried also, I believe, a bouquet of flowers."

"Really?" Jean said brightly. "Nights when rain blows onto the stage here I bet the Toscas wish they were carrying umbrellas instead of canes or flowers. One night it really poured, and a man sitting in the unroofed section in front of me put up a villainous-looking black umbrella, which isn't allowed because the people behind the umbrella-wielder can't see. He turned out to be John Ehrlichman, of Watergate memory."

"And to be both prepared and unprepared," said Dr. Weyland urbanely. He turned to Elmo. "Young man, I noticed that you have a seat on the aisle down in front. May I change seats with you? No reflection on Miss

Gray—she does not snore, scratch or fidget—but I have trouble sitting so still for so long, no matter how fascinating the occasion."

Jean smiled in spite of herself. The man had charm, when he chose to exercise it. She wished he didn't make her feel so silly and so—so *squat*.

Elmo said uncertainly, "I'm in the second row. It's pretty loud up there, and you can't see so well."

"Nevertheless, I would consider the exchange a great favor, I must get up and stretch my legs now and then. An aisle seat on the side would be a mercy for me and those around me."

The pit boys brought up a snare drum to set in the wings near the stage manager's console. Spiegel herself was momentarily absent, seeing to the administration of oxygen to a chorister from St. Louis. The Santa Fe altitude could be hard on lowlanders.

The assistant technical director circulated, hushing the chattering choristers who milled outside the dressing rooms. Behind the flat that enclosed the smaller, more intimate second-act set depicting Scarpia's office, a minuscule orchestra assembled on folding chairs. They would play music to be heard as if from outside, through an open window of the office. A TV monitor was positioned for the assistant conductor to work from.

In the small prop room a final test was run with the two candlesticks which Tosca must appear to light at the end of Act Two. The candlesticks were battery-powered, their brightening and dimming handled by a technician using a remote-control device adapted from a model airplane kit.

The house manager called in to Spiegel, back at her console, advising her to delay the start of Act Two: the lines outside the ladies' rooms were still long.

Elmo sat in his new seat, relieved to be at a greater distance from the stage. Down front, he had felt like a bystander trapped into eavesdropping on somebody's very private business.

Now as Scarpia mused alone on the anticipated success of his plans, Elmo felt safely removed and free to study the scene: the inlaid-wood effect on the stage floor, the carved shutters of the window behind Scarpia's curly-legged dining table, a fat-cushioned sofa placed across from a big writing table all scattered with books and papers.

Suddenly Scarpia's singing turned ferocious—bang, bangety-bang-bang, up and down. Shocked, Elmo stared at the man. Though large of frame, Scarpia was almost daintily resplendent in silk brocade: over knee breeches and lace-trimmed shirt, a vest and full-skirted coat of a delicate pale blue. From this Dresden figure came a brutally voluptuous voice. The words were close enough to Spanish for Elmo to catch their drift. They were about women: What I want I take, use, throw away, and then I go after the next thing I want.

Elmo squirmed in his seat, uncomfortably aware of Jean sitting between himself and McGrath. It seemed indecent for any woman to overhear from a man such a fierce declaration of appetite.

One of Scarpia's spies brought the news: they had not found the fugitive Angelotti at Cavaradossi's villa, to which Tosca had led them. They had, however, found, arrested, and brought back for questioning Tosca's lover, Cavaradossi. Scarpia began to interrogate Cavaradossi over the cantata performed by the unseen small orchestra and chorus.

Into a pause glided a familiar soprano voice, Tosca's voice, leading the chorus. Cavaradossi murmured impulsively that it was *her* voice. A glance passed between the two men: Cavaradossi's back stiffened slightly; Scarpia lowered his powdered head and pressed on with his questions, rejecting any complicity with the prisoner even in admiration for the woman who fascinated them both.

The stage director, watching from the back of the house with the standees, found herself delighted. Such a small bit of new business, and it looked great. Suddenly the triangle of Tosca and the two men flashed alive.

Jean thought back to the last part of Act One. If that had been a telling embodiment of the two-faced nature of society, here was something quite different. The choral work heard now from offstage was not, like the Te Deum earlier, a pretentious ceremonial of pomp and power. Instead, strings and voices wove a grave, sweet counterpoint against which Scarpia's interrogation, by turns unctuous and savage, gained in ferocity.

He was like a great beast circling his prey while outside was—Art with a capital A in the person of Tosca, Rome's greatest singer, whose voice crested the swell of the music supposedly being performed elsewhere in the building.

Scarpia turned suddenly, irritated at finding that voice so distracting, and slapped the shutters to, cutting off the choral background.

Jean whispered into Elmo's ear, "You're right about him being like an animal."

Behind the set a kneeling apprentice fastened the shutters with tape. There must be no chance they might drift open again or be blown in by a gust of wind.

"Places, judge's party," said the backstage speakers. The hooded torturers and scarlet-robed judge assembled at their entry point in the wings.

Weyland saw Cavaradossi taken out, marched downstairs among the judge and his assistants for the continuation of the interrogation in the torture chamber. Only two remained onstage: Scarpia, composed and watchful, and Tosca, newly arrived in his office and trying to hide her alarm. Scarpia began to question her with elaborate courtesy: Let's speak together like friends; tell me, was Cavaradossi alone when you found him at his villa?

Now the pattern of the hunt stood vividly forth in terms that spoke to Weyland. How often had Weyland himself approached a victim in just such a manner, speaking soothingly, his impatience to feed disguised in social pleasantry . . . a woman stalked in the quiet of a bookstore or a gallery . . . a man picked up in a park . . . Hunting was the central experience of Weyland's life. Here was that experience, from the outside.

Fascinated, he leaned forward to observe the studied ease of the hunter, the pretended calm of the prey. . . .

Tremain strolled on the smoking deck, feeling left out. The fictional Angelotti was supposedly hiding offstage in a well at Cavaradossi's villa. When next seen he would be a suicide, a corpse "played" by a dummy. Tremain himself had nothing to do but cool his heels in costume for two acts until the curtain calls. He would have liked to chat with Franklin, who played the sacristan and was likewise finished after Act One; but Franklin was in one of the practice rooms writing a letter to his sick daughter back in Baltimore.

Tremain went down to the musicians' area and out the passageway to the south side of the building. There were production people standing three deep on the stairs that led up to the little terrace off the south end of the theater. From the terrace you could see fairly well without being noticeable to the seated audience.

He turned away and headed downhill toward the paved road sunk behind the opera house.

To lunging music, Scarpia luridly described for Tosca how in the torture chamber a spiked iron ring was being tightened round her lover's temples to force him to tell where Angelotti was hiding—unless she chose to save Cavaradossi by telling first.

In the trap under the stage where the torture chamber was supposed to be, Cavaradossi watched the conductor on a monitor, crying out on cue and instructing Tosca not to reveal Angelotti's hiding place. Dressers stripped off the singer's shirt and substituted a torn one artfully streaked with stage blood (a mixture of Karo syrup and food coloring whipped up by the assistant technical director). They dabbed "blood" across his forehead and rubbed glycerine onto exposed areas of his skin where it would shine in the stage lights like the sweat of pain.

"Piu forte, piu forte!" roared Scarpia to the unseen torturers, demanding that they increase the pressure. Tosca cried that she couldn't stand her lover being tortured anymore. Her voice made a great octave leap down to dark, agonized chest tones.

In the trap Cavaradossi gave a loud, musical cry.

Weyland had made a mistake, exchanging his seat for one so near to pit and stage. This close, the singers in their costume finery were too large, too intense: Their violent music assaulted his senses.

Under locked doors in his mind crept the remembered odors of heavy perfume, sweat, smoking tallow, dusty draperies, the scent of fresh-mixed ink. He had been in rooms like Scarpia's, had heard the click of heels on beeswaxed floors, the thin metallic chime of clocks with elaborate ceramic faces, the sibilance of satin cuffs brushing past embroidered coat skirts.

More than once in such an office he had stood turning in his hands his tradesman's cap, or rubbing his palms nervously on the slick front of his leather work apron, while he answered official questions. When questions were to be asked, Weyland, always and everywhere a stranger, was asked them. Often from another room would come wordless shrieks, the stink of urine, the wet crack of snapping joints. He had grown adept, even brilliant, at giving good answers.

Another artful scream from the hidden tenor jerked

him back into the present. He tensed to rise and slip away—but the music, storming out of the pit, gripped him. Its paroxysms of anguish—deep shudders of the cellos, cries of horns and woodwinds—pierced him and nailed him in his place.

Tosca broke down and revealed Angelotti's hiding place; the blood-smeared Cavaradossi was dragged onstage, reviled her, blasted out a defiance of Scarpia and an allegiance to the Bonapartists that doomed him to execution for treason, was hauled away.

In the fifth row center a man turned off his hearing aid and went to sleep. He didn't like the story, and he'd eaten too much *carne adovada* at the Spanish restaurant. Later, hearing rapturous talk about what a great performance this had been, what a privilege to have witnessed it, he would first say nothing, then agree, and finally come to believe that he too had experienced the magical evening.

Scarpia's voice flowed smoothly again as the orchestra returned to the elegance of the lighter strings. He bade Tosca sit down with him to discuss how to save her lover's life. He took her cloak, his fingers crushing the russet velvet greedily, and draped it over the back of the sofa. Then he poured out wine at his table, offering her a glass in dulcet tones: *"É vin di Spagna . . ."*

Thrusting aside the wine, she stared at him with loathing and flung him her question: how much of a bribe did he demand? *"Quanto?"*

And the monster began to tell her, leaning closer, smiling suggestively: he wouldn't sell out his sworn duty to the State for mere money, not to a beautiful woman . . . while the orchestra's avid, glowing chords prefigured the full revelation of his lechery.

Elmo swallowed, stared, listened with a dazzled mind. He had forgotten Jean sitting next to him, as she had forgotten him.

*

This is the hour I have been awaiting! cried Scarpia.
The spare, almost conversational structure of the music
grew suddenly rich with the throbbing of darker strings
and brass as he disclosed the price of Cavaradossi's life.
In tones sumptuous with passion he declared his desire:
How it inflamed me to see you, agile as a leopard,
clinging to your lover! he sang in a voice itself as supple
as a leopard's spring. At last he claimed the brazen,
eager chords of lust in his own fierce voice.

Resonances from the monster's unleashed appetite
swept Weyland, overriding thought, distance, judgment.

The lady in the snakeskin-patterned dress glanced at
the professorial type sitting next to her in the aisle seat.
Heavens, what was wrong with the man? Sweat
gleamed on his forehead, his jaw bunched with muscle,
his eyes glittered above feverishly flushed cheeks. What
was that expression her son used—yes: this man looked
as if he were *freaking out*.

Jean sat groaning silently at the back of her throat for
the tormented woman on the stage, who now rushed to
the window—but what use was suicide, when the brute
would kill her lover anyway?

With the devotion of a romantic spirit, Jean gave
herself up to the beautiful agony of the second act.

Tremain strolled in the dark down behind the opera
house, cigarette in hand, head cocked to the music
above him. He drew a hot curl of smoke down his
throat: bad for a singer, but you can't be disciplined all
the time. Anyway, except for wearing this absurd
scraggle of glued-on beard and long gray hair and
staying in his ragged costume until the curtain call, he
could do as he pleased. Caruso had smoked three packs
a day, and it hadn't hurt him. Great appetite was a sign
of great talent, Tremain hoped.

From the opera house came a distant, explosive

crash. He identified it at once and smiled to himself: Scarpia and Tosca had finally overdone the pursuit scene and toppled the water pitcher from the dinner table. Must be having a wild time up there tonight.

One more smoke and he would go listen close up with the others. He looked out at the sparkling lights of Los Alamos to the west and mouthed Scarpia's words silently to himself.

With ghoulish delight Scarpia gloated, How you hate me! He strode toward Tosca, crying in savage triumph, It is thus that I want you! . . . Throes of hatred, throes of love . . .

The breath strained shallowly in Weyland's throat. His hands ached from clenching. Tosca's cries drew from him a faint whining sound: he too had been pursued by merciless enemies, he too had been driven to the extremity of desperation. Tosca fled Scarpia, darting behind the desk from which pens and papers scattered to the floor. The dance of hunting rushed toward a climax. Weyland trembled.

He could see the voracious curl of Scarpia's lips, the predatory stoop of the shoulders under the brocaded coat as he closed in on her . . . as she flew to the sofa with Scarpia a step behind her . . . as Scarpia lunged for her. To the urgings of the horns, Weyland's mouth twisted in a gape of aggression, his eyes slitted cruelly, small muscles started convulsively beneath his skin, as the prey was flushed into flight again—as Weyland sprang in pursuit, as Weyland roared, Mine!

Startled movement at his side distracted him: the woman sitting there jerked away and stared at him. He stared wildly back, then surged to his feet and fled past an usher who was blind to all but the drama onstage.

Hurdling a low gate between the patio and the dark slope beyond, he plunged down the hillside. The dry rattle of a military drum followed from the opera house. Impressions blurred in his molten mind: rows of pale tents, restless lines of tethered horses, smells of smoke and sewage and metal polish, wet rope, wet leather; and always, somewhere, the tapping of drums and the bark of voices. He heard them now.

Yet he caught no sentry's footfall, no gleam of white crossbelts marking the presence of solitary prey. Where was the camp whose tumult he heard—those lights to the west? Too far, and too bright. Perhaps a night battle? He sought the scent of blood and black powder; he listened for the muffled cries and weeping of a moonlit field in the battle's wake, where a vampire might feed unnoticed and unresisted among the tumbled casualties.

In that year of revolution and royalist repression 1800, Weyland had followed Bonaparte's Grand Army.

Tonight there was no need for the assistant technical director to trot about backstage hushing people as Tosca began her great aria, "Vissi d'Arte." Tonight people were already quiet, listening.

A percussionist who would ring bells for the beginning of the next act came out of the musicians' passage and headed for the already-jammed side terrace. Her attention was trained on the music. Anything that could be heard from outside the opera house she did not notice.

Impelled by unbearable tension, Weyland rounded the corner of the building and padded swiftly along the sunken road that ran behind it.

There was a man up ahead there; a spark in the darkness, an emanation on the night wind of body warmth, sweat, and smoke. Long hair, breeches, loose and ragged sleeves, a gleam of starlight on shoe buckles as the figure turned its back to the breeze—detail sharpened as Weyland closed the distance with silent strides.

A little flame jumped in the man's cupped hands.

Body strung tight on the rich, wild throbbing of his own heart, mind seething, compelled to strike, Weyland slowed for the final rush.

*

Tremain's concentration on the poignant strains of the "Vissi d'Arte" was interrupted. Turning, he glimpsed a tall form looming, huge pupils of the eyes shrinking rapidly like a cat's before the wavering match flame. Tremain's mouth moved to frame some startled pleasantry, and his mind said, It's only the night that makes this scary.

Hands of iron seized him and slammed him away forever beyond the singing.

The high notes of the "Vissi d'Arte" burned clear and steady, the low notes smoldered with emotion. Anders followed like a lover, breathing with the singer's breathing. Only once she faltered, and Anders's lifted left hand restored her while his right, held low and armed with the baton, translated for the players in the pit.

At the close of her beautiful, vain plaint, the audience exploded. They screamed, they cracked their palms wildly together—briefly. The pace of the drama had caught them up and would brook small delay.

Weyland's mouth was full of blood. He swallowed, pressing the limp form tighter in his arms, burrowing with greedy lips past the disordered neckcloth.

His stomach, irritated by his earlier, incompletely digested meal, rebelled. Retching, he let the body drop and tried to rise, could only stagger to one knee, heaving. He must not leave vomit for dogs to find, for hunters to examine by torchlight. He swallowed regurgitated blood, gagged, his throat seared; knelt panting and shivering in the darkness.

A droning sound passed high above him—his sense of present time and place flooded back. Looking up, he saw the sinking lights of the airplane pass out of sight behind the faintly lit mass of the opera-house wall rising above him.

And before him on the ground lay a man not dead but dying; quick exploration revealed a crepitation of bone shards under the skin of the temple where Weyland's fist had crushed the skull. Apart from one smudge on the throat, there was no blood. He crouched in panic above the dying man. He had struck without need, without hunger. From this man dressed as in an earlier time—costumed, rather, a performer in the opera surely—he had been in no danger.

He was in danger now. This kill must be disguised.

He rose and crossed the road. The hillside dropped steeply toward the brush-choked arroyo below. A man might fall—but not far enough or hard enough to smash his head in. Also, he could see a fence partway down which would break such a fall.

He looked back up at the opera house itself, which crested the hill like a vessel breaking forward from a deep wave. The south side reared up three stories over the roadway into a knife-sharp corner like a ship's prow against the night sky. From its deck a man might drop and crack his skull here below. And where the hillside sloped up to meet the north end of the opera-house deck, one might mount that deck as if stepping aboard from the surface of the sea.

Weyland shouldered his victim, ran along the road, and scrambled up the stony hillside onto the deck. Then he turned and, bending as low as he might with his burden, sprinted down the deck toward the high southern prow.

A woman in the balcony focused her glasses on Scarpia. Now that he had wrung from Tosca assent to her own rape, he was deceitfully arranging Cavaradossi's supposedly mock excecution in exchange. This was worth coming all the way from Buffalo. Scarpia was such a nasty brute, but so virile—better than Telly Savalas.

The assistant technical director, crossing behind the stage with some cables to be returned to the patch room in the north wings, was too close to the music to hear the faint susurration of movement out on the deck below. He was absorbed in checking for production people who might be lounging on the back stairs, making noise—but tonight there was no one.

Outside the patch room, for an instant he thought he saw someone sitting in the corner with drooping head. It was only the dummy, supposedly the corpse of Angelotti who had killed himself rather than be recaptured. The soldiers would hang up the "body" at the start of the last act, a bit of business special to this production. People needed something to watch during that long, delicate opening.

Every night of *Tosca* the assistant technical director saw the dummy slumped there, and each time for a second he thought it was real.

Weyland flung himself down with his victim on the veranda outside the costume shop. The windows of the shop were yellow with light but largely blocked by set materials stacked outside. He could hear no sound of footsteps or voices on the terrace above the veranda.

He rested his forehead against the low concrete rampart, pressing his sleeve against his mouth to muffle the rasp of his own breathing. His back and arms burned with strain, and a cramp gripped at his gut.

How long before the second act ended? Once again the music was quiet and conversational. Weyland could hear Scarpia gallantly agreeing to write the safe-conduct that Tosca demanded for herself and her lover before she would actually yield her body. A dirgelike melody began. It was not loud; Weyland hoped it would cover whatever noise he made back here.

The dying man was heavy with the quicksilver weight of unconscious people, as if any shift could send all his substance running instantly into one part of his body. Weyland hefted him by the arms against the low parapet. The man groaned, his head rolled on Weyland's shoulder, and one of his hands plucked aimlessly at Weyland's knee.

Looking down past him, Weyland decided: there,

between those heaped-up masses of rubbish, where the paving came right to the foot of the wall—a fall, he judged, of some thirty feet. Not a lot, but enough to be plausible.

Now, under the sobbing lamentation of the music, he rolled the man's upper body out along the rampart, bent and heaved the legs up—the man dropped. There came only a dull sound of impact from below.

No shout was raised, but during a performance, uncertain of what had been glimpsed in the dark, no one backstage would call out. They would simply arrive—and if Weyland had not been seen yet, he might be at any moment, for he had been aware of someone moving on the stage level above during his dash along the deck. He had to get off the deck at once. For fear of being seen, he didn't dare run the length of the deck again to reach the low end. And he couldn't risk trying to find his way out through the backstage area in the midst of the performance.

He looked over the rampart once more. Out of the piled-up theater trash below and to his left there thrust, end on, a huge structure made of two thick sheets of plywood joined by two-by-four braces, like the steps of a crooked ladder. Farther down was some sort of platform, warped and buckled, and—stage trees? He could make out sausagelike branches with bristling ends.

If he hung from the rampart at the full stretch of his arms, his rubber shoe soles would reach within perhaps five feet of the braced structure. And if the whole twisted heap didn't collapse under him when he landed on it, he might climb down.

Taking no more time for thought or fear, he lowered himself over the rampart and let go his hold, crouching as he dropped to grab at the pale wooden ribs below. His landing was unexpectedly solid and jarring; whether there was noise or not he couldn't tell, because suddenly the music burst into a thundering crescendo. He began to clamber down the crossed wooden struts.

The whole pile leaned and creaked and shifted obscurely beneath him. He smelled dust. Under the blaring music he was keenly aware of his heart pounding, his gasping breath, and somewhere below the cracking of wood. He caught hold of one of the spiny trees, which dipped drunkenly under his weight, and he let go and slithered down in a rush, fetching up breathless on all fours on the asphalt.

Hurriedly, he examined his victim. The skull was pulped, the man was dead. Weyland looked up: the circumstances would certainly suggest that the unlucky fellow had fallen from the veranda or the balcony above.

Still no sounds of alarm or investigation. The stormy music was dying away into falling tremolo chords under the soprano's furious shouts—Die! Die! Weyland listened to the deep sighs of the strings while his heartbeat slowed and the sweat of fear and effort dried on him. He was as safe as he could make himself. Even if murder were suspected, who would connect this dead performer and an Eastern professor, total strangers to each other?

He turned away without looking at the body again—it no longer concerned him—and walked back up toward the parking area. Just beyond the reach of the parking-lot lights he stooped to brush the dust from his clothing, in the course of which he struck his own knee a painful blow; his hands would not obey him with their customary precision.

The numbers on his watch face jiggled slightly with the tremor in his wrist: 10:40. Surely the second act would end soon and he could return to mingle with the crowd before the final act.

At last he allowed himself the question: what had happened to him? That blow was his oldest way: it paralyzed yet left the prey living, blood still sweet, while he fed. What had made him use that ancient method, when from these refined modern times he had learned appropriately refined ways?

But what elation in that instant of savage release! Thinking of it now he felt his muscles tingle, and his breath came in a sharp hiss of pleasure.

Onstage, Scarpia lay dead. Tosca had stabbed him with a knife from his dinner table when he turned, safe-conduct in hand, to embrace her at last. To his lust-motif, inverted and muted to a sinister whisper in the strings and flutes, Tosca set a lighted candle down at each of his outflung hands. On a sudden loud chord she dropped a carved crucifix onto his breast, and then as the snare drum rattled ominously again she snatched up her cloak and gloves and ran for her life. The dead man was left alone on the stage for the last stealthy, menacing bars of Act Two.

The lights blinked out, applause crashed like surf. Two stagehands in black ran from the wings to stand in front of Scarpia—Marwitz, the baritone—while in his pale costume he rose and slipped down through the trapdoor.

Marwitz hurried away to find Rosemary Ridgeway, his young Tosca. His chest was full of the champagne feeling that meant success. He had been in this business for a long time, and he knew what "perfect" meant: that somehow the inevitable errors had been knit into a progression of actions so rich and right that everything fused into a vivid, indivisible experience never to be forgotten—or duplicated.

He hugged Rosemary hard outside the dressing rooms. "I knew, I knew," he chortled into her disor-dered hair, "because I was so nervous. I could sing Scarpia in my sleep by now, so nervous is good—it means even after so many times something is still alive, waiting to create."

"Were we as good as I thought we were?" she asked breathlessly.

He shook her by the shoulders. "We were terrible, terrible, what are you saying? Pray to stay so bad!" With the jealous gods of theater thus propitiated, he made to embrace her again, but she stood back, looking into his face with sudden anxiety.

"Oh, Kurt, are you all right? You really fell tonight when I stabbed you—I felt the stage shake."

"I am not so heavy," Marwitz said with offended dignity. Then he grinned. "My foot slipped, yes, but don't worry—you killed me very nicely, very well. They will award you two ears and a tail for it, wait and see."

"I liked how the water pitcher was busted and she couldn't wash the blood off her hands like she's supposed to," said a woman in gold lamé, "so she just wiped it off on Scarpia's dinner napkin."

Her friend frowned. "They should call it *Scarpia*, not *Tosca*. It's not a love story, it's a hate story about two strong people who wipe each other out—along with a couple of poor jerks who wander into the crossfire."

A man in a raccoon coat shook his head vehemently. "You feel that way because this fellow played Scarpia too civilized, like an executive. He's supposed to be just a jumped-up hoodlum. Tosca's line about him after the torture was originally 'The dirty cop will pay for this.' "

"What is it now?" inquired the friend.

" 'A just God will punish him.' "

"Well, who changed the line?"

"Puccini did."

"Then he must have thought the 'dirty cop' line made Scarpia look too much like a hoodlum: he's meant to be smooth," the friend declared. "Myself, I never knew a hoodlum with legs as nice as this Scarpia's. Isn't it a shame that men quit wearing stockings and britches?"

The woman in gold lamé glanced around disparagingly. "No it isn't, not with the boring hindquarters most guys got. Maybe legs were cuter in days of yore."

McGrath had run into a client. He brought her a drink from the bar. She had taste: the plaster cast on her left arm was painted with a frieze of red-brown Egyptian tomb figures.

"Personally," McGrath said, "I think this opera's a bunch of cheap thrills set to pretty music."

The client, who had bought two bronzes from the gallery this year, reacted critically. "Other people do, too; they honestly feel that *Tosca*'s just a vulgar thriller," she observed. "I think what shocks them is seeing a woman kill a man to keep him from raping her. If a man kills somebody over politics or love, that's high drama, but if a woman offs a rapist, that's sordid."

McGrath hated smart-talking women, but he wanted her to buy another bronze; they were abstract pieces, not easy to sell. So he smiled.

He wished he'd stayed with fine silver, turquoise, and Pueblo pottery.

Jean and Elmo strolled around and around the fountain in the opera-house patio.

"Opera can really shake you up," Elmo ventured, troubled.

Jean nodded fervently. "Especially on a night like this, when the performers are going all out. And a responsive audience throws the excitement right back at them so it keeps on building."

"But why does the bad guy get such great music?"

"Listen, Elmo, do you read science fiction? Tolkien? Fantasy stories?"

"A little."

"Sometimes those stories tell about what they call 'wild magic'—magic powers not subject to books or spells, powers you can't really use because they're not good or bad or anything to do with morality at all; they just *are*, uncontrollable and irresistible. I think this music tonight is like that—deep and strong and nothing to do with right or wrong."

Elmo didn't answer. That kind of talk reminded him of his wife's relatives over near Las Vegas, New

Mexico, who sometimes reported great leaping wheels of witch-fire flying about in the mountains at night.

Soldiers assembled in the trap under the stage. When the third act opened, they would mount onto the platform of the Castel Sant' Angelo, where Cavaradossi was being held for execution. The dummy of the suicide Angelotti was prepared for them to lug onstage and hang from the castle wall according to Scarpia's Act Two orders.

Behind the set of the platform wall, the crew chief oversaw the placement of the landing pad on which the dummy, heaved over the wall with a noose around its neck, would arrive. The pad was two stacks of mattresses roped together side by side, twenty in all to cushion the fall not of the dummy but of Tosca, when she leaped off the battlement in the end.

Weyland came out of the men's room having cleaned up as thoroughly and unobtrusively as possible. At his seat down in front he put on the raincoat he had left folded there. The coat would conceal the split in the shoulder seam of his jacket and any stains or rips he might have missed.

Both terror and exhilaration had left him. He was overcome by lethargy, but he no longer felt ill; his hunting frenzy had burned all that away. A mood of grim pleasure filled him. It was good to know that living among soft people in a soft time had not weakened him; that adapting enough to pass for one of them had not damaged his essential lionlike, night-hunter nature. Even a flagrant misstep need not be fatal, for his ancient cunning and ferocity had not deserted him. He felt restored.

These thoughts passed and sank, leaving him spent and peaceful.

Rosemary Ridgeway took off the brunette wig, rumpled from her scuffle with Scarpia, and set it on its

Styrofoam head to be combed out afresh. How absurd to try to become the libretto's dark beauty of whom Cavaradossi had sung so meltingly in the first act: *"Tosca ha l'occhio nero."* Rosemary's eyes were blue, and she couldn't tolerate contact lenses to change them. On the other hand, she didn't quite have the nerve—or the force and reputation—to emulate the great Jeritza who, libretto be damned, had played the role blonde.

Rosemary knew she was young to sing Tosca. Yet tonight her voice had acquired maturity and control, as if all of Marwitz's encouragement and advice had suddenly begun to work at once. If only the miracle would last until the end!

She sat gathering strength for the final act and scratching at her scalp, which already itched in anticipation of the beastly brown wig.

Just before the house lights went down, the woman in snakeskin glanced nervously at the man beside her. She had hoped that he wouldn't return; he'd been so caught up in the second act that he'd scared her. You were supposed to appreciate the opera, not join in.

Now he seemed freed of his earlier agitation, and she saw with surprise that he was really a fine-looking man, with the strong, springing profile of an explorer, or an emperor on an ancient coin. Though he did not appear what she would call old, maturity had scored his cheeks and forehead, and he sat as if pressed under a weight of long thought.

He seemed not to notice her covert scrutiny. The curve of his upturned coat collar was like a symbolic shield, signaling a wish to be left alone.

She hesitated. Then it was too late for a conversational gambit; the last act had begun.

A horn called. Slowly, to the lighting-board operator's counts in the booth, the lights grew infinitesimally stronger, simulating the approach of a Roman dawn over the Castel Sant' Angelo.

Usually, once the Angelotti dummy had been flung over the wall and disposed of, the assistant technical director and his stagehand companion would stretch out on the mattresses and doze. The sound of shots— the firing squad executing Cavaradossi—would rouse them for the flying arrival of Tosca, leaping to her death.

Tonight these two technicians stayed awake and listened.

Tosca recounted to her condemned lover Cavaradossi the events that had led to her stabbing of Scarpia. At the swift reprise of the murder music, the woman in snakeskin felt the man beside her stir in his seat. But he didn't leap up and bolt this time. A sensitive soul, she thought, observing that he listened with closed eyes as if he wanted nothing to distract him from the music; perhaps a musician himself, a pianist or a violinist? She looked at his fine, long-fingered hands.

Holding Tosca's hands in his, Cavaradossi sang in a caressing tone, O sweet, pure hands that have dealt a just, victorious death . . .

Elmo, appalled, felt tears run down his cheeks. He didn't dare blot them for fear of calling attention to them. The doomed lovers were so sure the execution would be make-believe and then they would escape together. They sang with such tender feeling for each other, so much hope and joy.

How frightening his tears, how strange the pleasure of his tears.

The execution squad fired. Cavaradossi flung himself backward into the air, slapping a little plastic bag of stage blood against his chest. Red drops spattered on musicians in the pit below.

*

At the crack of the guns the tall man grunted, and the woman in snakeskin saw that his eyes had flicked open. He stared about for a moment, then shut them again.

For God's sake, the wretched philistine had been sleeping!

The opera was over, the singers took their bows. Rosemary, high on triumph, wanted no one to miss out. Fumbling for Marwitz's fingers in the fall of lace at his cuff, she said, "Where's Jerry Tremain? Isn't he going to take his bow?"

Amid a barrage of applause they all walked forward together on the stage, joined hands upraised. There were many curtain calls. Tremain did not come. No one knew where he was.

The ticket gate was jammed with slowly moving people still chattering excitedly or, like Elmo who made his way among them silently with Jean, trying to hang on to memories of the music.

Dr. Weyland was outside already, waiting by the ticket office. He looked sort of rumpled. Elmo spotted a clutch of burrs stuck to the professor's trouser leg and a long scrape across the back of his hand. He heard Jean's quick intake of breath as she noticed, too.

"Are you all right?" she asked anxiously. "It looks as if you've hurt yourself."

Dr. Weyland put his injured hand into his pocket. "I walked a little beyond the lights during intermission," he admitted. "I tripped in the dark."

"You should have come and told me," Jean said. "I could have run you back into Santa Fe."

"It's only a scrape."

"Oh, I'm so sorry—I hope this hasn't spoiled your enjoyment of the opera. It was such a wonderful performance tonight." Her dismay made Elmo want to hug her.

Dr. Weyland cleared his throat. "I assure you, I found the opera very impressive."

Elmo caught an undertone of strain in the professor's voice. He was relieved, glad that he himself was not the only man to have been moved by the experience.

Maybe being moved was good; maybe some paintings would come out of it.

While waiting for the parking lot to clear they picnicked on fruit and cheese laid out on the trunk of Jean's car.

"This is what opera old-timers do," McGrath said. He passed around cups of wine. "Here's a drink to get us started; I've lined up something special for us—a big party in town. Lots of Santa Fe people and some of the opera singers will be there. Jean, you just follow that blue Porsche over there—that's our ride, Elmo and me—and drop the professor off at the party with us. We'll find him someplace to bunk for tonight and bring him back down to Albuquerque with us tomorrow."

"No, thank you," said Dr. Weyland, turning away the wine in favor of water. "I'm tired. I understand Miss Gray is returning to Albuquerque immediately, and I'd prefer to go with her."

McGrath said heartily, "But people are waiting to meet you! I already told everybody I was bringing a famous Eastern professor with me. We don't want to disappoint folks."

Dr. Weyland drank. "Another time," he said.

"There won't be another time," McGrath insisted. "Not like this party. You don't want to turn your back on old-fashioned Western hospitality."

Dr. Weyland deposited his empty cup in the garbage bag. He said, "Good night, Mr. McGrath," and he got into the passenger seat of the car and shut the door.

"Well, up yours too, fella," said McGrath, throwing his own cup under the car. He wheeled toward the blue Porsche, snapping over his shoulder, "Come on, Elmo, folks are waiting!"

*

Driving down, Jean found her memory playing over
and over the final thunderous chords after 'Tosca's
suicide. They were from Cavaradossi's farewell aria in
Act Three, the melody of "O dolci baci, o languide
carezze." Sweet kisses, languid caresses. Puccini's closing musical comment, perhaps, on the destructiveness
of outsized passions.

In fact, Scarpia himself had remarked in Act Two
that great love brings great misery. That was just
before his paean to the superior joys of selfish appetite.
Yet he had been destroyed by his lust for Tosca, surely a
passion in itself? How to distinguish appetite from
passion? Or did art raise appetite to the level of
passion, so that they became indistinguishable?

Had Dr. Weyland been more accessible, she would
have loved to discuss this with him on the way home.
She wondered whether he was lonely behind his façade.

Moon-flooded countryside flowed past. On either hand
the rolling plateau was adrift with blunt constructions
that dawn would show as mountains. Weyland did not
miss his old car now, his whispering Mercedes. He was
tired and glad not to be driving under that immense,
glossy sky; better to be free to look out. The scenery
was silver with reflected moonlight. The cool wind
brought fresh night smells of earth, water, brush, cattle
drowsing at the fences.

The woman spoke, breaking his mood. She said
hesitantly, "Dr. Weyland, I wonder if you realize
you've made an enemy tonight. McGrath wanted to
show you off at that party. He'll take your refusal as a
spit in the eye of his beloved Western hospitality."

Weyland shrugged.

"I suppose you can afford to be offhand about it,"
she said, sounding resentful. "Not all of us can. Elmo
will bear the brunt of McGrath's bruised feelings
tonight. My turn will come tomorrow when they get
back. McGrath can't hurt you, so he'll hit out at anyone

within his reach. You haven't made things any easier for me."

His voice crackled with irritation: "Perhaps it hasn't occurred to you, Miss Gray, that I'm not interested in your problems. My own are sufficient."

Marwitz and Rosemary lay curled close, too tired for sex, too happy for sleep. They dozed on and off while shadows of moonlight inched across the flagstones outside the French doors.

She murmured, "When the water pitcher fell I was sure Act Two would end in disaster."

"I would wish many more such disasters for us both," he said. Silence fell. Too soon the season would end and they would go their separate ways.

At length he said, "I wonder what happened to young Tremain. How unlike him, to miss his bow and a party after."

Rosemary yawned and wiggled closer against his warm middle. "Maybe he came later, after we left."

"Which we did indecently early." He nuzzled her ear. "Surely everyone noticed."

Rosemary guffawed. "Anybody who hasn't noticed by now has got to be as stupid as a clam!"

Marwitz sat up. "Come, we have wine left—let's go out and drink in the moonlight."

They wrapped themselves in the bedspread and padded outside, arguing amiably about just how stupid a clam might accurately be said to be.

Weyland got out of the car. He said, "Thank you for bringing me back. I regret my ill temper." He didn't, but neither did he care to make another unnecessary enemy.

The woman smiled a tired smile. "Don't give it a thought," she said. The car with WALKING RIVER GALLERY stenciled on its side pulled away.

When it was out of sight, Weyland walked. The

pavement was lit by the late-risen moon. No dogs were
left out at night on this street, so he could stroll in
peace. He needed the exercise; his muscles were stiff
from exertion followed by long immobility. A walk
would help, and then perhaps a hot soak in his host's
old-fashioned tub.

Walking eastward on a hill-climbing street, he
watched a mountain rise ahead of him like a harshly
eroded wall. Its ruggedness pleased him—an angular
outline stark against the night and unmuted by vegetation. He could feel the centuries lying thick over this
country—perhaps a factor contributing, along with his
physical indisposition, to that headlong tumble tonight
through his own personal timescape.

The kill itself had been good—a purging of anxiety
and weakness. Catharsis, he supposed; wasn't that the
intended effect of art?

But the tension leading up to the kill—memory made
him shudder. The opera had broken his moorings to the
present and launched him into something akin to
madness. Human music, human drama, vibrant human
voices passionately raised, had impelled him to fly from
among his despised victims as they sat listening. He
feared and resented that these kine on whom he fed
could stir him so deeply, all unaware of what they did;
that their art could strike depths in him untouched in
them.

Where did it come from, this perilous new pattern of
recognizing aspects of himself in the creations of his
human livestock? Such mirrorings were obviously unin-
tentional. His basic likeness to humanity was the
explanation—a necessary likeness, since without being
similar to them he could not hope to hunt them. But
was he growing more like them, that their works had
begun to reach him and shake him? Had he been
somehow irrevocably opened to the power of their art?

He recoiled violently from such possibilities; he
wanted nothing more from them than that which he
already, relentlessly, required: their blood.

The mountain ahead of him was, he saw, to be envied; it could be wounded by these human cattle, but never perturbed.

The morning tour drifted out onto the concrete deck at the rear of the opera house. The guide pointed west: "On clear nights when we leave the back of the stage open, the lights of Los Alamos . . ."

A heavyset man standing by the rampart glanced down at the road below. He leaned out, not believing what he saw, his breath gathering for a cry.

Elmo made a painting of dreamlike figures from the opera dancing on a sunny hilltop, towered over by a tall shaft of shadow like a wellfull of night. In memory of the young singer who had died the night of *Tosca,* Elmo called the painting *The Angel of Death.*

V

The Last
of
Dr. Weyland

"FAT TIMES in Academe are over." Out of Irv's open office doorway drifted Alison's disconsolate voice. Weyland paused in the hallway to listen.

"Every sensible graduate student sees the handwriting on the wall," Alison continued. "Ph.D. and all, I'll wind up typing in an insurance office—which is probably no worse than spending my life diagramming kinship systems or arguing about how many languages are spoken in Nigeria."

Weyland recognized with amusement his own recent summation of the state of anthropology.

"Whoah, wait a minute," Irv said. "That's not the kind of work Ed Weyland has you doing." His chair squeaked. When he talked Irv habitually swiveled it for emphasis. Weyland could hardly avoid noticing: Irv's office was almost directly across the hall from his own.

"Dr. Weyland is an original, Irv, everybody knows that," Alison said. "He has this unique slant that makes his courses really exciting. But one mind like that does not a whole discipline make." Indeed it does not, thought Weyland, with a cold glance down the hall at the office doors. He did not think of himself as having much in common with those intellectual knitters. "This semester of work with him is ending, and I'm not capable of creating that kind of excitement for myself. I'm not an original. So it's back to comparing bride prices for me, and frankly I'd rather sell matches."

Irv said, "Alison, we need people like you, good thinkers with good hearts, to save the discipline from the statisticians and the jargonmongers. Oh, I wish you'd been up in Tres Ritos with me yesterday listening to Carlos Hererra talk about Indian raids on his father's farm. I know taking down oral history isn't large conceptual work, Weyland's style, but it's not sterile scholasticism either. We can rescue human lives and cultures from oblivion. We can snatch history from the jaws of death."

On the subject of his beloved oral-history project Irv waxed lyrical. He seemed fueled by animated conversation: his own, his informants' in the project, the conversation of the students and faculty who sought him out. Weyland had never known him to turn away anyone who wanted to discuss, debate, or just listen. How did the man find time for all that talk and his scholarly obligations too? By slighting the work, no doubt. Irv was the sort of man in whom much would be excused by those who enjoyed his warmth.

Alison Beader was Weyland's teaching assistant. He stepped into Irv's office and said, "Alison, when you have a minute, we need to talk about making up the final examination."

She looked up guiltily—because she had taken her complaints to Irv instead of him? The exact mix and weight of human reactions were often obscure. In fact Weyland rejoiced that she had not chosen his shoulder to wail upon. He waved aside her promise to come at once to his office. "Take your time."

Irv was leaning back, his arms folded behind his

head, his dark, welcoming eyes turned to Weyland. Taped on the wall behind Irv was a poster of a cartoon cat sitting on a stool strumming a guitar and singing. The poster was a gift from a student last Christmas. People wanted to be close to Irv.

Weyland did not. He had learned early that, because of a chronic health condition, Irv was always on medication. His blood was unfit to drink. However, Weyland took care to maintain a good-tempered relationship with him. To have treated Irv in the cool and autocratic manner that he treated most members of the department would have branded Weyland an obvious crank.

He said, "Have you persuaded Alison to spend the summer prospecting for the past in the sun-crazed brains of the aged? Irv is very seductive, Alison. He tried to recruit me, but when he showed me a parchment treasure map I fled."

Irv grinned. "You ought to come with me once, Ed, just for relief from books, journals, and the almighty printed word."

"My summer plans, thank God, are made," Weyland said. He meant to stay in Albuquerque, write, and hunt among the hordes of tourists. "Try again next year. For the moment, the printed word commands me." He tapped the handful of mail he had picked up at the main office.

Irv grimaced at the lesser heap of letters in the wooden tray on his own desk. "I'd trade mail with you, but would you want to take on the informant family I worked with in Ceylon? They write that they pray every day that I'll finance their third kid through college."

"I would answer as a god of wrath," Weyland replied.

Irv laughed. "I was afraid of that. Okay, no trades."

Weyland left them to finish their conversation.

This late on a Friday everyone else was gone. Without fear of being seen he slipped the latch of Arnold "Map" Oblonsky's door with a credit card and entered to search out a geologic map he wanted. Just as missing library books were generally found piled up in the sumptuous office of Eleanor Hellstrum, the department's emeritus, maps were hoarded by Map Oblonsky—ostensibly to protect them from being mishandled, stolen, or lost by other less loving borrowers. Weyland enjoyed recalling the exalted guest lecturer who, not recognizing the nickname as heard in conversation, had cordially greeted the map-miser as "Professor Mapoblonsky."

Taking the map he wanted, Weyland returned to his own office, where he too had begun an impressive hoard. Monopolizing materials was a sign of power, and power in the hierarchies of human beings was useful to him.

Foul stinks from the basement lab pervaded the building—doubtless somebody in a comparative-anatomy class cooking the flesh from an animal skeleton. Weyland opened his windows. Then, spreading the map on the small drafting table he had set up in one corner, he studied a spot in the Sandia foothills that seemed promising for cave exploration tomorrow.

He would look for a meal on the drive up. Spring had brought out the hitchhikers with their packs and guitars. Random travelers, when not rank with dope or disease, made excellent prey. He had developed several strategies to bring about physical contact with such passengers.

He heard Alison's rueful laughter from Irv's office. The situation with her required action. He did not want his relationship with Alison to go so far that people remarked on how peaked she looked, as they had remarked about his previous T.A. Now that spring provided the bounty of the roads, he need no longer depend so heavily on regulars like Alison for food. Wintering here in Albuquerque, he had constructed a network to supply him when hunting was poor: colleagues, students, and social companions—those whom he could approach without causing suspicion—made good victims at short notice. But there was always risk in repetition.

Alison was the most accessible, the most regular of the regulars, because of the personal relationship he had built on the working one. Now, happily, that connection could be ended. After several months, being her lover had become a strain.

He riffled through his mail: please review this book that should never have been published, please reply to this furious reply to your previous hostile review; would you be interested in contributing to our forthcoming issue on real and synthetic languages; an invitation to a craft show opening (more pots) inscribed in the curly hand of the Anthro Department head's wife; a request for a reference from a young woman whom he would consent to endorse, since she was brilliant and hard-driving and had gathered several illustrious names to back her.

Weyland had made his own name estimable enough so that others were eager to borrow its luster. Yet he gave them no sympathy. They hustled along trundling their little lives before them, panting and sweating to get ahead of others just like themselves with a pull from those who trundled still further ahead . . .

Here was something welcome, a practical query from the printer about Weyland's monograph, due out next month, on transformations of the self in dreams; an invitation to a conference in Australia next year—five days of soporific meetings and an overnight jaunt by kangaroo into the outback; a reminder of that outside lecture he was to give at the Indian School next week . . .

He must demand more secretarial help—another mark of status. The barrage of paper and the demands on his time were impossible.

He packed up his briefcase.

Alison came in and shut the door. She stood there in the bright print jumper that seemed to bring out the shadows in her face, and she said in a quavering voice,

"You may have noticed, Dr. Weyland, that I've been avoiding you lately."

Warily, he nodded.

She stared at him. "My God," she said. "I've spent a good number of nights in your bed this past winter, and I still call you by your title and surname. What have I been doing?"

A response seemed called for. He said, "Sharing your warmth and companionship with me." So she had begun to separate from him; how agreeable. He turned a chair toward her invitingly. She looked shaky on her feet. He was thinking of a time when he had been harsh in just such a situation and had been forced in consequence to deal with hysteria. It paid, he had found, to go gently sometimes. "Companionship was what I was looking for. I've never taken our liaison for more—how could I, a man more than twice your age?—and I hope you never did, either."

"What does age have to do with anything?" she said. She sat down. "Claire," she said, naming his former T.A., "was younger than I am."

"Yes." He seated himself behind the desk.

She looked confused, red-eyed: "I mean—doesn't that make it awfully easy for you? You get close to a girl and then whenever you feel like it you just— you can turn her off by telling her you're too old for her."

She seemed quite upset. He hoped Irv had gone home. "But it's you, Alison, who have come to do the turning off. And as for pursuing the young, I look for satisfaction where I have some chance of achieving it. You know how difficult it is for me, even with a youthful, attractive woman like yourself."

She sat back, frowning. "Difficult? You mean sex? Half the time we just drift off to sleep. I don't think you give a damn for sex, you know that? I guess when an older man pursues young women, he really wants them to keep him feeling young. And," she added bitterly, "there's no mystery in why a young woman falls for an older man, either."

He had understood his attraction for her and had used it. But he could not imagine what she felt like, seeking a lost parent, or how a man would feel in pursuit of his own vanished youth. The inward sensations of such compulsions were closed to him. He kept silent, hoping she would move on to some other subject.

"The point is, it's all over between us. I think it's been over for a while now. That's really a good thing—the timing, I mean, not too near the end of the semester, so it doesn't look as if we had some kind of lay-for-a-term arrangement. I don't want to get that kind of reputation. I did not start sleeping with you just to earn a boost up the professional ladder. I'm not like that."

"Nevertheless, I will of course do whatever I can for you," he said, "as discreetly as possible."

"Don't strain yourself," she said resentfully and blushed. "Sorry."

Ah; he saw that he should have shown some flinching of masculine pride. Too late. Suddenly the tears spilled from her eyes. Weyland shook out a clean handkerchief and handed it to her.

"God damn it," she gulped from behind the bunched and dampened cloth, "this would be a lot easier if you weren't—you have the face of everybody's dream-father, you know that? All rugged and worn and wise, and then there's this distance—it's irresistible, I can't explain it. But next time somebody says they climb mountains because they're there, I'll have some idea what they mean."

She took a deep breath and settled herself in the chair as if beginning over. "Anyway, it looks as if we're a pair of complementary neuroses that met, grappled, and are about to pass in the night. So I want to say goodbye on that score. I hope you won't hold it against me that I did this before you decided to do it yourself."

"On the contrary," he said gravely. "I'm grateful for your sensitivity and realism."

A "farewell fuck," to use Oblonsky's terminology, would be appropriate here if they were within reach of a bedroom instead of at the office. Thank God for small mercies. Sex, which Weyland had always found complicated, was a positive chore with Alison because of her recurrent desire to kiss and mouth him, practices which he detested. But he was willing to try now and again with her to keep up her hope that she would eventually "cure" him of his "difficulty" completely. How else could he keep her coming back? He had needed her for those other evenings, the ones that mattered—the evenings when, caressing her warm skin, with a pressure at the throat he put her straight to sleep and drank her clean, sweet blood. The thought stirred his ever present hunger.

Blinking, on the verge of renewed tears, she said, "I can't believe I've done it."

But you have, so let's not go over everything again. He got up. "Jennifer Chadwick is reading at Couche Hall—a paper on devil figures as instruments of social control. Would you like to attend?"

Alison shook her head slowly. "Poor Jennifer. You're planning some politely murderous questions for her, aren't you? All very courtly but right for the jugular. What have you got against her?"

"Sloppy thinking. Also, she drinks. You can see the veins on her nose."

She stared at him with a sort of dazzled bewilderment. "Sometimes you are positively inhuman, you know that?"

He held the door open for her. "A useful reputation to have," he said, "however undeserved."

After the colloquium Irv was waiting outside. His white sport shirt set off his swarthy skin. He was hairy—darkly furred arms and a black curl at the collar's opening—though balding on top. His face, folded onto a faintly simian bone structure, expressed alert middle-aged perplexity.

"Poor Jennifer," he said. "I was worried for a while that you weren't going to back off and let her recover."

Weyland shrugged. "I didn't intend to make an enemy, only to uphold some standard of scholarship."

"You do that so deftly and so entertainingly," Irv said with frank admiration, "that nobody could mistake your intentions, or even resent it too much that you decided to use them as an example, even if you do cut pretty deep in the process. Everybody knows that being too hard on other people means you're too hard on yourself too. A lighter hand in both cases would be a relief to everyone." His voice sounded gentle as always, dark-colored and faintly woolly in quality as if dense with thought.

Weyland did not reply, and, as he had expected, Irv chose not to pursue the subject. Having offered as much of a reproach as he was going to, he asked whether Weyland was going home. Irv lived in the same neighborhood. Sometimes they walked to or from the university together.

Weyland said, "I'm going over to the library."

"Then I'll walk you that far, though what you have to do over there that couldn't wait till next week I can't imagine. It's Friday, haven't you noticed? Alison says she doesn't know how you keep going, working as hard as you do."

"A roundabout way of complaining that I overload her?"

"Oh, no," Irv said. "I get the impression that though she's never found you exactly easy to work with, she definitely feels that the benefits outweigh the pains. It's not my business, of course," he added, "but people talk to me, they tell me things. And God knows being T.A. to a senior professor can be hard going in all sorts of ways."

Weyland had no intention of permitting the conversation to continue on that course. Irv could be expected to spot any false note in Weyland's remarks about the affair with Alison. As they walked through the campus in the fading light Weyland said, "Alison would be a valuable addition to your oral-history project this summer. The field work might do her good, too. She needs more self-confidence, a greater sense of independence and of her own strengths."

"Yes—I'd hate to see her drop out of anthropology. She's so discouraged about the future, scared she'll end up with no choice but to work for some state highway department on archaeological salvage."

"That would be a living," Weyland said.

"Sure. But she wants to be a scholar. You know the hunger."

Weyland glanced at him. "One must adjust one's hungers to the times."

Irv laughed. "How true, and for all of us, not just these youngsters. Next time somebody refers to the university as an ivory tower, I'll send them to you for a good, hard commonsense knock on the head.

"Weren't we lucky?" Irv sighed. "I mean, anthropologists of the last few decades. We've had the best of it, I think: field work in wild places before the wild places got paved with soda cans, cushy jobs while the universities were growing, an exciting young discipline busting with confidence and studded with stars . . . I feel guilty these days when I talk about my own professional experience to students because they know and I know that most of the good stuff is used up. What a future they have to settle for."

They crossed the artificial hills around the university's artificial duck pond. Weyland thought, The short trajectories of human lives predispose them to these anxious judgments that opportunities are insufficient, openings are unsatisfactory, the times are tragically lacking in this or that. If only I'd been born earlier, they say, or later. Alison can't wait a hundred years for some swing of events in her favor . . .

He said, "People seem to manage."

"Sure. But I worry about the ones I know. Don't you?"

They stood outside the library. Irv looked up mildly from under his heavy brows at Weyland. "We all concern each other, after all. Though maybe you wouldn't agree?"

Weyland considered. "We all keep watch on each other. I can agree to that."

Irv said nothing for a moment. He looked suddenly downcast and anxious, quite unlike himself. Weyland observed him curiously.

Irv said, "Never mind, I'm hardly fit to talk to lately. Too much on my mind, a mistake I made—several mistakes. Just now you reminded me of someone I knew—not your fault, it was the cautious way you said that. Keeping watch isn't enough, you know. You can watch things go wrong right next to you and never know why."

Weyland glanced about. In the dusk students were walking and biking over the mellow brick pavement. Feeling isolated with Irv in an unwanted intimacy, he said, "I've always found my work to be a good antidote to anxiety. How is your research coming?"

Irv was saying softly, "And when the crisis happens to someone you care about, you can really get torn up. I don't know what I'd do now without the oral-history project. Those marvelous transcripts—I get caught up in the vividness of all those voices, Ed, the actual stuff of history, our own connectedness with our forebears and their lives, a living past . . ." His hands sculpted the air as he spoke, his eyes shone.

"I'd like to talk with you about that sometime," Weyland said quickly. "I may venture into your territory from a different direction. My new book will be about predator-prey relations among human populations, and how those relationships influence human attitudes toward animal predators and prey. You're dealing, I suppose, with a frontier situation shared by groups as diverse as the Spanish, the Indians, the Anglos, and of course the once great animal predators of the West—grizzly bears, timber wolves, and the like. That should hold some interesting material for me."

A student on a bike halted beside them, nodded shyly at Weyland and turned to Irv. "Can I talk to you for a few minutes, Irv? I'm having a lot of problems with the reading for your class, and I thought—"

"Ed, excuse me a minute, will you?" Irv said to the student, "Do you have some time right now? Go on over to the Union, pick up a couple of cups of coffee, and I'll join you, all right?"

"Oh, great," the boy said on a sigh of relief. "Thanks." He pedaled away.

Irv said to Weyland, "Tell you what, let me think a little about the transcripts. I'll bet there's plenty of good stuff you could use. Might take me a few days to get to it, though—I'm feeling the end-of-term crunch as it is, and now I've been invited to join the folk-sing here on the mall tomorrow night, which will screw up my schedule royally.

"It'll do me good, though, to get out, leave books and trouble home, go shake the wrinkles out of the vocal chords, get the old blood moving, you know? When you live alone as I do, you have to make yourself be social. How about you coming, too?"

Weyland looked into Irv's friendly, expectant face. Their need for approval, for each other's presence, for endless conversation, seemed to drive them almost as hard as Weyland's hunger drove him. Yet what in them was actually fed?

He expressed regret that he was otherwise engaged tomorrow evening.

"Too bad," Irv said. "But you're going to the Indian dances at the pueblo on Sunday, aren't you?" That was better. Weyland had been meaning to reconnoiter the nearby Indian villages as potential hunting areas. He said he would certainly attend the dances at this village on Sunday. "Terrific." Irv smiled. "I've got to check some details with an informant first, so I'm leaving pretty early. I'll see you up there later on.

"Oh, and here's something I wish you'd think about: I'd like you to be an informant in a new project I'm setting up on academic origins—the backgrounds of people who wind up in anthropology, people of the older ranks compared with some of the younger crew. Are you interested?"

His look, his voice, his stance all said, I am interested; I am interested in you.

Weyland resisted the pressure. "No, I'm afraid that sort of thing isn't for me. I'm a private kind of person."

"I know, and I don't mean to intrude," Irv said gently, "but give it some more thought, will you? Privacy can be a burden that people set down with enormous relief—for a little while, anyway. Besides," and suddenly he grinned his self-mocking grin, "what'll I do if the major characteristic of all the academics I want to talk to turns out to be their love of privacy? See you at the dances."

Irv headed for the Student Union with his quick, athletic stride.

At the library desk Weyland paused to pick up a book they were holding for him, a description of a New Guinean group who were supposed to be able to synthesize supplementary proteins from intestinal flora. Dietary wonders like this fascinated him, hinting at an enlightening link with his own situation.

In the Southwest Room of the library he requested some of the oral-history transcripts to see if they might really be useful to the new book. Only then, for the sake of finding shortcuts through the huge mass of Irv's material, would he invite more of the man's insistent friendliness. Weyland's new book promised some popular success. Its subjects, spectacularly diverse, ranged from Vikings to multinational corporations, and he knew that human beings loved to read about the worst

in themselves. An appeal to local readership through a
chapter on the American frontier would do Weyland no
harm here at the university.

He read reminiscences of a public hanging at which
the victim was too tall to be suspended from the only
available tree limb, so the spectators had to climb onto
his body and weigh him down to complete the job; of a
family under siege watching its horses killed, one by
one, by Indians; of a bear hunt ended abruptly, in the
bear's favor, by a flash flood. The concrete details of
these accounts produced an effect of remarkable imme-
diacy. No wonder Irv was fascinated. People must
mourn the loss of such history in the same way that
Weyland sometimes felt robbed of his own past lives.

Yet he was not at ease with these narratives. He kept
interrupting his reading to look about him at the
shelves of books, the catalog cabinets, the tree shadows
on the illuminated lawn outside. After the experience
at the opera last summer, he felt threatened by these
vivid accounts.

The madness that inflamed him that night of *Tosca*
had not struck him since, nor did he expect anything
like it again. He was settled in, accustomed to this new
part of the world and his place in it, and he took care
not to subject himself again to such intense stimulation.

Nevertheless, he was uncomfortable now with these
transcripts. Even without music and stage illusion these
distinctly personal voices, slowed and muted in print,
disturbed him; they evoked the taste and feel of the
past so strongly.

Here was an anecdote from a Spanish witch near
Mora telling how he had transformed himself into a
coyote to follow an enemy and trotted along a wagon
track in the wild dark, ears pricked to the creak of
wheels and slap of reins up ahead . . .

Weyland pushed aside the transcripts and got up. He
had other work to do in the library tonight, dry work,
safely grounded in the modern world.

*

As usual, he walked home from the university circuitously, enjoying the crisp air and the quiet of the night. The only troublesome dog in the neighborhood, a nervous Doberman, he had attended to early the previous autumn. The animal had not been replaced.

Now whose car was this, parked around the corner from his own street? He did not recall having seen the VW hatchback around here before at night, and he tried to keep track of this sort of thing. Dark blue, a scrape along the rear fender, New Jersey plate—hadn't this very car roared past his own last week on Second Street? He paused to note down the license number on an index card. A black-and-white cat trotted quickly across the street ahead of him, head down, no catch.

Albuquerque had prettier streets, tree-lined and attended by gardeners. Weyland liked this block and its relatively old and established area east of and somewhat higher than the university. He enjoyed the unobstructed view of the mountains still farther east.

His house, sublet in September for a year, was a neat frame-stucco cube dressed up with a Mediterranean-style roof of red tile, dark foundation plantings, and a back yard bounded by a fence of warped wooden palings. His immediate neighbors were a pretentious adobe-style "ranch" enclosed in a high wall, and a brick house that looked as if it had been lifted, grounds and all, out of some Connecticut suburb.

Early and clearly he had impressed his preference for solitude upon his neighbors. Only Mrs. Sayers, across the street, continued her determined pitch for him; a fresh stack of used paperbacks from her, neatly tied up with string, awaited him by his front door. He tucked them under his arm and drew out his keys.

No one had laid an unfamiliar hand on his door. No faint shine of oil from a nervous palm's pressure gleamed on the door panel, no heel-ruck rumpled the loose rug on the living-room floor. He set down the books, turned on the lamp beside the living-room couch, and moved unhurriedly through the house savoring the quiet for what it divulged: soft hum of the electric clock, occasional whish of a car passing outside, faintest whisper of music from the pianist's house one street over.

In the kitchen the refrigerator began to grind its motor as he opened the door to get ice. He kept a basic food supply for guests and for appearances' sake—peanut butter, relish, pickled artichoke hearts, an egg carton, cheese, bottles of Bitter Lemon. One of his women visitors liked Bitter Lemon—the same one who had brought him, last week, that casserole wrapped in aluminum foil and these oranges going soft in the vegetable bin. Once, in order to excuse the refrigerator's sparsely filled shelves, he had told her that he ate out a lot at McDonald's. She had begun bringing him bags full of food, with the emphasis on fruits and vegetables.

He took a glass from the dish rack, polished off the water spots with a paper towel, and ran tap water in over two ice cubes. That first interwhirl of tepid and cold currents delighted him always, and he liked the mineral flavor of the local water. The house had a functional well which he had reconnected to the plumbing. Wasting good water on the grass while drinking chemically nasty stuff from the city mains was absurd. These days palatable water was often harder to find than clean blood.

In the living room, sipping water, he flipped on the television set: blank, blank, a shrill, silly movie, an ad for hamburgers. Off. What he liked to watch was ballet and basketball. Also occasionally *The Incredible Hulk,* which he had passed up this evening for Jennifer Chadwick's colloquium.

He was not yet hungry enough to hunt. Perhaps some work—he ran his palm over the fine-grained leather of his briefcase but set the case aside and picked up instead one of the new batch of paperbacks. Good, a Ruth Rendell mystery. Fictional depictions of the

criminal mind and its law-enforcement counter-
part always entertained him. He stretched out on the
couch.

When he stopped to think about it, for all its
pressures and demands this was a very comfortable life.

The phone rang; he had dozed off, book on his chest.
He came sharply awake: "Yes?"

Silence. Then low, distressed breathing.

"Alison?" he said. "Is that you?"

"Oh hell," she choked. "I swore to myself that I
would not do this!" She hung up.

How odd, he thought, looking at the telephone, if
one night it rang and when he answered he heard Floria
Landauer's voice. Now, what had put that into his
mind?

He got his bathrobe out of the closet and went into
the study, shrugging the robe on over his shirt and
pants. The nights were still chilly, and he hated the
stuffy smell emitted by the old-fashioned floor heater.

He had equipped the front bedroom with desk, filing
cabinets, typing table, metal bookshelves whose contents overflowed in neat stacks on the floor, and a
couch on which he often slept. He turned on the light.
The neighbors were used by now to the sight of that
light burning at all hours. Mrs. Sayers had offered him a
sleep-inducing herb tea.

Thinking of Floria Landauer reminded him; seated at
the desk, he took a thin file from the lower drawer and
opened it. Back in September, upon first occupying the
house and the job and the office at the university, he
had begun a letter to her. He had produced a series of
typed paragraphs, written at ever increasing intervals
and finally abandoned altogether.

Rereading them now, he recognized that these writ-
ings were a group of reflections, similar in form to her
notes about him which she had given him to destroy.
He had done so—but he had read those notes of hers
first. The novel experience of catching glimpses
through another's eyes of himself—and at a time when

he had been uniquely open to observation—had impressed him deeply.

Dear Dr. Landauer,
[Begin with conventional pleasantry, cordiality? No; but some gesture of appreciation?]

I learned today that the department head here has a machine called a "pacemaker" in his heart. Complete replacement of the body's systems by means of new technology in order to avoid death seems to be a current human goal. If my body systems do not, when damaged, repair themselves or regenerate, I cannot have them replaced. Someday, surely, I must die.

Imagine waking from a long sleep to find people totally mechanized, myself the only "human" (i.e., mortal) left. Speak for the mechanical men: *Clank. Please don't drink my oil.* If any oil remains.

I found this poem in a story by Saki:

> "Sredni Vashtar went forth,
> His thoughts were red thoughts and his teeth were white.
> His enemies called for peace, but he brought them death.
> Sredni Vashtar the Beautiful."

No stranger myself to red thoughts, I understand this poem well; but I could never have produced it. I can map ideas in words. I cannot make art with words. Perhaps words are the wrong medium. Speech is a human invention, used to trade endless scraps of gossip, complaint, desire. I have adopted speech, I think. It is not a tool that comes naturally to me. Do I have a medium of my own?

*

I have always used words for deception and manipulation (as I believe I once remarked to you). With you, words identified truths. To this I attribute some of the intensity and fascination of the experience.

Alison, dulled and dimmed by the dreams in which she floats, is a food source to be cultivated, nothing more. She was easy to approach. She never saw me at all, but rather the fatherly part I played. They are not difficult to victimize, these blind people, though some make their way—if they are fortunate—to your office, Dr. Landauer, where you attempt to focus their vision on the world outside. No wonder you were disconcerted when I came to you, as it turned out, for inward vision.

When I told you that I remember none of my dreams, I thought I sensed a degree of skepticism or at least reserved judgment on your part. Yet it is true that the much-praised freshness and originality of my writing on dreams springs from my own personal naivete with regard to the experience of dreaming. Sometimes when I consider the remarkable activity and inventiveness of the human mind in sleep I speculate: what might I learn of myself that the silence of my own dreams keeps from me? Still, although our work together led toward this very territory, I do not now attempt to explore further by the methods you showed me; a closure of inquiry that causes me both regret and relief.

Sometimes I think that in each waking life I learn the same lessons. How could I know, since on waking I have only shadows from past lives, no details? That is, languages and skills accrue from life to life; but what else do I discover and then forget? Do I progress over and over down the same path from ignorance to knowledge? I feel that I am in the midst of such a progress now.

Having a voice implies the existence of others. One does not need a voice to speak to oneself. Except for the need to entice my prey, I could be mute.

Moreover, without the necessity of outwitting clever victims I could be—not mindless, but unthinking. Sitting in the sun as a cat sits, its mind an effortless murmur of sensory input flecked with a point of attention here, a fragmentary memory there—but primarily a limpid stream merging with the palpable environment around it.

A neighbor brings me books, this time among them some stories by Ray Bradbury. I remember Mark telling me these stories one night soon after my imprisonment began, and how his voice lost its flat, guarded tone and grew supple, rich, and happy as he spun one fantasy after another. I think the vitality of his mind saved me then as the vitality of his blood saved me later. The stories, read tonight, provoked me to reflect that in such a tale I would be explained as—a device brought from some other planet in order to take samples of human history. Extraterrestrial origin is indicated by my long life, based on a premise of self-repair and self-replacement, in contrast to the multiple lives and rapid turnover typical of indigenous life forms. I look like human beings—I can pass for one of them. I must drink their blood for sustenance; thus I cannot go off by myself and ignore their history. Preying on them insures an outlaw status that prevents me from revealing myself to them.

And so on and so on, this sort of construction is

not difficult, but why bother? What reason would extraterrestrials have for an interest in the history of human beings? The obvious importance of humanity in the universe? A far from proven point. This kind of thinking can lead to nothing of mine.

I heard Oblonsky, learning of the destruction of a local Pueblo II site by bulldozers, mutter under his breath, "Thank God, that's one less to sift through." Even with computers to help, humans shrink from the entire weight of their past. I think my own long past would crush me to death, if I could remember its details. As it is, intrusions from past lives endanger me—consider *Tosca,* an involuntary look backward, and the consequences . . .

Irv asked me last week whether I could show his students how to make a knife from flint, as he invariably fails in the attempt. I said I could not do it, either—a lie. I do not recall making a flint knife, but I know I have done so, and the skill remains in my hands. My product would be too fine.

Such dangerous materials, and he had actually forgotten about them! What was the matter with him? These pages must be destroyed. The slight mystery of the blue hatchback reminded him: he must not let the security of this life lull him into recklessness.

First, however, he turned to the typewriter and made a final entry on a fresh page.

The sex occasionally required with Alison has been little different from conversation and other forms of social falsehood that I customarily employ in the hunt for my food. All are part of the performance of my present life. Of course the whole department knows about Alison and me.

They are supposed to. Our affair is a "convincing detail." I think sometimes of you and me, how different that was. Perhaps I desired, there at last, to repossess a part of myself I had unwittingly given you. At other times I think I wanted to touch a part of you that our speaking together had revealed to me.

Some experiences one seeks only once. I do not wish to do again what we did then. I never consider flying back East and visiting, or dialing your number on the telephone from here. What I like is that we were separate, and then together, and are now separate again, and can each separately think back on that time. I like the feeling of sharing a secret. Secrecy is natural to me, comfortable, reassuring.

He reread this several times. It satisfied him. He took all the pages into the kitchen, burned them, and flushed the ashes down the disposal unit.

Back in the study, he began drafting an article he had promised *The Journal of Human Wisdom* about vocabularies used to distinguish victims from aggressors in human relationships—an article destined to become part of his book. His records of the uncompleted Cayslin dream project, though still a plentiful source of raw material and ideas, would yield him only a series of papers and not the major work on dreams he had planned. Hence the predation study, a new labor that absorbed and invigorated him. Scholarship was the best game humankind had yet invented: intricate, demanding, rich with risk and reward—akin in many ways to the hunt itself. In the present instance he took special pleasure in elucidating a territory with which he was uniquely familiar.

As he worked, his hunger grew. It would not wait for a drive out to caving country tomorrow, and he did not wish to encourage Alison by calling her back and seeing her tonight. He left after midnight to hunt.

The mountains a dozen miles from his house were dotted with overnight camping sites. Nearing the campground he had chosen, he turned off his headlights and drove off the road by starlight, easing his car over the needle-carpeted, sandy earth into a concealing stand of brush and trees. Then he put on Indian boots with one-piece, upcurving soles that left scarcely a mark, an old black sweater from the Army surplus store, and a Navy watchcap over his gray hair.

He left the car and walked down from the ridge and along a stony, willow-lined arroyo. The arroyo sand was stippled with tracks—rabbit, snake sign, small rodents, marks of people's boots and sneakers, but no dog prints. Good.

Beyond, on a broad, sloping flat, the Forest Service had put in tables, latrines, leantos, and fireplaces of rocks and cement. He could see several cars and motorcycles parked there. The darkness carried air currents smoky from banked fires.

For a little while he stood among the trees at the edge of the camping area, watching and listening. Nothing stirred. He began to make owl sounds, loud enough to bring a light sleeper awake. Sure enough, after a time someone emerged from a shelter, a woman wearing long johns and shuffling along in unlaced hiking boots. She clumped over to a two-holer in the clearing, returned shortly. A bite, but the hook had not set.

Weyland gave her time to settle back into sleep. Then he picked up a dry branch and snapped it with a loud crack. Let that go for a while (picturing the open eyes of someone awakened by that sound, someone lying wondering—noises like that punctuated the forest night all the time—slipping back into sleep despite the vague discomfort of a full bladder) and then another owl hoot. This time, in a person plucked out of the top layer of sleep, bladder pressure might prevail.

It did. A man in undershorts and thong slippers came out shivering among the trees to urinate.

Weyland ghosted up behind him, caught him expertly by the neck, lowered him unconscious to the ground, and knelt beside him on the dry and slippery pine needles to feed. Afterward he rose and went light-footed away, leaving the man to waken later, groggy and chilled, wondering perhaps what in the world had led him out here to dream strange dreams among the tall pines . . .

The following afternoon Weyland found that a cave indeed existed where he had expected to find one. He had a good instinct for caves. This one proved well suited to his purpose: too high above the ground to be an attractive den to wild animals, and deep enough to reach a place where water slid over stone. He knew he needed moisture near him when he slept, although whether he actually arose in a stupor of sleep and drank or not he did not remember. He supposed that his lungs might take from the air sufficient water for his body's reduced needs.

The general location was excellent—an inaccessible area that even on this Saturday afternoon showed no signs of human invasion. The entrance to the cave was well hidden and difficult to reach. Though a determined team attack using sophisticated mountaineering techniques would succeed, casual explorers would not be able to reach the opening even if they perceived it. Climbing to the cave mouth Weyland had used the prodigious strength of his arms and hands to traverse a nearly vertical wall, exploiting tiny bulges and cracks in the rock not as holds—they were too small—but as leverage points. A human being, with strong lower but comparatively weak upper limbs, could not do the same.

He was well pleased with his good luck. A vampire could scarcely find a place to lay his head these days, unless he settled for the treacherous tunnels of abandoned mines into which no sensible caver would set foot. On the other hand, no sensible vampire would enter there either. During spring break he had located several possible sleep sites down at Carlsbad, in the vicinity of the famous caverns. In one of the most extensive cave systems in the world, any reasonably remote section had a good chance of not being invaded by explorers for a long time to come. But Carlsbad was a five-hour drive. Having a usable site closer to home made him feel more secure.

He looked out from the cave's mouth over the brushy foothills. The space, the quiet, the absence of people, were restful; the country invited him. Pictures drifting sometimes in his mind suggested to him that he had originated in some dark northern place of black forests and lush, gray-skied plains. How different from this spare, dry country, wide as the sea under its keen blue sky, harshly marked by time as he was himself. He felt kinship with these scored hillsides, he found some reflection of his own endurance and self-sufficiency. To go to ground in this part of the world would not be uncongenial.

At his back was the cool breath of the cave. It quelled his confidence and compelled his attention. Crouched on the dusty limestone floor, he turned and looked, not out the bright opening, but into the depths.

If I wished to sleep . . . but I do not, he thought.

Long sleep was his last resort, his refuge from otherwise inevitable disaster. Such sleep held its own dangers. No creature lies down at night assured of rising again in the morning to a livable day. For himself, he reflected, the odds increasingly favored calamity: cave-in, discovery, some change bringing loss of the moisture he must have—or waking to a world too complex for his powers of adaptation, or too poisoned, or too bare of human life.

He drew the smooth coils of his climbing rope between his hands. Waking was the worst part.

He woke a living corpse from some superstitious tale

in Irv's transcripts: skin colorless and shrunken over bone, mind like a cavern with consciousness rattling about in it looking for direction. He was a ghost, a phantom, without hunger but knowing that he must feed soon or die; knowing that he had lived before though not just when or how, and that the knowledge of previous lives would be available at need—but not specific events, not discreet memories; knowing that he must not seek to stir up those memories. Nothing must distract him from the immense task of learning his way about the new world facing him.

Suddenly there blinked into his mind a sign he had seen outside a garage downtown: "Re-treads cheap." His mood lightened into grim amusement. He gathered his gear and descended to head back toward his car.

As he passed the ruins of an abandoned homestead, only the stone-and-mortar hearth standing, he saw a small herd of deer. The wind was in his face. He paused, his body instinctively adopting a hunting tension. When the deer raised their heads, he was motionless in a grove of cedars, his backpack stowed behind a stump. They drifted nearer. He chose a young one with new horns, and when they passed he sprang out.

His momentum slammed the beast down as the others fled like quicksilver. He straddled the deer, wrenching the head back so that the twisting body could not gather under him and rise or the hard, sharp hoofs kick him.

Unthinkingly, he bent to the curve of the throat where the great artery beat—then drew back from that stunned and terrified life. He had not drunk animal blood since long, long ago, before humans, growing so numerous and strong, had become his sole prey. Drinking from the deer now would make him sick.

He let go, springing clear of the flying hoofs. Panting, he lay on his back, looking up into the blue pit of the sky as the earth beneath him drummed briefly with retreating hoofbeats. He had not landed on cactus or an anthill, by good fortune, but what foolishness he had committed: wasted energy was wasted food. He didn't care. Strength needs to be used, speed needs to be used. He felt better.

As he got into his car he saw a distant glint as if of sun on glass—perhaps the flash from a pair of binoculars. Alarmed, he cruised the area for almost an hour but found only the remains of someone's picnic.

He returned home to find a note from Alison thrust under his door. She would be going up to the pueblo with Irv on Sunday and hoped to see Weyland there, maybe to talk to him privately for just a few minutes. Much to think about there, but now he needed sleep. After a shower and a drink of water, he napped on the sofa in his bathrobe.

When he woke, he found he had jammed his forehead and knees against the back rest. His body was covered with a clammy sweat. He knew that he must have been dreaming, although he never remembered his dreams. It was as well. He had surely been dreaming of starving in the cell at Roger's apartment in New York and dreading the sadistic histrionics of Alan Reese.

Extraordinary, he thought: I provide their nightmares, and they provide mine.

After he had showered again and dressed, he went into the bedroom and opened a window which gave on the back yard, the tops of other houses, and beyond them the mountains. He sat and looked out, slipping into a mode of quiet attentiveness, senses alert, mind drifting. Smoke of burning leaves, car backfire, child voices, somewhere a rackety power mower, flowers, grass, dust, a trace more moisture in the air than last night . . .

He looked at his watch. An hour had passed. Nothing jarring, nothing out of place had registered with him. Yet he felt uneasy—a holdover from the unremembered dream, or nervousness at having possibly been observed in the canyon.

He went out to talk to Mrs. Sayers, whom he found

crawling about her lawn attacking crabgrass with vicious-looking pointed tools. Asked about the blue hatchback, she said she knew nothing about it but would inquire. A neighborhood should keep on guard against prowling strangers.

Weyland thanked her for the mystery novels. He went back in and made himself settle down to read about the social lives of wolves.

That evening he hunted on the campus, avoiding the central mall with its ruckus of massed voices and twanging instruments. Irv would be there. Weyland did not want to see or be seen by him.

He was not at his best, and the hunting went badly. He did not feed until the following morning, when, driving to the pueblo, he picked up a young woman in a long cotton dress and buckled boots heading for Denver with her calico cat in her arms. As Weyland fed, the cat arched its back and hissed at him.

In the brilliant afternoon light on the village plaza a long double snake of people danced. The women wore black dresses rimmed with borders and sashes of bright red and green, and at each step their flat wooden headdresses bobbed, their necklaces of silver and turquoise swung, the pine boughs in their hands quivered. The men wore white kilts, body paint, and trimmings of feathers, bells, and fur. They held rattles that spat dry sounds as gestures were made signaling a turn. All turned, turned back again, danced.

The singers, men in bright shirts with bandanas around their temples, moved alongside, following the drummer and an old man whose eyes were tiny squint-holes in his withered face—were perhaps even sightless. His knotted brown hands swooped toward the sky as he chanted.

At the ends of the lines children stumped along, dressed as the adults were. One of the dance marshals paused to kneel and retie a child's belt.

Alison murmured something, addressing Irv, but her

eyes glanced in Weyland's direction and away again. She had obviously been trying to nerve herself up for the private talk she had mentioned in her note. Knowing that she would not speak intimately with him unless they were alone, Weyland had made sure he stayed at Irv's elbow.

Unfortunately, Irv was standing in the sun. Weyland tugged down against the glare the brim of the old, battered, but still silky Panama hat he had found while hunting in a Goodwill store. He was tall enough to see over the crowd without effort. It didn't matter. He was bored. One group of dancers left, another arrived and danced what appeared to be the same dance to the same or a very similar chant. The dancing style was insistent, unvarying, and unindividual. One did what one's line of dancers did.

Weyland had already dismissed the village as a possible hunting ground. Anglos were far too obtrusive here, even on dance days. Today Indians, tourists, and a scattering of nuns stood around the walls of the low adobe buildings edging the plaza. Everywhere dogs slept, sniffed, or squabbled.

Irv seemed immersed in contemplation of the dance. Nearby a young Indian told an Anglo couple about having floated beneath polar ice while in the submarine service. Alison cleared her throat but did not speak. Weyland thought about leaving.

Alison said, "Give me the car keys, Irv, would you? I've got a headache. I'll go nap in the back seat for a while."

"You're not feeling well?" Irv emerged from his thoughts. "We've finished our business here, there's no reason we have to stay longer."

"No, you stay and watch. I just want to close my eyes." Alison looked at Weyland. He did not offer to accompany her to the parking lot. She left.

Irv said, "She was terrific this morning, so enthusiastic. I didn't realize she wasn't feeling well."

This time Weyland sensed that Irv would not accept

less than a confession from him. "She's sensitive," he said. "I'm afraid I haven't treated her as considerately as I might have, and right now we're at a difficult stage of our . . . our . . ." He trailed off, avoiding Irv's eyes.

Irv sighed. "Come on, let's stretch our legs a little. I'm awfully glad you said that. I have to admit that for a while I thought you were using your position to, well, take advantage. Female graduate students are so vulnerable to us. I'm glad your real feelings are involved, even though right now they must give you both a lot of pain."

Weyland said, "She's been a comfort to me in a new place, and I've meant . . . something to her, I trust." How Irv longs to hear honest love, or anguished compulsion, he thought; anything other than simple exploitation.

"I meant to ask sooner," Irv said, "but I've had so much on my mind—if there's anything I can do to help . . ."

Weyland shook his head. "Not for me, but if you can get Alison to talk to you . . ." Which was, of course, already happening. Irv had only to be there, to be his usual warm, welcoming self, and Alison would find it easier than she imagined to abandon Dr. Edward Lewis Weyland permanently.

But Irv was not his usual self. He kicked at stones as he walked, and now there was a tense, dark look on his face. He said, "I need to do some talking myself, Ed. Something happened that's eating me alive."

What's this? Weyland wondered. Am I about to receive some great, unwanted dump load of Irv's personal pain? No—the outward focusing so characteristic of the man was turned off, the light seemed gone from his face. He looked as blind as the old Indian singer on the plaza. The silence stretched, filled by the throbbing of the drum on the other side of the thick-walled church beside which they walked. What's the trouble? Weyland thought. But he wanted so firmly not to know the answer that he could not bring himself to ask the question.

They rounded the corner of the church, and two women, just out of the gate of the tiny graveyard, stepped into their path. "Irv!" they said. "What a surprise. How nice to see you." .

Irv made subdued introductions. "Dorothea Winslow, Letty Burns, meet my colleague Ed Weyland from the university. You two are a long way from Taos today."

The tall woman with the solemn face nodded so that the shadow of her wide hat dipped. She wore a home made-looking dress of moss-green cotton and a pink cardigan slung from her shoulders. Her shorter companion, Winslow, looked with a faint frown from one man to the other.

Weyland had heard that name before. There was money connected with it. One of the talents for which he had been hired was that of cultivating funding sources for the department. This visit to the pueblo, so far uncomfortably fraught with others' emotions, might be turned to good use after all. He bowed slightly, European style, over Dorothea Winslow's hand.

"Good to meet you, Professor," she said. "I heard your lecture in January on space and landscape in dreams." They traded gossip about university people Dorothea knew. Letty Burns talked to Irv about Chicago, where he had gone to school. She had just spent some time in that city.

Suddenly Dorothea, whose troubled look had deepened, turned and said, "While you two hash over Chicago, Dr. Weyland and I are going to have an intellectual discussion." She touched Weyland's sleeve lightly and led him ahead of the others, saying in a low, tense voice, "What's the matter with Irv?"

"Irv?" he repeated, startled. "Why, nothing."

"No. Something." She walked a little away from him, looking at him sharply. "Something."

He studied her. She was compact, sunburned, her

fox-narrow face framed in flying wisps of white hair that had escaped from her bun. She wore sandals, faded corduroy slacks, a buff shirt of doeskin, and a strand of red coral across her weathered throat. He guessed that she was about sixty.

"Irv has been worried lately," he offered reluctantly. "Do you know of some particular problem . . . ?"

She shook her head. "Nothing I'd care to talk about," she said. She moved nearer to him again as they reached the foot of the slope down from the churchyard and turned along the dirt road leading behind the plaza. The drum still sounded. For some moments they walked without speaking.

Then she said, "Even this far from the plaza you can feel the drumbeat drive right up out of the ground through your soles, can't you—the beat of a communal heart. It doesn't beat for you, does it, Professor?"

"No more than for any non-Indian," he returned steadily. Nothing to worry about in her remark, surely.

"You are not 'any non-Indian,'" she said. "If I were still painting, I'd paint you."

"You were a painter?" he said. Up ahead the blades of a windmill turned against the sky. He watched the windmill, wishing they were sitting and talking instead of walking so that he could look more easily into her face. "Why did you give it up?"

"To try something else: drawing with my eye, following the contours and outlines of the subject millimeter by millimeter, skipping nothing. When you've done that, the subject is fixed in your memory in a way that just doesn't happen when you transfer a mental image to paper or canvas."

He did not know what to answer. His mind cast back to the sketches Floria Landauer had made of him.

Dorothea said, "Why did you come out here, Professor?"

"I'd been ill in the East. I wanted a change."

"I came twenty-two years ago to paint, if you please, the mystery of the desert."

"And did you?"

"Hardly," she laughed. At the windmill they turned onto a tarmac road. "But painting led to looking, and that's led to—paying attention. I've paid attention to you, Dr. Weyland. In the lecture hall in January I tried to draw you with my eye, but I saw that you do not draw. You have a stylized, streamlined quality, as if you were already a drawing rather than a man."

Weyland looked back. Irv and Letty had stopped at the end of the unpaved road and were squatting by the windmill, doodling with sticks in the dirt as they talked.

He felt betrayed by chance in broad daylight. How did this woman walking the blacktop at his side see him so well? His mind raced. He said, "The range of variations in the human form must be wider than you thought."

"Apparently." She flashed him a look of ironical approval. "The range of variations in the human form —that must be the explanation. But then, suppose it isn't? I like a world with wonders in it. Mind you, just because you've noticed something doesn't mean it's yours to meddle with." She stopped and looked back at Irv and Letty Burns. "I wouldn't say anything to you now, except it rocked me, almost walking into Irv by the church, seeing all that hurt in his face—and there you were with him.

"But his trouble has nothing to do with you, does it? You're not a part of that. You're just made on a different mold."

"I beg your pardon," he said stiffly. "I don't quite understand . . ."

"Something's wrong, all right," she said. "I'll have to get him to talk about it." She walked back toward the others. He followed a few paces behind her.

". . . the last I heard," Irv was saying wearily, settled on his haunches with lowered head. Letty stood up, arms crossed, looking past Dorothea at Weyland.

"You have family here, Professor?" she said.

Dorothea said mildly, "Leave the professor his secrets, Letty. Everyone's entitled to their secrets."

The drumming had stopped. Dancers, jingling and rattling in costume, could be seen trooping out of the plaza. Irv said that the dancing would start again after a break, but that he for one had seen enough dancing for today. Weyland swiftly echoed this, and they all walked toward the broad dirt lot in which visitors' cars were parked.

What more would Dorothea say to Weyland, or of Weyland to the others? Possibly nothing. Possibly he had misunderstood, misread her, thrown off by these people's strong feelings about each other. His best course, he knew—his only course—was patience.

Art. They spoke of art and of the dancing as an art form. Repetitious, Letty said, from set to set, from year to year even. No, Dorothea said; each season's dance was a unique part of expressing over and over certain basic themes to insure continuity and regeneration. These themes could never be mined out, she said, they were so rich and full of power.

Then they were in the parking lot. Seeing Alison step out of Irv's car to meet them, Weyland thought, that at least has worked out as I hoped. She and I have had no quiet moments alone—of which somehow there have been more than enough today with other people.

Introductions were made; they lingered at the car, talking, talking. Irv described an oral-history tape made that morning with an old woman of the pueblo. Suddenly Dorothea put her hand on his arm and said in the middle of his sentence, "Irv, I have a terrific idea. Come home with us tonight. We haven't had a chance to just sit and gab away an evening in a long time. Bring Alison. You can show her the famous Libyan explorers' message on the rock in the arroyo." Her chuckling voice said this was a joke. Her face looked anxious.

"Thea, thanks, but the end of the term's coming. I've got everything to do that I've managed to put off until now."

"Forget all that," Dorothea said. "You need a break, even just overnight. Come back with us."

Letty said, "You do look beat, Irv. Come on, cut loose for a little."

Alison looked at Weyland. She said, "I ought to ride back to Albuquerque with you, Dr. Weyland. We still need to discuss those exam questions." Single-minded Alison, he thought darkly, closing in for a private talk he had been avoiding all day. What overbearing arrogance they had about the importance of their cursed feelings!

Irv put his hand over Dorothea's and said, "Honestly, I can't. I'm expecting a phone call at home tonight or maybe tomorrow night. It's important. Suppose I come up in a few weeks."

Dorothea said, "We're not going to wait that long. I'll be in touch." She held his hands and gave him a peck on the cheek. For Alison she had a brief, abstracted goodbye; for Weyland, a searching look and then a nod, a gesture of what he felt to be simultaneous acknowledgment and dismissal. She walked away kicking quick spurts of dust from under her sandals, Letty stalking alongside.

Alison did not press the suggestion of riding back with Weyland. Having made her bid, she had apparently lost her nerve again. She ducked into the passenger seat of Irv's car.

Leaning against the fender, his forehead furrowed above his dark, frank eyes in his usual expression of hopeful concern, Irv said, "Would you rather Alison went back with you?"

"She lives closer to you." Weyland was watching the two women's figures receding toward the far corner of the parking lot.

The anthro building still stank the next morning. There had been rain showers during the night. Weyland knew his windows would be swollen tight, assuming he could get inside to try to move them. For some reason his key would not turn in the lock of his office door.

He had been up all night listening to the rain and thinking: Had he been exposed? Had he somehow escaped exposure? What exactly did Dorothea know or suspect? Near dawn he had hunted, without finesse, in a motel he knew of that had particularly flimsy door latches. His first victim's blood had been spoiled with barbiturates, so he had run the risk of approaching another.

Driving to the office in a light rain, he had nearly run out of fuel and had yet again been outraged by the astronomical price of gas. At times like these he speculated gloomily that on his next waking he might well find the world reduced to muscle, wind, and water power, if not actually to postnuclear devastation. He was no longer sure that he had achieved the prime requirement of a successfully specialized predator: choice of an equally successful prey. He chafed at the thought of his own existence dependent on the feeble and undisciplined will of humankind.

If he didn't hold on to his temper, he would snap the damned shank of the damned key off in his damned office lock. Who had been tampering here, jamming the mechanism like this?

Alison came out of Irv's room across the hall. "Oh, Dr. Weyland, come in and join us. I've been cheering Irv up. I have those questions for you."

He pocketed his keys and went to sit in the overstuffed chair in the corner of Irv's office. Irv was at his desk, bowed forward on his elbows over a steaming Styrofoam cup. He seemed extraordinarily glum, for Irv. He said, "This isn't coffee, it's what drains out of the lab sinks downstairs."

Alison said, "The trouble with living in the sunny Southwest is that a little rainy weather throws everybody into despair."

Weyland scanned the page of questions she handed him. "These are good, except that I don't want two questions on social roles in subsistence-economy cultures. I realize that this was the topic of the lectures you gave the class, but too much emphasis on it in the exam will bring the students marching on my office—with justification."

Alison blushed. "Oh, sure, of course, I'll make up a replacement for one of those. We've been talking about my joining Irv's summer project. I can't hold out any longer, not after watching him yesterday morning with that lovely old woman at the pueblo. If I could get to be that easy and good with people doing work like his . . ."

Weyland said, "This is excellent news." Had she spent the night with Irv? Weyland hoped so. His temper was restored. He felt ready now to ask about the two women from Taos, but not in Alison's presence. "I don't like to interrupt, but I think you have office hours now, Alison?"

"Oh, yes—a couple of students are coming in for notes on lectures they missed. I'd better go. Lunch, Irv?"

"We'll see," Irv said. His eyes were sad and kind.

"You look tired," Weyland said when Alison had gone.

"So do you," Irv replied with a wan grin. "Anybody'd think we were dancing all day at the pueblo yesterday, not watching." He hesitated. "Alison . . ."

Weyland said, "Alison looks happier than she has in weeks. I'd like to ask you about Dorothea Winslow. I thought her very . . . intriguing."

"Ah, Dorothea. I'm glad you had a chance to talk with her. People will tell you that Dorothea Winslow is birdsy," Irv said fondly. "And they'll give you evidence to prove it. For instance, she once badgered the department into sending somebody out to her place up near Taos to look at a rock inscription that she thought might be in an ancient script—a sign of pre-Columbian contact, that sort of thing. Those fringe theories fascinate her. People don't notice, though, that while she'll pepper you with wild questions out of wide-open curiosity, she's damned rigorous about what she'll accept from you as a satisfactory answer."

"And how do you come to know her?"

Irv grinned. "I was the one the department sent."

"You didn't find her . . . 'birdsy'?"

"I found myself with two new friends," Irv said. "Those women are a remarkable pair. They've lived in Taos together for about fourteen years in an old museum of a place: fortress walls, carved beams, hulking Spanish furniture which Dorothea hates but keeps. She says it came with the place, so what the hell."

"Fourteen years," Weyland mused. "I can't imagine tolerating anyone's company for so long."

"No?" Irv looked sad again. He seemed to rouse himself to continue. "Dorothea was a painter—a good one—and Letty is a published poet. They're part of the established art community up there." He paused to wash down some pills with the remains of his coffee. "And then, they're just what you're thinking, of course, they wouldn't dream of pretending otherwise."

Weyland realized that he meant the two women were lovers. Whether a person slept with partners of one sex or the other was one of those distinctions humans invented and then treated as a tablet of the law. In this case, his own purposes were served. These women lived too eccentric a life to threaten him, no matter what they might know or guess about his own—eccentricities.

"Mind you," Irv added, "they don't cling. Letty gets itchy sometimes. She ups and goes, walking all over the country, hitchhiking. She writes cookbooks when she's home, good ones. I think when she needs cash on the road she takes jobs in restaurants."

Weyland was frantically searching his memory for any trace of that angular figure stepping into his car. Finding none, he breathed again.

Wistfully Irv said, "I wouldn't mind being able to

just get up and go when things start closing in." He leaned forward again, his blue-shadowed jaw propped in his palms. "But it's not my style. The few people I've known who could melt away and leave everything were like Letty—long, lean, always a little detached some- how, your quintessential drifters; rootless, inturned, melancholy, aloof, often brilliant but seldom happy, I think. Whatever 'happy' is—"

Suddenly he flushed a deep crimson right to the roots of his hair. "My God, Ed, I'm sorry. Of course I've heard something about your . . . your trouble back East, we all have. I wouldn't for the world want you to think that I—that—"

"That you feel sorry for me?" Weyland said, com- posed again. He was pleased with Irv's word picture of the sort of person whom he indeed attempted to embody, more pleased still that Irv found him convinc- ing enough to be classed in Letty's tribe of wan- derers.

"Irv," he said, "I'm not sensitive about that episode, or about my less than sociable nature. Don't apologize, you haven't hurt my feelings. Let me reply in these terms: Letty seemed to me, admittedly on the briefest of acquaintance, to be quite at ease, not melancholy, not aloof."

Irv studied him for several moments, the color receding from his face. He got up and paced the office, hands shoved deep into his pockets. "That's because, for one thing, Letty's an artist as well as a drifter. She makes art of what she sees out on the margins of society. If you can do that, you're not so horrendously isolated and cooped up in yourself. Letty's poetry is lone and cold enough to freeze the tears in your eyes, but it's addressed outward, it connects.

"And Letty always comes back home. She's lucky enough to have Dorothea, a human lifeline. Everyone needs a lifeline, drifters most of all."

"Why?" said Weyland, his interest thoroughly en- gaged. "They may simply be chilly souls who choose solitude and distance out of a preference for their own company."

"I don't think anyone chooses that kind of life," Irv said. "I think they're driven to it. We're social animals, Ed. It's too cold and lonesome for us out beyond the edges of the human herd."

Not for a lynx, Weyland thought; that is his place. He said, "What you began with was your own style. You speak as a man of the center, a warm man who thrives on close companionship. I think this distorts and darkens your viewpoint of life out here where I sit—or drift." He held up his hand to forestall Irv's demur. "A drifter's life doesn't seem nearly as bleak to me as it does to you from deep in the, ah, heart of the herd."

Irv stood at his desk, head lowered, jingling the change in his pocket. Finally he slung himself into his chair, stretching his arms above his head. "You're a remarkable man; and you're probably right. There's an element of sour grapes in my attitude, too, I think.

"The thing is, Ed, I've worked myself so deep into the herd that I wouldn't know how to move out again, even if some kind of wandering away alone was the healthiest thing I could do. Other people are just too important to me—friends, colleagues, students, especially students. They're some of my links with the future, I'm one of their links with the past. Connections like that make me know I'm alive, make me know how my life fits in with other lives.

"If you really don't need that kind of contact, I guess I envy you. The emotional heat in the herd can burn you up, and when I feel myself getting blistered, I can't just cut and run. I'm afraid I'd lose my place in the center—"

The door opened and a student looked in. Irv glanced at the wall clock and jumped up. "Can you come back after lunch?" he called to the student, who said yes and withdrew. "Damn! I have a committee meeting in two minutes. Listen, Ed, please come talk again. We still have those transcripts to go over, and I won't drop any more gloom on you, I promise. Dorothea phoned to say she's stopping by today before heading home to Taos. She's a tonic for my self-pitying moods."

Late that afternoon walking back toward the office after a seminar session in the Fine Arts Library, Weyland recognized Irv and Dorothea down by the duck pond. He paused by a dark pine grove to watch.

They walked slowly along the edge of the water below, clearly deep in discussion. Irv had opened his collar and rolled up his sleeves. He kept reaching one hand up to smooth back his thinning hair. Dorothea, in jeans and a knitted poncho, stayed close to him. Now and then she touched him, tapping home her words. They walked past the gliding, honking ducks and the young people crossing the fresh, long-shadowed grass. Irv sat down on a bench near the water. Bent over, elbows on thighs, hands dangling between his knees, he talked; Weyland could tell by the way Dorothea held her head cocked slightly, gazing out across the water. She put her hand down on Irv's slumped shoulder. They stayed that way a while, and once Irv lowered his head and rubbed at his face with both hands. Perhaps he was weeping.

There was no one else in the park now. They got up. Irv, glancing in Weyland's direction, said something that made Dorothea look also. Both their faces were turned toward Weyland. He thought they would come over the grass to him, and he considered moving on first. But Dorothea took Irv walking again, away from the pond, talking still, out of sight.

Feeling oddly empty but not hungry enough to hunt, Weyland drove home to do some work.

Returning on foot at a late hour, he approached the anthro building over the grass, keeping to the shadows. Judging by the undisturbed condition of his desk and the jammed lock on his office door this morning, whoever had attempted entry there had failed. Perhaps they would try again tonight. He was not averse to the idea of prey coming here to him.

But why was Irv's old Pontiac still in the parking lot, the only car? The library was closed, so he couldn't be working over there. His window was not lit.

Weyland let himself into the building, intending to wait in his own office for whoever might come. Across the hallway, the door was open to Irv's dark room. On impulse, Weyland entered.

His eyes adjusted at once to the darkness and the glow from the corridor. Irv was sitting with his swivel chair turned away from the desk so that he leaned on the sill of the open window, his head down on his folded arms. He made no sound of breathing. Weyland approached, leaned nearer, closer than he would ever have come to the man in life unless for blood. Irv's outreaching energy, which Weyland had felt as intrusive pressure, no longer held him off.

He looked into Irv's face. The face was vacant, eyes shut, mouth loose, cheeks slack and sunken.

In the wastebasket among the crumpled plastic cups was a small medicine bottle. Weyland did not touch it. He could see that the label had been scraped off. Irv had made sure that no one, coming upon him too soon, could telephone the Poison Control Center for an antidote, and he had sat dying in the dark to avoid so late a light attracting the campus police.

Weyland stood over him, hands in pockets to keep from inadvertently touching anything. On the blotter lay a stack of evaluation forms under a typed note that ran: "There will be no final exam in Ethnography 206. These evaluations are based on each student's entire output of class work, tests, and assignments so far during the term."

Beside this pile was a yellow legal pad. Weyland's name was written across the top of the first page in Irv's quick, strong script, followed by two sentences: "Try starting with these—the asterisks indicate materials on Indians and Spanish raiding each other for slaves. Hope

this points in the direction of what you're looking for."
Then came a column of some fifteen numbers, identifying transcripts in the oral-history series, and his signature. Below this, Irv had added a single line: "I am very tired of being strong."

Weyland sat down in the corner chair. He looked across the room at Irv's motionless torso in the rectangle of the window frame. Here was Irv at his last resort, despite his students' needs, despite Alison's cheer, despite Dorothea. Each little life had disasters in corresponding scale waiting to erupt from its secret depths.

No deep wisdom was required for Weyland to guess that Irv was dead as a consequence of his intensely emotional life at the center of the herd. He had died true to the logic of his nature, pressed past bearing by the strength of his own feelings—though what the feelings had been about might never be known. Was it what they called a "broken heart?" In any case, this life and death seemed proper for Irv and the very archetype of the brief, incandescent human span.

My inept picklock may arrive, Weyland thought, and if he finds me here I'll be mired in endless complications and explanations.

Yet he sat looking at Irv's corpse, and he put a riddle in his mind to the dead man: Now that you do not seek after me, why do I stay for you?

A fly buzzed in the room. Weyland left.

In the anthro parking lot next day he recognized the tall woman sitting in the pickup truck as Letty, so he was not entirely surprised to find Dorothea Winslow waiting for him at his office.

"Miss Winslow, may I—"

"I want to talk to you," she said. She entered behind him and left the door wide open.

He said, "May I express my sympathy—I know Irv was a close friend of yours."

"But not of yours?" She stood across the room from him.

"We were colleagues, little more."

"People say you two sometimes walked to work together."

"Yes, sometimes," he said.

"He talked to you."

Weyland was tired. Class today had proven more strenuous than he had foreseen. This on top of a harrowing session of questions with the police in the morning had worn his temper thin. He said irritably, "He talked to everyone."

"He must have said something to you," she persisted.

"You mean about killing himself? If he had, I would naturally have taken some action, Miss Winslow—I'd have telephoned you, for instance." He wanted to sit, but the woman had so clearly gathered herself for confrontation that he felt more secure facing her on his feet. Why was she angry with him? "Irv and I had a professional relationship, amiable but not close. He had, as you know, many good friends, many demands on his personal time, and I am myself a busy man."

She pointed out the open doorway. "His office is right there, right across the hall. You saw him every day, he saw you."

He set down the books he was carrying and spread his hands on the surface of the desk, bracing himself across from her. "Miss Winslow, what do you want?"

"I want to know why it happened, how he came to do such a desperate thing."

He shook his head. "We had no intimate conversation. If he confided in anyone, it was in people like yourself, people he was fond of."

She turned away from him slightly, her hot gaze fixed on empty space. "To people like me, he said that he had some bad trouble but that it would pass, he would handle it, he had the problem under some kind of control." Again the flashing glare at him, this time from reddened eyes. "He was used to us coming to him for comfort and encouragement, not the other way around. He turned to you."

"No," he said. She blames me, he thought, because she thinks Irv said something that should have warned me of what he intended. He wished she would go away.

"Damn it," she said with open rage and pain, "he wrote his suicide note to you! Nothing to anyone else, not a word, not a call, except to you. That line about being strong—I saw it, the police showed me the note when they talked to me."

He thought, She's jealous. "Please, Miss Winslow— sit down, listen to me. I can't help you. If you saw the note, you know that it was actually about business, some source materials we'd been discussing. The rest—I don't know why he added that sentence."

"He added it because he had warm feelings for you," she said. "He turned to you for the support one man should be able to give another. But you're not a man, and you gave nothing. You were no goddamn good to him."

The hallway was empty. He could stride over and slam the door shut, and then—

No, not her death on top of another death, and with her friend waiting for her outside! Ignore what she said. Keep calm. Give her something, divert her, placate her. He said, "Irv did make overtures of friendship to me. I'm afraid I wasn't very responsive. He told me no secrets, I assure you."

"You wouldn't know if he had," she retorted. "But I might, if I knew what he said to you. Tell me about your last conversation with him. Tell me what he said."

She would not be fobbed off with a two-sentence summary, repeated in endless variations, as the police had been. Irv standing with lowered head, furrowed brow, lower lip thrust out as he thought, came clearly to mind, but his words were gone, hidden in a blank mental silence. Weyland felt threatened, somehow, by his own inability to remember.

"So many questions have already been asked," he said. "I'm worn out with questions, Miss Winslow, my powers of recall are exhausted. The man is dead. What good—"

"Tell me!"

He straightened up. "This is very painful and quite useless. I must ask you to leave now. Perhaps another time, when the shock has diminished—"

"Ye gods," she said, "and he left you his last message!"

She was gone. He sank into his seat and leaned back, shutting his eyes. He could feel a vein jumping hectically in his temple. A feeling of defeat overcame him. He had fumbled the challenge, he had lost.

Dorothea was maddened by loss. Eventually her sight would clear again, but in the meantime her hostility might draw other attention to him—that of the authorities, of Irv's friends, relatives, colleagues, who could tell, even enemies, agents of whatever calamity Irv himself had fled. Irv's note had ensnared Weyland, and Dorothea, flailing about for a remedy for her own suffering, would undoubtedly embroil him more deeply still.

He could not afford the lightest scrutiny or inquiry into his own life. No spotlight, not even the outer edge of one meant to illuminate Irv's death, must fall on him. Therefore, he must not be found where such light would fall.

When he left the building the pickup truck was still there. Dorothea was sitting on the lawn. Letty knelt behind her, kneading her friend's neck and shoulders. They were facing away from Weyland. He slipped around the corner of the building.

He never liked to drive up to his own garage, observable by any lurking watcher. He preferred always to park at a comfortable distance and walk home, alert to unusual signs which he would not notice from behind the wheel.

Tonight he stopped the car in a deep pool of shadow under a sycamore three blocks from home. Turning off lights and motor, he sat a while with the windows open looking out on the night. The car was a decent machine —a Volvo sedan he had bought secondhand—though nothing like the beautiful Mercedes lost to him in the East. This one he could give up with much milder regrets, and give it up he must, along with the rest of the identity of Edward Lewis Weyland—he had made up his mind to it.

He reflected on the sour humor in the situation: at last that other woman, Katje de Groot the huntress whom he had so disastrously hunted at Cayslin College, was to have her way. Weyland would die. What a pity, to discard the pleasures and perquisites of a well-paid and respected career, the rewards of demanding work well done. The book on predation would never be finished now. That career was ended.

The first steps were taken. His errands this afternoon —laundry, groceries, and shoemaker—had enabled him to break the several large bills he kept by him into traveling money of smaller denominations. Yet he found himself oddly reluctant to go home and begin his final evening as Weyland.

The trouble was that an identity so well tailored as this one induced an inevitable reluctance to cast it aside. The fit was too perfect: the irascible, hard-working, brilliant scholar had expressed too many aspects of his real nature.

However, Dorothea had left him no real choice. She had seen through Dr. Weyland with her art-beyond-art, and her knowledge coupled with her lacerated feelings over Irv's death made her dangerous.

Fortunately, he was not without resources. He was in his own way an artist, a practitioner of the art of self-invention. Dorothea had seen him as the stylized performance of a man, and she had seen well. He would now set about redrawing himself as someone else, and he took wry pleasure in the thought that he could borrow his new role from Dorothea's friend—from Letty.

He had thought it all out during this afternoon of errands. If Letty could hit the road, so could he. He would be for a while, literally as well as metaphorically, one of Irv's taciturn drifters, someone who casually turns up cleaning out a dairy barn, digging sewer lines, working a loading dock, or sweeping a warehouse floor for his keep. He's heading for Seattle to see the Space Needle, this quiet, undemanding fellow with no attachments except to his battered old Panama hat. The sort who keeps to himself, perhaps he hints at a family deserted because of unnamable pressures. That would account for his avoidance of all forms of red tape and official questions. Maybe he has abandoned some career too commonplace to provoke curiosity: bookkeeping, something like that. A name—a fitting name would occur to him.

In a way he looked forward to this rougher life—too few baths, too much weather, too little money—because he knew that in such hard country he could hold his own. He was far stronger than the human beings whom its rigors often destroyed. And meanwhile all the impossible complications accreted around the person known as Weyland would be left behind.

From the vantage point of the center, Irv had spoken only half the truth. Art can be used to separate as well as connect.

A couple came out of the house down the street and drove away. Watching their taillights vanish, he felt his hunger push into the foreground of his consciousness. He would have to attend to that before long. When the street was silent again, he got out, locked his car, and walked homeward.

He saw the blue hatchback parked in the dirt alley that ran behind his house. The New Jersey plate was familiar. He had seen a similar vehicle somewhere in the parking lot at the pueblo on Sunday, he realized, but he had been too rattled by the encounter with Dorothea to attend to what his eyes had told him.

Now, flooded with the memory of lying caged and wounded in a tiny cell at the mercy of probing, hurtful hands and a vicious heart, he knew that Alan Reese had come after him at last.

He had risked precisely this danger by relocating West—and under the same name—instead of vanishing in New York into his chosen bolt hole there, a disused loop of subway tunnel. He had hoped Reese would be put off pursuit by the near-death of Roger, perhaps impeded by related entanglements with the authorities. The gamble was lost. Irv was not the only one with deadly secrets in his life.

The urge to flight fluttered in the pit of his stomach. He had money in his pocket, he could go now. He stood where he was, thinking, I will not flee in ignorance, in panic, I will not be harried like a fox before hounds.

He set down his briefcase under a privet hedge and, silently entering the alley, made his way to his own back yard. Searching outside the house, listening, studying the shadows, he found no trace of watchers. Someone was inside: the living-room blinds had been let all the way down. He stepped up onto the looped metal handle of the sprinkler system and leaned his head against the cool window glass.

After a little, someone moved in there, a shift of weight, a soft clearing of the throat. Only one, he thought.

He stood across the street again, invisible against the black mass of Mrs. Sayers's big spruce tree, looking at his own house and thinking, So, here is disaster, a mistake grown from other mistakes. What to do? Not talk, not think, none of their ways. Let go of reason, trust to buried memory. If he could release his grip on his human surface and sink back into the deeper, darker being at his core, his root-self . . . this was not so simple as in simpler times. He suffered a frightful moment of imbalance and disorientation. Then something hot and raw began coiling in his body.

I am strong, I am already bent on departure, and I am hungry; why should I not hunt the hunter in my own house tonight? He walked up the flagstone path to his front door.

As soon as the latch clicked behind him, a lamp flashed on. He flung up one arm to shield his eyes, pretending to be far more dazzled than he actually was.

"Stand still, listen to me!" Reese hissed. He half sat, half crouched in the wing chair in the corner, his thick torso tensed over the weapon he held braced in the crook of his beefy arm—an automatic rifle with a skeletal stock. The muzzle was trained on Weyland's chest.

With a shock Weyland remembered the tearing pain of the two little bullets from Katje de Groot's pistol.

Reese talked. From Weyland's entrance, he had not stopped talking. ". . . Of course I had a more civilized beginning in mind. I wanted to leave in your office an invitation to a more formal meeting than this, but I couldn't get in." His voice took on breath, deepened, slowed to an almost hypnotic smoothness. ". . . realizing that my previous approach was inadequate . . ."

An apology? More like a preamble to a new proposal, a kind of partnership . . . voluntary support network . . . steady blood supply . . . Church of Blood . . . carefully scripted and rehearsed ceremonies . . . nationwide organization . . . He used the word "worship," the word "devotee," the word "cult." An old tale, and to Weyland's unspecific but educated memory a transparent one. First they serve, then control, then destroy and replace you. Whether they label it religion or domestication, the process is the same.

Reese's tone smacked of oily self-congratulation. "Now this fellow you've been spending so much time with has killed himself and forced my hand—because he's forced yours. I am right, aren't I, in assuming that your flurry of activity today was set off by his death?

"An inquiry will be held, no doubt. What are you afraid they'll find out? Do you really think anybody will notice a little puncture wound on the dead man's neck?"

Weyland stared at him. This creature, fatuously ignoring the factor of departmental propinquity, had leaped to the conclusion that Irv had served as one of Weyland's sources of nourishment.

"Oh yes, you may well stand dumbstruck, vampire. I've been watching you. I was behind you most of the way today. It occurred to me that you might decide to discreetly remove yourself from the reach of any awkward questions, maybe even withdraw for a long sleep. I don't know how many other hiding places you've checked out besides the cave you went to on Saturday. I thought I'd better get in touch right away, while I still knew where to find you."

Softly Reese added, "You'd better believe that I'm both serious and formidable. I'd already made extensive preparations for this conversation." He tapped his jeans pocket.

"For example, I have here the letter that Katje de Groot left for the Cayslin College administration when she went back to Africa last winter. As for poor Roger, after he got home from the hospital the neighbors tried to get him put away because he was acting strange, but his family fixed things up. He's living with friends in Boston, more or less his old life, trying to write a book. We both know what it's about, but whether it ever gets published is up to you.

"Mark ran away after I talked to him outside school one day, and nobody has been able to find him. But the therapist, Landauer, is back in the city. A lieutenant of mine is keeping an eye on her for me. In fact, I have all these people under surveillance except for Mark, and he'll turn up.

"The point is, if you cooperate I can find ways to insure that they're no threat to you."

Rage took Weyland all in a rush. Spasms of his jaw

muscles shot pain into his temples, and the vision of his flaring pupils blurrèd. Reese saw or sensed this, for his voice turned harsh: "And if I have to cut you down right here, their testimony along with an autopsy will make a hero out of me."

"*I* can find ways," "If *I* have to cut you down . . .."; not "my men," "my followers." Weyland's mind cleared. Here is Reese cracking the whip to drive the tiger into its cage, but where is his audience? The man is a sadist and an exhibitionist; why has he come to me unattended?

Reese settled back slightly in his chair. "If you'd prefer the kind of partnership I mentioned, let me clarify the nature of the relationship I propose. Partnership implies trust. But you could say yes at gunpoint and then as soon as your partner's back was turned slip away and sleep for fifty years. I could end up spending my life looking for you.

"I don't think you realize just how fortunate you are. I'm sure you've lived through ages in which a man who didn't trust you would have no choice but to put out your eyes or cut your hamstrings to insure your obedience. However, in these more squeamish and ingenious times . . ." He took from his pocket a stoppered vial of fluid. "Thorazine. They use it at the State Mental Hospitals to keep the crazies docile. Tonight you take the first of many merry doses."

Weyland watched him set the glittering glass tube on the lamp table, and he felt Reese watching him in turn with those small, cold eyes like needles.

"You're sweating, vampire. Don't you like your good luck? At best this stuff will make you into a willing zombie who doesn't care what happens, and I won't have to experiment with other, stronger drugs. At worst, the Thorazine could react with your special chemistry and burn your brains out.

"Either way, I win. It's a funny thing about cults—sometimes they flourish better after their god is dead. Look at Christianity! A lot can be done with testa-

ments, spirit communications, physical relics—the
death of the deity gives the High Priest a free hand.
And there's no more risk of setting up a ceremony with
people coming from all over at great personal inconve-
nience and then finding that the star attraction has run
away." He twisted his fist around the gun barrel as if
the metal could bend. "I had a film crew come to
Roger's place on May Eve. On my word, people flew in
from New Orleans, from England. For nothing. A
fiasco.

"Everything you wrecked that night—influence, acceptance by important people, my followers' belief in
me—you're going to get back for me, all that and a lot
more."

More. Greed. Weyland knew about greed. He studied Reese.

How old was the man—thirty-seven, thirty-eight?
No longer young, and aging swiftly as human beings
aged. His cotton pullover clearly showed his heavy
body running to fat. Take away the extra padding, and
lines would show in his round, slick cheeks—
unchanged, that face, from the days in New York, the
freckled skin gleaming faintly with sweat, the thin lips
hungrily parted. His hair was freshly cropped, a sun-
bleached stubble: to hide new gray?

More. He wants more than his fair share of everything.

Offer it to him.

Weyland stepped to the couch and sat down.

Reese leaped to his feet with a guttural shout, the
gun flung up as if to fire—but there came no slam of
bullets, no deadly roar.

"Sit down." Weyland spoke firmly, driving his voice
past the fear-knot in his throat. "Cleanse your mind of
cheap theatrics; you've come to me for more than that.
I'll explain. Listen carefully. I'm not a patient teacher."

Sinking back onto the edge of the wing chair's seat,
gripping the gun with both hands, Reese said in a voice
thick with hate, "Fine, go ahead—you may never be

able to speak a clear sentence again. Talk while you can, entertain me. When I get bored, I'll see that you take your medicine. And meanwhile if you move again without my permission, I'll blow you apart."

A moment's breathing space, Weyland thought. Skillfully exploited, perhaps much more . . . What is my way here, what tone must I take?

When people came to see Irv privately, what did they come for? His warmth, his supportive advice, his healing sympathy. I am not warm, I am cold. Can I win Reese with my coldness? Does he want that for himself?

Try. I have nothing to lose.

Calmly he said, "While I'm nearly resolved that you are the correct choice, tests must still be passed. The first test is of your attentiveness, your self-control, your intelligence. Try hard. Success means a life like ours." Would Reese take the bait? "Long life, secret, and secure in the strength of the predator."

"Not very inventive," Reese said. "If I'm supposed to believe that there are more of you, you'll have to do better than that."

"A small number of us exist," Weyland lied. "We practice . . . birth control, figuratively speaking, and a very fine discrimination in our judgment of who is and is not fit to become one of us."

"Good," said Reese, "that's a much higher grade of bullshit." He laughed, but his little eyes stayed wide open, as though he were unwillingly engaged by vistas of immense time; Weyland began to hope.

He felt he had known men like this in other times— the ones who stood apart and manipulated others in fear and contempt. They pretended to be different, to be safe, to have achieved what they could only yearn for: the true, most secret of secret societies, the philosopher's stone, Faust's bargain. Reese professed to scorn what he was now hearing. Yet Weyland guessed that in his heart he longed to believe.

Weyland said with icy approval, "Your suspicion

does you credit; also your desire to take from me, not to be given. These are signs of the hunter in you. But you are not yet a wolf. Oh, a wolf among men, perhaps, but by our standards that's not much. You must drop your pose of authority and become a student. Otherwise, you get nothing from me, nothing you truly desire. And that would be a pity. On the day you first came to me at Roger's, your worth was manifest. By the touch of your hands I knew that you deserved more than a little human life."

"Liar! You were hurt and humiliated that day. Revenge is what you're after, not some phony blood brotherhood." The gun muzzle rose slightly as if Reese's hands had an eagerness of their own to repeat the hurt and the humiliation.

How well and with what profound hatred Weyland remembered the burning, rapacious grip of those hands. But facing such a shrewd and deadly adversary, hatred was a perilous indulgence. With immense effort he checked himself, putting away the force of rage in favor of the force of his own imposing presence. He made himself sit easily but not slackly, his hands relaxed on his thighs, only a mild flicker of scorn in his manner as he replied in a schoolroom tone, "Yes, I was hurt, but like the devil you profess to worship I can see good in what most consider evil. Now as then, you show the qualities that a predator must have: singleness of purpose, the sense of one's own advantage, the ability to be cruel. You came here to declare yourself my master. I want you to become my kin."

"How?" jeered Reese, gesturing with the gun held rock-steady in his two thick hands. "By putting down my weapon and coming over there to kiss your ass?"

Why this childish diction? Weyland seized on what Alison had said: You have the face of everybody's dream-father . . .

He said sternly, "The gun is unimportant, a sign of your human weakness, a toy. You may keep it if you wish. All I require from you is your consent to be made mature."

Reese guffawed. "Thorazine can't do your brain any harm, you're already crazy. Or is it just senility brought on early by panic?"

Swiftly Weyland shifted his attack. "Of course, you're afraid. I understand." Irv might have said that—but Irv was warm. Weyland's understanding must be cold. "You know how frail and unworthy, how merely human you are behind your carefully hardened exterior. Your weakness does not make you unfit in my eyes. I know that even in your childhood something cruel lived in you, not simple childish brutality but a core of ice for the sake of which you held yourself aloof . . ."

Reese licked his lips but did not speak. He must always have been physically unlovely, socially overbearing, avid for power. What childhood tales had lifted his sullen heart?

The child is lost in the woods, is taken in by wolves, becomes the leader of a mythic pack ranging the forest forever.

A stranger emerges from a great star vessel to say, "Come, you are not one of these wretched little mammals, this has all been a mistake. You are one of us, mighty, wise, and immortal."

Magic reveals that the dirty peasants around one are not family; one's real father and mother are immaculate king and queen of an enchanted land.

Weyland remembered none of his own dreams, but he had studied those of humankind. To the dream of secret superiority, of the potboy's princely destiny, he spoke. Not that he used such terms. To this deadly adult who proposed to create a new religion Weyland spoke of an ancient sodality; he touched on secrecy ruthlessly maintained, hidden wealth skillfully administered across the centuries, a hierarchy in which Reese would be a bare initiate for decades, a planned transfer from the outworn human identity that must be left behind, slow chemical changes and increasing powers.

No melodrama—that was Reese's own territory, he would not be taken in. Weyland spoke with the caution proper to one recruiting in such a cause. Where the desperate inventiveness of his mind failed, he hinted at secrets not so soon to be revealed.

All along ran the subtext, the fairy tales his lies were shadows of, so that he spoke both to the man and to the boy in the man.

Reese broke in at last, husky-voiced. "I don't believe you. I don't believe you." His hand moved stiffly on the mechanism of the gun, and Weyland heard a single, ominous click.

Time for one last, audacious gesture: moving slowly and deliberately, Weyland unbuttoned his cuff and began rolling back his shirt sleeve. He forced himself not to rush his words.

"As you observed in New York," he said, "I don't create another vampire by feeding even many times on one victim. But a grain of truth lies in the old tale of the vampire opening his own veins to an initiate. I must feed you not once but many times, until your change begins. This is risky for me, and I don't enjoy it, but there is no other way." He stood up. "Who was your father?"

"Don't move!" Reese commanded hoarsely. "Sit down!"

"I said, who was your father?" Weyland's voice sounded distant in his own ears. He felt dizzy with fear, with rage, with the tantalizing nearness of gratification.

Reese whispered, "My father was a motorman on the New York subway."

Weyland, startled, thought fleetingly of his old plan to go to earth in a Manhattan subway tunnel. The convulsion of feeling vanished. Now he must say the right words or lose all.

"That was the father of your human life," he declared in a clear, revelatory voice. "I am the father of

your life forever—if you are bold enough to acknowl-
edge me."

He put his lips to the thin skin of his own inner wrist
and thrust with the dart from under his tongue. The
taste of blood came into his mouth, shocking, familiar,
rich, and salty. His hunger surged, threatening to
overwhelm him in a feeding ecstacy such as once before
had nearly destroyed him. He made himself raise his
face and show that ecstasy to Reese: I invite you to
abandon mere mummery and tricks for what is yours to
claim—this sweet reality that I offer. He extended his
arm, feeling the warm trickle of blood curling down
into his palm.

"Come and drink."

Slowly, dazed, Reese rose and approached. His eyes,
in which Weyland saw the shine of tears, were fixed on
the bloodied wrist. The room seemed hardly to contain
Reese's hoarse breathing. The gun dangled in his slack
grip. He leaned forward.

Weyland put his other hand on the back of Reese's
head, guiding, reassuring, silently caressing with a
feather touch. Reese bent nearer. Weyland felt the
trembling lips against his skin.

With a roar of passionate triumph he seized his
quarry and flung him headlong, face down, onto the
couch, hurling himself atop him, entwining the frantically bucking body with iron limbs. The gun skittered
across the floor. Weyland's bloodied hand clamped
Reese's face, palm jamming the screaming mouth shut,
fingers crushing the nostrils, stifling the breath. He
bound tightly to himself the thunder of the frenzied
heart, the surge and strain of the massive back, until all
collapsed in an air-starved spasm.

Then he moved one finger, felt Reese's ribs heave for
more air—which Weyland gave, a sip at a time, enough
to support life and consciousness as he rasped into
Reese's ear, "Now I am going to drink your life. Take
good note, this is how I do it."

Reese's blood was pungent with adrenaline. Weyland

made not just a meal but a banquet, taking his time, permitting entrance of enough air to keep the lungs pumping. The futile lashing of the head and the lunges of the legs and trunk continued, but in time blood loss quelled all this commotion. He relaxed his hold and fed more slowly, savoring also the laboring of Reese's starved heart, his sobbing gasps at air now freely allowed but powerless to save.

At last, hunger and hatred both fed to repletion, Weyland knelt by the couch and looked into Reese's blue and liquid eyes that stared back from beneath drooping lids. The couch cushion was dark with Reese's saliva.

"Can you see me still?" Weyland murmured, drowsy and satisfied. "As you've surely guessed by now, you failed the final test. You're too human."

He lay down on the living-room rug and slept.

When he woke, Reese was dead. Weyland made his preparations, and with the body lying in the back he drove the blue hatchback toward the mountains.

Hands in pockets, the collar of the old windbreaker turned to the breeze's edge, he walked northward facing the sparse oncoming traffic. Now and then headlights would appear and draw on, and he would step back onto the shoulder of the road until the lights had whipped past in a buffet of wind.

Jacket, faded work pants, chambray shirt, even the heavy old hunting boots he wore, all had been lifted in darkness from the Goodwill store downtown an hour before. His own blood-spotted clothes he had deposited in various garbage bins around the city along with a pair of rubber kitchen gloves and the keys to Reese's car. Local jackals would soon dispose of the hatchback which he had abandoned, unlocked, with the gun inside on the floor, in a neighborhood of slums and light industry.

Reese's body lay tumbled in a brush-choked arroyo near a major hiking trail on the mountain. When eventually found he would be assumed to have lost his way and died of hypothermia. Little remained to show who Reese had been or what had been the nature of his errand to Albuquerque. Reese's identification and the letter from Katje de Groot had been burned and the ashes thrown to the wind.

Thrown to the wind like the ashes of Weyland's documents. Walking the verge of the highway, he altered his gait to the amble appropriate to the wanderer he meant to become. Wait, he had neglected the perfecting touch—a sober man of mature years does not go bareheaded. He pulled from his jacket pocket the rolled-up, time-worn Panama hat and put it on.

Inwardly he was exultant. Though the taste of blood was the sweetest in the world, much was to be enjoyed in the savor of victory. Out of blood and victory together he had fashioned a perfect climax and vindication of his Weyland life.

Now he could walk away from that life without regret.

Shreds of newspaper fluttered palely on the wires of the fence on his left. He imagined the headlines: DOUBLE MYSTERY ON CAMPUS—SUICIDE AND DISAPPEARANCE. Poor Alison, both her father substitutes lost within a few days. That didn't bother him, but something else disturbed his elated mood.

Word would get back to Cayslin, thence to Floria Landauer.

I care about this, he thought, alarmed. He stopped and turned off the road and stood staring west, watching the night depart. I care. What will happen to her?

He saw himself standing at some gas-station phone along the road, hunched away from the traffic noise and shouting into the mouthpiece—shouting a warning.

What if Reese had been telling the truth about having her watched? What might the watcher do, bereft of direction from Reese? Mark knew his danger and had flown, but Floria knew nothing. The thought of her innocent and unaware in the power of Reese's creatures was intolerable. She must be told so she could have the chance to save herself. She must be told so Weyland's mind would be freed of anxiety for her. Without a doubt, if the one in danger were himself and Floria knew, she would take her courage in her hands and find a way to warn him. Irv, similarly placed, would postpone suicide to do so.

Why, then, was it so clear to Weyland that he might imagine the phone call but not make it? Because by speaking to Floria he might compromise his own disappearance, and that he could not permit. Survival for people was at most a matter of decades, while for him centuries perhaps were at stake. The scale of time divided him from humanity irrevocably. Irv's passionate involvement, Floria's valor, were not for him.

The rough, dry wood of the fencepost he leaned on creaked in the grip of his hand, reminding him of the chair he had broken in a moment of alarm in Floria's office. This was not alarm. This was pain.

He spread his fingers, studying his hands with keen night vision: not the hands of a man, but the talons of a raptor. A raptor does not care. I used not to care.

What was it someone had asked once at a lecture he had given—a question about Satanic pride? He had seen Mrs. de Groot in the audience that night and thought nothing of it except that his efforts to lure her to him were succeeding. He ought not to have answered that question with sarcasm, for pride he had surely harbored, as well as the blindness that pride brings.

He had grown proud in the process of his long, successful struggle to forge the identity of Weyland: the years of working in all sorts of capacities at places where records were kept; the drudgery in libraries, small printing plants, a series of offices with computer links to certain information systems; the careful steps of an academic career begun in a mediocre Southern school and crowned at last with his prized position at Cayslin College. There running the dream-mapping project, he had settled down to perfect the regularity of his feeding and immerse himself in the absorbing routines of scholarship. His feeling of security had mellowed over several years into something like contempt. He had begun to take his prey for granted.

Until Katje de Groot with one utterly unlooked-for, devastating stroke had rent him open, body and mind, and left him vulnerable to these others.

Memory served him the pain and dread of Reese's butcher-hands first wrenching at him, Mark's blood offering, his own effort to refrain from crushing the boy's thin frame in the violence of his hunger. He remembered Floria's dazzled, growing awareness as she worked at revelation with her client, first in words, then in flesh. He remembered Irv's dark, warm gaze, his voice low and concerned, and Dorothea blazing with the anguish of having failed to save her friend.

Not cattle, these; they deserved more from him than disdain. And they had more. He had cared enough to preserve when it was no longer secure his Weyland identity and all its ties and memories. Tonight, in deadly jeopardy because of that recklessness, he had not owed his fury only to past pain or the promise of future suffering at Reese's hands. He had burned also at the thought of Floria Landauer caught unknowing in Reese's net; of young Mark flying into a fugitive's perils from the net flung after him; of Reese obscenely alive and Irv dead.

He burned still.

His breath came shallow and strained and his thoughts in dark, dizzying waves. He tipped back his head and drew air deep into his lungs. Why do I stand here? he demanded furiously of himself. I should be moving, soliciting a ride, jettisoning all futile reflection. He stared fiercely northward, the direction he had chosen to take.

There was no point. He could not leave that which he carried with him—these people, bright as flames. For how long would they dance in his memory even after they died in the world? Time was said to fade such visions. Suppose this was untrue for him—suppose other visions were added? Crippling damage had been dealt him, and all his plans were irrelevant. He could not hunt successfully among prey for whom he might come to care. His life had been broken into, anyone might enter.

Now he knew with bitter clarity why in each long sleep he forgot the life preceding that sleep. He forgot because he could not survive the details of an enormous past heavy with those he cared for. No wonder art, or dreams, or history brought too vividly to life in human speech, were dangerous. They could tap the reservoirs of feeling buried in him under intervening sleeps. He was not fit to endure grief, let alone grief piled on grief through centuries of loss. Short-lived human beings could themselves tolerate only so much pain—look at Irv.

The remedy lay where he had passed over it only a moment before in his own thoughts. Afflicted by attachment, he had recourse to a way out that had not been open to Irv. At some risk and a cost he had no way to measure, he could choose the oblivion of long sleep.

I am not the monster who falls in love and is destroyed by his human feelings. I am the monster who stays true.

The first weak light of dawn touched his face with a ghost of warmth as he turned eastward. Slowly, unwillingly, he raised his eyes toward the mountain; there was his retreat.

Perhaps hours had passed, perhaps days, since he had lain down in the cave. He had not even hunger to guide him, for the chill black air had begun to dim his body's systems.

This place in rock was the realm of his elder self, the animal core. From that center had welled up the clear, simple knowledge of how to proceed toward sleep:

within reach of water seeping over stone, make a pallet, undress, lie this way, be still, and wait.

No further action was required of him, and slowly anguish faded, calculation stilled. The past was immutable. For the future, it was enough to know that upon waking, if he did wake, he would rise restored, eyes once more as bright and unreflective as a hawk's and heart as ruthless as a leopard's.

The novelty of being free of all present necessity came to absorb him. He seemed to float some distance from himself in the darkness, although now and then he noticed the softness of worn cotton under his cheek where his folded clothing served as a pillow or the mixed fragrances of the brush, grasses, and pine boughs of which he had made his bed.

Then for a time came an unexpected gift. The voices of the people returned vividly to him, their faces, gestures, laughter, the swirling brightness of the opera crowd, the jingle of coins in Irv's pocket, Mark's warm, bony shoulder under his hand as they walked toward the river, the scent of Floria's skin. Intense pleasure filled him as he yielded himself to the mingled ache and joy of memory, as he gathered in his Weyland life.

At length, when possession of that life was achieved, all was effortlessly let go like a release of breath.

In the still vault of his mind darkness began to thicken and drift. Tranquilly he recognized the onset of sleep. He did not resist.